Terror at Trinity

Terror at Trinity

A Novel by

Jim Bornzin

iUniverse, Inc.
New York Bloomington

Terror at Trinity

This is a work of fiction. All of the characters, names, incidents, organizations, and dialogue in this novel are either the products of the author's imagination or are used fictitiously.

iUniverse books may be ordered through booksellers or by contacting:

iUniverse
1663 Liberty Drive
Bloomington, IN 47403
www.iuniverse.com
1-800-Authors (1-800-288-4677)

ISBN: 978-1-4401-6191-9 (pbk)
ISBN: 978-1-4401-6192-6 (ebk)

Printed in the United States of America

iUniverse rev. date: 8/25/2009

Contents

PART I **Paul's Terror 1990 . . . . 1**

Chapter 1 Not In a Church!. 3
Chapter 2 Terry's Tragedy 19
Chapter 3 A Mighty Fortress 25
Chapter 4 Paul and Cheri 31
Chapter 5 The Community Fair. 41
Chapter 6 Paul Visits Bob and Marge 47
Chapter 7 The Holloways' Grief. 51
Chapter 8 Marge and Cheri 63
Chapter 9 No Leads. 69
Chapter 10 $10,000 Reward 73
Chapter 11 One Good Lead 81
Chapter 12 Lunch in the Park 91
Chapter 13 Time for Confession 101
Chapter 14 A Good Day for Golf 107
Chapter 15 To Tell or Not To Tell 113
Chapter 16 The Holloways Are Gone 121
Chapter 17 Another Lead 129
Chapter 18 Search Warrant. 137
Chapter 19 Trinity's Grief 145
Chapter 20 Call in the Bishop 153
Chapter 21 The Bishop's Intervention 159

PART II **Terror at Trinity 2010 . . . . .169**

Chapter 22 Omar's Dilemma. 171
Chapter 23 The Plot Uncovered 181
Chapter 24 Trinity's Suspicions. 187
Chapter 25 Hassid's Plan 191
Chapter 26 Terror Strikes. 195
Chapter 27 The FBI Responds 207
Chapter 28 Foolish Bravery. 211
Chapter 29 Stalling For Time. 219

Continued...

Chapter 30 Allah Be Praised! 227
Chapter 31 Time's Up 235
Chapter 32 Meet The Press 239

PART III Terror Returns 2011 251

Chapter 33 Father's Day 253
Chapter 34 Brianna 261
Chapter 35 Brianna's Second Visit 271
Chapter 36 Please Don't Tell My Mom! 277
Chapter 37 Brianna's Third Visit 283
Chapter 38 A Major Interruption 293
Chapter 39 Triple By-Pass 305
Chapter 40 Trinity Hears the News. 311
Chapter 41 Paul's Recovery. 321
Chapter 42 A Time Apart 331
Chapter 43 Christmas at the Walkers' 339
Chapter 44 Brianna and Guy's Wedding 343
Chapter 45 The Trial 351
Chapter 46 Reward Ceremony 363

STUDY GUIDE. .373
ACKNOWLEDGMENTS 379
ABOUT THE AUTHOR 381

INTRODUCTION

TWO KINDS OF TERROR

"Do not fear those who kill the body but cannot kill the soul; rather fear him who can destroy both soul and body in hell."

- Jesus (Matthew 10:28)

There are two kinds of terror in human experience. The one we see in the horror genre of movies is the terror caused by an external threat. Americans experienced this kind of terror on 9-11-2001, when planes were flown into the World Trade Towers and the Pentagon. A second kind of terror is that which comes from within, a terror of the soul, a realization that one has betrayed all that one values most.

Paul Walker entered a Lutheran seminary in the Midwest, young and idealistic, never suspecting his life as a parish pastor would introduce him to both kinds of terror.

Jesus knew his followers would be persecuted, their lives threatened by religious and civil authorities. He knew some would die for their faith. Yet, he warned, the greater threat for each of us comes not from authorities or terrorists, but from Satan, the deceiver and the destroyer. The hell Jesus refers to in this imperative is not just the punishment of eternal fire, but the torment of guilt, the suffering of consequences, and the destruction of relationships that result from sin, or in more contemporary terms, poor choices. One doesn't have to believe in God, in Satan, or in the hell of fire to know the existential truth about the hell of betrayal and its consequences.

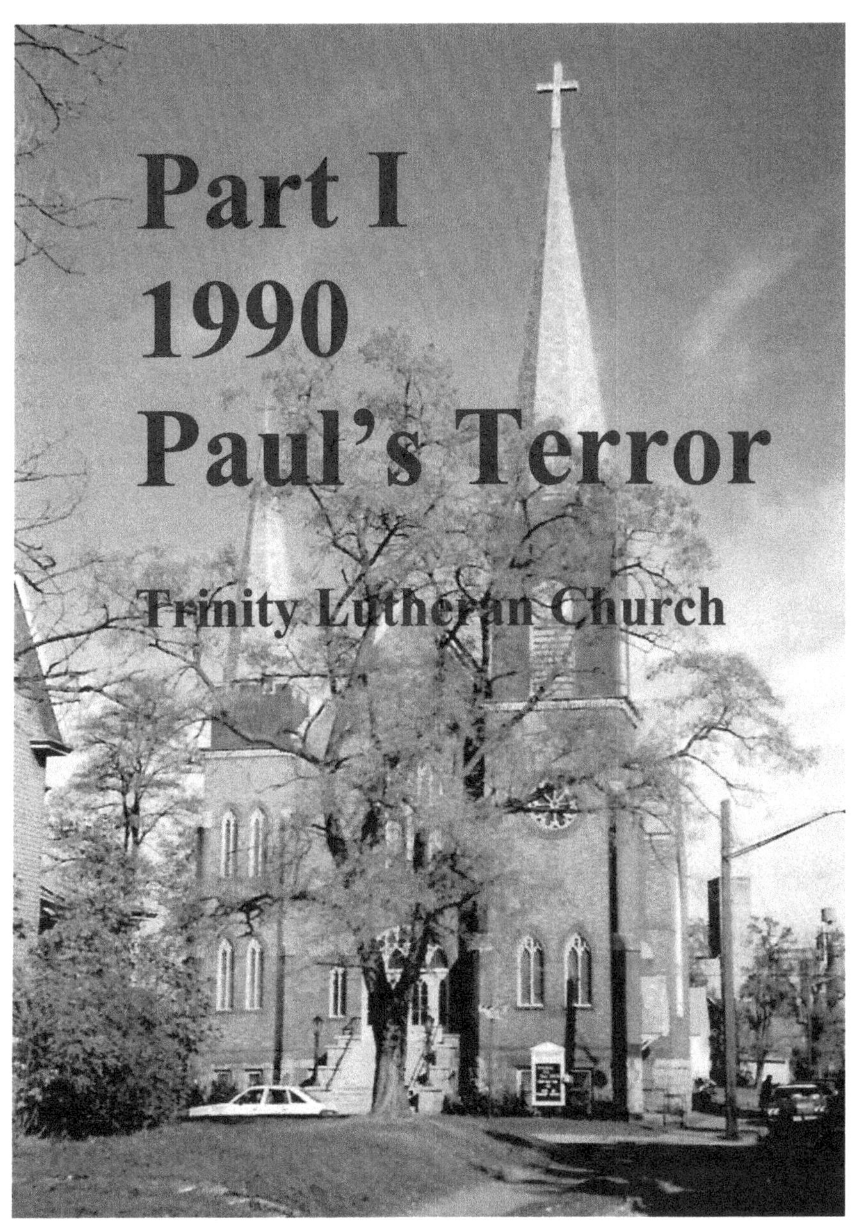
Part I
1990
Paul's Terror
Trinity Lutheran Church

1

NOT IN A CHURCH !

Members of Trinity were proud that their cross on top of the tall steeple could be seen from anywhere in Weston. Worshippers climbed ten old cement steps to enter the church sanctuary. The fellowship hall in the basement was half below ground and half above street level. Trinity Lutheran at 1590 Oak Street, had been established in Weston, Indiana, in 1922. A small frame church was replaced by the brick sanctuary in 1948.

Most of the members at Trinity were relieved when Ted Schackleby's contract was not renewed. He had been hired as janitor when the congregation council decided that the contract with a local janitorial service was simply too expensive. Ted was a World War II veteran whose wife had left him some twenty-five years ago. The first year on the job Ted seemed to be trying very hard to please. He made friends easily and adopted the church as his second home, which was not surprising, since his apartment in an old remodeled hotel was small and cluttered.

Pastor Paul Walker explained that his contract was for eight to ten hours a week, but Ted spent many mornings and afternoons puttering around the church, and visiting anyone who had time in the church office. The smell of alcohol on his breath was unmistakable, and on numerous occasions he had been found asleep in the church. No one knew where he hid the bottles of scotch, but nearly everyone had seen empties in the trash. After his first year the church began getting messier with each passing month. The property committee chairman gave him several warnings to no avail. The council agreed Ted needed to go. Telling old Ted that he could no longer be the janitor was one of the most difficult things Pastor Walker had ever done.

The council president suggested that the pastor put an article in the parish newsletter asking if any member was interested in the position. Within the week, two phone calls to the church office held some possibility. The pastor made notes about each caller applicant.

The first was one of the oldest men in the church, Lars Knudsen. He had been retired for nearly twenty years, but had time on his hands and told the pastor he'd be glad to tackle the job if no one else wanted it.

The second call came the day before the council meeting. Brian Holloway was sixteen years old, living at home with his parents and sister, and was in his junior year at Weston High. He hoped to become a veterinarian and was already working part-time in a vet's clinic on weekends. Brian was active in the youth group and often came to meetings early to help set up chairs or do whatever the pastor asked him to do. He was a faithful worker on clean-up days at the church. Brian said he needed another part-time job to help him save for college expenses, and that he would like to be the church janitor for a couple of years at least. Paul knew Brian would be a trustworthy worker.

When Pastor Walker shared the responses with the council, the decision to hire Brian was unanimous. The pastor agreed to write a thank you letter to Mr. Knudsen and talk to Brian about the job description and hourly wage. Within a week members were commenting on how nice the church looked and what a great job young Brian was doing.

A few months later Lent was in full swing and the church was being used more than usual. Brian was not deterred. An extra hour on Saturday night meant the church would be sparkling clean on Sunday morning. One Saturday, just a week before Easter, Brian was surprised to see a strange mess in the narthex. Someone had cut a bunch of branches and leaves and left the entire pile on the ushers' table. Conscientiously he scooped them up and dumped them in the metal burn barrel outside, stoked the large can with old newspapers, and set the barrel on fire. In less than an hour the fire was gone and nothing but hot ashes remained. An hour later, Brian locked the church and went home.

The next morning was Palm Sunday, when Christian churches around the world celebrate the entry of Jesus into Jerusalem, riding on a donkey. The head usher, Chuck Kushman, came into Pastor Walker's study. "Pastor, do you know where the palm branches are for the procession this morning?"

"I left them on the ushers' table as I always do," Paul replied.

"Well, they weren't there when I came in this morning. I've had my crew looking all over the building, but no one can find them."

"Why don't you ask Brian if he knows where they are," the pastor suggested. "He's always here on Saturday evening."

A few minutes later, Brian came bursting into the pastor's study. "I'm so sorry, Pastor. I guess I wasn't thinking. Last night when I cleaned up the church, I took the palm branches out to the parking lot and burned them."

Pastor Paul closed his eyes, said a quick prayer, offered an informal but sincere absolution to Brian, and went to tell the choir there would be no palm branches for the procession this year.

* * * * * * *

The following year Brian spent the entire season of Lent anxiously watching for palm branches to appear on the ushers' table. It was his senior year; he hadn't forgotten Palm Sunday last year. This year he was not about to let anything happen to the palms! When they finally arrived, he hid them in the janitor's closet and locked the door. On the morning of Palm Sunday, Chuck Kushman arrived early to unlock the doors, turn on the lights, and get everything ready for worship. He looked for the palm branches and threw his head back in disbelief! "Oh, no!" he hollered in the empty church, "Not again!" Brian arrived a few minutes later and reassured Mr. Kushman that the palms were safe. He unlocked the closet door and proudly presented the palms to Chuck. Everyone was thrilled to see the choir and children marching up the center aisle waving their palm branches!

After working at the church for a year, Brian was familiar with the liturgical year, and comfortable with the requirements of his part-time job. Members often complimented him on how nice the church looked. Many were saying he's the best janitor we've ever had. The small amount he earned each week was going into a savings account for his anticipated tuition at college the coming fall. The veterinarian for whom he worked part-time had written excellent letters of recommendation to two colleges. Pastor Walker had also written glowing letters. Bob and Marge were extremely proud of their son. Brian was accepted at both Purdue and the University of Indiana. He wrote an enthusiastic letter of intent to attend Purdue.

* * * * * * *

Friday, August 10, 1990

It was almost midnight on a hot summer evening when the phone rang at the Walker's. Paul and Cheri had just fallen asleep. The breeze coming through the bedroom window was blowing the curtains gently when Paul stumbled out of bed to grab the phone. Both their young sons, Chip and Randy were sound asleep in their toy-strewn bedroom.

"Pastor! This is Bob Holloway and I'm at the church! You've gotta come right away!" He was screaming into the phone. "It's awful, just awful! I've called 9-1-1 and asked for an ambulance and the police! Get over here, right away!"

Paul felt his heart begin to pound. Adrenaline was coursing through his body. "What's the matter, Bob? What happened?"

"I don't know. .... Oh shit, this is terrible! I came up to the church and found Brian inside. He's been stabbed! There's blood all over! Please get here as soon as you can!"

"Hang on, Bob, I'll be there as quickly as I can. Have you called Marge?"

"No, not yet. I couldn't. I can't believe it myself!"

"I think I can make it in about ten minutes. Hold tight, Bob, hold tight and pray." Paul didn't tell Bob that the phone had startled him out of the first hour of sleep. He whispered a few words of explanation to his half-awake wife, "There's an emergency at the church and I have to go over there right away." He hoped Cheri would be able to fall back asleep. Paul slipped on his clothes and headed to the church. He drove as fast as he felt he could, his mind racing. *Bob said he called the police. Blood all over? What in the world could have happened?*

* * * * * * *

Earlier that evening, Brian had talked to his girl friend on the phone, telling her that he couldn't come over because he had some cleaning up to do at the church. He gave his mom a kiss, jumped in his blue Chevy Caprice, and drove into the parking lot about 9:30 p.m. He unlocked the church door and went in. He didn't notice one of the basement windows had been broken until he went downstairs to clean. The first thing he always did was turn on all the lights. A church can be a little creepy in the dark. The fellowship hall had a few napkins and other scraps of paper on the floor, and the tables and chairs needed to be put away. One of the community groups that used the building had a dinner earlier in the week.

When Brian entered the kitchen, he noticed broken glass on the floor. His first thought was that someone had dropped a drinking glass. Immediately, however, he saw that the shards were flat, not curved, as they would be for a glass or vase. Looking up he saw that one of the windows above the kitchen sink had been broken, obviously from the outside, because all the glass was on the counter and floor. Brian pulled a broom and dust pan from the cupboard and swept up the broken glass. *Darn vandals*, he thought to himself. As he dumped the glass pieces into the garbage can, he wondered if he should report this to the pastor or someone from the building committee. "Somebody's gonna have to replace that window," he said aloud. Hearing a noise from the fellowship hall, Brian turned and saw something dark move past the kitchen door. It hadn't occurred to him that someone might have actually climbed in through the window.

"Hey, what are you doing?" Brian yelled. He dropped the broom and dustpan and ran after the fleeing figure. In the well-lit room he could see the person was a short, stocky male. "Stop, you creep!" he yelled again. But the person didn't slow down and didn't look back. Brian chased him across the fellowship hall and finally caught up with him when the intruder tripped running up the stairs. Brian reached toward the man, grabbing his sweatshirt, when suddenly the intruder rolled on his back and slashed with a knife. The blade nicked Brian's hand.

"You son-of-a-bitch!" Brian screamed. The intruder rolled to his knees and started up the steps. Brian regained his footing, jumped two stairs at a time and grabbed the man by the back of his sweatshirt. The intruder turned and jabbed his knife into Brian's stomach. Brian reacted by slamming him against the stairs. The knife flashed again, penetrating Brian's ribs and puncturing an artery. Brian fought for a few brief moments then fell as blood oozed from his wounds. He tumbled to the bottom of the steps. *Oh, shit!* he thought as he struggled to remain conscious. *I shouldn't have chased him. I'd better call someone…9-1-1… I guess… as soon as I get the strength to get up. I feel so weak and tired. Why did I chase that guy? That was stupid.* A few moments passed, and then there were no more thoughts. The pain in his stomach and chest receded as he drifted into a warm peace.

The intruder dashed up the stairs, found his way to the exit, ran across the parking lot, and faded into the dark shadows across the street.

* * * * * * *

At Brian's home his parents were beginning to worry. Marge called the church but got the message on the answering machine. "Bob," she said, "maybe you should go over and see what's taking Brian so long tonight. He's usually home by eleven, even ten-thirty in the summer."

Shortly before midnight, Bob drove over to the church to see what was keeping him. Brian's car was still in the parking lot and lights were still on inside the church. The vapor lamps in the lot cast eerie shadows on the church walls. It was so quiet. A lone car drove past the church. Bob went inside and called his name, "Brian!" Again, a little louder, "BRIAN!" Bob's heart began to pound. It was quiet in the church. Too quiet. He searched the office area and then headed for the stairs to the fellowship hall. "Oh my God!" He saw Brian lying at the base of the stairs, blood all around his body. "BRIAN!" he screamed and raced down the stairs. He grabbed his bloody hands and tried to lift him, but Brian could not respond. "NO! ...NO! ....NO!" he screamed. His body began to convulse. He wrapped his arms around his son's lifeless body and sobbed and screamed at God!

Sirens broke the stillness of the summer night. The pastor, the police, the ambulance and paramedics all arrived within minutes of each other. The parking lot was flooded with flashing lights, and neighbors peered out their windows. The paramedics moved quickly to the bottom of the stairs and determined that Brian was indeed deceased. They covered his body and waited for directions from the police officers. Detective Sean Asplund, the officer in charge from the Homicide Division, asked them to hang around awhile. "You might want to keep an eye on the dad who's pretty upset." Meanwhile, several other officers were taking photos, searching the building, the grounds, and securing the area.

Pastor Walker was greeted by the detective who introduced himself and asked Paul a few questions. "Does anyone work with the janitor, or is he usually here by himself? Is the church usually locked at night?" After a few minutes with the pastor, Detective Asplund pulled Bob aside and began his interview. "What time did you come to the church? What time did Brian leave home this evening? What did you do after you saw the body?"

Bob struggled to answer the questions flung at him. "I was pretty sure he was dead, so I ran up to the office and called 9-1-1," he said to the officer. "Then I think I called the pastor and asked him to come to the church as quickly as possible. I was going to call Marge, but decided to wait until the pastor arrived and ask him how to break the news to Brian's mom."

Detective Asplund was writing notes furiously. The phone rang in the church office and Paul ran into the office area to answer before the message machine clicked on. "Oh, Pastor, this is Marge Holloway, I'm surprised you're at the church this late. Are Bob and Brian still there?"

"Yes, Marge, I'm sorry they're so late getting home. We have quite a mess here at the church. Bob will be home in fifteen or twenty minutes to explain." Paul was not in the habit of lying, but he didn't feel right about giving her the horrible news over the phone.

"I can't believe it," Marge replied. "It's never taken Brian this long.... especially during the summer. There's hardly anything going on at the church. We were getting worried."

"Marge, I don't want to go into details on the phone. Please hang on. Bob will explain when he gets home. Just sit tight a few more minutes.... Marge, I've gotta go. Talk to you later." Paul knew he wasn't being quite honest, but he didn't want Marge to be alone. He also felt Bob should be with her when she learned the news about their son. And he wanted to spare her the horror of seeing her son in a pool of blood. Paul went to see if he could interrupt the officer's questioning. He stood obtrusively close to Bob staring at the detective.

Finally, Detective Asplund looked him in the eye and asked, "And were you in the church earlier today, pastor?"

"Yes," Paul replied.

"And what time did you leave?" the officer asked.

"I think it was a little after five," Paul responded. "Officer, Bob's wife just called and is very worried about their son. I think Bob and I should get to his house right away and inform her of this tragedy. They should be together as soon as possible."

"Certainly. I'll have the paramedics take the boy to the hospital emergency room. If the parents want to see him, that might be the best place initially. The staff there will help them make arrangements with a funeral home. Of course, there will have to be an autopsy. My name again is Detective Sean Asplund." "Here's my card," the officer said to Bob. "Call me if you have any idea who might have done this. I'll be in contact with you." Bob sat in stunned silence.

"Thank you, officer," Paul replied as he also took one of Sean's cards. "Bob, are you ready to go?"

Bob looked from the pastor to the policeman, "I hope you find the bastard who killed my son."

"We'll do our best, sir." There was no way that Bob could have guessed that for the moment, he was Detective Asplund's number one suspect. Bob and Brian were alone in the church together and there was blood all over Bob's hands and shirt. A father-son argument could not be ruled out. He would follow up on that later.

"Officer, may I ask how much longer you'll be here in the church?" Paul asked.

"A couple of hours at least. The medical examiner and our forensic officer are on their way and they'll be working here for a while."

"I was concerned about locking up. Just a stupid thing to worry about, but I assume you want it locked," the pastor mumbled.

"Hey, that's not a stupid thing," the officer assured him. "We'll want the building locked so no one disturbs the crime scene. Do you have an extra key?"

"Sure. I'll run into the office and get it. I just don't understand …O God… how could something like this have happened? Not in a church!" Paul glanced down the stairs. "Not Brian! O God, I'm so sad, and so angry…. that someone would break into the church in the first place … and then… oh, this makes me sick!" Paul went to his office to retrieve a spare key and gave it to the detective. Finally, turning to Bob, Paul said, "We'd better get going. This isn't going to be easy."

Bob had tears streaming down his face. "Marge, oh, Marge, this is gonna break her heart!" Bob and Paul walked to their cars. "I can't believe this is really happening," Bob said. "Wake me up, Pastor, and tell me this is just a goddamn nightmare."

"Bob, are you sure you're okay to drive?" Paul asked. "You could ride with me."

"Thanks, Pastor, I can drive. Why don't you follow me?"

"Sure thing," Paul replied.

When Paul and Bob arrived at the Holloways' Marge was frantic. She had just received a phone call from a neighbor near the church, who wondered if Marge knew why there were police and ambulance lights flashing in the church parking lot. Paul wondered if his wife Cheri had received any similar calls waking her from sleep. *Dear Lord, help me to be here for this family, and help me to say and do the right thing, even though nothing I can say will diminish their pain in this awful situation.*

Marge sat on the sofa in her nightgown and bathrobe. She wrapped her arms around herself trying to find some comfort and protection from the news she was about to hear. Bob sat down next to her and Paul took a chair across from them. Marge broke down as Bob struggled to speak. Slowly, haltingly, Bob began describing what he had found. The words lodged in his throat until he thought he would choke. Marge's cries of pain released a flood of tears for Bob as well.

What Pastor Paul had not expected was the sight he caught in the hallway behind Marge. There, with her hands over her mouth, stood Sarah, Brian's thirteen year old sister. "Sarah!" Paul whispered. Marge and Bob turned to look, assuming that Sarah had been asleep. They realized then, that their crying had awakened her.

Actually, Sarah awoke when the phone rang ten minutes earlier. She overheard her mother exclaim, "Police? Ambulance? Heavens no! I have no idea! Bob went up to the church to check on Brian. Pastor Paul is there too, I just talked to him. . . No, he said they'd be home in a few minutes. Oh, God… I hope nothing happened to Brian."

Sarah had no intention of going back to sleep. She lay on her bed listening. Now she stood in the hall, crying into both hands. "Honey, did you hear what I just told Mom?" her dad asked.

"Yes, Daddy, I heard it all." Sarah came and squeezed in next to her mom.

They continued talking and crying, bracketed by long periods of silence. "It might be best if you all waited until morning to see Brian at the hospital," Paul suggested. Marge insisted that she wanted to see him tonight. After nearly an hour Paul drove the three of them to the hospital, hoping Brian's body had arrived and that the staff had time to clean up his body as much as possible. They had to wait another twenty minutes before the nurse finally called them back to see Brian. Behind the curtain in the emergency room Marge laid her head over Brian's body and sobbed, not wanting to leave. Sarah sat on a chair next to the bed crying. Tears streamed down Paul's cheeks as he prayed. Bob pushed the curtain aside angrily, and paced between the examining room and the waiting area. Finally, Marge gave Brian a kiss good-by and was ready to leave.

About 2:30 a.m. Paul drove the Holloways home and went back to the church to lock up. There were three cars still in the lot: Brian's, the squad car of the detective, and an unmarked police car with the flasher inside on the dash. Paul guessed it might belong to the forensics person Detective Asplund had mentioned.

Inside the church Detective Sean Asplund told Paul it would be okay to hold worship in the sanctuary upstairs on Sunday. "I'd appreciate it if no one comes down the stairs or disturbs the yellow tape. We'd like to keep the crime scene secure for a couple of days. I'm sorry you won't be able to use the fellowship hall Sunday morning." Sean told Paul again to contact him if he had any questions. He would be doing the follow-up work on the case. He and the forensics officer, Raeann Sheeley, reviewed their notes, finished their discussion, and prepared to return to the police station downtown.

Paul bid them good night and locked the door. "It should lock by itself when you leave," he said. "You've got the key I gave you earlier?"

It was a little before four a.m. when Paul finally drove into his own garage, tired and in shock.

As he opened the kitchen door, he noticed the light was on. Cheri was sitting at the table with a half-empty glass of iced tea.

"You're up," he said, smiling weakly.

"Marge Holloway called about half an hour after you left. She wondered if I knew what was going on. I told her that you had gone to the church for an emergency, but I didn't know any details. She said there were police cars and an ambulance in the church parking lot. After that I couldn't sleep."

Paul shared a quick review of what had transpired since he left the house. As he finished his story he saw tears running down her cheeks. This was surely the most awful night of their lives. And how much more awful for the Holloways! They talked for an hour and finally crawled into bed exhausted. They said a prayer together and slipped into a restless sleep.

* * * * * * *

Weston, Indiana, is about forty miles from Chicago's loop, south of East Chicago, Gary, and Hammond, cities known for rough neighborhoods and high crime rates. Like most American cities, Weston has its share of urban problems. Gangs are organized along racial lines and are very competitive for territory and power. Driving through the streets around the church, one would say the neighborhood appeared much the same as it did fifty years ago. What had changed was the diversity of races and socio-economic groups living in close proximity.

When Terry Mankovic fled from the church a few minutes after ten, the lights in the parking lot seemed especially bright. He wished he could flee in darkness, but everything glowed in the bright orange of the sodium vapor lights. He slid the knife into its sheath beneath his sweatshirt. *I sure don't want anyone finding this knife with my fingerprints on it,* he thought to himself. A dark blue Chevy Caprice was parked near the entrance. It hadn't been there when Terry broke through the basement window. He glanced back at the bushes where he had crawled into the church and remembered a confrontation that had taken place on that very spot nearly ten years before. He remembered his buddy Jeff asking what to do with the items they had shoplifted from the store, and how he had suggested dumping them in the church parking lot. As he ran toward the darkened street he had a vision of an old man with white hair and a dark suit coming out of the church door and hollering at them. He remembered how he burned with anger when the old man said he was the pastor and was going to report them to the principal. His jaw clenched so tight it hurt as he remembered running from that same spot and hearing the old pastor's threat, "God's watching! God sees what you're doing!" The words echoed in his mind again tonight.

Terry ran across the parking lot and crossed the street, then slowed to a fast walk and glanced nervously over his shoulder and checked doorways, windows and the alley, to see if anyone was aware of his presence. The street was quiet and dark. At the next corner he made a quick right turn below the street light, and headed toward his apartment.

In the past several months Terry had been working the businesses from East Chicago to Michigan City to Valparaiso. He was a little concerned that he might be leaving a trail, so he had jumped from city to city, and was considering moving on to South Bend and Fort Wayne. Tonight, however, he was tired and didn't feel like driving that far to pull off a few more jobs. He did a mental review of the businesses in the neighborhood and thought of the church just a few blocks away. He remembered the tour the new pastor had led on the day of the Community Fair and decided the church was an easy target. Subconsciously, that incident from his middle school days had been bothering Terry for years. Robbing the church would kind of settle the score with that old coot who had chewed him out when he was in school.

"God's watching! God's watching!" the old man had yelled. Did God see what happened inside the church a few minutes ago? That was some bad shit. Why didn't God let me get out of there? Why didn't God stop that

guy before he caught me on the stairs? Damn! I didn't mean to kill him! The stupid kid is probably bleeding to death.

Terry's breath was slowing down, but his heart was still pumping wildly. *Shit! I've been so careful. I've never had to pull the knife; not in all these years. Never! Now, just four blocks from home ....this!*

He was approaching his apartment building. *Stay calm. Stay cool,* Terry said to himself as he unlocked the front door of the building. He made his way up the stairs to the second floor. It was dark in the hall. He unlocked the apartment door and fumbled for the switch. When the light came on, it seemed too bright, so much brighter than he remembered. He made his way to the bathroom, relieved himself, and stood at the sink staring at his image in the cloudy mirror. *How could I have done that? Why couldn't I have waited in hiding until that guy left? That was stupid. I didn't think he'd see me. I got impatient. Shit! Shit! Shit!*

Terry walked in a daze into his bedroom without turning on a light, flopped onto the bed and lay face up staring at the ceiling. He let his eyes adjust to the dark room. *I don't think I left any traces at the scene. I don't think the cops will find anything. I've got to stop thinking about this.* But of course, he couldn't. After a few minutes he got up and went into the bathroom again. He filled the basin with warm water, lathered his hands with soap and carefully washed the blood from his knife. He wiped everything with a towel, setting the knife on the back of the toilet. He threw his clothes in a pile on the floor. *Gotta wash the blood outa those tomorrow.*

Slowly he made his way back to the bedroom. *Tomorrow. What am I going to do tomorrow? I don't want to act any differently, or the brothers will know something's wrong. This will be in the papers. Shit! Maybe on television. I've got to play dumb. I've got to stay cool. Tomorrow I'll take my clothes to the Laundromat. I've got to stop thinking about it. I'll pretend it never happened. That's it! I'll just keep telling myself, it never happened! It never happened! I DON'T KNOW ANYTHING, because I wasn't involved. I was here all evening watching TV.*

Eventually, Terry's mind quit racing. His heartbeat slowed to normal, and he drifted into a fitful sleep. His dreams that night were more vivid than they had been for years. In slow motion he felt his foot slip on the church steps. He felt the janitor's hand grab him. He saw the knife plunging into the guy's shirt. He saw the blood on the knife. And over and over he heard an old man yelling, "God sees what you're doing!" And in his dream Terry could feel his legs kicking as he screamed, "I didn't mean to kill him!"

2

TERRY'S TRAGEDY

Terry Mankovic's father was employed at the local paint manufacturing plant in Weston. The plant was located in a dark industrial neighborhood, endless square blocks of dirty brick buildings surrounded by narrow, dimly-lit streets. One night, as he walked to work on the graveyard shift, he was hit and run over by a delivery truck. Terry's mom was distraught, and Terry was angry and afraid.

Tragedy among poorer families is always compounded by lack of financial resources. Terry's mother began working, but her meager salary was not enough to support the three children. Terry, in eighth grade when his dad died, found friends and a source of money in a gang of tough white kids from the hood. They were not nearly as powerful as the black gang that controlled the area, but they stuck together and kept a low profile. They were not the real movers in the drug market; they survived mainly by shop lifting, car theft, small business theft, and house burglaries.

* * * * * * *

Mr. Alford's math class was the most boring period of the day. Terry hated eighth grade. The halls of Lincoln Middle School were painted pea soup green. It made him sick just looking at the walls, the rows of lockers, the smell of the classrooms, and the superior attitude of the teachers and middle class students. It was all so oppressive. At one thirty on a Friday afternoon, Terry passed a note to his friend Jeff. "Let's cut out after math." Jeff gave him a high sign and Terry nodded. In the crowded hallway between classes the two boys raced for the parking lot exit.

They ran through the door, dashed between parked cars, and ran across the dead end street toward the nearby shopping center. "Hey, the weekend just started a few hours early!" Terry yelled.

"Let's go shopping!" Jeff yelled back. Terry understood what Jeff meant. Going shopping was their slang for shop lifting.

They strolled casually along the store fronts and entered a Payless store together. Just past the entrance they split up and headed down different aisles, looking for items they could slip into their baggy pants or sweatshirt. They met near the back of the store and discussed how they would get past the cashiers. "We need a distraction," Jeff suggested. "I can do that," Terry answered smugly. "Just follow me. When we get near the service counter I'm gonna get sick. You slip out the entrance door, okay?"

Jeff hung back just a little to watch Terry's act. As Terry strolled toward the Service Counter, he started coughing, loud violent coughs. He stumbled forward and grabbed the counter. He coughed a few more times, grabbed his stomach and started moaning. Customers moved back and several clerks came from around the counter to see if they could help. "Are you okay, young man?"

"Yes, ma'm, I think I'll be all right. (A few more little coughs.) I just need some fresh air. Something in here really kicked off my allergies."

Jeff had already slipped through the doors without being noticed.

"Are you sure you're all right?" the concerned employee inquired.

"I'll be fine as soon as I get outside," Terry assured her.

Out in the sunshine and the parking lot, Jeff and Terry doubled over with laughter. "We pulled it off!" Terry shouted.

"You were great!" Jeff acknowledged. "Now what are we gonna do with this stuff? I don't need any of this shit. Don't you know a fence who'd give us some cash for it?"

"Yea, but he got arrested. Let's just dump it," Terry said.

"Where?" Jeff asked.

"I've got an idea, c'mon," said Terry. After walking a block or two, Terry said, "There's a church around the next corner. Let's dump it there, and if anybody finds it there, they'll think someone from the church stole it!"

Jeff roared with laughter. Soon the two boys were walking along the sidewalk next to Trinity Lutheran. Behind the church was a parking lot, and there were bushes in front of the basement windows.

"Let's stuff it in here," Jeff said, as he began emptying pockets and reaching under his sweatshirt. Terry began to toss small items under the bushes. Suddenly the church door opened and a white haired man in a suit appeared. Terry and Jeff looked at each other and then at the man.

"What are you two doing?" the gentleman shouted.

"Oh, nothing!" Terry answered.

"Come here, I want to talk to you," the elderly man said as he began walking toward them.

The boys could have turned and dashed away, but that surely would indicate they were guilty of something. Terry decided to play it cool. "Honest, sir, we were just walking home from school."

"You boys are from Lincoln aren't you!" It wasn't a question; it sounded more like an accusation.

"Yeah, so what?" Jeff replied.

"Well, school isn't out for another hour. You two are skipping class and should be reported. What are your names?"

"I'm John, and this is my friend Mike," Terry lied.

"Well, I'm Pastor Bjornstad, and I'm a good friend of Principal McGuire. I think it's just awful how you young folks think you can get away with skipping school nowadays! Don't you know God is watching you and knows what you're doing? Now, what are your last names?" The pastor pulled a card and pen from his suit coat pocket.

This had gone on long enough. Terry grabbed Jeff by the arm and spun him around. The two of them took off running. "Stupid old coot!" Terry yelled over his shoulder.

"God's watching!" the pastor yelled back. "God sees what you're doing!"

"So what?" yelled Jeff.

Terry finally finished high school, though it took him five years. He was arrested several times for breaking and entering, and for attempted burglary. Terry avoided the use of drugs after seeing a friend die from overdose. He was familiar with the county juvenile detention facility and popular with the staff because of his sense of humor. Terry's wit had gotten him through some sticky situations at school and in confrontations with other gangs. When he turned twenty, Terry decided to leave his gang and petty criminal record behind by joining the Army. He enlisted, and because there were no felony convictions on his record, he was accepted for military duty. He was sent to Iraq to fight in Operation Desert Storm. He spent nine miserable months there and finally returned to the states and was stationed in Texas. He sent small amounts of money to his mother in Weston, and received a total of two letters in all that time.

After three years' active duty, he had enough. His CO encouraged him to attend community college, but once Terry returned to the old neighborhood, his reputation as a tough guy overcame his loftier intentions. He found a small apartment on South Meadow Street, on the second floor toward the back of the building. He was older now, and just a little wiser, and decided to work as independently as possible. He'd stick to burglary of small businesses. It was easy to break into stores and offices at night, rifle through drawers, and break open cash registers.

Terry could make anywhere from a hundred to fifteen hundred dollars a night depending on the business and their policies with regard to in-house cash. He always checked for alarm systems and knew how to disable some of the simpler ones. He watched for patrol cars, security guards, and dogs. He carried a knife for protection. He didn't want to be unarmed if jumped by members of another gang. He thought about carrying a gun, but because of its bulkiness, and the noise of firing it, he decided against it. He wore gloves, dark clothes, and a knit cap which he could pull down over his face if necessary. He was savvy, careful, and patient. At least he had been . . . until that stupid night in the Lutheran church.

Neighbors minded their own business and knew little of Terry's. When asked, he simply said he worked for Ace Roofing.

3

A MIGHTY FORTRESS

Brian Holloway's homicide created shock waves throughout the entire community as well as the church. Pastor Walker was pleased that the members of the church responded with an outpouring of kindness and sympathy. Flowers and meals were brought to the Holloways' home. Phone calls and cards expressed sympathy and support. And most important of all, the prayers of the faithful sustained Bob and Marge through this unimaginable time of emptiness and grief.

"We're praying for you," is an easy phrase to say, and a pious mouthing of words when one doesn't know what else to say. But the prayers that were said, both publicly in worship and privately in people's thoughts, expressed compassion, and motivated the worshipers to do something about the Holloways' situation. Because of the shock, and the prayers, and because Brian was "the best custodian the church ever had," attendance at Brian's memorial service was possibly the largest in Trinity's seventy year history.

The phone call on Tuesday morning was from the bishop in Indianapolis. John Ferguson had read about the death in the church in the Indianapolis Tribune. "Paul, I'm just calling to say how sad I was to read about your young custodian. I want to assure you that you and your congregation will be in my prayers."

"Thank you, Bishop. We really need them right now. This is the worst thing I've ever dealt with as a pastor."

"And this is one of the most terrible events in our synod's history. I've notified the cluster deans, so there will be a lot of prayers said in a lot of churches. Just be assured that you have my support and the support of the entire synod."

"Thank you very much. I really appreciate that. I'm sorry I haven't called you. I guess I've just been focused on arrangements here."

"Has a date been set for the funeral or memorial service?"

"Yes, it's going to be next Saturday. The family wanted to make it possible for Brian's classmates to attend."

"I think it would be good for me to be there. Would you like me to participate in the service?" the bishop asked.

"That would be wonderful. Let's see… would you be willing to read the scriptures?"

"No problem, Paul. And don't worry about which readings. I can get that information when I get to the church."

That afternoon Pastor Walker met with the Holloways to plan Brian's memorial. The autopsy had been completed and Brian had been taken to the Fairview Funeral Chapel. Bob and Marge had scheduled visitation for both Wednesday and Thursday evenings because of all the high school friends who wanted to see him one last time. They asked for a private family burial to take place on Friday with a memorial service on Saturday at one o'clock. Bob insisted that one of the hymns he wanted sung was "A Mighty Fortress" by Martin Luther. "That's a great hymn," agreed Marge, "but isn't it a bit too …too…loud or something…for a memorial service?"

"Maybe it would be fitting at the close of the service," Pastor Paul suggested, "as a kind of triumphant, victory recessional."

"I guess," agreed Marge, "if that's what Bob really wants."

The pastor also agreed to leave time for some of Brian's friends to share brief memories or stories about Brian. It seemed a good way for some people to express their grief, and often comforted the family to know that people had their own good memories. Paul asked Marge or Bob if they wanted to say a few words, but both of them concurred it would be too difficult. They were surprised when Sarah spoke up and said, "I think I'd like to."

* * * * * * *

The sky was dark and gloomy on Saturday afternoon, which seemed to fit the mood of the occasion. People arriving at the church after 12:30 found the parking lot full and had to drive a block or two to find parking on the street. As mourners gathered for the 1 p.m. memorial service it was sprinkling and the sky grew darker still. People were talking in the narthex and in the pews.

Someone mentioned Doctor Anderson's service back in 1963. In addition to being a popular family physician with a large and appreciative practice, Doctor Anderson was also a community leader, a member of the local school board, active in Kiwanis, and a volunteer for many civic causes. He had died rather suddenly, as his friends remembered, with an unexpected heart attack, shortly after retiring from practice. As it was for Doc Anderson, the church was filled for Brian's service. An extra row of folding chairs was added on the side aisle. People crowded into the balcony where the choir usually sat. Unlike Doc Anderson's service, however, the number of young people in their teens reminded the older members that Brian had a wonderful life yet to live, cut short by a stranger's wicked burst of fear and anger.

Paul was pleased to greet his bishop, John Ferguson, who shook his hand firmly. "Paul, it's a privilege to represent the other pastors and the sister congregations of the synod."

"Thank you, Bishop," Paul responded with a sigh. "It's really great that you came today. Here's a bulletin with the readings from the Psalms and John chapter 14. Will you please sit with me in the chancel?"

"Sounds good....and Paul, please call me any time, and let me know how things are going," the bishop said as he made his way into the crowded sanctuary. "Any time," he repeated.

Sid Thompson, the fire marshal, who occasionally attended church, approached Paul. "Looks like quite a crowd!"

"Yes it is. Probably the most people we've ever had here at Trinity."

"I'm sorry I won't be able to stay for the service, but I wanted to stop and express my condolences to Bob and Marge."

"You've got other duties to attend to?" Paul asked.

"No, the problem is that the church will be way over capacity for fire regulations. If I stay, someone will ask why I'm not enforcing the fire code. If I'm 'not here' I can say I didn't know how many people were in the building. Get it?"

"Sure, oh, yeah," Paul chuckled. "Now I understand. Thanks for dropping by. If anyone asks, I'll just have to say I never saw you!"

The service began with "What a Friend We Have in Jesus." Pastor Paul prayed and then introduced Bishop Ferguson. The bishop expressed sympathy and concern on behalf of the entire synod, and promised to keep the pastor and people of Trinity in his prayers. He read passages from Psalm 23 and 121, and John 14:1-6. Paul gave a short meditation on the place Jesus has prepared for Brian and the place Brian had in our lives. When he finished, Paul came to the chancel and asked for remembrances from friends and family.

One of Brian's high school buddies came to the lectern and talked about Brian's sense of humor. He told the story of a prank they had played on their soccer coach. The veterinarian for whom Brian worked told the congregation that Brian had shown great promise as a vet because of his love for animals, his bright analytical mind, his compassion, and his excellent work ethic.

When Sarah stood up to speak about her brother, it was hard to tell if she or her parents were the more nervous. "I loved my big brother … and Brian loved me. (There was a long pause as Sarah choked back the tears.) He also loved animals. When I was real little we had a gerbil named Roquefort. I loved holding him in my hand and watching him run on his wheel. Brian not only loved him, he seemed fascinated by everything about that silly gerbil! He wanted to know how his little legs worked and if he had … you know … male parts. (Chuckles rippled through the congregation.) He asked why he had whiskers and if gerbils were found in the wild.…all that stuff. When Roquefort died, we buried him in our back yard. I was so sad. Brian hugged me and held me for the longest time. I remember what he said. He said, 'It's okay, Sarah, all animals die sometime; and so will we some day.' But what amazed me was that he didn't seem scared at all.

"You know that Brian was studying to become a veterinarian. He was so smart! I don't know how he learned all that biology and chemistry. I just started algebra and it's hard!" Polite laughter floated through the congregation. "He told me about helping set a dog's leg at the clinic where he works. … I mean where he worked... He told me how the x-ray showed the shape and location of the fracture, and how the vet had to twist the leg just slightly so the bone would line up before putting a cast on it. Brian mixed the cast cement and everything. He was so smart. I'm really gonna miss my big brother. I love him a lot. (Again, Sarah paused to wipe away some tears and collect her thoughts.)

"Now I guess he won't be able to be a vet. But I think maybe in heaven he can be anything he wants. In fact, I've been thinking maybe he's in heaven right now, playing with Roquefort.… and Butch, our dog that we had put to sleep. I'll bet he'll help God welcome all the animals that die and help make them better again. Well, anyway …. I just have to think some good thoughts like that, otherwise …I couldn't stand it. I loved Brian and I know all of you did too. I'm sure gonna miss him. I guess that's all I have to say."

When Sarah sat down, there was not a dry eye in the church. Her friends were crying; her parents were crying. Pastor Paul needed several moments to compose himself before continuing with the service. During the quiet that followed the stories of remembrance, the congregation could hear the rain, now pounding on the church roof. It was good that a light luncheon was planned in the fellowship hall, and that the burial at the cemetery had occurred yesterday. At least no one would have to go out to the cemetery today.

The closing hymn began, and the ushers moved forward to escort the family down the aisle of the church. The congregation sang, *"A mighty fortress is our God, a bulwark never failing. Our helper, He, amid the flood, of mortal ills prevailing…."*

Marge and Bob and Sarah agreed to stand at the back of the church when the service was over. They wanted to thank everyone who came and who had called and sent cards and flowers. The congregation was singing the final verse: *"Though hordes of devils fill the land, all threatening to devour us. We will not fear, unmoved we stand. They cannot overpower us. Were they to take our house, goods, honor, child or spouse…"* Marge began to cry again. She had never really heard those words, though she had sung them many times. Now she knew why Bob had insisted on this hymn. *"Were they to take our house… goods, honor, child, or spouse; though life be wrenched away, they cannot win the day. The kingdom's ours forever!"*

•

4

PAUL AND CHERI WALKER

In the days that followed the funeral, Pastor Paul Walker struggled with his feelings. There was a profound sadness; he had truly loved young Brian. He also felt a gnawing guilt, wondering what he might have done to prevent Brian's death. He and the council knew the neighborhood was not as safe as it used to be, but everyone believed the church was a sacred place and should be the last place a violent crime would occur. At the September meeting of the council it was decided to install a security system with a coded door alarm and motion sensors inside the building.

Paul had been so excited five years ago about interviewing for the position at Trinity. He had been extremely impressed with the Call Committee, and was glad they had encouraged Cheri to participate in the interview. As the call committee reviewed the pastoral profile, they learned that Pastor Paul G. Walker was from Iowa. His father ran a small farm and was a professor at a small college. His mother was a nurse. Paul had graduated from the college where his father taught, and then went on to the Lutheran seminary in Des Moines. His first call was to a small town in Wisconsin where he had developed a strong youth program, and had demonstrated an interest in community service. He was married to Cheri, an office manager for a construction firm, and the mother of two sons, Chip and Randy. Paul's profile suggested that his strongest areas of ministry were outreach, youth ministry, and preaching.

What the profile could not describe was the pastor's maturity, the strength of his or her marriage, the dynamics of the pastor's family, and the depth of the pastor's faith. It is often these factors, as much as the professional qualifications, which determine the success of a working relationship between a congregation and its pastor.

Upon arriving for his interview at Trinity, Paul was glad to have Cheri at his side. A neighbor had agreed to watch the boys while Paul and Cheri traveled to Indiana for the interview. It was a sunny Saturday when they arrived in Weston to meet the call committee. They were offered refreshments and were seated at the head table. Two other tables, like the legs of a U, provided seating for the committee. Fred Wilson, chair of the committee offered a prayer and then began the interview. "Well, since I'm the chair of this here committee, I get to ask the first question. So here it is….how did you two meet?"

Paul was somewhat surprised that the first question would be about his personal life, but in the church, such questions are fair game and not unexpected. "I'd love to share that story," said Paul as he smiled at Cheri. "When I was newly ordained, a number of women in my first church tried to line me up with a daughter or granddaughter!" Paul said, shaking his head and smiling. The call committee burst into laughter, as they pictured the pastor's predicament.

Paul continued, "I dealt as gracefully as I could with a number of these well-intended but potentially disastrous situations. After about a year in the parish, a friend and I were having lunch together. There was a program where members of the school board were talking to community leaders about the upcoming school levy. As we sat down at one of the tables, I accidentally stepped on Cheri's purse lying on the floor. I stumbled slightly and apologized, and then she apologized sweetly for leaving her purse in the way."

Cheri interrupted to add her reaction, "He looked so embarrassed and contrite, like a little boy. I loved his innocent grin and I just wanted to hug him. I was attracted to him right away," she said, turning to smile at Paul. Members of the committee smiled in response.

Paul continued, "We chatted briefly during lunch and as I remember, I was pleased that she didn't react with nervousness when she learned I was a newly ordained pastor. She possessed an amazing self-confidence.... and the most amazing dimples! She told me she worked for Triangle Construction and her name was Cheri Schmidt ... and that both names were spelled with a *ch,* which made me stop and think a minute. Here's the funny part. Without thinking, I looked to see if she was wearing a ring. You know, I didn't want to be flirting with a married woman!"" The committee members chuckled again. "Well, I noticed a class ring on her finger, and I recognized the inscription. I leaned over and whispered to her, 'Quaecumque sunt vera,' that's a Northwestern University ring isn't it?"

Cheri spoke again, "I remember asking him, 'You speak Latin?'"

"Not really," I replied. "But when I saw the motto on your class ring I remembered those words and thought it was great that a Big Ten university used a biblical motto. She said 'Whatever is true' is biblical? And I said, 'Sure, it's from Paul's letter to the Philippians. Whatever is true, whatever is just, whatever is beautiful, think on these things.' I think she was impressed. But what impressed me," Paul continued, "was her smile... and her dimples! All through the lunch meeting, those words kept going through my mind: whatever is beautiful, think on these things. And all I could think about... were her dimples!

"So," Fred replied, "it sounds like love at first sight!"

"Well, it took me a few days to get up the nerve to call the construction firm where she worked. She sounded delighted that I called; so I asked if I could take her out to dinner. About a year later we were married, which I think brought as much joy to the church members as it did to our families. You know, we've been married almost five years, and I still love her smile... and her dimples!"

Fred, the chairman, spoke again, "Thanks, Paul, that was a great story. Now it's your turn to ask us a question; what would you like to know about us?"

Paul took a deep breath and relaxed, having weathered the first question. "In reading your mission profile it appears that the area around the church is a changing neighborhood. Do most of the members still live near the church? How do you feel about the neighborhood?"

After a brief silence, Bonnie spoke up. She explained that she and her husband were married at Trinity thirty five years ago, "and we still live in the same house. But a lot of our members have moved to newer developments and only come back to worship at Trinity on Sundays. We look forward to seeing these old friends and going out to lunch together after church is over."

Rick joined the conversation, telling Paul that several members are teachers at Weston High and Lincoln Middle School here in the neighborhood. "Dr. Anderson, a beloved member who died several years back was a member of the local school board. He lived right across the street from the church."

Fred Wilson added, "Some of our new members have come from the neighborhood, but the neighborhood is definitely changing. More ethnic minorities are moving in. We've had an influx of blacks and Hispanics, and recently some Russians."

Bonnie spoke again, "Pastor Bjornstad, our former pastor, did some house-to-house calling in the neighborhood, but he soon got discouraged because nobody came to church."

Pastor Walker responded, "I have some ideas from seminary and from my previous parish experience that I think might work in Weston. I really want to get to know the neighborhood and its people. When we learn what is needed in the way of help or services in this community, our church should partner with other organizations to provide for that need. The first step is getting acquainted and listening."

Fred was impressed that the candidate was already using the pronoun "we" and referring to Trinity as "our church."

"Pastor Bjornstad didn't think the Blacks and Hispanics would come to a Lutheran church," said one of the members.

"That all depends on how they're welcomed, and how they perceive what we are doing here," replied Pastor Walker.

Fred Wilson turned to Rick, "Rick, I think you've got the next question for the pastor?"

"Yes. Pastor Walker, everyone seems to mean something slightly different when they talk about faith. How would you define faith?"

"That's a good question, Rick," Paul replied. "In the Lutheran tradition, faith means more than just believing in God. Faith means trust and commitment. Lutherans believe that God is always the initiator in the relationship. Even when a person feels like they've found God, the truth is, God was there all along, waiting for awareness of his grace and mercy. I like how Martin Luther described the work of the Holy Spirit in the Small Catechism: 'I believe that I cannot by my own understanding or effort, believe in Jesus Christ my Lord or come to him, but the Holy Spirit has called me through the gospel, enlightened me with his gifts, and sanctified and kept me in true faith.' Faith, then, is our response, as we are moved by the Holy Spirit. Faith is the trust we place in God because God is 'gracious and full of compassion and abounding in steadfast love.'"

"Thank you, Pastor," Fred replied.

The call committee, council, and members of Trinity were impressed with the young pastoral candidate. There was a sparkle in his eyes and enthusiasm in his spirit. He was quick to smile and laugh. He listened well and spoke clearly and precisely.

Cheri, the young pastor's wife sat quietly during most of the interview with the call committee. Her answers to several questions were brief and to the point. "How do you see your role as a pastor's wife?" Bonnie asked.

"I hope you don't expect me to be an assistant pastor!" Cheri replied with a smile. "The traditional pastor lived in a parsonage owned by the church and his wife taught Sunday School, may have directed the choir or played the organ, and was active in the Women's Guild. I confess... I am NOT a traditional pastor's wife! My faith IS important to me. I'll be here for worship on Sunday morning, and I do enjoy singing in the choir. I also hope to work outside the home, but my first priority is as mother to Chip and Randy and as Paul's wife."

Later in the day, several women were responsible for giving Cheri a tour of Weston during the second part of Paul's interview. Cheri was even more animated as they drove around the neighborhood. She told them proudly about their two sons, Chip who was almost four, and Randy who was two. She talked about her career as a business woman, insisting that it was important but would not take precedence over her family. The women were impressed that she, too, was bright and friendly.

The following Sunday, the call committee made a unanimous recommendation to the congregation, and the members voted to call him as their next pastor. While some members remained skeptical, most hoped that Pastor Walker would indeed help their church to develop a successful neighborhood ministry.

* * * * * * *

Paul eagerly accepted the call and was excited to begin working in an older neighborhood and a more urban environment. His wife Cheri wasn't so sure. She was concerned about the schools their sons would attend, and whether or not she would be able to find a decent job. She was reluctant to leave the small town of Twin Lakes, Wisconsin, where both Chip and Randy had been born. Paul and Cheri found a three bedroom bungalow just five blocks from the elementary school. There was a swing set in the back yard and all it needed was a little sanding and a fresh coat of paint. Much to Cheri's delight, the boys adjusted quickly to their new home.

The first year in Weston passed quickly. Paul spent many afternoons and evenings visiting with members in their homes. It was not easy setting up appointments. With more and more women working outside the home, many couples were reluctant to give up an evening for a social visit with the pastor. Most, however, were polite and hospitable.

He wanted to be well acquainted with his parishioners. He also sensed that their trust and loyalty made leadership much easier.

One of his more intriguing visits was with Jana Nygaard and her daughter Carla. Jana was a single mom who divorced her husband when Carla was seven. He was a long-haul truck driver. He enjoyed the company of a female driving partner on his cross- country trips. He felt Jana should understand, but she didn't. Jana had done many hours of counseling with Pastor Bjornstad who urged her to forgive her husband and keep her marriage intact. She had tried, but when Carl began talking about the other woman in front of their daughter, Jana knew she could not go on living this way. She filed for divorce and explained it to Carla as best she could. Then with a smile, she explained to Pastor Walker how raising Carla as a single mom had shown her she had strengths she didn't know she had.

As Paul listened, Jana told how she had become inactive, because of the divorce. She wasn't sure what others might think, but she really missed teaching Sunday School. Paul said he was sure that God understood her decision to end the marriage, and would not hold that decision against her. He also suggested to her that he needed an assistant to lead parts of the confirmation program. Jana was thrilled at the possibility and during the next few years became one of his best education leaders. Paul admired her lively spirit and infectious laugh.

Carla joined the confirmation program and was always in the center of a circle of girls. She was bright and confident, and the other girls looked to her as a leader. Her voice and her laughter sounded so much like her mother's that Paul could not tell them apart on the phone. After being confirmed, Carla began organizing events for the youth group, with the help and support of her mother. Paul couldn't believe how fortunate the church was to have these two energetic women "back in the fold."

The other pillar among his education leaders was Marge Holloway. At his weekly Bible studies, she was always asking questions. No matter how he answered, she always had a follow-up question. Paul was patient and soon realized she was sincerely interested in growing in her faith. He was eager to get her husband Bob involved, but Bob politely declined the invitation to usher, to attend forums, or to help with maintenance of church property. Bob explained that he tried to keep the commandments, including worshiping God every Sunday. He simply didn't want to "get dragged into all that Christian fellowship stuff." Paul admired the Holloways who seemed to be outstanding parents. Their children, Brian and Sarah were among the most faithful at Sunday School and confirmation.

Fred Schmidt was one of Paul's first and most reliable supporters. He was quiet, but always present when there was work to be done. He ushered almost every Sunday. He frequently dropped by the office to visit with Carol, the secretary, and then would ask Paul if he'd like to go to lunch . . . and he always paid the tab. It was his personal ministry for his pastor.

As Paul was getting acquainted with members, they were observing and evaluating him. They found their new pastor to be quite a contrast to the former pastor who seemed friendly and pious, but slightly aloof from their everyday lives. Pastor Bjornstad and his wife had retired to Florida, and they were missed by many members, especially the older folks who hoped they would stay in Weston. Pastor Walker had a much more casual style, and to the younger people he seemed more approachable. He was genuinely interested in their everyday lives and experiences.

During the second year of his ministry at Trinity, Paul was most pleased when Luther and Joetta Harmon and their children joined the church. It was the first African-American family to become members. Luther confided that he had become uncomfortable with some of his Baptist brothers, and decided that with a name like Luther, he should check out this Lutheran church up the street. Joetta said she was really afraid that the children might be hurt by the racism they expected to find in an all-white church. But after several months of participation, they were surprised to be so warmly welcomed. The children reported one uncomfortable exchange, an unintentional racist remark from one of their classmates, which was gently corrected by the Sunday School teacher.

With Chip going into first grade and Randy enrolled in preschool that fall, Cheri began looking for a job as an office manager. She interviewed for a position in a law office with four attorneys. They had several legal assistants, but needed someone with experience to handle the business aspects of the firm, including payroll, billing, and purchasing. During the interview, the partners were pleased to learn Cheri had a bachelor's degree in Business Management, and several years' work experience as the office manager for a construction firm. When they questioned her lack of prior legal experience, Cheri burst out laughing! "My dad is an attorney in Milwaukee. I grew up listening to talk about depositions, briefs, and billable hours at breakfast, lunch, and dinner!" Her confidence impressed them and she was hired. The job provided some additional income and an opportunity for Cheri to make new friends outside the church. Paul was very proud of Cheri for landing such a challenging job and for being such a loving wife and mother.

In his third year as pastor, Paul knew the honeymoon period with Trinity was over. When he returned from his three week vacation in mid-August, the treasurer reported that offerings were down (as they always were during the summer) and that several bills had not been paid. One of the council members, George Downing, asked if attendance and offerings might be better "if the pastor wasn't gone all summer. I don't know of any job where the employee gets four weeks of vacation after working for only a couple of years," he complained.

The council president did her best to explain the terms of the pastor's call, and the pastor's need for rest and renewal. It was a good attempt at support, but the council meeting ended on a gloomy note. Paul was thankful the fall programs would begin in a couple of weeks, thankful that Sunday offerings and people's spirits would improve with the increase in activity.

What parishioners couldn't see was their pastor's prayer life, at home before meals, in his car as he drove to the church, morning, afternoon, and evening, and with his wife Cheri before falling asleep each night. Sharing with God his anxieties, his hopes, his concerns for others, seemed as natural as breathing. Paul knew he could not do the work he did without God's constant support and guidance. He prayed as he prepared his sermons. He prayed, not only in the hospital room, but again as he walked down the hall, sometimes with tears in his eyes. He thanked God for these people, his extended family, with whom he shared his faith each day and each week. He thanked God for his supportive wife and two healthy and energetic sons. He prayed for couples about to be married and for families in grief.

5

THE COMMUNITY FAIR

Pastor Walker continued to reflect on the mission of Trinity, wondering if some of his ideas might have contributed to Brian's tragic death. He remembered several years ago, how he had approached some of his leaders with the concept of a community fair. Various business and non-profit groups in the neighborhood would be asked to set up a table or booth in the church or in the parking lot on a Saturday to display merchandise, advertise, provide a service, or promote their organization. Fred Wilson, Bill Trogdon, and Bonnie Ledbetter, all thought it sounded like a great idea, a big "getting to know you" party! Paul asked Carol, the parish secretary, if she would be willing to help organize the event and she said it sounded like fun!

When Paul presented the idea to the council it was greeted with mixed reactions. Louise Downing said it sounded like a lot of work for nothing. Stan Malsberger had questions about liability and church security. Reluctantly, approval was given, and the council president, Bill Trogdon, agreed to contact the city for a permit.

The first community fair was scheduled for June, the first Saturday after school was out for the summer. Racial tension was high in the city even though integration of neighborhood schools had been in effect for years. The growing number of Russian and eastern European immigrants added to the tension. In the neighborhood surrounding the church there were many living at or below the poverty level. Neighborhood gangs often replaced families as the source of self-esteem and personal support for teenagers. The level of trust among neighbors was declining, including trust in institutions such as the church. Everyone held their breath.

For Paul, that first fair had been a big disappointment. He had hoped for a hundred kids or more, for tons of ice cream to be consumed, for adults to return to their homes and apartments saying what a good time they had. Only four businesses and four community agencies agreed to set up booths. Less than a hundred people from the neighborhood attended. Cheri consoled him by reminding him of the positive things. Church members met neighbors who had no church. Neighbors who did attend expressed appreciation for the booths and tour of the church building. And both the kids and adults loved the ice cream!

* * * * * * *

Saturday, June 23, 1990

Paul was now in his fifth year at Trinity. The Community Fair was, perhaps, the only bright spot in the church's outreach. It was a neighborhood event that had increased in attendance and participation each year since its inception. Each year, it had gained support both within the church and in the community. This year, the fair would be held again in June. Vacation Bible School would be the big event for July; and in August, Pastor Paul and his family hoped to get away for some vacation before gearing up for fall. A new participant this year, the owner of the bowling alley said he would set up a small bowling game which kids could play for 25 cents. He would offer prizes of free passes to the bowling alley located just two blocks south of the church.

Paul himself visited the local medical clinic to discuss the availability of nurses or doctors for brief clinical consultation. They discussed triage, diagnosing and prioritizing patients, and agreed that very simple medical conditions might even be treated at the church. Most would be asked to come to the clinic for an appointment. Sliding scale fees would be explained for those who could not afford treatment, and the simplest cases would be treated as charity without charge. On the day of the fair, one nurse sat at a table outside, and two worked in the Sunday School rooms set up as small consultation/examining rooms. One of the doctors agreed to come for a couple of hours in the afternoon.

Fred Schmidt, who was an avid blood donor, agreed to speak with the folks at the Blood Bank to arrange for the bloodmobile to park in the parking lot that day. Church members would sign up ahead of time for appointments, but drop-ins from the neighborhood would be welcome.

Pastor Paul and the worship committee planned the church tours, with a well-prepared lesson on Lutheran worship and the various symbols to be seen in the sanctuary.

The property chairman, Stan Malsberger, asked again about security. "You will keep the offices locked, won't you, Pastor?"

"Of course, Stan," the pastor reassured him.

Luther and Joetta Harmon talked about the neighborhood children and agreed to sponsor a clown who would entertain children with balloon tying. Joetta became so excited, she offered to do "face painting" with make up and decals. The women's group planned to serve ice cream in small disposable cups, and agreed with Pastor Paul that a simple sign asking for donations would be more hospitable than stating a price. This year, they were expecting about three hundred visitors, nearly half being children!

Some of the displays had been brought to the church on Friday. The parking lot was bustling with activity at nine o'clock Saturday morning. This was the kind of energy Paul had envisioned, members getting to know non-members, and the community getting to know Trinity. By ten, the sun had warmed the area around the church. Twenty or thirty children ran from the parking lot to the church doors, waiting for the ice cream being brought from the church freezer.

Chip and Randy were telling other kids about the clown and

bragging that their dad was the pastor. They also had to explain to some of them what a "pastor" is. Brian Holloway, Trinity's young custodian, was helping Curt from the bowling alley set up his game table. Several adults were already talking quietly to the nurse about what they suspected were head lice in their children's hair.

It was just after noon when the first small group hesitantly agreed to tour the church inside. There were only five people, an older black couple, two Hispanic young men, and an inquisitive ten-year-old friend of Chip's. Apparently the tour went well, because the word spread that no one had been pressured to "sign up for religion." Marge Holloway led several groups through that afternoon and was amazed at the diversity of ethnic groups, income levels, and ages.

Terry Mankovic wasn't a member of Trinity, but had lived in the neighborhood all his life, except for a brief stint in the army. As he ambled through the parking lot, he remembered an incident from his childhood and the old gray-haired guy who had yelled at him right here near the church entrance. He didn't know at the time that old Pastor Bjornstad was having a bad day. All Terry knew was that his father had died when he was in eighth grade. *Too bad my old man never had a chance to turn gray like the geezer who preached about God's love. Where was God when my dad got run over?* Terry was still bitter. He was angry at the old pastor for yelling at him, and angry at God for taking his dad. Maybe he could bum a free meal from the stupid Christians.

"Are you going inside?" asked one of the church members, interrupting his memories. "There's a tour of the church just starting."

What the heck, Terry thought, *it's not every day I get invited to case a job for a future burglary!* "Sure, why not," he said to the woman. *Christians sure are stupid,* he thought to himself.

Inside the church Pastor Walker introduced himself to the group and welcomed them to Trinity's Community Fair. "I hope you enjoy being inside the church; it's getting pretty warm out in the parking lot. I promise I'm not going to do an altar call and I'm not asking you for money. I just want to explain some things about our church and why we're here. And … I want to invite anyone who doesn't belong to a church to come and worship with us any Sunday morning." Paul answered questions about the altar paraments, and explained that the name "Trinity" reminded members that there was one God known in three ways, as Father the Creator, Jesus the Son, and God the Holy Spirit. Paul took the group through the Sunday School rooms, past the offices, and downstairs into the fellowship hall. "This is where we have coffee and church pot-luck dinners," he told the group. "We have a well-equipped kitchen, and the women here are wonderful cooks."

Terry noted the windows above the kitchen sink, and he could see people walking along the parking lot sidewalk outside. *Easy entrance,* he thought to himself.

Paul was happy when Cheri showed up at three that afternoon to get the boys. She invited Paul to come outside for some ice cream, and he was glad to take a break. They sat at a card table in the shade of a large old elm tree. "How's the fair going this year?" Cheri asked as she watched Randy and Chip playing with friends.

"I think we're going to have over three hundred people!" Paul answered excitedly. "It's definitely the most successful one so far! I can't believe how the response is growing to the mini-clinic they've set up. I never realized there were so many people who have no insurance and no access to health care."

"How are the tours going inside the church?" Cheri asked.

"I think that gets easier every year. I wish we could see results in terms of church growth, but even without new members, I believe we're building good relationships in the neighborhood." Paul looked again at the parking lot. Carla Nygaard was leading a group of children in a game of follow-the-leader. Adults stood next to their children waiting in line to have their face painted with crosses and butterflies. In a couple of hours this would all be gone … until next year. There was no doubt in his mind this was the right thing for Trinity to be doing.

"Can you imagine what old Pastor Bjornstad would say if he were here?" Cheri chided. She and Paul both shook their heads as they pictured the incongruous image of the controller in the midst of chaos.

"No I can't," Paul replied, "but I'll bet he'd like the ice cream!"

As they rose from the table, Cheri yelled, "C'mon boys, it's time to go home!"

Chip yelled back, "Do we have to?"

6

PAUL VISITS BOB AND MARGE

Labor Day, September 3

A couple of weeks after the funeral for Brian, Pastor Walker called the Holloways to express his continuing concern and to make an appointment to visit at their home. It was shortly after dinner when he dialed their number. Bob answered with a gruff, "Hello."

"Bob, this is Pastor Walker. I'm just calling to check in. I'm sure this has been a difficult time for you and Marge."

"Yeah, it has."

"I've had your family in my prayers. I was wondering if I could make an appointment to stop by and visit."

"Just a minute, I'll let you talk to Marge." Paul could hear him yell to the other room, but it sounded like Bob had put his hand over the phone, "Marge! Pastor wants to talk to you!" In a minute, Marge answered.

"Hello, Pastor Paul?" Marge asked timidly.

"Yes, Marge, I was calling to ask if I could make a visit with you and Bob."

"Sure. I guess that would be okay. Just a minute." Marge turned away from the phone. "Bob, it is okay if the pastor comes over?" Then, "Bob says it's okay with him. What night would you like to visit?"

"How about next Monday? Will you be out of town on Labor Day?"

"No, that would be fine. What time can we expect you?"

"About seven o'clock, if that's all right."

"See you then."

The next day in his office, Paul wrote the Labor Day appointment in his calendar and began working on a list of college students and where they were enrolled. Brian had been accepted at both Indiana and Purdue last spring, and planned to attend Purdue this fall. Paul paused a few moments to remember and to pray.

Paul was grateful for the Labor Day weekend. He knew that from now until Easter he would be working long days with very few breaks. He spent most of the day, Monday, mowing the lawn and working in his yard. After dinner, he drove to the Holloways'. They welcomed him into their home for the first time since the funeral. The evening was cooler and the days were getting shorter.

"Would you like some coffee, or juice or pop?" Marge asked him.

"No, thanks," Paul replied. He was not really thirsty; but wanting to be gracious he added, "I would like a glass of water, however."

"Bob, what would you like?" Marge asked her husband.

"Coffee," Bob answered. Marge started toward the kitchen. "And don't forget the cream!" he yelled irritably.

Marge went into the kitchen to prepare the drinks and fix a plate of cookies. Bob sat with his hands folded between his knees and his head drooping. Sarah came into the living room and greeted Pastor Paul with a hug. Then she went into the kitchen to help her mom.

Paul broke the silence, "Bob, I wish I knew what to say or do."

"Nothing you can do, Pastor." Again there was an awkward silence.

"This must be so terribly hard, I can't imagine," Paul offered. But there was no response. Marge came back with drinks and cookies, and she thanked Paul for coming. The conversation roamed back and forth between current happenings at church and the events surrounding Brian's death and funeral. Paul noted that Marge was not as talkative as she usually was. She kept glancing at Bob as though waiting for him to add something or enter the conversation. After about an hour, Paul asked Bob and Marge if they might be able to go out of town for a few days. "A change of routine might be helpful for both of you," he suggested.

"Hey, I'd love to go up north and do some fishing, but we're really busy at work, so I guess that'll have to wait," Bob replied.

"Would it be helpful if I came by once a week for a while, just to talk about Brian, or things in general?"

"No, I really don't want to talk about it," Bob answered, "but Marge.... if you want to meet with the pastor go right ahead."

"Is there anything else I can do for you folks?" Paul asked.

"I just hope they catch the bastard that did it; pardon my English, Pastor."

Paul offered a brief prayer, thanked Marge for the water, excused himself, and drove home.

7

THE HOLLOWAYS' GRIEF

Monday, September 10, 1990

Pastor Paul Walker was troubled. He stood in the parking lot, gazing up at the steeple of Trinity Lutheran. The cross glowed at night from the fluorescent light inside. Paul remembered that one of the bulbs had burned out and needed to be replaced. He wished they would all burn out! He felt the light degraded this sacred symbol. However, the cross was not the source of his troubled spirit. Though several weeks had passed, Paul realized he was still thinking about Brian Holloway's death. As Paul walked toward the church, his eyes dropped from the cross to the church doors. He glanced at the new basement windows which reminded him of the recent tragedy. He shook his head in disgust and sadness, and whispered a prayer, "God, how could you let that happen? Forgive me for thinking it couldn't happen in a church."

Paul grew up on a small farm in Iowa. He knew he didn't want to be a farmer. In Sunday School he heard the story of Jonah, and while the other kids loved the part about Jonah being swallowed by a whale, Paul liked the part where Jonah preached to the people of Nineveh and they repented. When Paul was in college and seminary he felt called to be a pastor, and challenged to bring the gospel to people living in the city. He had visions of working with street gangs, talking with them about the love of God and the blessings of belonging to a church. Now, at the age of 36, his dream seemed so naïve. *How quickly my idealism has faded,* he thought, as he pressed the security code, entered the back door of the church, and climbed the steps to the church office.

His youthful vision of "saving" gang members had been shattered by the recent events at Trinity. *My fifth year as pastor of an inner-city parish and I haven't even met a gang member!* Graffiti was everywhere. The scribbled words and symbols made no sense to Paul, and when he found it sprayed on church property, as he had last week, it made his blood boil. Graffiti, he realized, was just the tip of the iceberg. The real problems of the city lie much deeper.

Paul stopped at the office door and saw the parish secretary busy folding newsletters. "Good morning, Carol!" he said, forcing himself to sound cheerful.

"Good morning, Pastor!" Carol replied. "Would you like some coffee? I just made some."

"Sure, that would be great."

"I'll bring it to your study in a few minutes; as soon as I finish the newsletter."

"Thanks," Paul replied, as he opened the door to his office across the hall.

Five years ago, when Pastor Paul Walker accepted the call to Trinity, he had been excited about his new opportunity. He felt like he could fly! But today he felt like he weighed five hundred pounds and was sinking in quicksand. Cheri was working now at the law firm of Etheridge, Juarez, Fuscio, and Barkley. Paul appreciated Cheri's desire to work professionally. They continued to negotiate parental responsibilities for Chip, who was about to turn nine, and Randy who was seven. Carol walked in and placed a cup of hot coffee on his desk. "Is there anything else you need right now?"

"No, not right now, but thanks for the coffee." As he carefully sipped the steaming brew, he looked at his desk calendar and realized*....today is exactly one month... exactly one month since that terrible night at the church, when, as some people say, "All hell broke loose."*

He picked up the phone and called Marge Holloway. "Hello, Marge? This is Pastor Paul. I was just looking at my calendar and realized that ... it's been a month since ...since Brian ... died." It had also been a week since Paul's "post-funeral" visit with Bob and Marge at their home Labor Day evening.

Marge began sobbing. Paul could hear her futile efforts to calm herself. Finally, she managed a few words, "Thank you, Paul, for calling."

"Marge, I wish there was something I could do. Losing your son is just the most awful thing."

"It hurts so bad, Pastor. It just keeps hurting and hurting..."

"Is there anything, anything I can do to help?"

"Could you possibly ... come by the house? You said last week you'd be willing to do that. I always feel better after we've talked and prayed together."

"I have some commitments this morning, but I could come by about one o'clock." Paul wasn't sure what he could say or do to ease Marge's pain. As uncomfortable as he knew he would be, he knew he should go. There were other church matters on his mind, but the Holloways were a priority at a time like this. He met with the stewardship chairman at 11:30 to discuss plans for the Every Member Response in November. At 12:35 he stuck his head in the secretary's office to let Carol know he was leaving. He pulled into a fast food place, drove to the drive-up window, and ate in his car. The afternoon sun was making it very warm in the car, so he gulped down the cheeseburger, said a prayer for Marge and Bob, turned on the air-conditioner, and drove to the Holloways', arriving at 1:15.

Marge opened the door. Her eyes were red and wet, her face puffy from crying. As soon as Paul walked into the living room, she leaned against him and began sobbing. She was wearing jeans and a light blouse, and she was barefoot. Paul held her and felt her warm body pressing tightly against his.

"Thank you, Paul, for coming," Marge sniffed between her sobs. She pressed her head against his chest and continued crying. It seemed she would never let go. Perhaps it was only a minute, but Paul was becoming uncomfortable about the prolonged closeness. Finally, she looked up and gazed into his eyes, put her hand behind his head, stretched on her tiptoes, and kissed him on the cheek. It startled him and he felt his heart pounding.

Whoa! Paul thought to himself. *Marge is a beautiful woman. She may be a few years older than me, but her body feels so warm against mine.* Her brown eyes sparkled with the moisture from her tears. Her lips were parted slightly as she breathed against his cheek. He felt a hunger stirring within him. Gently, he took her arms and pushed her away. He didn't know what to say; he wanted her to talk. He moved her toward the sofa and sat down next to her and took her hands. "Marge, I keep wondering if my naivete was in some way responsible for Brian's death."

"No, Paul, please don't feel that way. I don't know what's happening to me," Marge spoke barely above a whisper. "I'm not myself anymore. I'm not sure what's happening to Bob. He won't talk to me at all. I've talked and talked about Brian, about our grief, about little everyday things, but he doesn't answer me. I've begged and pleaded with him. I've asked him to go see the doctor, or make an appointment to talk to you, but he won't do it. He walks around here like a zombie. There's a wall or canyon between us and I can't reach him, and he doesn't seem to care about me. I'm so lonely. I don't know who I am or what I'm doing."

"Marge, Marge, first of all, let me assure you, you are not crazy, you are grieving. And what you and Bob are experiencing is what many couples experience when they lose a child. The way Bob is behaving is not uncommon. Everyone grieves in different ways. Because of the trauma of your loss, however, it would be advisable for both of you to see a doctor, and possibly get some medication to help your nerves, your depression, to help you sleep, that sort of thing."

"Thank you, Paul; I'm sure you're right. I guess I should go even if Bob won't." She stared into his eyes. She had been sitting with one leg under her body. She moved closer, then reached out and wrapped her arms around his neck and kissed him, first on the cheek and then gently on the lips. Paul grabbed her arms and gently pushed her away. Her kiss felt good; too good. He rose from the sofa and mumbled, "I think I'd better go."

"Please Paul, hold me," she whispered as she stood, moving close again.

"Marge, you're really vulnerable right now. And I'm not feeling too strong myself. I think it would be best if I left."

"Maybe you're right," Marge said, dropping her head in resignation. "But I appreciate all you've done for me and my family."

Paul made his way out the front door to his car. His face felt flushed and he was shaking from the deep feelings of desire Marge had stirred in him. He was amazed at how strong Marge's grasp had been.

* * * * * * *

Marge Holloway had become one of Trinity's most active members since Pastor Walker and his family came to Weston. Paul appreciated her keen interest and perceptive questions during his Bible studies. She seemed fascinated with the historical background of the Hebrew Scriptures, encouraging the pastor to share all he could remember from his seminary classes. She was often puzzled by actions and traits attributed to God which seemed contrary to her Christian understanding of a loving God. The former pastor had always put her off with statements like, "Sometimes, Marge, God's Word is beyond our understanding; we just have to accept it on faith." But whenever Marge asked Paul, "Why would God....?" he would struggle to answer, admitting it was speculation, or providing a Jewish perspective which helped Marge grow, both intellectually and spiritually. Marge became very fond of their new pastor and admired his compassion; and he seemed so wise for a man several years younger than her husband. Not only that, but he was very good-looking as well. His slim, athletic build from his college baseball days was still intact.

For the past three summers, Marge had been coordinator for Vacation Bible School. Her son Brian had graduated from high school and would have attended college in the fall. Her daughter Sara was about to enter high school. In July Sara had been a great help as her VBS Assistant. Marge enjoyed calling and recruiting women and high school students for teachers and helpers. She loved working with the children who were so eager and full of energy! This was the most complex and challenging job Marge had ever done, outside of being a mom; and even though she wasn't paid, it gave her such a sense of satisfaction and pride!

Bob Holloway seldom attended Bible studies, but was very faithful about coming to church for worship. He was a hard-working blue-collar foreman for a local asphalt company. He was respected for his integrity and work ethic. In his oversight of the paving crew, the other workers respected his knowledge and experience. They considered him fair and helpful, and knew he would not ask them to do anything he hadn't done or wouldn't do himself. Bob believed that being a Christian meant believing in God and being a good person. His faith was just that simple, and he could see no reason for all the questions and studies which seemed to interest his wife and other members of the church.

Bob was proud of the fact that he had worked for the same company for twenty-three years, since high school in fact. Bob was handsome, had a good steady job, and seemed like such an honest, good man, that Marge had fallen head over heals for him. They met when he was twenty-one and she was only seventeen. As soon as she graduated, they were married. Brian was born a year later, and Sarah four years after that. Bob was insistent that Marge would never have to work. He would support his wife and family like a good Christian man. Marge was impressed with his strength at first, but when she spoke about wanting to work after the kids were in school, he wouldn't hear of it. She discovered a very stubborn side to his strong character which would require a lot of tolerance and patience on her part.

Bob also believed that being a good person meant controlling one's temper. He had had problems with that, even as a kid. It had gotten him into trouble at school. He had seen his dad hit his mom on several occasions and he swore he would never hit his wife or beat his kids. Once, when Brian and Sara were twelve and eight, after a particularly difficult day at work, Bob came home about an hour late. Dinner, which had been ready an hour earlier, was cold. The kids had already eaten and were playing noisily. Brian was chasing Sarah around the living room with a frog he had found, saying, "Froggy wants a kiss!" Sarah ran screaming. And Bob lost it. Rising from the dinner table, he grabbed an empty pot and flung it across the living room as he yelled, "STOP IT!" The pot hit the wall with a loud clang. Both kids froze and stared at their dad. The look on his face terrified them both. Throwing things, or banging a fist on a table or through a wall, was not uncommon. All Bob knew was that he had never hit Marge. He could not understand their fear of his anger.

With Brian's death, the stress in their relationship hit an all time high. Bob was angry, but had no clue what to do with the rage inside. He held it in, denying how terrible it was. Bob was like a silent robot at work and at home. Marge's grief was like the tide. One day she would feel a wonderful peace, knowing that Brian was in heaven with God. *Surely this is the peace of Christ that passes all understanding,* she thought to herself. The next day she would collapse on the bed in wave after wave of tears. Her thick reddish brown hair fell recklessly about her face. She struggled to get off the bed, take a shower, and get dressed by noon. She shook trying to get a cup of hot water out of the microwave. *What's wrong with me; I can't do anything! I'm shaking so bad. I need something to do. But if I had to do something, I know I couldn't do it! God, how am I ever going to get through this?*

The hardest part of her day was when Bob came home from work. "Where's dinner?" was the question on days she hadn't fixed anything. When she did, it was even worse. "Barbequed ribs again?" No matter what she did, Bob was angry. Sarah avoided her dad, and Marge found herself wanting to avoid him too. Marge was thankful that Vacation Bible School had been finished in July this summer. At least she didn't have to wonder if she could get through that! She was thankful for

September, knowing that the fall schedule at church would include Bible study where she would find caring and support from her friends.

The past few weeks had been the most traumatic of Marge's life and Pastor Walker's as well. School had begun in the Weston School District right after Labor Day. Paul tried to focus on the everyday events of his church and family. Chip was beginning fourth grade and Randy was going into second. Paul and Cheri had shared the boys' excitement on the first day of class. Paul made a point of coming home early in the afternoon to hear his sons' stories about their first weeks of school. Cheri saw the boys off in the morning; but after getting dinner and tucking them into bed at night, she seemed preoccupied with problems at the law firm. Paul listened to his wife as well as he could, but his mind kept going back to Bob and Marge.

His church was in turmoil, and everything seemed out of control. He knew he should be a "non-anxious presence" representing the "peace of the Lord," but his anxiety had never been higher. Perhaps his emphasis on neighborhood ministry had left the church too vulnerable. Perhaps he was responsible, in some way that he couldn't understand, for Brian's death. Everyone expected him to hold things together, but who would hold him together? Paul prayed, wishing he could erase the past month, asking God to give him the strength he needed and couldn't find. He had never felt such a strong attraction to another woman. The more he tried not to think about it, the more the vision of Marge intruded upon his mind. *So wrong, yet such an exciting possibility. Forbidden, yet so inviting!*

* * * * * * *

Tuesday, September 25

Two weeks after his first visit, Paul called Marge again, and asked if he could stop by to see her. He told himself it was out of concern for her, but suspected that a more selfish motive was lurking. She told him she would like to see him, so he scheduled another afternoon meeting. He wondered if she would be more reserved this time, yet secretly hoped she might still be as full of desire as she had been before. Had she been thinking about him as much as he had about her?

Driving to Marge's house, Paul nearly ran a stop sign. He realized he was thinking about what might happen when he was alone with her again. *What would it be like? Stop it! You know it isn't right to entertain fantasies. You know you're putting yourself at risk.* His heart was racing as he pushed the doorbell.

As soon as he slid through the door, she reached up and put her arms around him. "It's good to see you again," she whispered. She was wearing a silky green rayon bathrobe, tied at her waist.

Paul responded by wrapping his arms around her. He could feel there was nothing underneath the robe but her bare skin. "I've wanted to see you again," Paul whispered back.

Slowly they released each other and moved toward the sofa. "I'm sorry I didn't have time to get dressed. I just got out of the shower," Marge explained. She put one knee on the sofa and sat down, pulling her legs up under her.

"Oh, that's okay," Paul replied nervously. They sat facing each other, making small talk; Paul even said a prayer. Each began looking for signs from the other, waiting to see who would make the first move. Marge was the first to stand. She reached out and took Paul's hand. He stood to face her. Her bathrobe clung loosely to the curves of her body. They gazed at each other, not speaking a word. She wore no lipstick. Paul thought her lips were exquisite. They embraced again. She was nearly a foot shorter than Paul. He could smell a sweet fragrance in her hair, freshly shampooed. The thick reddish brown waves splashed gently upon her shoulders. His hands moved to hold her waist. She kept pressing. Her mouth was open. She pressed her hips against him. She wanted him.

Paul mumbled, "Marge, no," not sure if he meant it. She wasn't listening. Her breath was hot in his ear. Her hands moved across his clerical shirt. She pulled the white plastic tab from his collar and dropped it on the floor. The symbol of his ordination lay powerless at his feet. He felt aroused and felt his resolve slipping. He knew the truth of why he was here. Even though he knew it was wrong, he wanted her. He wanted to make love.

His hands pressed hard on her back which felt firm and slender. He moved his mouth to hers. Her lips were moist and delicious. Her hair brushed casually against his face sending shivers down his spine. She pulled back slightly; her robe parted revealing the shadow between her breasts. She unbuttoned his shirt, and he pulled his arms from the sleeves. They kissed again. Marge untied the bathrobe and let it drop to the floor. She began fumbling with his belt. She opened his pants and her hand moved inside. Paul pulled his pants down to his ankles. Marge wrapped her arms and legs around him as they fell together to the sofa. In a few terrible, wonderful moments, he yielded himself to her, and she to him. It was over in a matter of minutes, and Paul knew that he had crossed a boundary, and failed a sacred trust.

"That was wonderful!" she exclaimed breathlessly. "Thank you. Thank you, Paul. You're a beautiful man!"

As his body relaxed, the heat of passion turned into a flood of embarrassment and shame. "You're beautiful too, Marge, but I shouldn't have come here. I'm sorry; I'm so sorry," Paul whispered.

"Don't be," she whispered back, her arms still wrapped around him.

"This was wrong, very wrong on my part," Paul insisted as he began to pull away.

"Shh … shh ... don't talk. Just hold me."

"Oh, Marge, no. I mean, I want to, but this isn't right."

"But I need you," Marge urged.

"No, not in this way," Paul argued, finally getting to his feet.

"Shhh … it'll be okay. I'm sorry too; it's my fault, not yours." Marge handed Paul his shirt and the white plastic tab, then slipped back into her bathrobe.

"I should have been stronger, Marge. Please forgive me."

"Of course. Of course. Let's pretend it never happened."

"I'd like to, but I'm not sure I can," Paul answered as he pulled up his pants.

"Will you try?" begged Marge.

"Yes, I'll try."

"Good, then you'd better clean up and get out of here."

Paul started toward the bathroom, then stopped and looked back, "Marge, I am truly sorry."

"I'm not. I'm glad you came. I thank you for being such a caring man. And I promise, I won't say a word to anyone....ever!"

"I'd appreciate that. I certainly won't say anything." Paul went into the bathroom and washed his hands and face and finished tucking in his shirt. He couldn't stand to look into his own eyes in the mirror. As he walked past Marge to leave, he stopped to apologize again, but she put her finger against his lips, rose on her tiptoes, kissed him on the cheek, and whispered, "Good by."

As Pastor Paul Walker drove away from the Holloways' home, he could not escape the realization of what he had done. An inner terror launched its attack upon his soul. *So wrong...so wrong! How could I have done that? It felt wonderful; but it's so wrong!*

8

MARGE AND CHERI

When the Holloways lost their son, Cheri and Paul both experienced a sadness and depression that seemed unending. For many weeks, Paul struggled with feelings of guilt. *Surely this wouldn't have happened if the church was more secure, or if Brian hadn't been there alone that night, or if… if… There must have been something I should have done that I didn't.* Cheri did her best to love and encourage him through this traumatic time. "Learn from this, but don't beat yourself up," she said.

Cheri was also doing what she could to be a supportive friend to Marge. She had always admired how patiently Marge interacted with Brian during his challenging teen years, and how beautifully she related to Sarah, four years younger. "How do you do it?" Cheri asked. "I mean, talking almost a different language to each child?" Marge would just grin and say, "I just play it by ear!" After the funeral Cheri made a point of calling her, sometimes on her lunch hour and sometimes on weekends. Paul didn't even realize how often they talked. Occasionally Cheri would mention something Marge told her, if she felt Paul ought to know, especially Marge's concern about how Bob was handling the loss of his son.

On Tuesday morning, September 18th, Cheri looked at the calendar on her desk at work and saw her note to call Marge. She had marked the date exactly one month after Brian's funeral. Cheri called during her lunch hour and listened as Marge just cried for several minutes. "Would you like to meet for lunch one of these days?" Cheri asked.

"Oh that would be wonderful! I'd appreciate that. You're such a dear!"

Two days later they were sitting at a restaurant sipping coffee and waiting for their order when Marge said, "Cheri, why do I feel so guilty? I keep asking myself what I could have done that might have prevented Brian's death."

"Strange you should put it that way, Marge, because that's exactly what Paul keeps asking me. He feels that somehow it was HIS fault!" It was enough to bring a little laughter to both of them. "Have the police got any leads on who might have done it?" Cheri asked.

"I was really impressed with the detectives who interviewed us right after Brian was murdered. They seemed so sympathetic and they conducted such a thorough and detailed interview. They wanted to know everything about Brian, especially who his friends were and if he had any enemies. They even asked about our relationship with Brian. Were things going well at home? Did he and Bob get along? We assured him we had good family relations. They seemed to agree that it was probably someone who didn't know Brian, but just got caught after breaking into the church. They suspect the reason for breaking and entering was robbery. He must have been hiding somewhere hoping Brian wouldn't see him, but you know, Brian always turned on all the lights. Apparently Brian and the intruder fought on the steps; there were a few drops of blood half way up the stairs, but most of it, of course, was at the bottom where Brian fell."

"Have you heard how the investigation is progressing?" Cheri asked again.

"Well, we had one visit from the chief himself about two weeks after the memorial service. He said they had most of the reports together, but no leads on the perpetrator. He promised to let us know if anything developed and said again that he was very sorry for our loss." Marge's eyes filled with tears.

"O Marge, it is just so awful! I can't imagine what I would ... Marge, if there is anything I can do, please don't hesitate to ask." Cheri offered.

After a few moments, Marge wiped her eyes and cleared her throat. "Well, I thought of one thing you might do, but I'm afraid it's a silly request."

"Don't be ridiculous, Marge, just tell me."

"Well, would you mind talking to the lawyers in your firm, and see if they have any ideas of how we might find Brian's murderer? Like I said, I don't think it will do any good; lawyers don't solve crimes, do they?"

"Maybe not, but it couldn't do any harm either," Cheri replied brightly. "I wouldn't mind at all. In fact, I'd be honored to give it a try. Who knows what they might suggest?"

"Oh, Cheri, you are such a great friend! I don't know what I'd do without you and Pastor Paul."

"I'll put it on the agenda at next week's meeting with the partners," Cheri responded.

* * * * * * *

Tuesday, September 25

On Tuesday, at the regularly scheduled meeting of the law firm, Cheri added a note to the agenda which got everyone's attention: Brian Holloway's death –suggestions? The "old man" (as they affectionately called the head of the firm, Scott Etheridge) asked if a memorial fund had been established.

"Yes, certainly," Cheri responded, "it was set up at the church right away. The family wanted gifts to go to the Scholarship Fund."

"Well, I don't see any reason why our firm couldn't make a nice donation, do any of you?" Scott asked his partners. They all nodded their heads.

"Thank you very much, Mr. Etheridge, I'm sure the Holloways would appreciate that very much. And speaking on behalf of my husband, which I try hard NEVER to do, I'm sure he would appreciate any gift to the church as well."

"What do you think, gentlemen? And Mrs. Barkley, of course." Mr. Etheridge was still learning how to deal respectfully with a female partner. "I should think we could put $500 into that fund. Does that sound reasonable?"

Again, there were nods around the table. "Very generous, Mr. Etheridge," replied Cheri. "But may I ask one more question about this matter?"

"Certainly," Scott replied.

"What I really wanted to know was if anyone in the firm would have a suggestion for Brian's family about how this crime might be solved, or how the murderer might be found?"

There was a long silence. Mrs. Barkley finally spoke up. "Has a reward been offered? Like, for any information or leads?"

"I don't think so," answered Cheri. "But that's a wonderful idea!"

"I have an idea," suggested Miguel Juarez, "what if we put up a thousand dollars for a reward leading to the arrest of a suspect, and if it's not claimed, that money would go to the scholarship fund at the church?"

"Yes," said Mr. Etheridge, "not bad, not bad. What do you think Mrs. Walker? Would the Holloways go for that?"

"I imagine they would; I can't imagine why they wouldn't!" Cheri replied. "And I thank you all for the offer." Cheri appreciated the use of her last name, at least during formal business meetings. Scott Etheridge even referred to the receptionist by the title "Miss" whereas the younger attorneys usually called her Sandi. "Are there any other ideas?" Cheri asked.

"I was just wondering," said another partner, John Fuscio, "if the family was planning to hire a private investigator?"

"Oh, I think it's way too soon to think about that," said Cheri. "I'm sure they'll want to give the police some time to solve this and bring the person to justice."

After a little more conversation, Mr. Etheridge asked if everyone was ready to move on. Cheri was pleased with her friends' responses and couldn't wait to get home and call Marge. Not only that, but she would have some excellent news for her husband as well, a possible donation of $1000 for the church scholarship fund! And if the money helped to catch Brain's killer, so much the better!

That afternoon, while Cheri typed the report of the meeting, Paul was making his fateful visit with Marge Holloway. Cheri could hardly wait to get home to share the good news with Paul!

* * * * * * *

A great day for Cheri had not been a good one for Paul. After leaving Marge's home, he drove to the city park to pray about his transgression. He knew he had been double-minded when he called her. He knew he had been double-minded when he rang the doorbell. His motives were selfish, far outweighing the genuine sympathy he felt for Marge. How could he have allowed himself to deceive himself this way? Where were his boundaries? Where was his good judgment - his integrity?

Paul felt physically sick. He had betrayed Marge; and then he realized, not just Marge. He also betrayed Bob...and Cheri...and God....and the church....and himself...*If Marge tells Bob, he'd be angry enough to kill me. If Cheri finds out, she'll file for divorce. And who could blame her? If the bishop is told about this, I'll be asked to resign. I may never be able to work as a pastor again.*

The terror was building. As he sat in his car staring at the trees, he knew that thinking about it was only making him sicker. He needed to get going…do something…focus on something else.

He remembered Mrs. Ogilby, one of the shut-ins he hadn't seen for over a month. He pictured her wrinkled skin and sparkling smile. And he knew that today, he needed to see her much more than she needed to see him. He started the car and headed for Lake Crest Nursing Home. After giving her communion, he returned to the church office, and told Carol that he had been to visit Mrs. Ogilby.

* * * * * * *

Paul was home in time to greet the boys after school. He began preparing hamburgers from the meat Cheri had left thawing in the refrigerator. The boys watched a couple of their favorite cartoons until Mom came home. Paul grilled the hamburgers and was trying to keep them warm without drying them out when she finally walked through the door. His stomach was in knots. She wrapped her arms around him and gave him a kiss. "Honey, I've got some wonderful news!" she said. "Our law firm is putting up a thousand dollar reward!"

9

NO LEADS

The police investigation continued at the church with photos, interviews, evidence collection, observations, and notes. Blood samples were taken from the stairway and a couple of drops were found upstairs in the entry. All of them proved to be the victim's blood and no other. No footprints were detectable outside the church near the broken window. The area was covered with bark dust and left no clear imprints. A large rock was found near the window, but no prints could be lifted from it. Pieces of glass from the trash can were gathered and bagged. Traces of bark were found on the kitchen ledge inside but were of no help. A four by four block area around the church was searched for the murder weapon, presumed to be a knife, but to no avail. There seemed to be little in the way of physical evidence to aid the investigation.

Neighbors were questioned, and several responded that the first indication they had that something was wrong at the church was when they saw emergency lights flashing in the parking lot a little before midnight. When asked if they saw the custodian's car in the lot that evening, one elderly couple said they had noticed it pulling into the church about 9 pm as they were getting ready for bed. When asked to identify it, the husband said all he could remember was that it was dark blue. They didn't recall seeing any other cars there. Sean put the neighborhood canvass on hold. He checked back with the County Medical Examiner who had finished the autopsy.

Discussions with the pastor and parents yielded no clue as to the killer's motive or identity. Detective Asplund did follow up by interviewing the friends who were mentioned. All agreed that Brian was a great guy, very smart, and had a good future as a veterinarian. Ironic that Brian's final thoughts about himself had been, *How stupid! I shouldn't have chased him.*

Everything about the crime scene indicated a random act which began as a church break-in and ended, unfortunately, in a desperate escape and murder. The perpetrator probably did not know the victim, but was discovered inside the building when the janitor came in. The autopsy report indicated death from abdominal hemorrhaging caused by multiple stab wounds. There was some superficial bruising in the abdominal area and on one arm, possibly where the victim was kicked or hit with a fist or something blunt. Time of death was estimated to be between 9 and 10 p.m. which his parents said was shortly after he left the house. The pieces all fit, but there were no leads that would help identify the killer.

About a month into the investigation, Detective Asplund gave his preliminary report to the Chief of Police who called Mrs. Holloway and made an appointment to visit her at home. He said he wanted to express his sympathy on behalf of the police department and give her an update on the investigation. When he got to the door, he rang the bell and waited. He surveyed the house and yard and saw a well-maintained home. When Marge finally opened the door, the chief removed his cap and greeted her, "Good afternoon, Mrs. Holloway. I'm Chief of Police, Jed Wilson. You may know my brother Fred; he's a member at Trinity."

"Please come in, officer," Marge said, stepping back from the door. "Yes, I know your brother. He was the chairman of the call committee a few years back when Pastor Walker interviewed here. Fred ushers quite often also."

Marge sat down on the sofa and pulled out a hanky to wipe her tears. The chief shared condolences, "All of us are very sorry for your loss. We have a couple of our best detectives working on this case, and I'm confident they are doing everything possible to solve Brian's murder."

"Have they got any clues yet? Or do they have any idea who did it?" Marge asked.

"No ma'm. I'm sorry to say they haven't found much to work with. We're hoping, with all the publicity, someone will come forward with information we can use."

Marge's spirit sank again. After telling the chief about Brian's memorial service, she thanked him for stopping by and showed him to the door. When Bob came home from work, she told him about the visit. He was angry all over again. He didn't say a word. He just retreated into the living room to watch TV.

* * * * * * *

Detective Sean Asplund was an experienced officer. He was thorough, and believed in doing everything by the book. He had cracked some tough cases which had begun just like this one. But the truth was he also had to let a lot of cases go cold and unsolved. In such instances he would feel extremely disappointed. It was especially hard to visit the victim's family with nothing to report and to tell them frankly that the investigation was being dropped. He hoped this case wouldn't end this way.

Shortly after the chief's visit with Marge Holloway, Detective Asplund received a phone call from her. She informed him that a scholarship fund had been established at the church. "And I have some other exciting news which I think you'll be glad to hear. A local business has offered a reward of $1000 for information leading to the capture of Brian's killer. Actually, it was the law firm where Mrs. Walker works that offered the reward! Isn't that great!"

Sean was elated! It wasn't especially large, but it would be enough to get some more coverage on the evening news. Reward money wasn't always successful, but at least there would be some calls to follow up.

They were usually from publicity hounds or nosy neurotics who simply wanted some attention, or who harbored fantasies about winning reward money... or the lottery. Sean had heard it all, but he was willing to do the legwork to get a glimmer of a lead and the hope of results.

The days following the news report brought seven phone calls and one anonymous letter. After detailed questioning, most proved unreliable or fruitless. Several calls pointed to suspicious parties with known criminal records, or just plain bad reputations. These were worth the effort of exploring. Perhaps someone was willing to rat on a former friend. The most promising lead was from an anonymous caller who suggested that Amad Fumatah might know what happened at the Lutheran church. Mr. Fumatah had a rap sheet a mile long and had done time for assault with a deadly weapon.

The last known address of Mr. Fumatah turned out to be a vacant rental which looked like an abandoned drug house. Reports from the neighbors expressed unanimous relief that the former residents had moved on. It took Sean more than a week to finally track down the owner whose name and address were in the county tax records, but that address was also vacant. When he finally found Mr. Velasquez, owner of the rental, the slum lord had no forwarding address for Mr. Fumatah. Sean gave the name to his partner Chad Skiles, asked him to do a computer search to see if he could find him, and scratched another lead off the list.

10

$10,000 REWARD

Monday, October 1

It seemed like an unusually hectic Monday morning in the office of Etheridge, Juarez, Fuscio and Barkley. The staff meeting at 9:30 lasted longer than usual. Cheri's calendar was screaming, "the first of October!" Cheri had to have payroll checks ready today. Just before lunch, Scott Etheridge appeared at the door of Cheri's office. "Cheri, there's someone I'd like you to meet."

Cheri rose from behind the pile of papers on her desk and stepped around to meet a tall stranger who towered behind "the old man." Scott stepped aside, "Cheri, this is Brian Randall, an old friend of mine from Chicago."

Cheri shook his hand, "How do you do?"

"It's a pleasure to meet you; Scott has told me good things about your work." Brian was not only tall, but smiled with gorgeous lines in his cheeks and a dimple on his chin; and he had a mustache that was beginning to gray. He seemed much younger than Scott Etheridge, but his thick dark hair was also turning prematurely gray. "I was talking to Scott about an idea I have and he suggested I discuss it with you; do you have time for lunch?" Brian asked.

"Oh, that's sounds wonderful, but I'm really swamped today. Could we possibly do it tomorrow?" Cheri replied.

"Hmm.... I've got an important noon meeting tomorrow and I'll be out of town on Wednesday, how about Thursday?"

"Let me look at my calendar, yes, I guess that would work for me. Let me put it on my calendar so I don't forget."

I'll look forward to seeing you...about noon?" He reached into his pocket for a business card.

Cheri jotted a note on her calendar.

"Noon, Thursday .... and DON'T forget," Brian smiled and winked and placed the card on Cheri's cluttered desk.

As Scott and Brian left her office, Cheri thought to herself, *how could I forget a smile like that? Whew! I'd better get back to the payroll. I haven't even had time to eat that ham and cheese sandwich hiding in my desk drawer! I'll have to remember NOT to pack a lunch Thursday morning!*

* * * * * * *

Thursday, October 4

Thursday was bright and sunny. Cheri glanced nervously at the clock, 11:55 a.m. She reached into her desk drawer and pulled out the business card the handsome business man had left on the corner of the desk a couple of days ago. **Brian Randall, Chairman and CEO, Jerusalem Steel Corporation, Gary, IN.** *Wow! Pretty impressive credentials.* A few minutes later she saw Brian Randall approach the reception desk. Her phone blinked and she answered. "Tell Mr. Randall I'll be right there." Cheri hated to sound too anxious, but she was really curious. *What* *kind of business would a steel executive have to discuss with her, an office manager?*

A moment later she was at the front desk. "Mr. Randall, it's good to see you again."

"And I'm delighted you are making a little more time for me today. You looked a little harried on Monday."

"A little more than usual....first of the month....payroll deadline, you know..."

"I thought we might walk over to Francesca's; Scott says they have excellent salads and pastas. Would that be all right with you, Mrs. Walker?"

"Please call me Cheri; yes, Francesca's would be fine."

"Then you'll have to call me Brian."

The two left the office and walked about a block and a half to Francesca's. After a brief wait, they were shown to a table near the front window. "Isn't this weather just wonderful!" Cheri mused.

"Couldn't be better! I've always loved October; it's one of my favorite months."

"Mine too," Cheri agreed. The waitress came and took their order. Cheri chose the chef's salad and Brian ordered fettuccini alfredo with a small salad on the side.

"I suppose you're wondering what I wanted to talk to you about," Brian began.

"Well, I was a little curious," Cheri admitted.

"Let me start with a little background on myself so you know where I'm coming from. I grew up in Chicago; my dad was a sheet metal worker and later became a shop foreman. My mom raised five of us, two girls and three boys. I think I inherited a love of steel from my dad. I was interested in his work and he seemed to enjoy talking about it. I finished high school, started college, business degree at the

University of Illinois, but couldn't wait to get going on a career. I was enjoying my summer jobs in a steel foundry, Jerusalem Steel, in fact. The foundry work was really hard, physically, but when you're young ....hey, the money was good. After a few years they let me work in the office so I could learn the business. When I finished college I was sent out with one of the guys as a sales assistant. It was a great introduction to the company; so of course, without the least bit of modesty, after a few years, quite a few years actually, I worked my way up to CEO."

"Quite a story! I'm impressed!"

"Well, that's not why I told you all this. I also wanted to mention that I've been an active member of my church in Gary, and it happens to be a Lutheran church."

"Is that right? I'm a Lutheran too." Cheri interjected.

"I know. Scott told me that your husband is a Lutheran pastor. In fact he's the pastor of Trinity Lutheran here in Weston, right?"

"That's right. I'm very proud of him; he's a wonderful pastor and a very good dad. Oh good, here comes our lunch!"

As they began to eat, Brian Randall continued, "Well, about a month or more ago I was reading the newspaper and saw an article that really grabbed me. It was about a murder that took place in your husband's ... I mean ... in your church." Brian paused.

"Yes, it was the worst thing we've ever had to deal with. We feel so badly for the Holloways. Their son was our church custodian and such a fine young man."

"It must have been awful. I was shocked by the horror of it, of course, but for other reasons, I couldn't get it out of my mind. First, as I'm sure you must be realizing, because I share the same name as the boy who was killed. And second, because it happened in a Lutheran church, and I've always felt safe in church. I guess the fact that it happened at Trinity made me realize it could happen anywhere."

"Your name is Brian, of course," Cheri said. "That would be kind of creepy."

"The other day, when I was visiting with Scott, I mentioned the newspaper article and asked if he knew anything about it. He said, 'By coincidence, the pastor's wife is our business manager.' I told him I'd been thinking of helping the church and the family in some way, but wasn't sure what would be best. He suggested I talk with you about it."

Cheri nodded. And there was a long silence between the two of them. Her eyes were dark brown, large, and with a hint of moisture as though she might be about to cry. She looked into his eyes, grayish blue, intense and caring. *One might even say they were a steel blue, which would be appropriate for someone in the steel industry.* She became a little uncomfortable. "That's very nice of you....I mean...to want to do something for the Holloways. Marge is a very dear friend of mine. She was so thrilled when Mr. Etheridge approved a thousand dollars for reward money."

"Scott's always been a generous guy." Another pause. "So I guess what I was thinking was that I would like to make an anonymous donation, say $10,000, to add to what has already been given."

"What?" Cheri was awestruck... speechless....unsure how to respond.

"I really would like it to be anonymous;" Brian repeated, "just a secret between you and me. You can say it was a client of the law firm, but no more than that, okay?"

"Okay....sure....I just don't know what to say....that's a wonderful offer!"

"I know there is no way to bring their son back, but if this gift helps to find the killer, then it's money well spent."

"Oh, I just thought of something. Our law firm agreed that if the reward is not claimed, the money would go into the church's scholarship fund as a memorial to Brian. I don't know if you'd be willing to do that with your offer? Or would you want the money back if it isn't claimed? .....I'm so embarrassed, I'm not sure I said that right," Cheri stammered.

"Oh, that was perfectly clear." Brian smiled. "Like I said, I'm a Lutheran and like to help our Lutheran churches in any way I can. If the reward isn't claimed, it goes to the church."

"I still can't believe it! Did you say $10,000?"

"Yes, that's right. And just so you know, that's a personal donation; it's not from Jerusalem Steel."

"That is very generous, Mr. Randall."

"Uh, uh, uh… I said I preferred Brian."

"Sorry."

"How's your salad, Cheri?"

"Delicious! How's your fettuccine, BRIAN?" she couldn't help but giggle. It seemed to relieve the stress of the prior conversation. There was that magnificent smile and his deeply dimpled chin that seemed to invite a caress. *O God,* Cheri prayed silently, *what in the world is happening? What kind of miracle have I just witnessed? Marge is going to be so moved! Paul says he is always amazed at how much people care. This is certainly proof of that!*

"So, if you'll just send me a written description of the reward details, and some information about the scholarship memorial, I'll get a check off to your husband. But please keep this as confidential as possible. I'd rather the Holloways not know, at least not at this point. Just tell them that others do care."

"Brian, I don't know how to thank you. You are so kind! Thank you from the Holloways too. I'm sure they'll be overwhelmed." Cheri was feeling overwhelmed herself. Brian Randall was not only one of the most handsome men she had met in a long time, but also one of the most kind and generous!

"Do you care for any dessert?" Brian asked.

"No, thanks, I'd better be getting back to the office."

"In that case, I'll take care of the check and walk you back."

What Cheri didn't know was that Brian was equally charmed by her smile, by her warmth, and her shy look of embarrassment. It had been a dreamlike conversation; and it had been years since he had met anyone so charming. They chatted casually as he walked her back to the office. They shook hands at the firm's front door. Brian wanted to wrap his arms around her, but he restrained himself. He sighed deeply as he thought to himself how much he would like to see her again.

At her desk, Cheri called the church office to tell Paul about this amazing man and the $10,000 reward donation!

11

ONE GOOD LEAD

Friday, October 5

Detective Sean Asplund filled his coffee cup before going into the meeting with the chief on Friday morning. It was time for weekly reports, and Sean hated it when he had nothing to say. Well, he could say, "I worked hard all week and accomplished nothing." There were too many times he had tried to say this creatively to make it sound a little better, "Been following up on some great tips!" But the chief could see through that one. Fortunately Chief Wilson was familiar with the frustration of empty leads, and exhausting and unrewarding leg work. He had done enough of it himself.

Sean's partner, Chad, took the phone call while Sean was in the meeting. It was the Lutheran pastor, Paul Walker. "I've got some great news to share with you guys!" The pastor sounded really excited. "My wife informed me yesterday afternoon that a client from their law firm was offering $10,000 more in reward money!"

Chad took down the information and promised to share it with his partner. He and Sean spent their lunch hour talking about the news coverage the reward might generate. The local TV station in

Gary jumped on the report and began making phone calls. They sent a crew out on Sunday to interview the pastor of Trinity about the now $11,000 reward for information leading to the arrest and conviction of a suspect in Brian Holloway's murder. On Monday they interviewed Scott Etheridge from the law firm that had provided the anonymous donor. The Monday evening news report also included a scene at the Holloway home. Brian's parents made an emotional plea for assistance from the public. A couple of the Chicago TV stations picked up the story and ran it the following night.

* * * * * * *

Monday, October 8

The phone call came into the station at 6:35 p.m. Monday. The dispatcher listened to a very nervous older woman who said she had just watched the six o'clock news and had some information about the boy who was killed at the Lutheran church. He told her that case was being handled by Detective Asplund who would be in the office in the morning.

"May I take your name and phone number?" he asked.

"No, señor" she replied nervously. "I call back tomorrow."

When Sean Asplund came to work Tuesday morning he found a message in his box. It was a brief note scribbled by the night dispatcher: "Woman called... information on Holloway case. Said she will call back." Sean was dumbfounded, both excited and angry that there was no name or phone number. He settled at his desk to review reports and paced nervously to the water fountain and restroom for a couple of hours. Finally, at 10:08 am, his phone rang. "Asplund, Homicide," he answered.

"Are you policeman in charge of murder at Lutheran church?" a shaky voice responded.

"Yes, this is Detective Sean Asplund, and I'm the investigating officer for the Holloway death. Who is this?"

"I no tell you my name, but I hear about the beeg reward on the news las' night." It was the quavering voice of an older woman with a strong Spanish accent.

"Yes, there is a reward for information leading to the arrest and conviction of the person who killed young Brian Holloway at Trinity Lutheran Church. Do you have some information for us?" the detective asked.

"I not certain, but I hear someteen' you might wan' to know about."

"Yes ma'm, what did you hear?"

"Promise me… you no tell nobody who tol' you dees."

"Yes ma'm, this conversation is strictly confidential."

"You t'ink I jus' a crazy ol' woman, but several weeks ago, I remember it very clearly. I was sound asleep in my apartment. My bedroom is nes' door to a young man; he comes and goes at all hours. Anyway, I hear dees loud THUMP on my bedroom wall and a man screaming! It woke me up! Estupido! I hear him scream, 'I deedn' mean to kill him!' He hollered it several times; I sure da's wha' he say! I t'ink it was the same night that young boy got killed at the church. It give me a creepy feeling so I couldn' go back to sleep."

"Did your neighbor say who he killed?"

"No, he just say, 'I deedn' mean to kill him.' Dat's all I could hear."

"This information may be very helpful in our investigation. May I come to your apartment to take a sworn statement?" Detective Asplund was nearly holding his breath. Each step of this exchange was crucial in establishing evidence in a trial.

"Oh, no, señor! I wouldn' wan' my neighbor to know the police was here! Can't you jus' use what I tol' you on the phone?"

"Well, ma'm, what you've told me could be very helpful, but I really must speak to you in person. Would you be willing to come down to police headquarters to make your statement?"

"I have no way of getting there! And besides, I am old woman. I t'ink I do all I can."

"Just a minute, please don't hang up!" Sean was afraid he would lose her before getting her name. His mind raced for something to keep her on the line. "Are you still interested in the reward money?"

"Of course, señor!" she replied indignantly.

There was a long pause. Sean slowly suggested, "How can we get the reward to you if we don't know who you are or where you live?" There was another long pause.

"I understand," the woman replied. "Is it necessary, you mus' talk to me in person?"

"Yes ma'm. And in case you were wondering, I could come to your apartment in an unmarked car and park a block away. I'm a detective, so I don't wear a uniform. And if you'd like, I could wait until you call to tell me your neighbor has gone out. That way, he wouldn't even be there to see a stranger come into your building."

"Sí, that might work. What deed you say your name was again?"

"I'm Detective Sean Asplund, and I've been assigned to this investigation. The number to use to call directly to my office is 776-0386. Will you write that down? 776-0386. And once more, before we say good by, would you be willing to give me your name and a phone number?

"You sound like nice young man. I guess I can trust you not to come here til I call. My name is Maria Olivera. I promise I call you soon. Good by."

Sean heard a click and the buzz of the disconnected call. He sat at his desk sweating and wrote her name in his notebook. This just might be one of those amazing breaks every detective hopes for. He gathered his thoughts and wrote a few more notes. Maria Olivera. He grabbed a phone book from the drawer, but her number was not listed. He was tempted to pursue it further, but decided to trust Maria to call again. *Sometimes it's better to just wait and let things come to you,* he thought to himself. Maria had already shown him that. She had called back today as she said she would.

Every tip or lead to this point had led nowhere. Maybe this was the one. Sean and his partner Chad went to the nearby Wendy's for a burger at lunch time. When he returned to the office there was another message in his box. Call Maria Olivera, 723-8111. "Hallelujah!" he yelled. "First the name, now the number! Yahoo!" He threw his fist in the air! Everyone turned to look at him, but he was too intent on getting to the phone to explain his excitement.

"Ms. Olivera, this is Detective Asplund. I just received the message that you called."

"Sí, I call you about half hour ago. I t'ink my neighbor will be out for a long while. He usually goes out to eat about this time and not come back for several hours; sometimes not til late evening or the middle of the night."

"May I come over for a visit?"

"Sí, but please be careful. Jus' press the buzzer at the fron' door for apartment 6 and I buzz you in."

"I'll need your address."

"Oh sí, how foolish of me! I live at 1694 S. Meadow Street, Apartment 6."

"It will take me about 10 minutes to get there. Thank you very much for calling."

The neighborhood was definitely showing signs of deterioration. Sean drove up Oak Street and past Trinity Lutheran Church, turned left on 16th, and continued three blocks to Meadow. He turned left again, then realized he had to double back a block to 1694. He found a parking place and approached the two story brick apartment building and the locked front door. He pressed the button for Apartment 6, noting that there were eight apartment numbers. *The suspect must live in 5 or 7*, he thought to himself.

"Sí, who is it?" answered Maria.

"This is Sean," the detective replied, hoping she would remember his first name, "Sean Asplund."

"Please come in," she said, as the buzzer sounded unlocking the door.

It appeared that there were four apartments on each floor. He climbed the stairs to the second floor and saw the number 6 on the door to the right. He knocked and the door was opened by a wrinkled little woman who stood about 5' 1" at the most. "Please come in, detective," she said politely. She glanced down the stairs to see if anyone was watching. She motioned to a tattered old sofa, "Please sit down."

"Thank you," he replied. He removed a small cassette recorder from his inside pocket and asked, "Do you mind if I record your statement?"

"I suppose. If it's really necessary," she replied.

"Oh, yes ma'm, it really is essential for us, and it insures an accurate record of your testimony."

"I understand; go ahead. Like I say to you before, I don' know if it help you much, but I tell you what I hear dat night." Sean pushed Record and the tape began recording. Maria kept talking, "I mean he woke me from dead sleep. He mus' have kick the wall or somet'ing. It scared me very bad, very bad!

"Let's back up a little, may I ask you to state your name and address?" Sean asked.

"My name is Maria Olivera; I live at 1694 S. Meadow Street, Apartment 6."

"And do you swear that the testimony you are about to give is true?"

"Absolutely! I no tell a lie about somet'ing like dees!"

"Go ahead. You said you woke from a sound sleep when you heard something thump on the wall."

"Like I tol' you on the phone, his bedroom is right nes' to mine.... right through dat wall over there." She pointed to her bedroom. "On the night of the murder, I was sound asleep by 10 o'clock. Nes' t'ing I hear was him kickin' the wall and screamin', 'I deedn' mean to kill him! I deedn' mean to kill him!' He say it two or tree times."

"Do you know what time it was?"

"No, señor, I don' know exactly, but it was the middle of the night, you know, after midnight."

"Did he say a name? Who the victim might have been?"

"No. He jus' scream in the most frightenin' voice, 'I deedn' mean to kill him!'"

"You heard nothing else?"

"No. I laid there awake; I was very frightened, Señor. I thought maybe he was goin' to kill me! Then I thought maybe he jus' havin' a nightmare; you know how sometimes you yell somet'ing when you dreamin'?"

"I guess," replied the detective, "but I usually yell 'Help!' or something like that." They both chuckled. "Do you know your neighbor's name?"

"I don' know his firs' name. He is a young man, lots of muscles, not very tall. By the buzzer downstairs it say Mankowitz or somet'ing like that."

"What is his apartment number? I don't remember seeing that name," Sean asked.

"Apartment 8, right nes' to mine!" Maria replied testily.

"I thought apartment 5 or 7 would be next to yours."

"No, estupido." Maria began pointing through the walls to the other apartments. "Across the hall is apartment 5; dees is 6; across the hall nes' to 5 is 7; and the nes' door pas' mine is 8. Even on dees side, odd on other side."

"Oh, now I see! Thank you, Maria, for straightening me out." Sean smiled; and she shook her head wondering how he could ever solve a crime. "Just a couple more questions. Do you remember what night this incident occurred? Did you mark the date on a calendar or anything?"

"Ah, Dios, no! But when I hear the news reports about the boy at the church, I remember t'inkin' it was the night I hear my neighbor screamin'. I deedn' write it down, but it mus' have been the night that boy was murdered."

"One last question. Does the manager live here in the building?"

"Oh, Dios, you not goin' to tell her about dees, are you? You promise dees conversation was confidential."

"No ma'm. I won't tell the manager I talked to you. I'll just tell him we need some information about one of his renters."

"Our manager is a woman!" Maria sighed with frustration, wondering if this detective could get anything right. "She doesn't live here. It's Mrs. Schonmeier. I have her number here somewhere." Maria retrieved the number from a cluttered desk. Detective Asplund thanked her for her help and turned off the tape recorder. "When do I get the beeg reward?" she asked.

"It may take quite a while, Ms. Olivera. This investigation is just beginning. If your lead is a good one, I promise you, you'll be hearing from us again." Sean rose to leave.

"Oh, I'm so sorry, I forgot to offer you a cookie! They are on the table in the kitchen. Would you like one?"

"That's quite all right," Sean grinned as he eased his way toward the door.

"Jus' a minute. You mus' take a couple of cookies weeth you," Maria said as she hurried into the kitchen to retrieve them. In a moment she was back with several cookies wrapped in a paper napkin.

On the way out of the building Sean glanced at buzzer #8 and jotted in his note pad: Mankovic, Apt. 8. He climbed into his unmarked car, pulled a cookie from inside the napkin, and took a bite. Mmm…not bad!

12

LUNCH IN THE PARK

Thursday, October 25

Sometimes in the fall in northern Indiana, a day comes along which brings every color of the natural world to its peak of brightness and clarity. The trees that lined many streets in Weston glowed bright yellow and orange and deep red. Even the oaks seemed proud of their elegant brown. It was late-October and the first frost put a sparkle on the leaves that morning. The air was brisk, the sun was low and bright, and there was just a hint of a breeze. Hoosiers were going football crazy for local high school teams and state colleges! It was the kind of day when strangers are suddenly neighbors, and every one breathes deeply, knowing that the dark days of winter are just around the corner.

Paul made sure Chip and Randy had their backpacks, their lunch money, and got out to the school bus on time. Cheri had left for work at 7:45, but Paul didn't have to be at the church office until 8:30 or 9:00. As he backed the car out of the garage, he thanked God for the glorious beauty of fall, and for a job which brought a level of satisfaction most working class people never know. On days like this it was a joy to go to church knowing he had a full agenda, including a text study with local pastors, hospital and shut-in visits, and a few hours in the afternoon for study and sermon preparation. Best of all, there was nothing on his schedule for this evening. He and Cheri could put jackets on the boys and they could all go for a drive or a long walk through the neighborhood.

Paul checked in with Carol, the parish secretary, to see what she had scheduled and if there were any phone messages from yesterday or early this morning. She reminded him that she would be working on Sunday's bulletin and still needed his input before running off copies on Friday. A few minutes before ten, Paul left for the text study which was always held on Thursday morning, and was meeting this month at the Methodist church.

* * * * * * *

Cheri was enjoying the morning in her office as well. An order of supplies had just come in from the printer for paper, envelopes, and legal forms. She was busy dividing and distributing various supplies to the four secretaries when Sandi, the receptionist, caught her eye and signaled a phone call for her. She returned to her office and set several boxes on her desk and picked up the phone.

"Mrs. Walker, you have a call from Brian Randall. Please hold."

Cheri was caught just slightly off guard. *Why would Brian Randall be calling?* Cheri noticed her heart racing as she picked up the phone, "Hello, this is Cheri."

"Good morning, Cheri, this is Brian Randall with Jerusalem Steel. How are you?"

"Just fine, Brian, and you?"

"Couldn't be better. We'd better enjoy these lovely fall days because the snow will be coming soon enough."

"I certainly agree; aren't the trees beautiful this year?"

"Yes, and that's why I'm calling."

"Because the trees are beautiful?" Cheri asked, puzzled.

"Because I think today would be a beautiful day to have lunch in the park across from the court house. I'll pick up some sandwiches and a salad and meet you downtown as close to noon as I can make it. How does that sound?"

"Lunch in the park? What's the occasion?"

"I told you ....the beautiful trees. Not only that, but I'd like to hear how the investigation is going into Brian's death, and how the Holloways are holding up. How 'bout it? Are you game?"

Cheri thought for a moment and decided it was just too beautiful a day to pass up such a pleasant invitation. "Sure, why not?"

"May I pick you up at the office?"

"Oh, no, that's not necessary. It's only about six blocks and the walk would be good for me."

"Oh, I almost forgot," Brian interjected, "I'll bring the food and what would you like to drink on this crisp October day?"

"Well, I guess a cup of hot coffee would be fine. I take it black."

"Hot coffee it is; see you at noon."

As soon as Brian hung up Cheri had a funny feeling inside, like a young girl who had just been asked for a date by the captain of the football team. No, she said to herself, it's just business....nothing to be embarrassed about. Still, it seemed her heart was beating just a little faster than normal.

* * * * * * *

Paul was at the Methodist Church laughing, as his friend and colleague, Pastor Ryan Jacoby was describing Peter in the gospel for the coming Sunday. "And Jesus came to them, walking on the sea. And Peter said, 'Lord, if it is you, bid me come to you.' And Jesus said, 'Come.' Peter got out of the boat. Stop right there. Peter got out of the boat. Can any of you imagine anything more stupid than that? Look at Peter, staring at Jesus, full of faith and amazement! Look at Peter's face, full of piety and sincerity and TOTALLY UNCONSCIOUS!' He didn't know what the hell he was doing!!! He was just walking over to meet Jesus. AND …he was doing just fine, walking just as proud as you please, until he started to think. You know, fellas, (Sharon Mallory, the only female pastor there this morning, let the sexist address go by without interrupting) that's what always gets us into trouble …we start to think…and thinking leads to analysis and analysis leads to questions and questions lead to doubts and ….before you know it, Peter began to sink. Look at his face now! Peter is just beginning to realize what he's doing. He's walking on the SEA! And the water's deep….awful deep….and cold….awful cold…and Peter's thinking to himself, 'I must be crazy!'

"Peter looked down at the water. You know, my friends, I think we could preach a whole sermon on that one idea right there. Peter took his eyes off the Lord and looked down. And if we take our eyes off the Lord and look down, the same thing is gonna happen to us; we're gonna sink! Look at Peter's face now! He's got the shit scared outa him! He's sinking! And in those loose fitting robes, it's gonna be mighty hard to swim! Peter screams, "Lord, save me, I'm sinking!" And Jesus, being the softy he is, reaches out and grabs Peter by the arm and helps him into the boat. Look at Peter's face again. Now what do you see? How do you spell RELIEF? How do you spell embarrassment? Wanna get away? Peter had no where to go. Face your buddies, Peter. Lift your head up; don't be ashamed. At least you tried. At least you dared to get out of the boat. Hold your head up, Peter, and look them in the eye. And tell them what faith is all about. It's not about who's smartest, or who's got their act together, or even who's got the most faith! It's about excitement, and risking, and trying, and wanting to be with Jesus. It's about trying and failing. And most of all, it's about trusting God to reach out and grab you when you realize you can't do it on your own! Tell 'em, Peter; tell 'em what faith is all about."

Paul loved these text studies! The conversation that flowed between the pastors provided insights and inspiration which often lead to some very fine sermons. Some weeks it was worth coming just for the give and take between the pastors, even if he left without a single sermon idea. In the privacy of their pastoral group, they could swear occasionally, confess their weaknesses, tell some jokes, make fun of each other, and simply be themselves. They could argue about the meaning of a text because they respected each other deeply. It was in these sacred acts that faith was expressed in love. It was in these intimate rituals that they encouraged each others' faith and ministry. In these moments of honest sharing, they became healthier pastors for the people they fed.

Paul knew that Ryan was right about trying and failing, and about trusting God with every aspect of his life and ministry. Half the time Paul wasn't sure if he was doing the right thing. It often seemed he was either in the right place at the wrong time, or at the wrong place altogether. He almost envied the evangelicals who seemed so sure of right and wrong, so sure they were doing what Jesus would do. Paul believed he and most Lutherans had a more profound understanding of the sinfulness of the human condition, and a more radical belief in God's grace. Now, however, there was guilt in his life, the likes of which he'd never known. Now, HE was sinking and needed some help from Jesus as he never had before.

The momentary hope and well-being Paul felt as he drove from the Methodist church toward the hospital was short lived. One of his favorite widows, Clara Sooty, had just received word from her doctor that her CT scan showed the cancer was spreading through her bones.

* * * * * * *

At quarter to twelve Cheri put on her sweater, left the office, and walked toward the court house. The park was more breath-taking than she had ever seen it! The noonday sun set the trees ablaze, and the wind had disappeared. She walked slowly along a paved pathway, checking out the familiar picnic tables, looking for Brian. She finally spotted him sitting on a blanket on the grass beneath a grove of maples.

"Ah, there you are!" he hollered and waved. She felt like skipping as she walked across the lawn toward him. Brian rose to meet her, dressed in khakis and a handsome tan and brown sweater. "I'm so glad you could come today," he smiled and reached out to give her a hug. She fell into the embrace and wrapped her arms around him, then gently pushed him away.

How could she feel this familiar after meeting only once? She glanced around nervously to see if anyone was watching them. "How have you been, Brian?" she asked. "What's it been, a month since we met?"

"Fine, just fine. And yes....a little less than a month, I believe." They both sat down on the blanket. Cheri tucked her legs under her, and tugged her skirt down to her knees.

"So what did you bring?" Cheri asked. "I'm starved! This cool air does wonders for my appetite."

"Let's open the bag and see what's in it! I think there's a ham and cheese, and a club sandwich, and my favorite, roast beef and provolone. What'll it be?"

"Aww... I wanted the roast beef and provolone," Cheri teased.

"You can have the beef and provolone; I'll eat the ham and cheese," Brian replied.

"No, I was kidding. I'm perfectly happy with a club sandwich." Cheri said reassuringly.

"How about some salad?" he asked.

"That would be great!"

"And here's the coffee; be careful not to spill it."

As the two settled on the blanket to eat, the conversation slowed and finally came to a stop. There was a long silence and Cheri began to feel uneasy. The day was perfect; the setting was intimate; everything seemed uncomfortably grand! As she struggled to get the conversation going again, their eyes met and Brian smiled that gorgeous chin-dimpled smile.

It was Brian who broke the silence, "You are such a beautiful woman, Cheri!"

Cheri's heart started pounding. *I knew it; I knew it; I could feel it coming. This isn't just a business meeting; Brian wants it to be a date.* Cheri smiled, "Thank you, Brian." Again, there was an awkward silence.

"I'm sorry if I'm being too forward," Brian sighed. His eyes dropped.

Cheri thought he looked sincere… *Or was it part of an often-played act?*

"Last time, when we met," Brian continued, "I told you about my business career. But I didn't say anything about my personal life."

"I guess you didn't. I assumed you were married," Cheri interjected. "Was I wrong?"

"I was married…..WAS..." Brian's voice dropped so that Cheri could hardly hear him. It was not the confident CEO voice she had been hearing until now. "About eleven years … to the most beautiful woman on earth ….or at least in Chicago….sorry, a little attempt at humor there. Nancy and I were introduced by her cousin who worked at Jerusalem in the sales office. My career, as I told you last time, was just getting started, and Nancy was the most enthusiastic woman I had ever met. She was working for a dress designer on Michigan Avenue and was so excited about her work. Anyway, to make a long story short, we were married, never had any kids, and just before our tenth anniversary, she was diagnosed with melanoma. At first we thought we had it beat. She got really sick from the treatments, but the doctor said the cancer was in remission. I thought that meant she was fine. Less than a year later she got sick again, and this time it spread very quickly and didn't respond to the treatments. She was only thirty-six when she died. We were married eleven years, two months and fourteen days."

"Oh, Brian, I'm so sorry. How long ago did she die?"

"Almost four years ago. I was three years older than Nancy. She died right before Christmas. This December it'll be four years. Christmases have been terrible ever since."

"And you had no children?"

"No....maybe that was for the best. We wanted kids eventually. But when we were first married, we were both into our careers. It seemed like we were both just too busy to start a family."

"Paul and I are so lucky to have two boys. And each other."

"I haven't met Paul, but I'd say he's a mighty lucky man to have a wife like you."

"You're very kind."

"So now you know.... I'm also very lonely." Brian stared sadly at Cheri.

"I hope you find someone...someday..." Cheri replied, "not quite like Nancy, but someone you can love just as much."

"I never thought I would..." Brian gazed into Cheri's eyes, "until I met you last month."

"Oh, Brian, now you're really making me uncomfortable."

"I'm sorry. I just thought...I don't know what I thought." Brian shook his head. "I guess it's time to change the subject."

"That would be a good idea."

"Did you get enough to eat?" Brian asked.

"Yes, and thank you very much for bringing the salad and sandwiches...and the coffee...which tasted really good when it was hot."

"It has gotten rather cold, hasn't it. Cheri, tell me about the Holloways and what's happening with the investigation."

"Well, first of all the Holloways were thrilled to hear about the reward money you offered. And so was my husband. And so were the police! They were able to get more TV coverage and hoped that would generate more calls and leads. I haven't heard any specifics about the investigation, though." Cheri paused to think.

"What about the Holloways?" Brian asked. " I imagine they're still having a rough time."

"Yes, I spoke to Marge last week and she just seems so depressed. Paul's been over to see them, and he says Bob has totally withdrawn. Apparently there's just no communication between them."

"That's too bad. I can't imagine what it would be like." Brian stared at his empty coffee cup and put it into the basket.

"Perhaps I should be going," Cheri suggested. "Mr. Etheridge will wonder if I got lost!"

"Tell Scott it's all my fault! And thank you again for spending part of this beautiful day with me."

Brian helped Cheri to her feet, felt the strong grasp of her hand, glanced at her legs as she rose, and wanted to hug her… but thought better of it. "May I call you again?" he asked, like a puppy begging for table scraps.

"I'm not sure that would be a good idea, Brian. But thank you for today."

"You're probably right. And thank YOU for today. Thanks for listening to my story about my wife. I think I told you before, you're a great listener."

"I can't remember if you did, but thanks for yet another compliment."

Brian finished closing the picnic basket and folded the blanket. "And just because you know how vulnerable I am, don't think for a minute that I'm not a tiger at work," Brian joked, struggling to regain his composure as Cheri turned to leave.

"Oh, not for a minute!" Cheri replied over her shoulder as she hurried back toward the office. It was an awkward parting, but under the circumstances she felt she had been courteous and respectful. She really did feel badly for him, losing his spouse so early in their marriage. She prayed a prayer of thanks for Paul and her boys. She wondered if

Brian would be contacting her again. *I certainly hope not,* she thought to herself. *And yet. . . he had been very polite. Maybe I will see him again . . .probably not; certainly not unless he initiates it. And he probably won't. . . Or maybe he will.* Cheri struggled with her feelings all the way back to the office.

"How was lunch?" Sandi asked, as Cheri came through the door.

"Fine, just fine!" Cheri replied, not really wanting to talk about it.

13

TIME FOR CONFESSION

After supper that evening, Paul offered to do the dishes. Cheri said she'd help the boys with their homework. When he finished cleaning up the kitchen, Cheri was reading the newspaper. He sat down in his favorite chair and wondered whether he should turn on the TV or grab a section of the paper. In these quiet moments, he was aware of the inner knot of guilt and shame and fear, constantly there in the pit of his stomach. *What if Cheri finds out what happened with Marge? Would Marge tell her? If Marge said something would Cheri believe her? Would he deny it? Should he tell Cheri?* He looked over at Cheri and stared at her for a few moments. Her eyes were not moving. They weren't focused on the paper. Paul realized that she hadn't said a word during dinner. That wasn't like her. Did she already know what had happened with Marge? The knot in his stomach grew tighter. Was this the moment he had been dreading?

"You're awfully quiet tonight, hon'," Paul ventured.

Cheri came out of her own thoughts. "I was just thinking how crazy life can be," she responded.

"That's for sure," Paul replied.

"You've been kind of quiet yourself lately." Cheri looked him in the eye.

"I've had a lot on my mind, but I didn't want to burden you. I know you're busy," Paul sighed, hoping he could shift the subject back to her.

"Church stuff?" Cheri asked.

"Yeah, this is always a busy time of year with all the fall programs. I really hope our stewardship drive goes well next month. I know a lot of members are still upset about Brian's death; I know I am."

"You haven't mentioned the Holloways for quite a while. Have you noticed they haven't been in church for several Sundays?"

Oh, oh, here it comes, thought Paul. "Yes, it must be hard for them to worship and be reminded of Brian every time they come into the building."

"Have you talked to Marge or Bob?" Cheri asked.

"I've seen Marge at Bible study, but we haven't talked much."

There was a long silence. Paul tried to prepare himself for the worst. It seemed that Cheri was approaching the subject but didn't know quite how to break through. Or was she waiting for Paul to confess?

After several minutes Cheri spoke, "I had lunch today in the park near the courthouse." Cheri often packed a lunch and ate at the office, so there was nothing unusual about her taking her lunch outside to the park.

"Beautiful day for a picnic!" Paul feigned enthusiasm. "With others from the office or did you eat alone?"

"No, actually....with Brian Randall....the guy who put up the reward money."

"Oh, yes, that reminds me, did I tell you I sent him a thank you a week or two ago?"

"That's nice." Cheri's eyes glazed over again.

"Just the two of you?" Paul asked.

"It was so strange. Did you know he lost his wife? Just a few years ago?"

"No, how would I know that?"

Cheri took a deep breath and spoke slowly one word at a time, "Paul... something's bothering me.... something.... I have to talk to you about."

Paul's stomach wrenched tight again. I thought we had changed the subject. But here it comes. Paul's guilt and shame was growing with each passing word. *She knows. Somehow, she found out.*

"Paul, I had the strangest feelings when I was with Brian. First of all, you know I love you. You mean the world to me, and there couldn't be a better husband in the entire world. You know that's how I feel, don't you?" The newspaper lay crumpled on the sofa and Cheri's eyes locked on his.

"Yes, Cheri; and I love you," Paul spoke with all the sincerity he could muster.

"This afternoon, I felt like I used to feel in high school when boys flirted with me or when I was asked on a date. I never expected to feel that way after I was married, but it's been bothering me all afternoon, and I was trying to decide if I should tell you about it."

"Oh, Cheri," Paul sighed. "That's nothing to worry about. I can understand your being attracted to another man. And I can certainly understand other men being attracted to YOU." Cheri smiled, and Paul continued, "I know you love me, and I trust that you would never do anything inappropriate. You didn't actually DO anything, did you?"

There was another long silence. Paul waited uncomfortably, reviewing his words. *Maybe I shouldn't have used the word "inappropriate."* He winced slightly. Cheri caught his facial gesture and realized how uncomfortable they both were feeling.

"No, I didn't DO anything, as you put it. I guess what I'm trying to say is that I was really scared by what I was feeling. I don't think I did anything inappropriate, but maybe I'm kidding myself. Maybe it WAS inappropriate to even accept his invitation to lunch."

I don't believe it, Paul thought to himself. *My wife is feeling guilty about having lunch with a business acquaintance. That's nothing compared to what I've done. But I'm glad we're talking about her, not me.* It began to dawn on him what an amazing confession she had just made and what awesome courage she possessed. He suddenly felt overwhelmed and humbled by her trust in him.

"Cheri, my amazing wife, I am thankful you love and trust me enough to share these scary and intimate feelings. I admire you for your honesty." He wondered momentarily if this would be the appropriate time to tell Cheri of his indiscretion. Cheri smiled, grateful for Paul's tenderness. Paul couldn't bring himself to do it. His eyes fixed on the dimples he loved so much. He spoke again, "If I could be half the person you are... Let me just say that I forgive you for whatever attraction you felt for....for Brian what's-his-name. Please don't feel guilty about it any more. Just think about how much I love you. Will you do that?"

"Paul, you are the most understanding man I've ever known. I am so lucky to be married to you. I promise; I will try to be just a little easier on myself. And believe me, I won't be doing any more one-on-ones with Mr. Randall." Cheri sighed, then grinned. She felt tears welling in her eyes. She sighed again. She had done it. What a relief!

Paul got out of his chair and stepped toward the sofa. She reached up to him and he bent down to hug her. She grabbed him with an amazing strength and pulled him to her and kissed him. *Oh what a fool I am!* Paul thought to himself. *What an idiot I've been! How did I ever get blessed with a wife like this?* All of Paul's thoughts led to one deep feeling, *How I would hate to lose her!*

"I think we'd better get the boys ready for bed; it's getting late," Cheri whispered. "Then maybe you and I could snuggle into bed a little early." She grinned again, and gave him a teasing tug on his shirt collar. "Are you playing golf tomorrow morning?"

"Yes, thanks for reminding me. I'm meeting Isaac at 8:30 at Weston Hills."

"Then let's not waste any more time tonight," she said as she rose from the sofa and kissed Paul again. "Randy and Chip, time for bed!" she hollered.

14

A GOOD DAY FOR GOLF

Friday, October 26

Friday is a good day for golf for pastors who have their sermons ready early in the week… or for those who write them on Saturday! On Thursday, Paul had called his friend Isaac Chevitz, the Jewish rabbi, and asked if he'd like to play nine holes on Friday.

"It doesn't get light until eight o'clock," Isaac reminded Paul, "so why don't we meet there at eight-thirty."

"Sounds good to me," answered Paul. "See you at eight-thirty tomorrow!"

Paul had heard that golf is a reflection of the game of life. For instance, there are many ways to hit a ball wrong. Any variation in a golfer's swing may cause the ball to deviate from the intended path. At the same time, there is only one way to hit it right. In the game of life, there are a lot of ways to screw up. It's much harder to do what's right every time. Paul's mistake with Marge Holloway certainly proved that to be true. And then, there is another lesson from golf: If you make a mistake, you can often make up for it by hitting well on the next shot. Paul wondered if there was any way to make up for what he had done with Marge.

The sun was shining brightly over the tops of the trees lining the first fairway when Paul pulled into the parking lot. Weston Hills, the county course near the synagogue, was their favorite place to play. It was not a long course, but the doglegs were challenging, and the greens were always in good shape. A few billowy clouds made the sky picture perfect. Birds were singing everywhere, and a flock of Canada geese honked loudly as they passed overhead. There was a chill in the air. Isaac was already on the practice green working on his putting.

"Paul!" Isaac hollered, "What took you so long?"

"Had to spend some time helping Cheri get the boys ready for school."

"I'm glad Kathy isn't working right now. She fixed me a hot breakfast and told me she'd clean up the dishes; I should get out and have fun."

"If I was paid as well as the synagogue pays you, Cheri wouldn't have to work either!" Paul joked.

"Cheri loves her work and you know it, you schmuck; so don't give me this 'have to work' crap."

As the twosome prepared to tee off, Paul's mind drifted back to the conversation the previous night about Cheri and Brian Randall. It had taken a lot of courage for her to tell him about her feelings toward Brian. He wondered if he could find the courage to tell her about Marge Holloway. Isaac pulled his first drive to the left side of the fairway and Paul sliced his into the trees on the right. He managed to pop his second shot back onto the fairway without hitting the tree trunks. Isaac's second shot was straight and rolled onto the edge of the green. "Great shot!" hollered Paul.

As they holed out on number one, they realized they had nearly caught up with the foursome in front of them. Paul sat down on the bench near the second tee as Isaac took some practice swings, waiting for the group ahead of them to move out of driving range. *When you make a bad shot, you can often make up for it by hitting the next shot well.* Paul was thinking again about the day he went to visit Marge Holloway. *Maybe it was time to come clean about what happened. It would be a big risk, but there were also risks in not telling Cheri. Perhaps it would be better to tell her than have her find out from someone else.*

"You're really lost in thought today, Paul," Isaac said, shaking Paul awake.

Paul looked up and glanced down the fairway. "Looks like they're out of range. I guess we can tee off."

"I already hit, so I guess you're up," Isaac replied.

"You already hit?" Paul asked, astonished that he had not been watching.

"Right down the middle!" Isaac answered.

Paul's drive faded slightly again, but he was in the fairway. As they walked together, Isaac asked, "Something troubling you, good buddy?"

"Yeah, there's something I need to talk to Cheri about, but I've been putting it off."

"Sounds like you have some conflicted feelings. Anything you want to tell me about?" Isaac asked, concerned.

"No, not really. Just an issue between me and my wife."

"Those things aren't good to leave hanging. Whatever it is, you'd better talk."

"I know you're right. Tell you what you CAN do for me. Why don't you call me some time next week to hold me accountable. Just ask if I've talked to Cheri. With your call coming, I'll know I can't put it off. Would you do that for a friend?"

Isaac smiled. "You got it."

* * * * * * *

That afternoon, Paul developed his plan. First, he arranged for one of the girls from the church youth group to come over at seven that evening to keep an eye on the boys while he and Cheri went out for dinner. Then, he called their favorite restaurant and made a reservation for 7:15. After that he called the florist and ordered a dozen red roses. A half hour later he called and canceled the order. Roses before dinner would be a delightful gift, but they would surely seem like an attempt to buy Cheri's mercy after he told her what he had to tell her. No roses this time.

When Cheri got home from work, Paul explained that he would like to take her out for dinner. "What about Chip and Randy?" she asked.

"That's all taken care of; I called Carla Nygaard and she'll watch the boys."

Cheri was delighted to be going out, and asked about his golf game. "Did you beat Isaac today?" she queried.

"No, my game was off. But we had a good time. A lot of trees have dropped their leaves, and the leaves were blowing and dancing across the greens. When you leaned over to putt, it looked like the green was moving! And when the ball rolled through the leaves it looked like a snow plow!" Paul said, laughing.

"It will be snowing before we know it," Cheri mused. "How much time do we have to get ready for dinner? Can I take a quick shower and change clothes?"

"Sure, we don't have to be there until seven-fifteen. You've got almost an hour."

Paul trembled as Cheri went into the bathroom. Tonight, he would tell her. It might end their marriage. But he hoped they could get through it somehow. He realized again how lucky he was to have such a beautiful wife.

The thought occurred to him that this "second shot" could never make up for how badly he had messed up. All he could do was take his best swing. After dinner he'd park somewhere away from home and away from the restaurant. Then, he'd talk. After that, it was all up to Cheri.....and the grace of God.

15

TO TELL OR NOT TO TELL

Monday, October 29

The phone rang at the church office for the seventh or eighth time just before noon on Monday. Carol, the church secretary answered and heard a familiar voice. "This is Rabbi Chevitz, is Pastor Walker in?" "Just a moment, Rabbi," she replied. Pastor Paul heard his phone buzz and picked it up. "It's Rabbi Chevitz calling for you," Carol said. Paul pushed the blinking button for line 2.

"Good morning, Isaac, this is Paul."

"Good morning to you Paul, how are you doing? Getting ready for Christmas?"

"Not quite yet, Isaac. We've got to get through Thanksgiving and Advent first."

"Tell me again, how long is your Advent season?" Isaac asked.

"Four weeks, the four Sundays before Christmas," Paul answered.

"And Hanukkah will be here for us."

"What can I do for you?" Paul asked.

"Oh no, it's what I can do for you," Isaac responded.

"What can you do for me, then?"

"Don't you remember? You asked me to keep you honest."

"Oh, that…" Paul's voice dropped.

"Well, did you talk to Cheri?"

Paul hated to answer. "Well, no, I guess I didn't."

"Dear Moses," Isaac responded, "it's either not that important, or you're really afraid to talk about it."

"I think it's the latter," Paul answered.

"Wanna get together?" Isaac asked.

"Yeah, maybe. Have you got any time this afternoon?

"How about three or so?"

"Is it okay if I come over to the synagogue?"

"Sure, you're always welcome here."

"I'll see you about three then."

"Okay, Paul, see you at three."

"And Isaac, thanks ….I guess."

"Think nothing of it, big guy."

Paul wasn't sure why Isaac always called him "big guy," but it had an endearing ring to it, and he was about four inches taller than Isaac. He wasn't sure he wanted to talk either, but his guilt wasn't going away, and something needed to be done.

* * * * * * *

The synagogue was a modern building, all brick and glass. It seemed a little cold at first, but to Paul, it also had a feeling of honesty and safety. He went to the office area where the receptionist greeted him with a friendly smile. "Hello, Pastor, you know where the rabbi's study is."

"Yes, I've been here before," Paul replied.

"Then go right ahead, he's expecting you," she added.

Paul was nervous with anticipation, but he trusted Isaac and was certain he would never tell another person anything Paul confided to him. As he glanced around Isaac's office he thought how similar this felt to his own office. The number of books on the shelves behind Isaac's desk astounded him. There were several pieces of art work on the desk and hung on walls. *The symbols are different, but the ministry is very similar,* Paul reflected. The Jewish membership is also called a congregation, just as it is in the Lutheran church. He liked the Jewish candles, the breadth and depth of Jewish history, and rabbinic theology, and considered if he weren't a Christian, perhaps he might become a Jew.

The two men shook hands then sat in comfortable chairs perpendicular to each other. Paul looked into his friend's eyes, noticed a little gray in his beard and the slight grin; then Paul's eyes dropped to the floor. "So what's troubling you, Paul?" Isaac asked without hesitation.

"I did something I am very ashamed of," Paul responded.

Isaac waited a moment then responded, "So did I." He paused another moment and added, "I shot a hundred and twelve last year." Paul broke into laughter and Isaac joined him. Both were grateful for the comic relief. Isaac spoke again, this time more seriously, "If you want to confess something, I promise you strict confidentiality."

"I know, and I trust you, Isaac. I guess that's why I'm here."

Isaac waited respectfully, and after a long, long silence, the dam burst. Paul could hold it inside no longer. Weeks of pent up feelings began flowing through a torrent of words.

"The first visit was with Bob and Marge. It was about two weeks after the funeral. I'm telling you, Isaac, I've never felt such a strained visit in all my years as a pastor. Marge is usually a very open person, you know, she shows her feelings easily. But that night she was reserved, emotionally flat, like she wasn't feeling anything, which I attributed to her grief, but later decided was due to the strain in her relationship with Bob. And Bob? I don't think he spoke more than a couple of times the entire hour! Not a word about Brian, or his grief, or anything. Oh, yeah, I remember the last thing he said was, 'I hope they catch the bastard,' or words to that effect."

"So you figured the uncomfortable visit was due to the grief you all were feeling; is that right?" Isaac asked.

"Yeah, I chalked it up as one of my 'duty calls,' you know, something you feel obligated to do, but secretly you dread."

"I've done some of those," Isaac responded.

"Well, a week or so later, I called Marge and she cried on the phone and asked me to come over, so I did. "I was feeling so bad for her," Paul explained. "This time was more like what I expected. She was crying, really feeling the grief. She started telling me how awful she felt. She said that Bob wouldn't talk to her, wouldn't listen to her, and wouldn't hold her. I wanted to hold her and make her pain go away. I knew I couldn't remove her pain, but she wanted to be held, and … and…I don't know. It started feeling so good, so warm, if you know what I mean."

"I think I get the picture." Isaac waited. Finally he asked, "How far did you go?"

"Oh, I was all right that time. I kind of pushed her away and told her I should leave."

"And did you?"

"Yeah, like I said ….that time." Paul paused before continuing. Isaac waited. "But a week or two later, I called her again ….and I know

I was struggling with temptation. I knew I probably shouldn't have gone over there ... but I wanted to see her again."

The atmosphere in Isaac's office was heavy with anticipation. Isaac didn't really want to know the details of what was coming, the details of his friend's failure, but Paul needed to get this out. Isaac knew he had to listen. He felt tightness in his chest. He could hear the clock ticking on the wall.

Paul continued. "When I got to Marge's she grabbed me and held me tight. I was willing to do whatever she wanted. It was a stupid loss of control. I don't think I have to be graphic, but you get the picture."

"So, how far did you actually go?" Isaac asked.

Paul hesitated, not wanting to say the words. "We had intercourse ...in her living room."

There was a long silence. "I've been trying to get up the nerve to tell Cheri," Paul finally whispered.

Isaac was again aware of the tightness in his chest. He was pretty sure he had heard what Paul had whispered. He was grappling with the reality of Paul's confession, the tragedy of Brian's death compounded by the tragedy of Paul's weakness. "What happened this weekend? When we played golf, I thought you said you were going to talk to her?" Isaac asked.

"Oh, man! Remember what a beautiful day it was last Friday? I really enjoyed the golf, by the way, even if you did beat me by four strokes." Paul seemed relieved for the change of subject. He had done it. He had openly confessed to another human being, the awful sin that had plagued him for months.

"Yeah, it couldn't have been nicer. We won't get many more days like that!

"Well, I made reservations at a nice restaurant for Cheri and me. I lined up someone to stay with the boys. And I planned to tell her after we finished eating, on the drive home. I figured we might stop at the park and talk in the car." Paul's head dropped.

"And then what happened?" Isaac waited for Paul's reply.

"I guess I just turned chicken," Paul admitted as his head dropped even further.

"I can understand your being afraid," Isaac said, "but there's another way to look at it."

"What do you mean?" Paul asked, looking up into Isaac's gaze.

"Well, it seems to me you feel that telling Cheri is the right thing to do; you just don't have the nerve to tell her. You're too afraid of what might happen."

"Exactly."

"Maybe you shouldn't tell her," Isaac said.

"Shouldn't tell her?" Paul repeated. "Why's that?"

"You want to do what's right, don't you?"

Paul nodded in the affirmative.

"So, what is the right thing?" Isaac asked. "There are two possibilities. You can tell her, knowing she will be hurt, and not knowing if she will forgive you. OR, you can avoid hurting her and losing her trust in you by keeping it to yourself, and finding a different way to be forgiven."

"I hadn't thought about that," Paul admitted.

"I'm not telling you that's what you SHOULD do. I'm just suggesting that you give that some consideration."

"But then, how do I get rid of this guilt?" Paul begged. "My stomach's been killing me."

"You're a Christian pastor, and you don't know the answer to that?" Isaac almost laughed.

"C'mon Isaac, help me here," Paul asked again.

"You need to confess to someone, and receive the assurance of forgiveness from that person, speaking on behalf of God. Isn't that what a priest is supposed to do?"

"Yeah, I guess you're right." Paul thought to himself for several moments. "I just confessed to you, didn't I?"

"I believe you did," Isaac answered.

"And do you think God can forgive me?" Paul asked.

"Can forgive you? Or will forgive you? Or has forgiven you?" Isaac responded.

Paul thought again. "I guess... I mean, of course I believe God CAN forgive me. And I believe... that when a person confesses their sin, and is truly repentant, God promises He WILL forgive. I'm not sure yet... about that last question... whether God HAS forgiven me."

"Then let me answer it for you," Isaac said. "I believe that you are sorry for what you did. You broke your vow to Cheri. You transgressed against Mrs. Holloway and her husband. You did not behave according to the guidelines of your profession. All that, and maybe more. Oh yes, you betrayed yourself; and you broke God's commandment forbidding adultery. Do I believe God has forgiven you for ALL of that? YES, I do." Isaac paused to let his words sink in. "I believe God is just and merciful. If you need to be punished, let God worry about that... you don't need to punish yourself. God is also merciful and takes pity on his children. God loves you dearly and doesn't want you to suffer, just as God doesn't want Marge to suffer..." Isaac paused for a long moment. "...or Cheri to suffer."

Paul stared at the floor, thinking about what Isaac had just said. "I agree. God doesn't want anyone to suffer." Paul looked up at Isaac. "Maybe I have been punishing myself. ...So, you believe God has already forgiven me?" Paul asked.

"Yes, I do," Isaac answered. "The last, and sometimes hardest, step is up to you. Will you forgive yourself?"

"Hmm, I'm not sure I can do that yet," Paul responded.

"It takes some work, but I'm confident in you, Paul."

"Thanks, Isaac." Paul's throat was tight, and he felt tears welling in his eyes.

"To tell, or not to tell. That is the question. And don't forget to examine your motives. Your motives for doing what you did with Marge. And your motives for telling, or not telling Cheri. Remember, telling her because you hope it will make YOU feel better is not a good reason. And punishing yourself for being afraid is just stupid. God put fear in our hearts for a very good reason."

"Jeez, I've got a lot of work to do on this. I don't know how to thank you. You've given me some good insights."

"Happy to help if I can," Isaac said.

"I feel a real sense of relief already. I guess I really did need to talk to someone about it."

"I'll be checking back with you, if that's okay," Isaac added.

"Okay? Okay?? Listen, Isaac, I can't tell you how much I appreciate what you've done already. I'd really like to talk with you again, maybe in another week or two."

"Any time, Paul, any time." Isaac rose and embraced his troubled friend. "Shalom, my friend. Shalom."

"Shalom," Paul replied. His heart was still heavy, but he felt the whisper of hope and healing in his friend's kind words. As Paul returned to his car in the parking lot the sun was low in the sky and dark clouds hung heavily over the roof tops. *Wouldn't surprise me if it snowed tonight,* Paul thought to himself. As he drove back to his office, the word "shalom" kept repeating itself in his mind. In Hebrew, the word meant more than peace, the absence of conflict or stress. It meant well-being, justice in the community, peace among neighbors, and a deep sense of contentment that comes from knowing one's relationship with God is secure. *It may be a while before God's shalom returns, but I'm hopeful it will,* Paul reflected.

16

THE HOLLOWAYS ARE GONE

Marge was glad when October came and Bible study began again on Tuesday mornings. Pastor Walker announced a study of the Psalms, the Jewish prayer book and hymnody. The first Bible class was scheduled for 10 a.m. on October 2nd. She arrived at the church that morning and chatted briefly with Carol in the office before going to a classroom in the basement. Carol expressed her sympathy, and Marge thanked her for her help in preparing the memorial service for Brian.

Several women were already in the classroom chatting and laughing when Marge entered. A hush quickly followed as all turned to greet her. "Oh, Marge, our hearts just ache for you!" She was thankful to have such caring friends, and she hoped being here at church would ease her pain. "Brian's service was just beautiful! I don't know how you got through that." "How are you, dear? It must be so hard!" Pastor Walker entered the room a few minutes later. She gave him a quick smile which still conveyed a sadness and weariness.

As her pastor, Paul was glad to see her in class, but as a man, he was definitely uncomfortable. When their eyes met, he glanced away nervously. He still felt guilty about his last visit with her, and he didn't want to encourage any further intimacy.

"The Psalms are sometimes called the Jewish hymn book," Paul began. "Most of us associate the Psalms with King David who we know was a shepherd and musician before becoming king. Many of the psalms are ascribed to David as author, but many were written by others. In fact, the book we call Psalms was a collection that spanned hundreds of years. No doubt many were used in worship, in the temple built by Solomon, David's son. Many were written by temple musicians, by scribes, and by unknown men of faith who poured out their deepest feelings to God in these very personal writings."

It seemed to Paul that Marge was quieter and more reserved than she had been in the past. It was probably her grief, but he wondered if she felt guilty too, or angry. When Paul was describing the different types of psalms, Marge asked a question about psalms of lament. Paul promised to pass out a list of the different types of psalms. He suggested to Marge that reading and praying the psalms of lament would be a good way for her and her husband to express the grief they were feeling. The morning passed without any other conversation between them. Paul hoped she would return the following week.

Paul looked for Marge and Bob in church the following Sunday but did not see them in their usual pew. About half way through his sermon, he spotted Marge near the back of the church, sitting alone and very inconspicuous, behind a large family with five busy children. *She may have come in late,* he thought to himself, *or I just didn't see her behind the kids.*

****

Several weeks later, Paul arrived in the office at 9 am and overheard Carol talking on the phone. "Yes, he just walked in. I'll give him the message right away. I'm sure he'll be there as soon as he possibly can."

"What was that about?" Paul asked.

"That was your friend at the hospital in Gary, Chaplain Meyer," Carol replied. "He wanted you to know that Ernie Patterson was there in ER. Apparently he was in a car accident on his way to work this morning. He said he may have a whiplash injury to his neck but otherwise seems okay. They're doing x-rays and keeping him for observation."

Paul grimaced, "Ooo…those can be nasty. I'll get over there right away. Tell my Bible study ladies to read and discuss Psalm 8, 23, and 103. I may be late getting back here."

Gary Memorial Hospital was a twenty minute drive from Weston. Paul remembered the funeral he had for Ernie's wife about three years ago. He was only in his fifties and much too young to be a widower. He made his way to the Emergency Department and asked for Mr. Patterson. The nurse walked him to a small examining room and pulled back the curtain. Ernie was resting but opened his eyes when Paul said his name. "Ernie, how are you doing?" Paul asked. "I heard you were in an accident this morning."

"Not too bad, Pastor, considering what happened," Ernie answered. "In fact I'm lucky it wasn't any worse. I was hit from behind and that knocked me into the car in front of me. The car's a total wreck! I think the good Lord was watchin' out for me though. The doctor says I have a whiplash. All I know for sure is I've got one heck of a headache!"

"You look pretty good, considering…" Paul chided. "I'm sorry to hear about your car, but I'm glad YOU weren't totaled!

"Me too," Ernie replied.

"You'll have to take it real easy for a while. I've heard that whiplash injuries can cause problems for a long time. Are they going to keep you here at the hospital for a while?"

"No, I don't think so. They've taken x-rays of my neck. They said they'd give me a neck brace. They just advised me to take it easy for a few days, and to notify my doctor if my symptoms don't go away."

"How are you going to get home?" Paul asked.

"The nurse said she called my daughter at work. I'm expecting her any minute now."

"That's good," Paul sighed. "May I say a prayer for you? I hate to rush off, but there's a Bible study class waiting for me at the church."

"Oh, please do. I'd appreciate that very much, but I don't want to keep you here. There's really no need for you to stay."

Paul placed his hand on Ernie's shoulder and prayed, then left to drive back to church. He was only five minutes late for his class on the Psalms.

Marge was there, which made Paul somewhat apprehensive. But again, there was little conversation between him and Marge. When class was over Paul thought about his conversation with Rabbi Chevitz. *Maybe it would be best not to say anything to Cheri about what happened at Marge's. It was one time, and clearly because of her grief, and his feeling of helplessness. Knowing how weak I was would only upset Cheri and disappoint her terribly. Perhaps this is one of those burdens I will just have to carry on my own. God, I hope I can forgive myself.*

* * * * * * *

Marge had her own thoughts after class. She was embarrassed about her infidelity. She was glad that Paul hadn't contacted her since that weird day. What had happened between them was, for her, a release of so much pent up emotion. It was a spontaneous reaction on her part; nothing more than that. She hoped Paul was not suffering too greatly from his part in the indiscretion. She decided again that she would not add guilt and regret to her already overburdened soul.

By November Marge found that concern for her had been expressed and now the group's attention was focused on their study and discussions. Some of the women felt that bringing up the issue of Marge's grief might be unkind, so they avoided speaking to her or about her. The days were long and there seemed to be no relief from the ache of missing her son. Bob was still angry and there was no breaking through the emotional wall he had built between them.

She tried to concentrate on the Psalms, and to read the ones which Pastor Paul assigned each week. However, her mind kept drifting during class. At home, as she read psalms of lament, she broke down crying time after time. It also seemed that Pastor Paul had become more distant. Not that she blamed him. Perhaps he was angry at her for being so emotional and for what had happened between them.

Bob came to church with her and Sarah for two or three Sundays, but he was quiet and seemed reluctant to be there. Marge missed her period in October. At first she thought it was just a few days late, but when two weeks had passed, she began to get nervous. Another week went by with no sign of bleeding. Suddenly, it was November. It hardly seemed possible, but she felt like she was in the early stages of pregnancy. And because she and Bob had not had sex since Brian died, that could only mean one thing. If there was a baby growing inside her, Pastor Paul Walker was the child's father. She scheduled a doctor's appointment for the second week in November.

Marge also called the church office to make an appointment to talk to Paul. "Hello, Carol, may I speak to Pastor Walker?"

Carol buzzed Paul on the intercom and told him that Marge Holloway was on line 1.

"Hello, Marge," Paul hesitated, unsure what to say next, and afraid of why she was calling.

"Hello, Paul, I was just calling to ask what time the service will be for Thanksgiving?"

"7:30 on Wednesday night," Paul replied.

"Thank you. I'm not sure if Bob will want to go." Marge hung up, too nervous to make the appointment with the pastor, or to say anything about the pregnancy.

The week before Thanksgiving, she had the confirmed report that she was indeed pregnant. Marge was surprised that the news did not shock or disturb her. She realized she had been thinking about the situation for several weeks. She felt a sense of calm, a new focus for her own life, perhaps a new reason to live. Marge told Bob she wanted to spend Thanksgiving with her parents in Chicago. He said he wasn't interested, but she could go if she wanted. So Marge and Sarah spent three days with her parents, lovingly wrapped in their warm embraces. The grandparents were concerned about both Marge and Sarah, but didn't want to pry with too many questions. Marge talked about her growing separation from Bob, but did not mention the pregnancy.

When they returned to Weston, Marge prayed constantly, asking God for direction. She found it difficult to concentrate on the Bible study; and she continued to feel a growing distance from the pastor as well as from Bob. Finally, she knew…she would not tell Bob…or the pastor. So, in December, Marge stopped coming to the Bible study.

* * * * * * *

Saturday, December 15th, was Marge's birthday, just ten days before Christmas. Marge waited all day for Bob to say something. They listened to Christmas music. Together with Sarah, they trimmed the tree. A little after seven that evening, with Bob's face buried in the Sports section of the paper, Marge started singing, "Happy Birthday to me! Happy Birthday to me! Happy Birthday, dear Margie, Happy Birthday to me!"

Sarah joined her on the last two lines, singing "Happy Birthday, dear Mommy, Happy Birthday to you! …Oh, Mom, how could we have forgotten? I'm so sorry. I bought a birthday card for you last week. It's in my bedroom. Just a minute, I'll go get it!"

When she had left the room, Bob started his defensive harangue. "Very funny, very funny. Sing to yourself and embarrass us. You act like you're the only one around here who matters."

"No, I'm NOT the only one who matters. I just hoped you hadn't forgotten. I am your wife, remember me?" Marge asked on the verge of tears.

"So, I forgot!" Bob yelled. Sarah was about to enter the room, then stopped at the doorway. "Tough shit!!" Bob screamed at Marge. "You think you're little Miss Perfect. Why don't I cry? Why don't I talk? Why don't I care? Well, screw you!" Bob pushed his way past Sarah and went out the back door. Sarah ran to her mom crying, her tears falling on the envelope on which she had written, "MOM, Happy Birthday!"

The next morning none of them felt like going to church. They were embarrassed about the argument, but that was only part of it. It was hard to face people, and the memories of Brian were especially strong there. A week later, with Sarah begging and pleading, her parents reluctantly agreed to attend the late Christmas Eve service. Members were kind, and seemed glad to see them; but Marge wondered if just seeing the Holloway family would spoil their Christmas joy. She and Cheri chatted briefly after worship, before Randy, Cheri's seven year old, began begging to go home to open a gift or two. It was their last conversation.

Marge knew she could not go much longer without Bob finding out about her pregnancy. It was beginning to show, but so far Bob had not noticed her baggy clothes; after all, it was winter. Marge tore off the December calendar in the kitchen. It was a new year and time for some difficult decisions. The first, and in some ways most painful decision, was that she could no longer live with Bob. She called her parents and asked if they could give her some financial help because she was leaving Bob. They were sad, but promised their support.

Next, she had a long talk with Sarah, who cried and then said she understood. It was amazing that a fourteen year old could be so mature. She was still grieving her brother's death, and now would grieve the loss of her father as well. Sarah even seemed relieved. "I get kinda scared sometimes when dad gets angry. At least I won't have to worry about that any more." She promised to help her mom in any way she could. Marge decided to wait until they were away from Bob to tell Sarah about the baby she was expecting.

January was the longest, coldest, most challenging month in Marge's thirty-seven years of life. She found an apartment in Chicago, got Sarah enrolled in school, and began looking for a job. Her resume was brief and full of generalities, based mainly on her experience organizing Vacation Bible School. Nevertheless, she soon had a job in a local fabric shop at slightly more than minimum wage. Each step gave her more confidence. She knew that with the help of God, she would make it. Summer would come and she would soon have a new baby to care for.

****

In Weston, Bob drew unemployment for several months. There was simply no asphalt work being done in the winter. His child support payments for Sarah were inconsistent. He never returned to church, and never returned the pastor's phone messages. When spring came Bob took another position with an asphalt company in Ft. Wayne. Word in the congregation spread that he and Marge had left town. No one seemed to know a forwarding address, and eventually, the Holloways were simply dropped from the active membership list.

With the passing of time Paul's guilt and fear subsided. Apparently, Marge had said nothing to Bob. There was no call from the bishop. The wastebasket in his office reminded him constantly of Brian, Trinity's best custodian. He would always think of him on Palm Sunday and smile. He still wondered what he might have done to prevent Brian's death. He still felt ashamed about what had happened between him and Marge. Now that the Holloways were gone, it seemed pointless to tell Cheri. There was little he could do but try to forget. Focus on the present. Trust he was forgiven. Do his work as pastor.

17

ANOTHER LEAD

Detective Sean Asplund was grateful to Maria Olivera for giving him the name and phone number of the apartment manager. He called and left messages for several days. It was the middle of October when he finally made contact and was able to set up an appointment with Mrs. Randa Schonmeier who managed the apartments on Meadow Street. Mrs. Schonmeier worked out of a small rental office located in downtown Gary. The sign on the door read "Northwest Indiana Properties." She was Jewish, about fifty years of age, and her black hair was streaked with gray and tied back in a bun. She explained to Detective Asplund that she managed about two hundred units in Weston and Gary.

Sean informed her that he was doing a routine police investigation and needed some information on one of her renters. "No one else needs to know about this," Sean assured her.

She gave him all the information she had, and promised to be very discreet about his inquiry. "I've never helped the police before. Happy to do it; I'm happy to do it," Mrs. Schonmeier replied. "I sure hope one of our renters isn't in trouble!" she added, hoping the detective might spill some dirt. Sean took the information but revealed nothing about Terry.

Basically, all he had now was the full name, Terry Alonzo Mankovic, a social security number, an address and phone number, and an employer, listed as Ace Roofing. According to Mrs. Schonmeier's records Terry was always prompt with his rent payments. It was a good start. He had a lot of work to do. Sean met with Chief Wilson to discuss this new information and how to proceed with it. The chief was glad to hear they had a suspect's name, but an old woman's testimony about a man screaming during a nightmare didn't sound like much of a lead. He had other problems on his mind. "Have you got any leads on the shop lifting ring? And have you made any progress on the gang-related assault last week? That kid was beaten pretty badly." The chief was frustrated with lack of results; too many cases to follow and not enough staff.

"Chad is chasing down some leads on the shoplifters. And no, we don't have anything further on the gang violence. But I really think we could break this Holloway case, Chief. I thought we might do some more canvassing in the neighborhood around the church. What would you say to the idea of questioning our suspect Terry Mankovic?"

"Too soon, too soon. I suggest gathering as much data as possible before bringing him in for questioning."

"Exactly what I thought you'd say, Chief. Chad wants to tail the suspect, to check out his daily routines. He's confident he can get a photo of the guy without being seen. I plan to check with Terry's employer, Ace Roofing."

"Go for it! And next time we meet, I want some results!" The chief pointed at the door.

Chad agreed they didn't have enough on Terry to make an arrest. First, Sean would check with the employer, hoping to get some information without revealing that it was a police investigation. Sean didn't want word getting back to Terry that he was a suspect. Not yet. Chad, who liked action, was excited about tailing the suspect. In the department he was known as "Mr. Invisible." He could follow a suspect and never be seen. If he was spotted, he had a way of blending into the environment. "I bet I can get a photo with one of our new mini-cams," Chad bragged.

"Give it a try, but keep a low profile," Sean reminded him. "We don't want to spook ol' Terry."

Sean let his beard grow for a couple of days, put on his dirtiest old clothes, and walked the final block to the office of Ace Roofing to apply for a job. He would pretend to be an old acquaintance of Terry's. He would hope above all that Terry was not working that day, and that if he was, he would already be out on a job. He shuffled along the street, entered the office door, and leaned over the reception counter.

"Anybody workin' here?" he yelled toward the back offices. A wiry, gray-haired fellow with dark leathery skin came out.

"Yeah, whaddaya want?" He was wearing dirty overalls and had both hands buried deep in the side pockets.

"I need some work. Ya hirin' anybody right now?" Sean growled.

"Maybe," the tough old guy replied. "Who sentcha?"

"Used to know a guy named Terry, said he worked here. Terry Mankovic, you know him?"

"Yeah, Terry works here sometimes. Depends on how busy we are."

"Ya busy now? I done roofin' in Ohio some years back." Detective Asplund hoped his tough guy act was convincing.

"How long you been in Weston?" This was apparently the beginning of a job interview.

"Not long; I'm stayin' at the Y," Sean responded.

"What kind of roofin' you do?" the boss asked.

"Shingles mostly. Helped with a commercial tar job once. What kind of roofin' you do here at Ace?"

"Commercial mostly, a lot of rolled roofs."

"Did you say Terry still works here? I ain't seen him in a couple years. Not even sure I'd recognize him. Has he gotten any taller, or is he still a runt?"

"He may be short, but he's stronger'n an ox. We call him when we need extra help. Funny thing is, he don't seem to need the money too bad. I don't know what else he does to pay the rent. None o' my business really."

"So, you got any work for me?" Detective Asplund didn't think he could wrangle any more information without the boss getting suspicious, so he decided to wrap things up.

"Not right now, but if you want to fill out one of our forms, I could call ya when we get busy." The boss started looking for an application form.

"I need some cash pretty quick. Guess I'll just keep lookin'."

"What'd you say your name was? I'll tell Terry you stopped by."

"Jim Olson. Doubt if he'll remember me, but say hi." Sean pulled himself off the counter and turned to leave.

"Good luck….. Jim." The way the boss said it, made Sean wonder if he was suspicious about the name. The best thing to do now was just keep going. He pulled the door open and sauntered down the street toward his car without looking back.

When he got back to the office, he found his partner Chad sitting at his desk. Chad looked up, "Hey, I've got some good news. I've been tailing Terry for a couple of days and I think I got what you were hoping for," he said excitedly.

"A photo?" Sean asked anxiously.

"You bet! And a good close up. The film's in the lab being developed right now."

"Did he see you tailing him or did he spot the camera?" Sean questioned.

"Heck no. You know me, Mr. Invisible," Chad said proudly. "And that's not all. I found out where he eats most of the time, a little diner on Main, six blocks or so from his apartment. That's where I got the picture. Today I went in and ordered lunch while he was there. It seems like the waitress and quite a few of the regulars know him pretty well. I didn't ask any questions, just listened. Figured you could do the follow up. I didn't want anyone getting suspicious."

"Great! Absolutely, friggin great!" Sean high-fived his partner.

"So, how did your masquerade go at Ace Roofing?" Chad asked.

"Didn't learn much, but it seems Terry gets along all right there. Works off and on depending on how busy they are."

"So what're you gonna do with the photo? Put it in the newspaper or staple it to the neighborhood utility poles? We know where he is. Why don't we just pick him up? See if he's got an alibi for the night of the break-in?"

"Not so fast," Sean replied. "The chief said to learn all we can before we bring him in. Remember the canvass we did around the church the month after the incident?"

"Yeah, a big waste of time. A lot of people weren't home and those that were couldn't tell us a thing."

"Well, that was September, and now it's November, and we still haven't got anything new. Somebody in that neighborhood must have seen something. We're going around again; this time with the photo. Maybe we'll get lucky."

"I don't know, Sean. I hate that door-to-door stuff, but if you say so, we can try again."

Off and on during the last two weeks in November, the partners worked the homes and apartments around the church. They agreed to canvass for two hours, from five to seven p.m., hoping to catch people after work. They expanded the canvass to six blocks in every direction, and most importantly, kept records of every contact, going back over areas they had covered before. They showed the photo of

Terry Mankovic to hundreds of neighbors, but everyone shook their head. "Never seen that guy," was the usual comment. They were tired and they were getting nowhere. Tomorrow would be their final attempt to speak to neighbors near the church.

* * * * * * *

Friday, November 30

The next evening they pulled into the church parking lot at 5:30 pm. It had been dark for over an hour. The parking lot was empty. Sean took the north side of the street and Chad took the south side. This block was mostly apartment buildings. It was tedious work, pushing buzzers, calling on security phones, and knocking on doors. Again, they were surprised how few people were home. They referred to their prior notes on which apartments had responded on previous visits. At the second apartment building on the south side of 16th Street, Chad got lucky. A gentleman from apartment D came quickly down to the front door. "You say you're a detective?" the man said excitedly. "What's going on? Something I should know about?"

"Yes, my name is Detective Chad Skiles. My partner and I are investigating the stabbing of Brian Holloway over at the church back in August. We're looking for someone who might know what happened over there. Do you know anything that might help us?"

"Hmm, maybe..." he paused as if trying to remember something. "Did you say somebody got stabbed at the church?"

"Yes, the young janitor came over to clean the church and apparently found an intruder inside the building. The victim was stabbed and died in the church."

"In August?"

"Yes, August 8th, almost four months ago," Chad answered.

"Whoa! I do remember something strange that happened back in

August. See my white Jeep parked over there? That's exactly where I parked when I came home that night. It must have been about ten o'clock 'cause I left the theater at 9:15, stopped for an ice cream cone and then drove home and parked right there. When I got out of the car, I checked to make sure the doors were locked; you know this isn't too great a neighborhood, and I saw a guy running across the church parking lot over there. He crossed over to the houses on the other side and I couldn't see him around that corner. I thought it was so strange to see someone running away from the church like that. So I walked up to my door here and started to unlock the door. That's when I saw him come walking around the corner and right up that sidewalk across the street. See the street lamp there on the corner? Well, I got a real good look at him when he walked under it. I kind of hid in the shadow here by the door, so I don't think he saw me. I watched him walk up the street a little ways, then he stopped and looked back. He looked all around then kept walking pretty fast. He seemed kinda suspicious to me. He kept going up the street. I unlocked the door and went up to my apartment."

"Why didn't you report this sooner?" Chad asked.

"Well, the next day I had to fly to New York for a meeting. I didn't know anything happened at the church."

"Didn't you see or hear any of the news reports about the stabbing?"

"I was in New York for three days! When I got back I guess it wasn't in the news any more. Like I said, the guy looked real suspicious, but when I got home from New York I guess I just forgot about it."

"You said you got a pretty good look at the suspect as he ran around the corner there. Do you think you could identify him in a line up?"

"Yeah, I think so. Unless you had a bunch of guys that looked a lot alike."

"Does this photo look familiar?" Chad asked, pulling the photo from his coat.

"That's him! That's the guy I saw! I'm positive!"

"Are you sure about the date?"

"I could check my calendar. I know for sure it was the night before I left for New York."

"Great, I'd like to get your name, address and phone number."

"Do I have to go to court or anything?" Anthony asked.

"Eventually, you will be called to testify, I'm sure. Are you willing to help us?"

"I don't know. I've never been in court. I had a speeding ticket once, but I just paid it."

"The court can issue a subpoena requiring your appearance, but don't forget it takes all of us working together to keep the streets and city safe," Chad reminded him.

"Yeah, I feel bad somebody got stabbed. And in a church? Man, what a shame! Like I said, this isn't too great a neighborhood. I can see why people want to move out to the suburbs."

Chad could hardly wait to catch up to his partner and share the good news: Anthony Montano, 201 16th Street, Apartment D, could put Terry Mankovic at the scene of the crime on the night of the murder.

18

SEARCH WARRANT

Monday, December 3

“C’mon Chief, go to bat for us here.” Detective Asplund was presenting his report to Chief Wilson. “We’ve got two very credible witnesses who link this guy with the Holloway murder. It’s taken us several months to get this far. Don’t let it end without a search of the suspect’s apartment.” Sean Asplund had scoured the neighborhood for witnesses and clues. Based on the circumstances of the homicide, he suspected from the very beginning that the crime had been committed by someone local, someone perhaps with priors for theft, robbery, or burglary. He had a suspect. Now all he needed was physical evidence linking the suspect to the crime scene. Although he knew his chances were slim, he needed the murder weapon.

“Judge Svoboda doesn’t like us snoopin’ around people’s houses without some pretty compelling reasons,” Chief Wilson argued.

“Well, try Judge Mendez then. She’ll be sympathetic. She’d love to help us put away Brian’s killer.”

"Judge Mendez is in Washington, D.C. this week; do you want to wait?"

"Shit NO!" Sean fumed. "We've probably spooked our suspect already, with all the snoopin' we been doin' in the neighborhood. The word is out that we're looking locally, so it's probably gotten back to Terry."

"All right, all right, I'll see what I can do," the Chief sighed.

* * * * * * *

Tuesday, December 4

The next morning a search warrant was on the desk of Detective Sean Asplund, Homicide Division. Waving it in the air, he shouted, "We got it! Let's go guys!" Sean's partner Chad was off his chair in a flash.

"I'll grab Rick and Sharon!" Chad shouted as he ran toward the locker room. Rick was Chad's cousin, and they looked for every opportunity to team up and work together. They both loved hockey, big trucks, and beer. When they were together, that's all they talked about. Sean shook his head as Chad disappeared around the corner. "Hey, Rick!" Sean heard Chad yell, "We got our warrant!"

Sean made a phone call to Maria Olivera who lived in the apartment next to Terry Mankovic. "Ms. Olivera, this is Detective Asplund. How are you today?"

"Oh, Dios, my arthritis is giving me a lot of pain; and I t'ink I might have pneumonia. I been in bed for tree days, hackin' and coughin'. My temperature go down in the mornin' and then go back up every night."

"I'm sorry to hear you're not feeling well. Have you seen or heard your neighbor, Terry Mankovic, the past day or two?" Sean asked.

"No, Señor, I haven't. Like I say, I been in bed for several days, and I haven't been payin' attention to anythin' goin' on aroun' here."

"Do you know if he's home right now?"

"No, but I could go nes' door and see."

"No, no, don't do that, Maria," Sean said hastily. "We're still keeping an eye on him, so don't trouble yourself. You just stay in your apartment and take care of yourself. I hope you're feeling better soon."

"Thank you, Detective, I will."

* * * * * * *

The four police officers were at the apartment about half an hour later. They parked down the street a short distance from the apartment building to discuss their strategy. "Do we just do a search today?" asked Rick, "Or are we going to bring him in?"

"Depends," said Sean, "on what we find in the apartment. If Terry is here, I don't want him to get away. I'm thinkin' now or never."

"Me too," agreed Chad. "We've got those two witnesses who make me pretty sure Terry's the one we want."

"In that case, Chad, why don't you and Rick take a position as close as you can to the front door without being too easily observed, in case our suspect is out and returns to the building? If he shows up, grab him. I'll take Sharon with me and we'll check out the apartment. If Terry's not at home, we'll try to get inside to do a preliminary search and see if we find anything. If he is there, we'll call you up to help with the search."

"Sounds like a plan," Rick replied. "Chad would probably recognize him more easily than I would. You guys have been looking at his photo for weeks."

"Okay with me," said Chad. "But how're you gonna get in? Doesn't the manager work in an office somewhere? You got a key?"

"No, but I've got an idea that might work," said Sean with a grin.

"I'm ready," Sharon said. "And I get to go inside with numero uno!"

"Look who's suckin' up for a promotion," her partner Rick jabbed.

Sean and Sharon checked their weapons, vests, and the warrant, and approached the building. Sean briefed Sharon on his plan. "The apartment manager is a Mrs. Schonmeier, according to Maria Olivera who lives in apartment 6. Doesn't that name sound a little Jewish to you?"

"Olivera sounds Hispanic to me," Sharon said quizzically.

"No, no, Schonmeier! Schonmeier sounds Jewish!"

"Yea, I suppose it does," Sharon replied, feeling rather foolish.

"She is VERY Jewish. I would guess from New York, with a really thick accent. When we get to Terry's door, apartment 8 on the second floor, I want you to knock on the door and with your best Jewish voice say, 'This is the manager, I need to talk to you about the rent.' And hopefully, he'll open the door." Sean buzzed Mrs. Olivera in apartment 6, and she unlocked the front door from her apartment buzzer. "No need to come to the door, Mrs. Olivera. We're just checking on your neighbor." Sean and Sharon headed up the stairs.

"Jewish accent, huh? I'll give it a try." Sharon shrugged as they moved down the hallway. They held their guns ready. At door 8, she knocked. They waited. She knocked again a little harder.

"Yea, who is it?" someone shouted from inside.

"Ms. Shonmeier, the manager, I need to talk to you about the rent," Sharon said, hoping her Jewish accent was convincing.

"I already paid my rent; go away!" he replied, sounding annoyed.

Sharon looked at Sean and raised her shoulders. "Now what?" she whispered.

"Say, 'It's about a refund,'" Sean whispered back.

"It's about a refund!" Sharon shouted.

They heard movement inside and then the door opened. Sean pointed his gun at the suspect and said, "Weston Police, step back and put your hands against the wall."

Terry raised his hands slightly. "What's goin' on?" Terry asked.

"Get over there," Sean pointed with his gun, "and put your hands against the wall!"

Terry did as he was told. "Sharon, cover him while I frisk him." Sean patted him down then snapped handcuffs on Terry's wrist. "Put both hands behind your back!" Sean barked. He cuffed the other wrist and ordered Terry to sit down in the chair.

"We have a warrant to search your apartment," Sean said as he pulled the warrant from his pocket. "Would you state your name?"

"Terry Mankovic," he snarled. "What are you looking for, drugs? I don't use that shit. Go ahead, search."

"Sharon, why don't you go downstairs and get the other officers while I keep an eye on Terry."

"Sure thing," she replied and hurried down the hall and down the stairs. In a few moments she returned with Chad and Rick. The three of them began going through the kitchen, bedroom, and bathroom.

"Some good porno here in the bedroom," Rick yelled. Sharon went through every kitchen cupboard.

Chad checked the bathroom, opening cabinets and lifting the toilet lid. "Nothing in here!" he shouted.

"So, Terry, what's been keeping you busy lately?" Sean asked. Terry fidgeted in his chair and wouldn't answer. "Been going to church like your momma told you to?" he asked. Terry wouldn't look at him. His leg kept jiggling. "So if we don't find any drugs, what should we be looking for, huh, Terry?"

"Bingo!" Rick yelled from the bedroom. "Bottom dresser drawer!

Looks like a pretty wicked knife!" Carefully pulling the sheath and knife from the drawer with his gloved hands, Rick bagged them and brought them out to show Sean.

"Terry Mankovic, you are under arrest for the murder of Brian Holloway," Sean said, looking Terry in the eye.

"Hey, I didn't do it! You got the wrong guy!" Terry complained.

"Killing an innocent kid in a church is about as low as it gets, Terry," Sean replied.

"You're nothin' but scum," Rick added.

"Fuck you!" shouted Terry.

"You have the right to remain silent, and I hope to hell you will.... at least 'til we get you to the station." Sean began reading Terry his rights. "You have the right to an attorney. Anything you say, can and will be..."

"Yeah, yeah, I know; ...used against me in a court of law." Terry twisted and resisted slightly as they led him down the hall toward the stairs. As they passed the next door, Sean heard the sound of violent coughing coming from Apartment 6.

Jeez, I hope she doesn't die, Sean thought to himself. *Ms. Olivera will be a key witness if we get this thing to trial.*

****

The following Monday, Detective Asplund called the Lutheran church to notify the pastor that a suspect was in custody. Paul was relieved, and pleased that this terrible chapter in Trinity's history might finally be drawing to a close. The detective promised to call again when a trial date was set. The detective also called Bob and Marge Holloway's home to inform them of the arrest. There was no answer during the day, so he called after work hours on Monday evening.

Bob answered the phone, "Hello."

"Good evening Mr. Holloway, this is Detective Asplund. I'm calling with some good news. We've captured the man we believe killed your son."

"Good, I hope the damn killer will be fried!

Sean told Bob his testimony would be helpful in court, particularly at the time of sentencing. Bob simply hung up without responding.

19

TRINITY'S GRIEF

Not much was said publicly that winter about Brian's death in the church. But behind the scenes there were many private conversations among the members. Many of the women were reluctant to come to the church for evening circle meetings or committee meetings. Those who had thought the problems of crime were in other parts of the city could no longer deny there was crime in this neighborhood as well. Two couples in particular were critical of Pastor Walker's efforts to serve the neighborhood. Stan and Beth Malsberger were extremely protective of their church building; and George and Louise Downing never had cared for Pastor Walker.

One Sunday in January, Cheri was standing in the hallway after church and overheard Louise talking to Beth. "Maybe Pastor Bjornstad was right when he said that the Lutheran church wasn't the right kind of church for these people." Cheri wondered exactly what was meant by "these people." *Did they assume Brian's murder was committed by someone of another race or color? Or was it just an angry reference to anyone who didn't belong to their church? Or were they referring to poorer families now living in the neighborhood?*

Beth responded, "I wonder if Pastor Walker is having second thoughts about his ministry in the neighborhood." Cheri's anger grew.

It wasn't just "his" ministry; it was the church's ministry! The criticisms were growing, and some members talked about leaving to attend other churches in safer neighborhoods. Some speculated about where the Holloways had gone. Beneath all the conversations were the common feelings of fear and anger.

The annual meeting was held the last Sunday in January following a shortened worship service. Pastor Paul was pleased to see a record attendance in spite of the cold temperatures and snow-packed streets. He assumed everyone was there to lend support to Trinity's ministry of outreach. How wrong he was!

After worship, coffee was served at the back of the church; then members returned to their seats for the beginning of the meeting. Children were all invited to one of the Sunday School rooms where a movie was being shown. Paul sat down next to Cheri, about four pews from the front, and waited while Bill Trogdon, the council president, called the meeting to order.

Bill asked the pastor to lead an opening prayer. Pastor Walker was invited to comment on his report, after which the congregation clapped politely. The committee reports were presented without much discussion. The Property Committee reported the change of all locks and installation of a security system in response to the break-in and Brian's death. They also replaced all ground level windows with tempered glass. The budget for the coming year was presented along with a small cost-of-living increase for the secretary and the pastor. Then the questions and opinions started to fly.

Stan Malsberger rose from his seat. "How can we give our staff, especially the pastor, a raise when we are losing members? Maybe we should be cutting staff. We'll never make this budget."

Cheri looked at Paul and whispered, "Is he saying the church should eliminate the pastor's position to meet the budget?"

"I suppose that could be inferred," Paul whispered back.

Louise Downing stood up. "Who wants to belong to the church

where the janitor was murdered? Nobody'll join Trinity after all the negative publicity we got last year."

George Downing stood when his wife sat down. "I think we need to talk seriously about relocating this church to a safer part of town."

"Maybe having a Community Fair in this neighborhood is just asking for trouble!" someone shouted.

The president wasn't sure how to handle all the questions and comments. People were not raising their hand to be recognized; they simply stood and spouted off and then sat down, one after another. It appeared that people needed to vent frustration, so he let the comments continue.

"On a more positive note, I hear the police arrested a suspect," Fred Schmidt offered.

"Yeah, but for all we know, another killer could be waiting to stab somebody right here in our parking lot!" Louise Downing spoke again.

"I think we need a pastor who can really make a difference. I mean, Pastor Walker means well, but he just doesn't seem to know what to do in this situation." Charlie Schoen looked toward George and Louise for agreement.

With that remark, Cheri was ready to scream. For the past five minutes there had been nothing but fear and criticism, and most of the criticism seemed aimed at her husband. She shook her head and stared at Paul. *Isn't anyone going to talk about the good things Paul's done? Isn't anyone going to rise to my husband's defense?* she wondered. Cheri was reluctant to speak out. It would appear to be self-serving to defend her husband.

Paul was thinking similar thoughts and finally decided he had heard enough. He stood and asked the council president for permission to speak. Bill was relieved to have someone actually ask permission from the chair.

"Friends in Christ, it is evident that we are still grieving the loss of Brian, and that there is a lot of fear and anger that we need to work through. It's natural that we should look for someone to blame for Brian's death. I hold myself partially responsible for allowing him to be in the church alone at night. I've asked how God could allow something so tragic to happen in our church. There is no satisfactory answer to that question."

"That's what I mean, Pastor. You don't seem to know what to do in this situation." It was a sudden interruption from the previous speaker, Charlie Schoen, repeating his accusation.

"I do have some ideas about how to deal with our fear and anger. We need to talk about them and get our feelings out in the open. I'll admit you all have caught me a little off guard, but it is obvious from some of the remarks you've made that there are still a lot of unresolved feelings. I would propose a forum in which we all have a chance to talk about our grief and our fear, and remind ourselves that our ministry has not changed. It is still the gospel of Jesus Christ, a gospel of healing and reconciliation that shapes our ministry, not our fears."

"What good is it gonna do to just talk about it?" Stan Malsberger complained.

Bill rapped on the pulpit to regain control of the meeting. "We've drifted away from the motion which is on the floor, to accept the proposed budget. I believe the pastor has a good suggestion, and I promise the council will have some serious discussion about the concerns that have been raised today. Are you ready to vote on the budget?" He waited a moment to see if there were any objections. "All in favor say 'Yes.'" A majority of members quietly replied, "Yes."

"All opposed, say 'No.'" A vocal minority shouted, "No!"

"I believe the budget passes," Bill declared.

"I demand a written ballot!" someone shouted. A fearful silence followed.

"That IS a legitimate REQUEST," Bill replied, emphasizing the word 'request.' "We don't want anyone intimidated by having to raise their hand, so will the ushers please distribute pieces of paper to the congregation?"

It took a few minutes for the ushers to go to the office, cut sheets of paper in half, and return to distribute them to the members. Paul and Cheri whispered their dismay that the meeting had become so confrontational. "Bill sure is handling it well," Paul commented.

"Does everyone have a ballot now?" Bill asked. "Please write on your ballot using your own pen or a pencil from the pew. Write 'yes' if you are in favor of accepting the proposed budget. Write 'no' if you want to reject the proposed budget. Ballots were folded and collected by the ushers, then taken to the office to count. Bill asked if there were any other motions to come before the congregation. There was a rustling among the members, but no one spoke. Bill thanked the pastor, the secretary, the treasurer, budget committee, the council members, and all who helped put together the annual report. Then he thanked everyone for coming out for the meeting. He looked to see if the ushers had returned with the result of the ballot. "It may take a few more minutes to hear the result of our vote, so in the meantime, Pastor, would you lead us in prayer?"

Pastor Walker stood up again and walked to the front of the church. "Dear Lord, you know us better than we know ourselves. You know our weaknesses and our fears. Be with us and with the Holloway family as all of us grieve the loss of Brian. May your Holy Spirit grant us comfort; and may your Spirit inspire us to continue our gospel mission. Use this tragedy to pull us together, not to divide us. Give us strength to face the days ahead, led by your Son Jesus Christ. Fill us with the hope that comes from knowing the power of the risen Lord. Help the police and the courts bring the guilty person to justice, and then show him your mercy, even as you have shown mercy to us for our sins. Bless the members of Trinity and the ministry of this congregation so that we may go forth from this annual meeting with a renewed commitment to love and serve you. These things we ask in Christ's name. Amen."

When Paul finished, everyone noticed the ushers standing in the doorway. The council president beckoned them to bring their tally. He took the paper and read the results, "The proposed budget passes by a vote of 119 in favor and 23 opposed."

"I object!" shouted Stan.

"Point of order!" shouted George Downing.

Bill acted as though he hadn't heard. "This concludes the business on the agenda. Thank you all again for participating in the annual meeting of Trinity Lutheran Church. This year's meeting is officially adjourned."

Members rose from the pews and began moving toward the exits. Most were rather subdued and glad the meeting was over. Cheri gave Paul a hug and whispered in his ear, "Don't let the S.O.B.s get you down!" Paul laughed and hugged her, grateful for her support. Cheri headed for the Sunday School room to pick up Chip and Randy.

Paul greeted several members, then turned to Bill Trogdon, shook his hand, and received a hug in return. "Thanks Bill, you did a good job chairing the meeting."

"For a few minutes there, I thought we might have a lynch mob on our hands," Bill whispered.

"You handled it well, and I don't think either of us made any personal comments against any member. At least, I hope I didn't," Paul added.

"No, I don't think so. But you should have seen the look on Cheri's face after that one comment about you!" They both burst into laughter.

* * * * * * *

On the way home from the meeting, while the boys chatted in the back seat about the movie they had watched, Paul confided in Cheri that he was hurt by the criticism. Cheri tried to minimize it, but Paul warned her that it wasn't over by any means. "I just pray that our frightened members won't continue organizing a rebellion. I believe we have enough members who believe strongly in our mission to help the others work through their fear and anger. I guess I was naïve to think that the incident was being forgotten."

"That kind of trauma takes a long time for healing and recovery," Cheri commented.

"We've got a lot of work to do; that's for sure," Paul added. "Maybe I need to focus on the members and relationships within the church for a while. Otherwise I may not even be the pastor here for long."

"That may be wise," Cheri agreed. "Do you really think there will be more trouble?"

"Do you mean from the neighborhood or from the members?"

"I meant from the members," Cheri answered.

Paul shrugged, "I don't know; we'll just have to wait and see."

"And pray," Cheri added.

20

CALL IN THE BISHOP

"Hey, George, this is Stan Malsberger calling. How 'bout that snow we got last night?"

"I spent half the morning shoveling our driveway and the neighbor's."

"Why ya doin' the neighbor's?" Stan asked.

"She's an old widow and her kids never come around. I figure a good Christian should help his neighbor."

"Hey, that's nice of you. Say, I was thinkin', aren't you the one that got cut off at the annual meeting?"

"Yeah, Stan, I was. Irritated the hell outa me!" George replied.

"Yeah, me too. I thought the president had to recognize a point of order; isn't that in Roberts Rules of Order?"

"Sure it is. What burned me up more than anything was to see the pastor and council president huggin' and laughin' after the meeting was over; like they pulled a real fast one on the rest of us." George Downing was fuming!

"I didn't see that, but it doesn't surprise me. Those two are real buddies! I still don't think we got a fair hearing."

"That's what Louise said to me on the way home that day," George responded. "Bill just wanted to get that budget passed; and he didn't want to hear any objections."

"My wife's upset too," Stan added. "Say, why don't we get together and see if we can figure out what to do about this mess at the church? Would you and Louise like to come over to our place Thursday night? I think Al and Donna are gonna be here too...and Charlie Schoen."

"Sure, why not. I'll talk to Louise, but I'm sure she'd be interested."

"We'll see you both about seven, Thursday evening," Stan concluded.

This wasn't the only phone call that took place after the annual meeting at Trinity. Beth, Stan's wife, was calling her friends to discuss "the problem with the pastor." Anyone who sounded interested was invited to their home on Thursday.

* * * * * * *

Pastor Walker was also making phone calls, first to members whom he knew would be supportive, and then to those who had spoken out at the annual meeting. He wanted to garner support for the forums that were being planned by the council. He also wanted to give his critics a chance to speak to him personally about their concerns.

He met over lunch with his council president to review plans for the forums. "Bill, I think it would be best if some of the forums were held in the homes of council members. Do you think they would mind hosting a couple of meetings?" Paul asked his council president.

"No, Pastor, I think that's a great idea," Bill replied. "Maybe for those who can't attend home-based forums we should offer opportunities for discussion at the church during the education hour."

"Good suggestion," Paul responded. "I'm thinking of three topics for discussion: first a review of Trinity's history; second, a discussion devoted to Brian Holloway's murder and the grief process; third, a discussion focused on the future of Trinity."

"That sounds good," Bill agreed. "For Trinity's future we need to talk about any further actions that might be taken to make the church safer and to calm the members' fears."

"Right, and secondly, we need to review the congregation's mission plan, especially in relationship to the neighborhood," Paul added.

After his meeting with Bill, Paul also tried to set up as many home visits as possible with those he believed to be antagonistic to the neighborhood mission plan or to the forums. Most of the people he called made excuses why this was not a good time for a visit. The few whom he was able to visit were cool in their reception, and constantly steered conversation away from their true feelings about the mission, or about their fear, or about Brian's death. Paul was frustrated. *What's going on?* He wondered. *Are they in denial about the tragedy? Don't they believe that Christ calls us to love our neighbor (even if our neighbor isn't Lutheran)? What's going on?*

* * * * * * *

All the members were concerned about recent events at Trinity. Some prayed for more neighborhood outreach. Some prayed for reconciliation within the congregation. And some prayed for a new pastor. Before their meeting Stan researched the congregation's constitution to see how to fire a pastor, only to discover that a pastor in the Lutheran church can't be "fired." One article said that if the pastor was guilty of misconduct, the bishop could declare the pulpit vacant, and appoint an interim pastor. An anonymous call to the bishop's office resulted in disappointment. "Misconduct" referred to immoral or unethical behavior. Fortunately, or unfortunately, Stan didn't have any evidence of that.

Stan and Beth Malsberger welcomed a dozen disgruntled members into their living room on Thursday evening. Guests helped themselves to coffee and cookies and found a seat in anticipation of the meeting. Stan greeted their friends and explained that he and Beth had invited them there to share their concerns about what was happening at Trinity. "I've been thinking it's time for a pastoral change," he began. "But I found out it's not easy to get rid of a pastor in the Lutheran church. Is the pastor having an affair that anyone knows about?" Stan asked, grinning. Everyone glanced nervously around the room. "Molesting kids?" he asked in joking exaggeration. "No, I'm half-serious. We need something more than difference of opinion about his leadership." After a brief silence, it appeared no one had heard any juicy gossip.

"Has he taken any money from the church?" Beth asked.

"We're not in great shape financially, but the treasurer's report was audited; so I don't think we'll get anywhere with that approach," George replied.

"What about that other article in the constitution, the one about 'ineffective ministry'?" Louise inquired. "It says if the pastor's leadership is deemed to be ineffective, the bishop can replace him."

"Well, that's what I've been saying all along," Charlie Schoen spoke up. "All his darn outreach to the neighborhood has resulted in only one thing, our best janitor getting killed!"

The group spent the rest of the evening discussing all their gripes and complaints about the pastor. Beth took notes furiously to document the problems for the bishop. At the end of the evening, Stan volunteered to go to the bishop and present "their concerns." It seemed there was reason to question the pastor's effectiveness. "Would anyone like to come with me?" The group was quiet. "How 'bout you, George? Will you come along so it doesn't look like I'm the only one who has a problem with the pastor?"

"Sure," George agreed, somewhat reluctantly.

"That settles it then; I'll call the bishop and set up an appointment." Following a little more conversation, Stan concluded the evening. "Good night, everybody, and thanks for coming." The guests rose to leave.

"Stan," said Beth, loudly enough for everyone to hear, "didn't you forget something?" Everyone stopped in mid-conversation to hear what had been forgotten. Stan glanced at her with a puzzled frown. "Aren't we going to close with prayer tonight?" she asked.

"Oh, yeah, let us pray." Stan bowed his head. "Dear God, you know how concerned we are about our church. We only want what's best for Trinity. It's where our kids have been baptized and married; some of us were even married here. It makes us sad to see things going downhill. We know, with the right leadership, Trinity could be strong and vibrant once again. Help us not to get discouraged, but to keep trying to do all we can to save our congregation. Amen."

A week later, Stan and George made a trip to Indianapolis to visit with the bishop. Armed with Beth's notes and the newspaper clippings about the murder, they felt well prepared for the conference.

21

THE BISHOP'S INTERVENTION

"Good morning, Trinity Lutheran Church!" Carol's voice was calm and sweet. Trinity's secretary sounded the same every time she answered the phone, and members often commented what a nice first impression that gave first time callers.

"Good morning. This is Janet from the synod office. Bishop Ferguson would like to speak with Pastor Walker. Is he in?"

"Yes, just a moment please." Carol buzzed the pastor's phone. "Pastor, there's a call for you on line 1. It's the synod office. The bishop wants to talk to you."

O God, it's happened! Paul's heart began pounding. *Marge or Bob called the bishop.* "Good morning, this is Pastor Walker."

"Good morning, Paul, this is Bishop Ferguson." The bishop insisted that pastors call him John in personal conversations and "Bishop" in public. He usually introduced himself on the phone as Bishop Ferguson because there are so many John's."

"Hello, Bishop, how are you?" Paul asked.

"Just fine, and you?

"Doin' okay;" Paul lied, "what's new?"

"I was calling because I thought you and I needed to have a little visit."

"Am I in trouble?" Paul asked, trying to disguise his panic.

"No…no, not with me….but maybe with some of your members."

The Holloways did call. I'll just have to face up to what I did. Paul's head dropped to his desk. He waited for the terrible accusation.

"I'm calling because I thought you might appreciate a little support," the bishop continued.

"Your support?" Paul asked incredulously.

"Yes, my support. Unless you don't want my support," the bishop joked.

"No, no, of course I want your support."

"Well, I've been contacted by some of your members who are still upset about the janitor's death, and your neighborhood ministry."

Paul lifted his head and took a deep breath. "I guess I should have called you after our annual meeting, but I didn't want to bother you; and I thought we could handle the conflict," Paul confessed.

"What did I tell you after your custodian was killed?" the bishop asked with a kind voice.

"I remember, you said you were available; you said if I ever needed to talk, to call you."

"And….?" the bishop paused.

"And I thought I was getting through the grief pretty well. I didn't think about calling you in this situation," Paul confessed again.

"I think we need to talk, Paul," the bishop replied.

* * * * * * *

The following week, Paul drove to the synod office in Indianapolis to visit with the bishop. They talked briefly about the turmoil surrounding Brian's death and how Paul had assumed the members were moving beyond that. The bishop asked about the young man's parents and how they were coping with the grief. Paul talked about how difficult it was for them and said that he had encouraged them to seek professional counseling. He became very nervous as he thought about his visit with Marge. He told the bishop he hadn't seen them for a couple of months, and they hadn't returned his calls. The bishop then asked about the congregation. Paul told him about the conflict at the annual meeting and the council's plan to hold forums. He explained how he had tried to visit the disgruntled members, but they didn't seem to want to talk.

Bishop Ferguson folded his hands on his desk and leaned forward, "Paul, I had a visit last week from two of the men from your church. They talked about your leadership and how ineffective it has been, especially your attempts to reach out to the neighborhood. They presented a list of concerns, mostly petty complaints, which they said indicated that you didn't know how to handle the situation following the death of the janitor."

"I heard some of that at the annual meeting, but I was hoping they wouldn't take it any further. There's still a lot of anger, which I attribute to grief over Brian's death," Paul replied.

"After listening to these men, Paul, I got the feeling that they weren't grieving the death of Brian as much as they were grieving the changes in their church, the death of the church as it used to be." The bishop paused for a minute, then added, "Do you hear what I'm saying?"

"The death of their church… as it used to be," repeated Paul.

"Exactly. The neighborhood around Trinity is changing. The urban culture is changing. The world is changing! The cozy congregation of European immigrants huddled together doing the Lutheran liturgy is disappearing all over the country." The bishop paused again, then continued, "If Lutheran congregations don't adapt to the cultural changes going on, if we don't become part of the neighborhoods we serve, if we don't reach out to diverse ethnic groups, if we don't experiment with new forms of ministry… we simply won't be here twenty or fifty years from now."

Paul was stunned, but thrilled, by the bishop's emotional speech. "I agree completely," he replied. "Those are the things I've been trying to say and do at Trinity."

"I know, Paul, and that's why you're running into opposition," the bishop smiled.

Paul thought for a few minutes, "So am I doing the right thing? What should I do about these members who are, as you said, grieving the changes that are happening all around them?"

"Maybe I can help a little," Bishop Ferguson smiled sympathetically. "Here's what I'd like to suggest. We have a team of trained lay people who will come and meet with your lay people. They're less threatening than pastors," the bishop said with another grin. "They'll listen to complaints with a grain of salt, and try to help members understand what's behind their 'concern.' Then the team will make a report to the bishop, and I will come back to the congregation with recommendations. Those recommendations will be discussed between you and me, before I present them to Trinity. I would also like to schedule a visit to Trinity and be invited to preach. Can that be arranged?" the bishop asked.

"Of course, John, we'd be honored to have you."

"Trust me, Paul, you have my full support."

"What should we be doing in the meantime?" Paul asked.

"Go ahead with your forums. From what I understand of their purpose, they should provide many members the opportunity to express their feelings and opinions."

"Thank you, John. It's great having a bishop like you."

"And it's good having a pastor like you in our synod," the bishop responded.

During the three hour drive back to Weston, Paul felt greatly relieved. He was aware again of the paranoia spurred by his guilt. His suspicions had been verified about what some members were trying to do. But it felt good to have the bishop's support. He knew Cheri would be relieved as well.

* * * * * * *

That Lent was the busiest of Paul's life. In addition to Lenten services, there were forums with the council. Unfortunately, the critical members would not sign up, and participation was limited to the more supportive members. Just the reverse was true for meetings with the synod's task force. Those who were unhappy with the pastor and changes at Trinity were eager to share their concerns with the task force, while the more supportive members seemed unsure of what to say.

Stan and Beth talked frequently with George and Louise. There was a growing confidence that things were going their way. When the task force finished interviewing members of Trinity, Stan stopped by the office one morning to visit with Pastor Walker.

After shaking hands, Stan offered his condolences. "I'm sure sorry things have gotten so difficult for you here at Trinity," he said with sincerity. "You gave it a good effort here in Weston, but have you given any thought to seeking another call?"

Paul bristled with Stan's use of the past tense. "Quite frankly, Stan, I haven't considered it. I realize some members disagree with my vision of community outreach, but I'm not as discouraged as some of you may be."

"Having our custodian killed doesn't mean anything to you, Pastor?" Stan asked sarcastically.

"Stan, that's not fair. You know how awful I feel about Brian. I believe we have a mission here, and I believe most members support my ministry."

"Paul, I'm speaking to you as a concerned friend. This congregation is badly polarized, and you're caught in the middle. I just hate to see you hurt any further. Maybe you should just resign and let the bishop find a better… a healthier place for you to serve."

"Thanks for your concern, Stan. If you're right, and if that's what the bishop recommends, I certainly will seek another call. But for now, my commitment is to Trinity. Is there anything else you wanted to talk about?" Paul asked calmly. He was extremely irritated by Stan's duplicity, but didn't want Stan to see it.

"No, that's about it. Just hope you'll give it some thought," Stan added, smiling.

The two of them shook hands, a civil formality. Paul couldn't bring himself to pray with Stan. He knew he'd do plenty of praying after Stan left.

That evening, he couldn't help but share the conversation with Cheri. It seemed only right to keep her informed. Cheri was furious. Again, Paul was so grateful for her passionate support. There was never any doubt about where she stood when it came to her husband or her sons.

* * * * * * *

Sunday, April 7, 1991

When the bishop did come to Trinity a few weeks later, the attendance at worship hit a post-Easter high. Bishop Ferguson was the guest preacher and celebrant at the Eucharist. A potluck dinner was scheduled to follow worship, and the bishop was scheduled to present his recommendations to the council at an afternoon meeting scheduled for 1 p.m. Cheri, Chip, and Randy were in their favorite pew. Across the aisle and a few rows back, Stan and Beth, George and Louise were very happy to see so many of their friends. They could hardly wait to hear the bishop's report.

Bishop Ferguson delivered a powerful Easter message about the post-resurrection church as described in the book of Acts. "The disciples might have dispersed in fear after their leader was crucified. No doubt some of them did, while other would-be followers simply went their own way. But those who caught Jesus' vision of the kingdom, and those who believed in the power of his resurrection, could not abandon the mission. I hope you realize I'm not talking just about first century disciples; I'm talking about YOU, the members of Trinity Lutheran Church in Weston, Indiana. Jesus has given you a life-saving, church-changing, neighborhood-shaking, world-transforming mission! Are you walking with the resurrected Jesus? Are you standing with your courageous pastor? Are you performing miracles in the neighborhood?"

After his sermon, two couples walked out of the church vowing never to come back. They knew already the direction of the bishop's recommendations. He was apparently as blind and naïve as the pastor.

* * * * * * *

After worship Cheri took the boys to a friend's house for the afternoon. "Thanks so much, Holly, for watching the boys today. I really appreciate it. And let me know when I can watch Teddy for you!"

As Cheri drove back to the church, she prayed that the boys would have fun and prayed that the meeting at church would go well. When she arrived at the church, the potluck dinner had been blessed; some folks were already seated and eating. She joined Paul and the two of them followed a friend in line for food. Near the conclusion of dinner, the bishop asked Paul if he could speak to the members who had stayed.

"Certainly," Paul replied. He stood and rapped on a water glass with his spoon. "May I have your attention? Please continue eating and help yourself to dessert over there. Bishop Ferguson would like to say a few words." A few members were still talking quietly, but became silent as the bishop stepped to the microphone.

"My formal report will be presented to the council this afternoon; however, I would like to share a summary with all of you who have stayed for the dinner…which was very good, by the way. Trinity Lutheran Church has a proud history of proclaiming the gospel and serving the people of Weston," he began. "You, and the members who have gone before you, have worked tirelessly on behalf of the gospel. You have served faithfully in the name of our Savior, Jesus Christ, not for your glory, but for his. Some months ago, one of your members fell victim to a terrible crime. The tragedy of Brian Holloway's death in the church should not, and will not be forgotten. As I did at the time, I extend to you again, my sympathy and the heartfelt prayers of the synod. I urge you to remember that the gospel is proclaimed to sinners, which includes both victims and criminals. All are in need of the grace and mercy of God. That is precisely why Trinity's ministry is needed in this neighborhood, now more than ever.

"While Pastor Walker may have disturbed or offended some of you, unintentionally, he has not, and should not apologize for his ministry to the community. Pastor Walker has my full support. It is my recommendation that you continue with the forums, openly discussing the congregation's mission. I recommend that all activity, whether informal conversations or organized meetings, which disparage the pastor's ministry and personal reputation, stop immediately. If you have been a part of such activity, I urge you to lay aside your differences and focus on what you DO like about Trinity. The bishop's office will not accept further petty complaints about pastoral leadership. I urge you to pray for your pastor and his family, and to support the mission of Trinity under the leadership of your congregation council. If you cannot accept the direction of the mission and ministry of this church, I urge you to seek a community of believers more to your liking and support that ministry. This is a brief summary of my recommendations.

"I have a written report from the synod's task force and a copy of my report which I am submitting to your council. Thank you very much for the delicious dinner and the privilege of worshipping with you this morning."

The congregation broke into applause for the strong stand taken by the bishop. Pastor Walker thanked the bishop for his words of encouragement and thanked the members who had brought food for the potluck. Many of the members stayed a while to visit and discuss what had been said. The council members left the fellowship hall and went to the conference room for their meeting with the bishop.

* * * * * * *

With conflict in the congregation finally resolved, a more normal rhythm returned to life at Trinity. Paul's ministry gained momentum as the congregation now stood solidly behind his ideas for mission and outreach. Paul felt rewarded by small gains in membership, and noted in his annual reports that several new families were of non-Anglo ethnic origin. Luther and Joetta Harmon were thrilled when two other African-American families joined the church. Much to everyone's joy, Maria Olivera, who had given the police their first lead in the murder case, also became a member of Trinity. Slowly, and not too steadily, Trinity's membership began to reflect the ethnic diversity of its neighborhood.

Paul and Cheri, Chip and Randy, became well-known in the schools and throughout the community. In spite of the pain and turmoil of that fifth year, the Walkers considered Trinity, and the city of Weston, their home. They felt blessed with many deep and lasting friendships. Each year, the bishop inquired how things were going and asked Paul if he had any desire to seek a new call. Paul's reply was always the same. "Things are going well. Cheri and the boys seem quite content. I don't feel any need or desire to move."

Nearly a year after Brian's death, a trial was held which brought some degree of closure for Paul and Cheri and for the congregation. Painful memories are not forgotten, but no one likes to talk about them. The story of Brian Holloway's death and the trial of Terry Mankovic would be told again years later, following another series of strange events.

Part II

Terror at Trinity

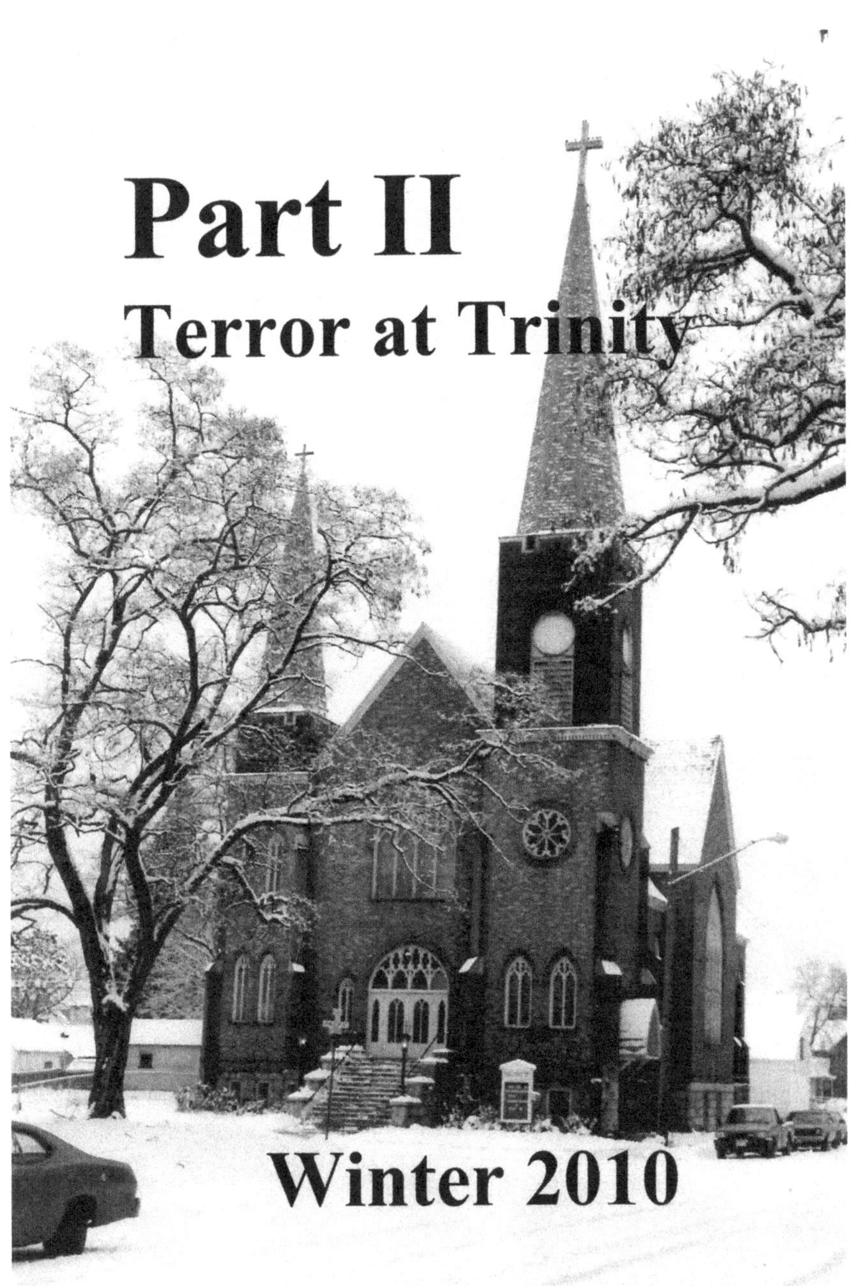

Winter 2010

22

OMAR'S DILEMMA

Pastor Paul Walker stood in the freshly plowed parking lot staring up at the steeple. There had been a lot of snow so far this winter. Snow banks were already three feet deep surrounding the parking lot. February weather was always unpredictable. Paul watched the moisture from his breath drift slowly upward in the cold morning air. The cross high above the church still looked as it had nearly twenty-five years ago when he first came to Trinity. Paul smiled as he thought of the changes that had occurred in those years. For one thing, the fluorescent lights had burned out in the cross, and the original sheet metal cross had rusted through several years ago. The property committee reported that the old cross was dangerous and could possibly be dislodged from the steeple by a strong wind and come tumbling down. Some research on the problem led to a recommendation to replace the old cross with a new fiberglass cross which would be stronger, lighter, and yet have the same appearance as the old one. Spotlights mounted at the base of the steeple could be pointed upward to light the cross and the steeple at night. They would be easier to replace than the old fluorescent bulbs inside the cross. The estimates to complete the work were expensive, but there was more than enough money in the Memorial Fund to cover the cost. Everyone was pleased with the proposal, even Paul.

Pastor Walker's family was changing too. After eleven years with the law firm, Cheri "retired" in order to have more time with the boys during their high school years. It was a nice break, but after a few years, she found herself missing the work environment. She and Paul agreed that a second income would really be helpful for Chip and Randy's college expenses. Cheri interviewed for a position with the county library and was hired. They weren't looking for another librarian, but for a business manager, and Cheri's resume impressed them. Her new job didn't pay as well as the law firm, but it was much less stressful.

Chip, their older son, discovered his musical talents when he began playing the trumpet in junior high. He tried out and was accepted for marching band at Weston High School, and he was soon playing first chair trumpet in the symphonic band as well. His favorite high school memories were of football games, half time shows, school spirit, and band rehearsals after school in the crisp autumn air. His childhood dream of being a Hoosier at Indiana University was realized, and he graduated with a degree in Computer Science. During his senior year at Indiana a recruiter from Silicon Valley in California practically offered him a job on the spot. They even flew him to San Fernando for an interview. He couldn't wait to share his decision with his dad and mom. "Guess what? I'm going to work in California!" They were happy, of course, but sad that he would be so far away.

Randy was more athletic, like his dad. He became the point guard on Weston's basketball team during his junior and senior year. He was ranked third in the league, but not listed in the state rankings. Randy majored in business at the University of Iowa and was able to make frequent visits with his grandparents, Paul's parents, who were retired and living in Des Moines. Randy's real talent was a gift of gab. His easy-going personality and great sense of humor made him a natural for sales. After graduating, he took a position with Iowa Mutual and began selling insurance in Des Moines.

Paul and Cheri were proud of both their sons and were delighted to attend their college graduations. A year after Randy's graduation they celebrated another exciting development in Randy's life when he married Gail whom he had dated at Iowa. A year later Chip was married at a Catholic church near his fiancé's home in California. Randy and Gail were the first to have children, presenting Paul and Cheri with grandchildren, Trevor and Joy.

Paul walked toward the back doors of the church, packed snow crunching beneath his feet. With Paul's long-term ministry in Weston, Trinity took on a different character. Mission and ministry groups multiplied. Miguel Juarez, from Cheri's law firm, had helped the church sponsor an immigrant family from Mexico several years ago. Then, last year, the refugee committee welcomed Omar, an Iranian Christian from Tehran.

There were now two well-attended Sunday services. Membership had doubled. The annual budget was nearly three times as large as it had been when Paul came to Trinity. Paul's first secretary, Carol, had moved with her husband to Chicago, necessitating the hiring of new office staff. The ministry team consisted of an Associate Pastor, Barbara Lambert; Jeannette, the full-time secretary; and Sheila Gordon, the part-time Minister of Music. A new office area, conference room, and entry from the parking lot had been added to the east side of the building. The work load was heavy, but Paul felt blessed to be the lead pastor at Trinity and foolishly thought he could handle almost anything!

Paul punched the security code at the parking lot entrance, climbed the back stairway to the office area, and said good morning to Jeannette.

"Oh, Pastor, I just talked with Pastor Barbara. She called on her cell phone from the hospital. She said to tell you that Arda Johannsen had her hip replacement yesterday and is doing okay this morning."

"Thanks, Jeannette. That recovery is going to be hard for her and for Elmer."

Paul spent the morning making phone calls and writing his annual report for the synod. He called Cheri and agreed to meet her for lunch at the Subway Sandwich Shop. After lunch he returned to his office and met with Barbara to review the visitation plans for the week. "I'd like to visit Arda and Elmer at the hospital tomorrow if that's all right with you."

"That's fine," Barbara agreed. "I've got a lot of planning to do for the high school snow trip to Michigan. And who's going to lead confirmation class next week?" Together they worked out the plans for confirmation classes for the next several weeks. Barbara liked everything set in stone, as far in advance as possible. When she was finally satisfied, she got up to leave. Paul turned on his computer, checked his emails, and began doing some research for the coming Sunday's sermon.

* * * * * * *

Sunday, February 7, 2010

The strange phone call came shortly after 7 p.m. on Sunday evening. Cheri and Paul had just finished eating and were relaxing in the living room when the phone rang. Cheri picked it up. "Hello.... Yes... FBI? ....Yes he is; just a moment please." She handed the phone to Paul with a puzzled frown on her face.

"Hello, this is Pastor Walker...Yes, I know Omar. He's what? There was a long pause. "No, that's ridiculous! ....Where? ...Yes, I suppose I can," Paul replied, glancing at his watch. "Would you give me the address? ....Yes, I've got that. It will take me an hour or so to get there. Please tell him I'm on my way. ...Yes, thank you for calling."

"The FBI?" Cheri asked, frowning. She wasn't happy to overhear that Paul would be leaving the house, driving in darkness, with snow blowing.

"An FBI agent calling from the Federal Building in Chicago. They've arrested Omar!"

"Omar? What on earth for?" Cheri asked, bewildered.

"They're holding him pending an ongoing investigation involving national security."

"That's insane!" Cheri said indignantly.

"That's what I said," Paul replied. "The officer said he couldn't give me any details over the phone. Apparently, Omar asked them to call me because he didn't know an attorney."

"Oh, for heaven's sake! I can't imagine… national security? How could that possibly involve Omar?"

"Guess I have to drive to Chicago tonight to see what's going on. Poor Omar! I'll bet he's scared out of his mind. …Say, would you like to come along for the ride?"

"No, thanks, I think I'll stay and clean up the dishes. I was hoping you and I could talk while we did them together, but you always seem to find a way to avoid work around here!" Cheri was only kidding; but she did feel angry that Paul's work was again interrupting an evening at home together.

"I'm sorry, hon'; I'll be back as soon as I can." Paul leaned over to give Cheri a kiss on the cheek.

"Go! Duty calls!" Cheri said as she began clearing the dinner table.

* * * * * * *

Omar Kushti was a nineteen year old refugee from Iran. He was a handsome, idealistic youth whose reading of the New Testament had led him to faith in Jesus as the Savior. At his college in Tehran he began meeting with several Christian friends and was secretly baptized. Another student, a faithful Muslim, had reported the group to school authorities, and the young men were threatened with expulsion and then prison sentences, if they continued to meet, or were caught speaking publicly about their faith.

Omar talked and prayed with his Muslim family who disapproved of his new faith, but they didn't want him to be arrested. They urged him to flee the country and gave him the address of an uncle who lived in India. He dreamed of coming to the United States, and through the Lutheran Immigration and Refugee Service, he was eventually approved for refugee status in the U.S. He lived for a few months in New York City, alone and afraid; and then Hassid, an old family friend who had left Iran six years earlier, invited him to come to Weston, Indiana. Hassid had an extra bedroom in his apartment, so LIRS agreed to pay the transportation cost of Omar's move. They also contacted Trinity to ask if the congregation would sponsor Omar and help him find a job.

Omar's dream had come true. He was living and working in America. He had a job at a local bookstore. He had a friend; someone he knew from Tehran. He felt badly declining Hassid's invitation to the mosque; and he explained how he had become a Christian after Hassid left Iran. To prove his sincerity about his new faith, Omar joined Trinity Lutheran Church. He spoke with the pastor about his gratitude and his faith in Jesus. Pastor Walker and the members of Trinity were impressed with his story. After attending the orientation class for new members, Omar was officially received by affirmation of faith. He had been in Weston just a little over a year. His job was going well. His English was improving. And he was thrilled to be so well received in his church. Though he was often homesick, church members were becoming his American family.

Paul watched the snow falling as he drove up Lake Shore Drive to the loop. Because it was Sunday night, traffic was light. When Paul arrived at the Federal Building, he found the parking garage and showed his I.D. to the guards on duty at the gate. He was asked to stand outside the car while it was being inspected. After explaining why he was there, he was allowed to enter the garage, told to park in the Visitors' section and to report to the information desk inside the lobby. The officers on duty inside checked him through security and told him to sign his name on the visitors' log. They also recorded his Indiana driver's license number. Finally, they directed Paul to a bank of elevators and told him to report to Agent Robinson on the sixth floor.

Robinson was a burly FBI agent who reminded Paul of the Pillsbury Dough Boy stuffed into a tight brown suit. Robinson also checked his I.D. then explained that the young man in custody needed an attorney. "Omar is being detained, pending official indictment which will be presented before a grand jury at a later date. The FBI is holding him for questioning and has informed him of his rights. Omar told us he didn't have an attorney, but wanted to talk to his pastor, so you were called. You will be allowed thirty minutes for visitation, and I remind you to secure an attorney for him first thing Monday morning."

Paul was escorted to a visitation room and seated at a table with one chair on each side. The walls were off-white enamel. One large fluorescent fixture on the ceiling lit the room. A mirror on one wall was probably a one-way glass window for observing suspects. Paul wondered if there was a microphone under the table or somewhere in the room. After a few minutes Omar was escorted into the room, handcuffed and chained. He awkwardly lifted the chain above the table and sat down. The chain rattled back down between his legs where it was attached to ankle bands. Agent Robinson stood unobtrusively in the corner.

Paul watched as Omar folded his hands and bowed his head in prayer, or in resignation, Paul wasn't sure which. After a moment, Omar looked up at Paul and said simply, "Thank you for coming, Pastor." Paul had expected him to be frightened by this ordeal, but he seemed only sad.

"What happened?" Paul asked, leaning forward with his hands also on the table.

"I don't know why I am here?" Omar replied, his English thick with accent.

"Speak as quietly as you can," Paul whispered, "and tell me what you were doing when you were arrested."

Paul waited while Omar took a deep breath and then paused, looking down at his handcuffs. Paul was uncomfortable with Omar's hesitation. Could he be involved in something Paul didn't know about?

Slowly, Omar raised his eyes. "I was reading Playboy magazine." He looked at the pastor, his eyes pleading forgiveness. "Will I go to prison for that?"

Paul stifled a giggle. "No, no, you can't be arrested for reading that in the privacy of your own home."

"But I'm a Christian now, and I know I shouldn't have been reading that kind of book and looking at those pictures! I didn't buy it, honest.

It belongs to my roommate. I saw it on the table and I couldn't believe my eyes! There's nothing like that in Iran!"

"Oh, Omar. In this country, sex is everywhere. Magazines, TV, movies. As a Christian, you should be careful about what you buy and see, but such magazines are not against the law. They didn't arrest you for that!" Paul could see him sink slowly back into his chair. "So you were at home? And the police came to the door?"

"Yes. Yes, I was in the living room at the apartment. It was about two o'clock. I heard the doorbell and quickly put the magazine under the cushion of the sofa; then I went to the door. The police were there. They asked if I was Omar Shufti. I said, 'Yes, I am Omar Shufti.' They said, 'Please turn around and put your hands behind your back. We are placing you under arrest.' They took me out to a police car and brought me here."

"They told me on the phone it was a matter of national security. Is that what they told you?" Paul asked.

"Yes. They said they were from the F…B…I… I think those were the letters. They went through Hassid's desk and took his computer and disks, but Hassid wasn't home or they might have arrested him too."

"Omar, I am so sorry this has happened to you. Since 9-11 the entire country is paranoid. Do you know what that means? …. Paranoid means afraid. There is a general fear of anyone from the Middle East, Iran especially, or of anyone who might be a Muslim extremist."

"But Pastor I'm not a Muslim any more; I'm a Christian now."

"Yes, I know Omar. But people hear your accent and just assume you may be a threat."

"9-11 was terrible, Pastor, I understand that. But why was I arrested? I'm not a terrorist."

"I know, I know. We have to get an attorney for you…first thing tomorrow morning. I'll make some calls and get someone here to talk with you and explain your rights and what might be done to get you released. Omar, try not to be frightened. Pray and trust God. I'll pray for you. And our congregation will be praying for you."

"I won't be afraid, Pastor. I believe God hears our prayers. I read in my textbook in Tehran that in American courts, a person is innocent until proven guilty. The teacher said that's why there are so many criminals running around free in the U.S. But I thought to myself, America is a wonderful land; innocent people aren't thrown into prison. I never thought I would be in prison in America! America is the land of the free! Isn't that right, Pastor?"

"You're right, Omar. It is the land of the free. I'm sorry you have to go through this. Hopefully, you will be released in just a day or two. Try not to worry. I'll be in touch with you again tomorrow." Paul leaned forward and whispered, "Omar, is there anything you've done that would make the police or FBI suspicious of your actions?"

Omar leaned toward Pastor Walker, "How did they know, Pastor? How did they know?"

"How did they know what, Omar?" Paul whispered.

"About the magazine," Omar whispered.

Paul shook his head. "Give me your hands; let's pray."

Pastor Walker prayed for Omar, bid his friend good-night, and was told to wait while Omar was escorted from the interrogation room by Agent Robinson. In a few minutes, Robinson returned for the pastor. They walked in silence past several empty offices and out into the main hallway. "Agent, can you tell me anything about the charges you're bringing against Omar Shufti?" Paul inquired.

"No sir, not at this time."

"Not even what he's suspected of doing?" Paul insisted.

"No sir. The agent in charge of the investigation will explain the procedure, the right of the government to detain, and the rights of the suspect when he meets with him and his attorney." Stopping near the elevator doors, the agent turned to face Paul. "All I can tell you is… your boy is in big trouble."

Paul wanted to object to his paternalistic use of the phrase "your boy," but decided not to provoke the agent, nor indulge his own frustration. The agent turned and walked beneath the long row of fluorescent lights back to the office area. Paul stared at the reflections on the marble tile floor. Finally, he pushed the down button and entered the elevator to take him to the main floor and the parking garage. When he started his car, he noticed the dashboard clock said 9:26 p.m. It would be close to 11 by the time he got home. Thankfully, it had stopped snowing, but the chill in his bones was as much from the evening's events as from the cold air.

23

THE PLOT UNCOVERED

The agent who discovered *2hot4u* was reluctant to bring his suspicions to his superior. Scanning through internet chat rooms was part of his assignment, but he knew he had spent an inordinate amount of time eavesdropping on lewd conversations. Sexual chat rooms were not off limits, but ever since his first suspicions in early December, he had spent days tracking and recording sexually explicit dialog which … how could he explain it…lacked sensual integrity. The partners in the conversations were suspicious for several reasons. First, they were in different countries, which, in and of itself, would not be significant were it not that most of the countries had large Muslim populations. Second, they were sometimes joined by a third and fourth partner in the chat room. And third, and most perplexing of all, although the words being used were sexually explicit, the sentences and replies didn't make sense; they seemed to have no erotic flow. Questions and answers didn't seem to connect.

Agent Richard Burrows printed pages and pages of intercepted instant messages, and studied them at home trying to figure out why the conversations seemed so phony. It might be that something was being lost in translation into English. Messages had come from Malaysia, Lebanon, Iran, Saudi Arabia, Libya, even France and England, New York and San Francisco. One night, after laying his work aside to watch a late action movie on TV, Rich dozed off and then awoke when he heard the main character say something about a coded message. Suddenly his brain was fully awake. That was it! That would explain why the sexual conversations didn't make sense as erotic dialog!

Now he was certain that he had to share his suspicions. He struggled to write a report about suspected terrorist communication, but all his recorded data related to foreign erotic websites and sexual chat rooms. What if there wasn't a code? What if there was, but it couldn't be broken? What if the agency branded him a pervert and sent him packing? His dream of a career in the CIA was about to turn big time or turn south. Only time would tell.

Fortunately, Burrows' supervisor felt his report raised enough red flags to merit further consideration. The data was turned over to the decoding experts and their computers. Within twenty four hours the word code was broken and Burrows was a hero. The messages definitely represented a clear and present danger. Homeland Security and the FBI were notified, and several agents from each agency were assigned to track future communications to and from the internet users Agent Burrows had identified.

At the center of the network in the United States, two identities were prominent in frequency, *bigdick* in San Francisco, and *2hot4u* in New York City. Terrorist groups around the world were agreeing that a coordinated attack against civilian targets in the U.S. would disrupt American society and throw the government into confusion. Each cell group in the U.S. would choose its own target, and for secrecy and security, not tell anyone else about their plan. The only thing they would need to agree on was a date for the attack. Coordinated attacks all across the U.S. on a single day would create the greatest fear and chaos. Citizens would no longer be able to trust their government to keep them safe.

As the weeks went by Christmas came and went, and there was less and less communication from overseas. New names began appearing – *jst2hot* in Atlanta, *jesusluvr* in Chicago, *sknnydppn* in St. Louis, *lonenude* in Dallas, *spaceprik* in Seattle, *milehiboobs* in Denver, and *crzyone* in LA. Each was "looking for action" and asking for "a date."

While the CIA worked on the messages and deciphering transcripts, the FBI was working on identities: names, addresses, telephone wire taps, employers, etc. Local FBI field officers were assigned to investigate the possibility of cell groups and meeting places. The investigation was named "TransAm" because of its nationwide scope. Files grew rapidly.

Homeland Security was getting more and more nervous. The cell groups would have to be identified and penetrated in order to find out more about specific plans. Also key to any future action was the amount of time available. "Has a date been set?" Director Harold Bellenkamp asked this question several times a day to anyone and everyone. Finally the CIA found the answer. The date for the attack will be 14 February, Valentines' Day, which would fall on a Sunday this year. Bellenkamp called CIA Director Owens and FBI Director Brown to set up a meeting to coordinate the TransAm investigation, now involving suspected terrorists in nine major cities. Timing would be crucial. The agencies had just a little more than one month to complete the investigation. The goal was to uncover all suspected terrorists and their plans. Finally, a nationwide sweep of arrests would have to be conducted in all nine cities on the same day, or suspects and cell groups in other cities, knowing their plot had been discovered, would simply disappear. All three federal agencies agreed to set February 7, one week before Valentines' Day, as the deadline for Operation Clean Sweep. It was agreed the FBI, with field offices in those cities, would lead and coordinate the final stage of arrests.

Throughout the month of January, agents wire-tapped, eaves-dropped, and followed suspects, tracing their daily habits, learning as much as possible about their plans. The initial reaction in each agency was similar to Rich Burrows' disbelief that sexual conversations were being used to plot subversive attacks. Male agents made raunchy jokes about what might happen if *bigdik* made a video of *spaceprik* together with *milehiboobs*! The fun waned quickly as the seriousness of the threats sank in. In New York a cell group planned to strike several large power transfer stations, causing a blackout through most of the city and hopefully shutting down large portions of the northeast power grid.

In Chicago eight young Muslim radicals agreed to form two teams.

They had been stockpiling explosives for weeks. Their plan was to blow up runways at O'Hare and Midway International Airports. Team A studied flight schedules at O'Hare and Team B did reconnaissance at Midway. Some time after midnight on Saturday, under the cover of darkness, each team would cut through a perimeter fence and place explosive charges across the main runway in use that night. If time and darkness permitted, they would proceed to set charges on other runways as well. The team would then retreat to their getaway vehicle and wait until the next commercial flight came in for a landing. As the plane touched down on the runway, a cell phone call would detonate the explosives, hopefully destroying the plane as well as the runway.

The terrorists in St. Louis decided that the city's water supply would make an ideal target, especially since the code name, *sknnydppn*, had become a great source of jokes and laughter at their meetings. In Los Angeles, *crzyone* suggested a high profile attack against network TV stations. Each building was scouted for potential weaknesses in security, and it was decided to try poisonous gas in one, fire at another and explosives at the third. An attempt to topple Seattle's Space Needle was the exciting plan of the Seattle cell. By February first, the FBI had uncovered the terrorists' plans in eight of the nine cities.

The FBI investigation in Chicago was headed by Agent Ron Keller. His team began tracing phone calls among members of a Muslim mosque in northwest Chicago. Leader of this cell group was Hassid Al-Akkbah, an Iranian who had come to the U.S. legally in 2003. He shared his residence in Weston, Indiana, with Omar Shufti, also from Iran, who arrived only one year ago. Omar's immigration record stated he was a refugee fleeing religious persecution for his Christian faith. Agent Keller recognized this as a convenient "cover" and linked him immediately with the internet user known as *jesusluvr*.

On Sunday morning, February 7, FBI agents and police officers gathered in cities across the country for final instructions in Operation Clean Sweep. Telephones and computers were linked with FBI headquarters in Washington, DC. Director Brown paced nervously in the central command station trying to be nine places in the country at once. The plan in each city was to send out teams of police and FBI agents to positions near the known locations of all suspected terrorists, which now numbered a total of sixty-three. In New York, Chicago, San Francisco, and Los Angeles the terrorist groups consisted of eight or ten cell members. Other cities had four, five, or six. Preparation and instructions were to be completed by noon Eastern Standard Time. Three hours would be allowed for personnel to reach positions near the arrest sites. Arrests would take place as close as possible to 3 pm EST on the east coast, 2pm CST, and noon on the west coast. Secrecy and timing were critical.

Agent Ron Keller's teams in the Chicago area headed to the south side near the University of Chicago, to an apartment on the northwest side near the Muslim mosque, to an athletic club in LaGrange, and to an apartment in Weston, Indiana. At precisely 2 pm Central Standard Time, Omar Shufti, who was reading a Playboy magazine at the time, heard a knock on his front door and quickly tucked the book under the sofa cushion.

24

TRINITY'S SUSPICIONS

Pastor Walker pulled out of the Federal Building and drove carefully to South Lake Shore Drive which was slushy with melting snow. He simply couldn't believe Omar was involved in anything as serious as a national security threat. His car radio was tuned to an FM station with classical music playing softly. A piano concerto became a little annoying, so Paul turned off the radio and prayed for Omar. Meanwhile, Cheri turned on the TV at home to listen to the ten o'clock news wondering if there might be any information about a national security threat.

At the top of the broadcast for all three major networks was the story of Operation Clean Sweep. All three federal agency directors had appeared for a news conference in Washington, D.C. at seven p.m. EST. Homeland Security Director Bellenkamp shared how relieved his agency was to have interrupted plans for nine different attacks against the homeland. CIA Director Owens proudly announced that it was their agency which discovered the internet communications and broke the code used by the terrorists. FBI Director Brown made the final statement, taking credit for Operation Clean Sweep and announcing that fifty-eight terrorists were in custody. Their reports were followed by dozens of questions. Network analysts were still discussing this threat to the homeland and the government's well-coordinated response when Paul pulled into the garage. Cheri heard his car and couldn't wait to share all this news with Paul. She still couldn't believe that Omar was involved in this terrible plot.

The fact that five suspects had not been found on Sunday was embarrassing to the agencies. It was agreed this information would be kept confidential. It was also agreed that the case would be presented before one federal grand jury, since the attacks had been coordinated, at least in terms of the date. There would be weeks needed to sift through the evidence gathered during the arrests, a time that would also be used to search for missing suspects and to question the detainees.

****

Monday, February 8

Early Monday morning, after a brief conversation with Jeannette in the church office, Paul called Miguel Juarez, the attorney from Cheri's former law firm, who had provided so much legal counsel for Trinity. Paul made an appointment for ten o'clock at the law office. There, he began to explain what had happened to Omar.

"Have you seen the news reports on this thing?" Miguel asked.

"Not first hand," Paul replied. "I was in Chicago last night visiting with Omar, but when I got home, Cheri told me it was on every news broadcast. She filled me in pretty well."

"Pastor, this is high profile stuff….a nationwide network of terrorists broken up by the FBI, Homeland Security, and the CIA. I think they said fifty-eight terrorists had been arrested in nine cities from New York to LA."

"I'm as shocked as everyone else; but I can't believe Omar was involved. He's not a terrorist!"

"Yeah, right. But who knows what any more? What do you and I really know about Omar Shufti? Do you have any verifiable information on his life in Iran?"

"Well, no...but I know Omar. He's a gentle kid. I believe he's sincere about his faith. I've known him for almost a year now. I really don't think he's an undercover terrorist! You've talked to him. What do you think?"

"Please Pastor, don't get me wrong. I'm not saying I think he's guilty of anything. I'm just being an attorney... you know, keep an open mind, get the facts, don't jump to conclusions..."

"Okay, Miguel. I'm sorry if I sounded defensive. I just feel bad for Omar. Will you talk to him?"

"Sure. Do you have anyone else in mind to represent him?"

"No, not really. You're the first person to come to mind, Miguel, and I really trust you."

"Thanks for your confidence. I'll see what I can do. I'll give'em a call at the FBI office in Chicago. I'm sure you've got plenty of other things to worry about."

"I really appreciate this, Miguel." Paul reached over the desk to shake the attorney's hand. "Keep me posted, will you?"

"Sure thing, Pastor. I'll take it from here."

* * * * * * *

Attorney Miguel Juarez met with his client, Omar Shufti, and the representatives of the FBI in Chicago. They would not share with him at this time, any of the evidence they had gathered. Miguel's conversations with Omar pretty well convinced him of Omar's innocence. One troubling fact remained an unresolved issue for them. The list of fifty-eight suspected and arrested terrorists did not include Omar's roommate, Hassid Al-Akkbah. Omar seemed relieved. When the attorney brought this to the attention of FBI agents, they replied that this list was the only one they could make available. "The investigation is still ongoing," they said.

Miguel agreed to take Omar's case pro bono and did his best to reassure Omar that everything would work out in the end. It was hard to explain to the young Christian believer and recent immigrant why he had to remain in custody, and why it would take so long before the case would go to trial. Miguel called Pastor Walker and explained the situation to him as well. Paul was relieved to know Miguel would take the case of Omar's defense.

* * * * * * *

Valentine's Day, February 14

At Trinity Lutheran Church the following Sunday, everyone was talking about terrorism. Pastor Barbara made a point in her Valentines' Day sermon about God's love and its beauty compared to the ugliness of hatred manifest in terrorist plots to kill and destroy. Pastor Paul included Omar in the prayers of the people, and prayed that God would keep the community and nation free and safe from violence in every form.

After worship, the coffee hour was buzzing with the news of the attempted terrorist attacks. Everyone was thankful the government had been so effective in its vigilance. And, of course, everyone was talking about Omar. Most expressed surprise and disbelief that Omar could possibly have been involved. Some questioned whether he might have known what was being planned. A few ventured that "we may have been fooling ourselves all along."

"Perhaps Omar deceived us and the pastors as well. The government wouldn't make a mistake on something as serious as this."

On Monday morning, Paul called Miguel to thank him for representing Omar and ask if anything new had developed.

"Not yet, Pastor. The FBI still thinks he was involved, and Omar still claims he knew nothing about the planned attacks."

25

HASSID'S PLAN

Hassid and two friends were meeting at the mosque on Sunday afternoon when Operation Clean Sweep took place. Hassid had left Omar alone at the apartment about noon, then drove into northwest Chicago. His friends, Abdul and Ahmid were excited to see him. They had stolen several pounds of plastic explosives from the construction company they worked for to be used for detonation. Hassid had purchased twelve inexpensive cell phones. Abdul had drawn sketches of the roads around Midway and O'Hare and they discussed the best place to park to unload explosives without being seen. Getaway routes and other details were discussed. Everything was ready for the airport attacks the coming Sunday.

As they drove out of the mosque parking lot at 2:15, two dark sedans and one unmarked police car passed them coming into the lot. Hassid grew suspicious. His nerves were already on edge. The men in the sedan appeared to be Caucasians. They were clean shaven and were wearing suits. There was just too much going on for this to be a coincidence. He pulled the cell phone from the console and dialed his home number. There was no answer. Omar was gone. That was a bad sign. The three men discussed what might be happening and agreed it was possible that the feds were aware of their plans.

"They might be looking for us," Hassid suggested. "Let's wait until tonight to go back to our apartments. Check for law enforcement stakeouts at your place before going in. It could be a trap." They all agreed to wait and be very cautious about returning to their apartments.

That night, it was as they had suspected. Unmarked cars were parked within sight of Ahmid's apartment in Chicago and Hassid's apartment in Weston. They were unable to locate other cell members. The three of them decided to rent a cheap motel room Sunday night.

That night, as they watched the news on the TV set in their room, the story of the terrorist plot was on every station. They watched in anger as Homeland Security Director Harold Bellenkamp, at a press conference in the capital, boasted about the work of his agency, the CIA, and the FBI. Hassid and his friends were sick! They prayed to Allah and began planning revenge.

* * * * * * *

By the following Saturday, Hassid, Abdul, and Ahmid had recruited five more angry Muslim friends. Hassid was convinced that his roommate, Omar, the Jesus Lover, had betrayed them. Omar was just learning how to work the computer, but all of Hassid's internet access was protected by a password. Perhaps Omar had overheard something. It seemed obvious that the FBI had taken Omar into protective custody and that he would be a government witness against them. Hassid began thinking of how he could get even with the Christian betrayer.

During the week Hassid's plan took shape. He shared the idea with his seven comrades on Saturday night. They would strike at America. They would strike at Omar and his Jesus-loving friends. And they would win the release of Islamic warriors now in custody. They would attack and hold hostage the congregation of Trinity Lutheran Church where Omar worshipped.

Hassid shared a sketch of the church and neighborhood he had made earlier in the week. "The explosives will be put to better use than killing strangers at the airports. We will place them around the perimeter of the church sanctuary at the base of the columns I have marked. Memorize this drawing! We will have to work quickly. We will take our van and one other car. We will park in the west parking lot and move like cats around the building while the Christians are worshiping their Jesus inside.

"After the charges are placed you will each have an assigned position inside the church sanctuary. Except for Esau; he will stand guard on the front steps of the church. We will demand the release of our friends or we begin killing Christian hostages. After we have word that our Islamic brothers are free, we will leave the church and detonate the explosives, killing everyone inside. Hopefully, we will all be able to leave the building safely; but if that fails, we must be willing to die as martyrs along with the Jesus lovers." His friends swore their readiness to be martyrs for Islam.

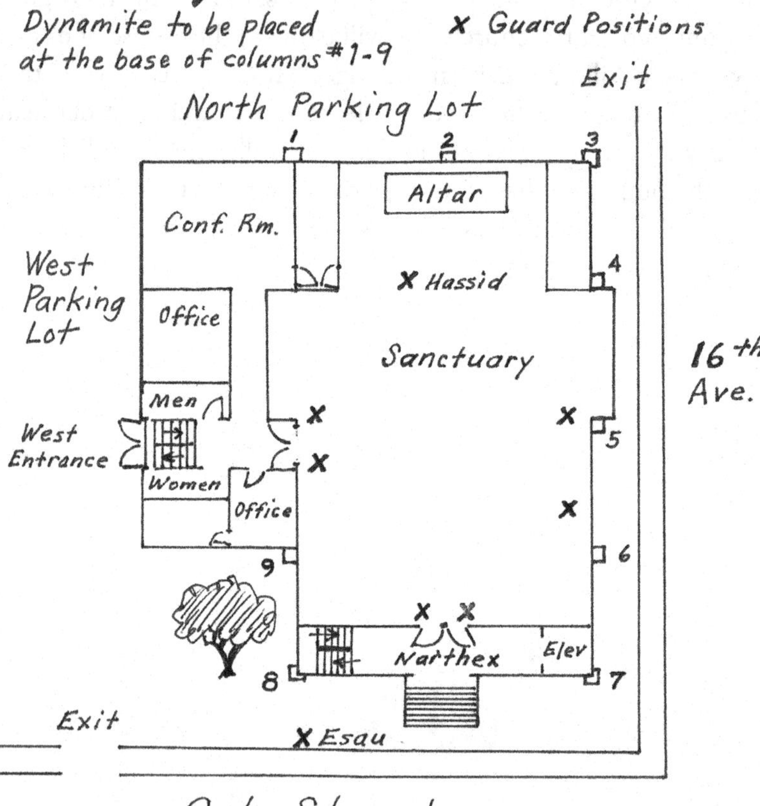
Trinity Lutheran Church
Dynamite to be placed
at the base of columns #1-9
X Guard Positions
Exit
North Parking Lot
1
2
3
Altar
Conf. Rm.
West
Parking
Lot
4
Office
X Hassid
Sanctuary
16th
Ave.
Men
West
Entrance
Women
5
Office
6
9
Narthex
Elev
8
7
Exit
X Esau
Oak Street

26

TERROR STRIKES

Sunday, February 21

A thin coating of frost on the birch trees shimmered in the morning sun as Pastor Walker pulled into the church parking lot the following Sunday morning. Spring was still a month away. Paul was looking forward to Easter. As he walked toward the church doors he noticed that Sheila Gordon's car was already in its usual spot. It was a forest green Buick Riviera, and it also was covered with a sparkling layer of frost. Sheila was a capable organist who also directed Trinity's twenty-four member choir. She was always the first one at the church on Sunday mornings. She was forty-five years old, a peroxide-blond, divorced, slim, and always dressed provocatively. And she was extremely flirtatious. She made the married women in the congregation uncomfortable; she knew it, but she didn't care. She made some of the married men even more uncomfortable; she knew it and enjoyed it! It was all a game to her, in church on Sunday, at the office on Monday. Despite the discomfort of the members, her musical talent was undeniable. As the pastor at Trinity, Paul was wary of her flirtations. He had been tempted in the past and wanted no part of any scandal, real or imagined.

Cheri would arrive later as usual, in time for the second service.

Paul always felt better when she was nearby. They had been married for twenty-nine years. Cheri loved talking with church members about her sons and her two young grandchildren.

As Paul entered the church he could hear Sheila practicing on the organ. He went to his study and read through his sermon notes, then walked out to the narthex to greet members as they arrived. Everyone seemed to be in a good mood. About five minutes before worship began Paul went to the sacristy to put on his robe and pray with the acolytes. Pastor Barbara Lambert was already there. As Paul put on his vestments, Pastor Barbara prayed with the acolytes and sent them into the sanctuary to light the candles.

"Good morning, Barbara, how are you this morning?" Paul asked.

"Fine; and yourself?" Pastor Lambert was a heavy set young woman with a no-nonsense approach to everything. Paul was trying to get her to take herself and her ministry a little less seriously, but had made little progress.

"Have you got a good sermon for today?" Paul asked.

"What?! You're scheduled to preach today, aren't you?" she asked with panic in her voice.

"Yes, yes, I was just kidding," Paul replied.

"Why do you do that?" she asked angrily. "You know I'm always prepared. And I never know when you're joking!"

"I'm sorry, Barbara, I shouldn't do that right before worship." Paul clipped on his lapel microphone and they entered the sanctuary together. Paul greeted the congregation, and Sheila played an introduction to the opening hymn.

The first service went smoothly, and after worship Pastor Barbara greeted folks in the narthex. Paul removed his alb and ambled down to the fellowship hall for a cup of coffee. Sheila came up behind him and squeezed his arm almost causing him to spill his coffee. "I just wanted to remind you there will be a choir anthem at the second service." Leaning close to his face, she whispered in a most intimate tone, "It's an old gospel spiritual; I think you'll like it!" She saw him nervously switch his coffee cup to his other hand and look down to see if he had spilled any on the floor. *Just enough to keep him off balance,* she thought to herself, with no intention of apologizing.

Paul reeled from the scent of her perfume. "Thanks, Sheila, I'll look forward to it." She gave him a wink and a smile and disappeared into the crowd.

As people from the early service made their way to the parking lot, others were arriving for the 10:30 service. Once again, Paul, Barbara, and the acolytes gathered in the sacristy. When everyone had their robes on, Paul prayed that Trinity would continue expanding its ministry, strengthening the faith of its members, and reaching out to others in the community. The acolytes were sent to light the candles.

When the organ prelude finished, Paul walked to the center of the chancel to welcome worshippers and share opening announcements. His wife Cheri was sitting in her usual place in the fourth pew. As his eyes met hers, she gave him a smile of encouragement. Although other members were unaware, she knew, in spite of all his years of experience, Paul was always nervous as the service began.

"Welcome to Trinity!" Paul announced enthusiastically. "We are pleased that you've come for worship today, and we invite you to stay for coffee in the fellowship hall after church. Communion will be served by intinction. You may dip the wafer into the red wine or white grape juice. Please stand for the opening hymn, 'All Are Welcome,' 641 in the red hymnal." Everyone rose to their feet to sing.

Pastor Barbara began the opening liturgy; her voice was strong and clear as she led the Kyrie and Song of Praise. Pastor Paul moved behind the altar to lead the Prayer of the Day. "Renewing God, as you send living waters to bring forth new life upon the earth, send forth your Word and Holy Spirit, that we, your people, refreshed in the waters of baptism may live the new life to which you have called us, through...." Paul's prayer was cut short by a shout from the side entrance.

"Everyone sit down and stay calm!" Men with automatic weapons began filing into the sanctuary waving their guns from side to side.

"Everyone sit down!" the leader shouted again, firing five or six rounds into the ceiling. People sat immediately in their pews. The church rang for a moment from the sound of gunfire. Plaster dust drifted downward from the ceiling. Then a child started crying. Her mother wrapped her arms around her and tried to comfort her. Otherwise, the room grew quiet. The gunmen quickly circled the sanctuary.

Paul counted two gunmen at the rear doors, two at the side door, and two on the outer wall aisle. They were dressed in camouflage fatigues and several wore checkered head cloths. The seventh, apparently their leader, approached Paul. "Sit," he commanded Paul. He pointed his rifle at the front pew and motioned for him to sit there, and to give him the microphone.

Holding the small lapel mike, he addressed the congregation, "We are here in the name of Allah, the Just One, the Mighty One, Allah the Righteous. We have come to bring the wrath of Allah against you infidels!" He surveyed the congregation and saw eyes filled with fear. A few stared at him; their faces tense in anger. "The Jesus you worship is an abomination to Allah. No man can BE God! You are fools! Now we will see if your Jesus can save you!"

"What have we done to hurt you?" Paul spoke boldly.

The leader stared at him for a long minute, slowly pointing his rifle directly at Paul. "You are a fool! EVERYTHING you do hurts us. You steal our oil. You pervert our children. You steal our brightest students for your universities. You promote a way of life that is immoral and corrupt. You and your multi-national corporations are destroying our culture." He paused a moment and stared at Paul. "And YOU, you Christians in particular, teach an abomination, a lie! Of all the sins of your country, your teachings about Jesus are the worst of all in the sight of Allah."

Emboldened by Paul's question, Pastor Barbara spoke up. "Does Allah approve of killing innocent children?" She still had her microphone clipped to her stole, so her voice sounded clearly throughout the sanctuary.

The leader swung his weapon, and pointing angrily at Barbara, he screamed, "AND WHAT MAKES YOU THINK YOU OR YOUR CHILDREN ARE INNOCENT?" Barbara suddenly realized she might have been too bold. Looking at the barrel of the weapon just ten feet away, she wondered if that moment might be her last. She held her breath, waiting for him to pull the trigger.

"The atrocities of the United States in Muslim nations can not be weighed." The leader turned and faced the congregation. His voice suddenly became cold and hard. "Allah has seen the domination of your way of life over ours; Allah has seen enough. Now…the tables are about to be turned…Allah be praised!"

"ALLAH BE PRAISED!" the gunmen shouted in unison. Now she would die. Barbara waited to hear the burst of gunfire.

A hush fell over the sanctuary. The only sound was the sniffles and sobbing of the child near the back of the church who still sensed that something was very wrong.

"Now I will tell you what is going to happen. My men have placed explosive charges around the perimeter of the building. They are well hidden, and set to detonate simultaneously at my command. We have a number of demands which I'm sure your authorities will be happy to meet. If they cooperate, no one needs to die. If they will not negotiate, YOUR BLOOD will be on their hands."

"You…what are you called?" the leader shouted, pointing his rifle again at Paul.

"My name is Paul; the people call me Pastor."

Barbara was relieved the gun was no longer pointed at her. But she was still frightened. Now it was pointing at Paul.

"Pastor, I am commanding you, ask someone for a cell phone. Do it! Now!" he said, waving his weapon toward the congregation.

"Does anyone have a cell phone I could borrow?" Paul asked.

His wife Cheri, pulled hers from her purse and held it up. Paul walked over to her, smiled, stared into her eyes a moment, thanked her, and walked back to the chancel.

"Dial 9-1-1, and tell them who you are and where this church is located. Then hand the phone to me."

Paul did as he was told. "This is Pastor Paul Walker and I'm calling from Trinity Lutheran Church in Weston. Yes, the address is 1590 Oak Street." He handed the phone to Hassid. As he did so, he studied the man's eyes and face. He was definitely of Arab descent, dark intense eyes and dark complexion, with deep wrinkles radiating from the sides of his eyes. His black beard was of medium length with no trace of gray hairs. Paul guessed his age to be early to mid- thirties.

"My name is Hassid Al-Akkbah." Although he was staring at Paul, he was speaking into the cell phone. "We are holding this pastor and his people hostage. If you want them to live, connect me with someone in the FBI, and do it quickly. There are close to two hundred people in this church and they will die unless you act quickly."

Paul was amazed that Hassid had only a slight accent. "You speak very good English; where are you from?" Paul asked cautiously while waiting for the 9-1-1 operator to dial the FBI. Paul wanted desperately to humanize this enemy. He also hoped that simple conversation might lower his own level of fear and nervousness; perhaps the gunman's as well.

"I was born in Iran, but went to college in England. I came to the U.S. in 2003..." "Yes, I'll wait," he said into the phone, "but I am serious; someone will die if you are not quick about it." Looking at Paul he said, "No more questions."

Someone in the middle of the congregation hollered, "Pastor?" Everyone turned to see Elmer Johannsen standing with his hand high in the air. "Elmer, what's the matter?" Paul asked.

"I have to go to the restroom!" Elmer shouted. Paul was thankful that Elmer's wife, Arda, was not with him this Sunday. She was at home, still recovering from her hip replacement. Elmer and Arda were both in their eighties, faithful members, and strong of spirit.

"You'll just have to hold it, old man!" Hassid shouted. "You're not going anywhere."

"It's going to get really messy and SMELLY in here if I don't get to the john soon," Elmer yelled back, desperation in his voice.

Hassid thought for a few moments. Should he send one of the gunmen with him? Should he let him go and ask him to return voluntarily? Should he call his bluff and see if the old man really messed his pants?

The 9-1-1 operator was back on line. "Sir, I am putting you through to FBI headquarters in Chicago."

"Get out of here! And don't come back!" he shouted at Elmer. Releasing one old man seemed harmless. Elmer excused himself and made his way carefully around the gunmen standing at the door, and disappeared down the hall.

Paul breathed a thank you prayer and a sigh of relief. For the moment, Elmer was safe. Not only that, Old Elmer might just be able to help from "out there." At least he knew a little about what was happening. Paul prayed Elmer would use this opportunity to call for help…and keep a cool head. He prayed that Elmer might remember how many gunmen were inside the church… and about the explosives.

"Hello, this is Agent Ron Keller from the Chicago office of the FBI. I've been told you are holding hostages in a church in Weston."

"Yes, I am Hassid Al-Akkbah and I represent the Islamic Liberation Front. There are two hundred people here who will die unless our demands are met. Are you able to negotiate for your agency, or should I be talking to someone higher up?"

"I am the highest ranking official on duty today. We are not at full staff on Sunday, but I'll listen to your requests."

"DEMANDS! These are not requests! They are demands. And unless you cooperate, PEOPLE WILL DIE; do you understand? You haven't forgotten 9-11, have you?"

"No," Agent Keller responded soberly, "we haven't forgotten."

"First, we want you to release all of the Islamic warriors you took prisoner two weeks ago. Second, you will prepare passports and papers granting them immunity from prosecution, and a chartered commercial plane to take them from New York to Tehran on Monday. Third, you will not send agents, or any kind of law enforcement to this address, or we will BLOW THIS CHURCH TO HELL! Is that clear?"

"I'm sorry, but the local police and sheriff's office have already been notified of the situation. I'm sure they are already on their way."

"Call them off," Hassid said calmly. "Do you hear me? Call them off . . . or people start dying in here." Paul could only hear one side of the conversation, but the urgent threat and the coolness in Hassid's voice sent chills up Paul's spine.

"I'll do what I can, but don't panic if you hear sirens." Agent Keller was doing his best to keep Hassid talking and to keep him calm.

"I won't panic. I'll just tell my men to kill a woman… then a child… then an old person….about one every ten minutes until the police are gone." Hassid was serious, and Paul was trying to think of any possible way to get people out of harm's way.

"I'll do everything in my power to call them back," Keller responded. "Let me make sure I have your demands. First, to order the release of the sixty detainees who are suspected of terrorism. Second, to provide passports and a charter plane for them. And third, to keep law enforcement away from the church. Is that correct?"

"You've forgotten something," Hassid replied.

"What's that?" Keller asked.

"Official documents granting immunity and protection until my friends are out of the U.S."

"That's a tough one, Hassid," Agent Keller replied. "I'm not sure I can arrange that in just a couple of days, let alone a few hours."

"Oh, I'm sure you can Mr. FBI Agent. You have one hour to get as much arranged as possible. Call me back at this number and report on your progress. And remember, if I am not satisfied with your effort, we will begin killing hostages. I look forward to hearing from you. You have one hour." Hassid pushed the button to end the call. He could hear sirens approaching.

* * * * * * *

Elmer Johannsen hurried to the men's room. He was 83 years old. He had served four years in the Army at the end of WWII, but he wasn't in the mood for any more youthful adventures. He wasn't bluffing about his bowels. Under stress he was vulnerable to a sudden release, and he didn't relish trying to clean himself up in the church rest room. Fortunately, he made it there in time, and as he sat on the john, his mind was racing. What should he do next? He said a prayer, thanking God that his beloved Arda was safe at home.

Suddenly, he heard gunshots being fired in the sanctuary. He wrapped his arms across his stomach, bent forward on the toilet, and fought back tears of terror. He prayed for the congregation and his pastors, both Paul and Barbara. He sat silently, his eyes closed, his heart pounding… he waited. He felt like he was twenty again, not in the church men's room, but on the battlefield in France. He prayed for guidance, whom to notify, and for physical and mental strength. This was a combat mission. The enemy was inside his church, and he would do all he could to defeat them. Elmer slowly opened his eyes. What could he do? An unarmed 83 year old veteran. He'd call for back up and stand ready to assist. It was all coming back to him; he had a plan. He steeled himself for action.

In a few minutes he was out and moving toward the church office. No one was in the hallway; no one in the office. The door was unlocked so he let himself in and went to the phone. He lifted the receiver, but there was no dial tone. Had the terrorists cut the phone line? No, it was one of those darn fancy business phones with buttons of all kinds. He wasn't sure what to do, but he pushed a button labeled Line 1, and got a dial tone. He punched the numbers 9-1-1. An operator answered in a matter of seconds, "9-1-1, how may I help you?"

Elmer slid off the chair and hid behind the secretary's desk. "There's armed terrorists in our church! Must be eight or ten of 'em. They're threatenin' to blow up the church. Send the police. Send help! And hurry please!" His left knee was hurting, so he sat on the floor.

"May I have your name please?" the operator asked.

"Johannsen, Elmer Johannsen, but that's not important; send help, please!"

"Thank you Mr. Johannsen. Where are you, can you give me an address?"

"I'm at Trinity Lutheran Church. It's on Oak Street. I don't remember the number."

"Are you being held hostage?"

"Yes… well, no… I mean, I was, but they let me go to the bathroom and now I'm in the church office."

"We had a call just a few minutes ago from your pastor and one of the terrorists. I put them through to the FBI. Perhaps it would be best if I put your call through to them also."

"The FBI? How soon can they get here? The leader, the guy talking to the pastor, said he might blow up the church and kill us all!" Elmer was feeling more and more panicky.

"Mr. Johannsen, please hold on and stay on the line. I'll patch you through to the FBI."

Elmer waited for what seemed like an hour; it was perhaps a minute at most. "This is Agent Weissmuller with the FBI; may I help you?"

Elmer explained again about the hostages in the church, how he had been released to go to the men's room, and was calling from the church office to get help to come. He told the agent there were eight or ten…no, seven or eight gunmen. He told him about the explosives placed around the church that would blow up the whole place and kill everybody. After a few minutes of questions and answers, Agent Weissmuller handed the phone to Agent Keller who questioned him again about the explosives. Finally, Elmer couldn't stand it any more. "Are you coming or not?" he yelled impatiently.

"Elmer, we are on the way. Do you hear me? Help is on the way. However, for the safety of everyone inside, we don't want to get too close to the building. Can you get out of the church, preferably without being seen?" Keller was looking at a map of Weston and the location of the church.

"Yes, I think so," Elmer replied. Elmer began to hope. The FBI said they were coming. Maybe things would be okay…if they got here in time.

"I want you to help us, if you're willing, Mr. Johannsen. I want you to exit the building. Walk casually away from the church, and walk west on Oak Street about two or three blocks. We are setting up a perimeter around the church. An FBI agent or a police officer will be looking for you. Can you do that?"

"Yes. Yes, I'm sure I can. I want to help in any way I can. This is a terrible situation." Elmer's spirits rose a little. He wanted to do something, anything to help his friends. Elmer crawled out from under the desk and slipped quietly out the office door and down the steps into the parking lot. He ducked behind parked cars and walked up Oak Street trying desperately to appear as if nothing was wrong.

27

THE FBI RESPONDS

At the FBI office in Chicago, a level one alert was issued immediately following Agent Ron Keller's talk with Hassid Al-Akkbah. He got on the phone with superiors in Washington, DC. All agents who had been working on the TransAm affair were notified. Homeland Security posted a red alert, the highest possible threat. Operation Clean Sweep had been anything but a "clean sweep." Agency Directors, speaking at press conferences, all claimed it had been a successful and well-coordinated operation. Fifty-eight terrorists had been arrested and were awaiting grand jury hearings and trials in federal court. The number sixty-three suspected terrorists under investigation had not been released to the public. It was also unclear whether additional suspects might have been involved who had not been detected in the nationwide investigation. Now, however, it was clear that those not arrested were striking back.

Keller began contacting law enforcement in Weston and the sheriff's office for the county. He briefed them on the hostage situation and the threat to blow up the church. Former Police Chief Jed Wilson had retired three years ago, and Chief Warren Shinn was now in charge.

"Agent Keller, we've had several 9-1-1 calls already," Shinn replied. "The dispatcher said that kids are text-messaging their friends. All available units are on their way to the scene."

"Chief, there are several things you need to know. First, since this is a national security threat, the FBI will be in charge of negotiations. I'm in touch with my superiors in Washington, and I'll be the commander for all law enforcement agencies on the scene. Is that clear?"

"Absolutely! I'm glad to have someone else calling the shots on this one." Shinn sounded genuinely relieved.

"The next thing you need to know is that one of the conditions laid out by the terrorist leader was 'no law enforcement.' Have your dispatcher relay the following orders: First, no sirens! Second, set up perimeter barriers two blocks distant from the church. We don't want the terrorists to know where we are. One more thing: I don't want anyone playing hero. No one is to approach the church until I get there. Seal off the area! Got that?"

"Yes sir! I'll notify all units right away. Turn off sirens. Establish and maintain two block perimeter."

Next, Keller called the Chicago Police Department and asked for their assistance. He informed them of the terrorists' threat to blow up the church in Weston and gave them the address. He warned them to use no sirens once they were within a mile of the church. He wanted a SWAT team and the Bomb Squad. They would join the SWAT team from the FBI. The FBI would set up a command center near the church as quickly as possible, and all responding units would wait at the perimeter until commanders agreed what action would be taken. All county hospitals were also put on alert. Available ambulances would be stationed at the perimeter.

A decision was quickly agreed upon in Washington that standard policy would be followed and no prisoners released because of threats being issued. This was always the first response. Stall for time until the threat could be evaluated.

After the phone call from Elmer Johannsen, Agent Keller called the Chief of Police in Weston again. "How many units do you have in the vicinity of the church?" Keller asked.

"Six squad cars, plus two from the sheriff's office," the Chief replied.

"As per your instructions I've ordered all units to stay at least two blocks from the church. They're putting up barricades as we speak."

"Good. I've just spoken on the phone with one of the hostages who managed to escape from the church. He's an elderly gentleman. His name is Elmer Johannsen. I told him to walk west from the church on Oak Street. Can you have a patrol car and officer there to meet him? I imagine he'll be pretty shook up."

"Sure, I'll get on the radio right away."

"Thanks, Chief. Oh, and by the way, I'm heading to Weston in the next few minutes. I'll stay in touch by radio through the dispatcher here." Would you be thinking of a location where we might set up a command center? A school gymnasium, VFW Hall, even another church might do... something big enough and not too far from the Lutheran church?

"Gotcha, Commander, I'll get to work on that too."

"Thanks again, Chief. See ya soon."

Within minutes, police officers met Elmer walking west on Oak. Other police and sheriff's units had taken positions on various streets around the church. They set up barricades and closed off every street within a two block radius. One street was designated and reserved for fire and rescue units. 16th Avenue was lined with ambulances from nearby hospitals. Police Chief Shinn's assistant was talking with school officials about opening the gym at Lincoln Middle School for use as a command center. Since it was Sunday, they wouldn't have to evacuate students. News reporters and vans would be arriving soon. They would be directed to the school parking lot and warned not to approach the church.

Several cars with Agent Keller and other FBI personnel were streaming south on Lake Shore Drive with sirens blaring. SWAT teams and bomb defusing personnel were also heading out from Chicago.

28

FOOLISH BRAVERY

David Turner was an angry kid. He was mad from the moment he saw the Muslim sons-a-bitches coming into the church. He was a senior at Weston High School and was seriously considering enlisting in the Army, or trying for the Marines if they'd take him. He was sitting next to his wrestling coach, Bob Warmowski, in a pew about half-way back in the church. In grade school David was small for his age. The kids at school had called him a wimp and a "momma's boy" for as long as he could remember. David's mom was an unwed teenager. She was still in high school when she had the baby, leaving most of the infant's care to her mom and dad. Several years later, they insisted she get a job and move out. She finally did. But to her, David was just a doll to be played with. He was sick of being bullied at school, and swore some day he would be tough enough not to be pushed around.

He began growing during his freshman year at Weston High and decided to go out for wrestling. The coach was a hard-ass ex-Marine who had David pegged after two practices. The kid was skinny but had a fighting spirit. David was angry and took his aggression out on any wrestling partner, bigger or smaller than himself. The coach's challenge was to harness and discipline that anger and resentment into a focused wrestling style. Coach Warmowski pushed him, yelled at him, demanded he work harder…lifting weights, running laps, doing push-ups. And in spite of the rough treatment, David liked the coach. He sensed a change in himself. He could feel his confidence growing. He would be tough, like his coach. He wouldn't let anybody push him around any more. He ran laps, he lifted weights; and he wrestled, practicing moves over and over and over until his strength was gone. He slept hard and ate well; he lived to wrestle. His problem was his anger. He couldn't stand being overcome by the strength of another. If he was taken down, he would kick and claw his way free. The coach would yell, "You can't do that. You'll be disqualified." If his partner pinned him in practice he would kick, pinch, or bite him if necessary. Coach Warmowski temporarily suspended him from the team and from practice on several of these occasions.

Another incident which upset the coach and scared his partner occurred when he finally managed to pin the more experienced wrestler. With an arm around Mike's head, another arm under his opponent's leg, and his body firmly on top of Mike, he began twisting and pulling on Mike's head. Driven by years of pent up rage, David wanted to break Mike's neck. He could feel the power in his own body, and it felt wonderful! Mike began to scream. Coach Warmowski had to dig his fingers into David's arm to get him to release his hold. After his shower, David endured another one of Coach's lectures, and another suspension.

In his sophomore year he won his first match in a district meet. By his senior year, his anger was under better control, and he was ranked second in state in his weight division. Bob Warmowski liked the kid and understood his inner turmoil. David filled a void in his life. The coach lived alone, had never married or had any kids. Bob met David's mother and despised her for what she had done to her son. It seemed to the coach no wonder David was filled with resentment. When school began in the fall of David's senior year, Bob had an idea. Maybe the kid needed more than he could give him in terms of love, respect, and hope. He wondered if David would respond to an invitation to come to Trinity Lutheran Church with him. He decided to try.

David was reluctant at first, but he didn't want to disappoint Coach. At first, Coach Warmowski would call David on Saturday night and tell him he would pick him up at 10:15 Sunday morning. They attended most Sundays together in October and November, but it wasn't until Advent and Christmas that David began to really appreciate what was happening in church. Several other students from school greeted him enthusiastically. A couple of older members made a point of trying to get acquainted. And at the late service on Christmas Eve, David became choked up during a traditional Christmas hymn and felt tears flowing from his eyes.

David invited his mother to come to Trinity with him and his coach on Valentines' Day, but she refused. Bob picked up David at the usual time and when David's mom did not come out the door, the coach wisely said nothing. On the Sunday after Valentines' Day, they were sitting in their usual pew when the terrorists came into the sanctuary. David's first reaction was to stand and fight. Coach Warmowski put his hand on David's arm and whispered, "Stay cool." When Hassid waved his rifle and yelled, "Everyone sit down!" they sat down. David's mind, however, was racing. He was trying to think like a Marine. He wondered what Coach was thinking, but under the circumstances, it was impossible to talk.

Everyone in the sanctuary was listening intently as Hassid told the FBI his demands. David watched the guard nearest their pew. When the guard looked away, David slowly lay down on the pew with his feet on the floor. After a minute he slid quietly off the pew and lay prone underneath the pew in front of them. Bob wondered if the kid was scared, but sensed that wasn't the case.

David listened as Elmer left to go to the bathroom. A few minutes later he watched as the guard near him took a couple of steps back toward his pew. He rolled slightly forward so the gunman would not see him on the floor. He had a clear view of the gunman's legs and feet, just inches from his face. David began figuring a move, how he might grab the man's legs and pull him down between the pews. It would be a tricky move, and the motion would have to be swift. He waited. He heard the leader's threat to begin killing hostages if the FBI did not act quickly. He waited. He rehearsed his move carefully in his mind. His anger grew. He could feel the adrenalin and his pulse quicken. Then he struck.

Rolling perpendicular to the pews and bracing himself against the pew supports, he wrapped his arm around the gunman's left leg, locked his hands together and yanked the man's knee forward between the pews. The terrorist crumpled, his right knee hit the pew support, his right hip hit the corner of the pew back and he screamed in pain. Falling forward with his rifle across his chest, his right wrist hit the top of the pew and his hand released the trigger. Tumbling to his left, his rifle hit the pew seat, then his left shoulder hit the pew, tossing him to the right as he fell between the pews and over the top of David who was still twisting his leg. His right arm cushioned his head as he hit the floor. He was aware of pain in every part of his body, but he still held his rifle with his left hand. It was pointing straight up between the pews with the butt end on the floor. The coach saw his opportunity, reached over the pew, grabbed the rifle by the barrel and yanked straight up, which slammed the gunman's left hand against the bottom of the pew. He yelled again in pain and released the rifle. People were screaming. Gunmen were running toward the commotion but couldn't see their companion who had disappeared beneath the pews. Coach Warmowski spun the rifle to his shoulder and fired a round into the terrorist's head. As he lifted the rifle and turned to face the onrushing terrorists, he heard rifle shots and was knocked forward as several rounds of ammunition hit him in the back.

David released his hold on the dead terrorist's leg and rolled as fast as he could beneath several pews toward the front of the church. He hit a woman's legs from behind. She let out a startled shout. David pulled himself up onto the pew next to the woman; put his finger to his lips, "Sshh." It was the pastor's wife, Cheri. She nodded her understanding. David buried his face in his hands and began to sob; his body shook with terror and grief. He knew his beloved coach was dead; and he knew his anger had caused it.

They both kept their heads down as two gunmen rushed by. The terrorists stopped and stared at the two bodies - their fallen companion on the floor, and the dying ex-Marine on the pew behind him.

It had happened so quickly, no one was sure how it started. Coach Warmowski could barely breathe; blood was filling his lungs. He couldn't see David on the floor; he hoped he was safe; he heard no more gunfire. The kid would make a good Marine. He was proud to have had a part in his growing up. He prayed for David's future, and slipped away into God's hands.

Hassid surveyed the sanctuary, counted his men and noted their positions. People were crying and most had ducked below the back of the pews. A few were standing up, trying to see who had been shot. In their faces he saw fear. Their eyes bounced back and forth stricken by panic. The angel of death circled overhead, like a hawk searching for its next victim. Terror had come to Trinity.

One terrorist could not take his eyes off his friend whose face lay in a pool of blood. Those in the congregation who were watching saw him raise his face toward heaven and scream, "Naaaaah!" Then he fired several rounds into the ceiling. People ducked again below the level of the pews as chips of plaster showered down.

Slowly Pastor Walker stood up and began to walk back to where his wife was sitting. "Where are you going?" Hassid demanded.

"I want to make sure my wife is okay," Paul replied calmly. Hassid watched him sit down next to a woman who had her arm around a teenage boy. Paul sat next to Cheri and squeezed her left hand. Her right arm was wrapped around David's shoulders. Several children were crying, and several adults were conversing in whispers about the violence which had claimed the life of Coach Warmowski. No one was sure what had caused it, but a lot of people saw gunmen fire in his direction and watched as he fell into the pew. It was a moment they would never forget.

Most were glad that Bob had killed one of the terrorists. The sanctuary grew quiet as gunmen pulled their fallen comrade from beneath the pew. They lay him reverently against the aisle wall. His friend knelt down and kissed his blood-soaked cheek.

"Get back to your positions!" Hassid shouted. The men responded slowly. The congregation grew even more silent.

After a few moments, a soft, but strong voice came through the PA system. "Our Father, who art in heaven, hallowed be thy name." It was

Pastor Barbara. Members of the congregation joined in. "Thy kingdom come. Thy will be done, on earth as it is in heaven…" Every soul in the church prayed with her, the words of that prayer touching their hearts as never before. "Forgive us our trespasses as we forgive those who trespass against us." Could this attack against our sacred church ever be forgiven? "Lead us not into temptation; but deliver us from evil." Lord, we really do need your help…to deliver us from the evil that has come into our lives today. "For thine is the kingdom, and the power, and the glory…" O Lord, we hope so. "Forever and ever. Amen."

The minutes that followed seemed to last forever. People whispered quietly. The gunmen paced back and forth, their eyes scanning the congregation for trouble.

One woman pulled a cell phone out of her purse, held it below the level of the pew top and dialed her husband at home. She bent low and began whispering about what was happening in the church. She was spotted by a terrorist who quickly rushed over and demanded she give him the phone. She handed it to him; he threw it on the floor and stomped his foot on it, smashing it to pieces. "No more cell phones or we smash them," he hollered. Several teenagers had already sent text messages to friends, telling them to call the police or send help.

After twenty-five or thirty minutes, Pastor Walker asked Hassid if they might sing some hymns to help pass the time. "No singing!" was the curt reply. Then he asked if the children might be released and sent out of the church with just one adult. Again the reply was brief. "No! No one leaves until our demands are met."

During the hour Paul realized that there was at least one gunman posted outside. At ten or fifteen minute intervals he came through the front door of the church. Hassid would go down the main aisle and out to the narthex. They spoke in hushed voices. Then, Hassid would return to the front of the church and the guard would go back outside to keep watch.

Paul whispered to Cheri that it was strange that everything seemed so still. "Perhaps the police have barricaded the streets around the church. I guess I'm used to the movies where the police surround the building and negotiate with a bull horn, 'Come out with your hands up!' The only communication I can see is the cell phone Hassid took from you."

"I pray there's no more shooting," Cheri whispered back. "I sure hope they have some kind of plan to get us out of here."

29

STALLING FOR TIME

Agent Ron Keller rolled into Weston with two other FBI agents in his car, two in a second car, and the FBI SWAT team in an armored van truck. The bomb squad and SWAT team from the Chicago Police Department were just a few minutes behind them. By radio, he was told where to meet the sheriff and chief of police who were waiting at Lincoln Middle School, four blocks west of Trinity Lutheran on Oak Street. One escaped hostage, Elmer Johannsen, sat in a police car waiting to talk to the FBI man from Chicago. He was trying to remember everything that happened before he left the sanctuary. He watched as the FBI cars pulled into the school parking lot. He looked at his wrist watch and realized he had been out of the church for fifty minutes. He also realized that in all the excitement, he hadn't talked to his wife Arda. She would be worried sick that he wasn't home!

Talking with FBI Director, Bob Brown, in Washington, D.C., Keller was told that under no circumstances would any of the suspected terrorists in custody be released. Ron Keller would not say that to Hassid Al-Akkbah. He would say they were working on it. He would stall for time. And his entire team would be looking for alternatives. Tear gas, shock grenades, and a SWAT team assault were under consideration. Keller hoped to frustrate the terrorists inside the church to the point that they would finally give up without lives being lost.

Elmer watched helplessly as law enforcement personnel surrounded Agent Keller, contributing observations and suggestions, and waiting for orders. Large armored vehicles arrived with the SWAT teams and bomb technicians. Finally Elmer saw the Chief of Police pointing at the squad car, and the FBI commander coming his way. Lieutenant Hanson from the bomb squad was at his side.

"Are you Elmer Johannsen?" Keller asked.

"Yes sir. I'm the one who called you from the church office."

"I'm Agent Keller, and this is Lieutenant Hanson from the Chicago bomb squad."

"Nice to meet you. I'm sure glad to see you guys."

"Elmer," Lieutenant Hanson spoke, "I understand the leader of the terrorists, when making his demands, threatened to 'blow the church to hell.' We need to know all you can tell us about the explosives."

"All I remember is what he said when they first came bustin' into the church. He said ....let's see...he said, 'we've hidden explosives all around the church'....I think that's what it was."

"Hidden....all around the church..." Hanson repeated. "Do you remember anything else?"

"Well, I remember there was one or two guys with guns at both doors and in the side aisles. So that makes seven or eight...best I can remember. Oh, and the leader told me to get out and don't come back. Was I relieved to hear that!"

"He didn't say anything else about the explosives or where they were hidden?" Agent Keller asked.

"Just that they were all around the church," Elmer repeated.

"Thank you very much, Elmer. You've been a big help. Why don't you come into the school to wait? You'll be more comfortable in there. We'll do our best to get your friends out safe and sound."

"Agent Keller, I hate to bother you, but could I ask a favor?"

"What is it, Elmer?"

"Could I call my wife? Church should have been out half an hour ago, and if this gets on TV, she's gonna be worried sick."

"Sure, Elmer. I'll send an officer over here who can patch you through to your home phone. Thank you for your help." Keller and Hanson both shook Elmer's hand and returned to the crowd of officers.

* * * * * * *

Everyone inside the church was getting extremely nervous as the hour approached for the FBI to call back. Even Hassid seemed to be pacing a little more than before. He kept looking at his watch. When his cell phone chimed, everyone grew tense.

For Agent Keller the first hour was up. Much of it had been spent driving to the scene. Keller dialed the cell phone number given to him by the FBI technician in Chicago. He prayed a silent prayer that this would go well.

"Yeah, I hope you've got some good news for me and for the folks here in the church." Hassid was not in the mood for small talk.

"This is Agent Keller from the Chicago field office of the FBI. I've been working on your demands, and I've got a couple of good things to report." First, Keller wanted Hassid to believe he was still in Chicago and not four blocks from the church. Second, he wanted Hassid to believe he was putting forth a good faith effort to meet the demands.

"Have any of my Islamic friends been released yet?" Hassid interrupted.

"We're working on that," Keller replied. "You know how slow things move in Washington."

"Gee, what a shame. Ahmid.... kill a hostage."

Everyone looked around the sanctuary to see which gunman was Ahmid, their hearts pounding, not believing the order they just heard.

A guard near the narthex door stepped forward, raised his rifle and fired three bullets into Maybelle Stewart. Screams of horror filled the sanctuary as Maybelle fell forward onto the pew in front of her and toppled to the floor. The only blessing was that she hadn't turned around and didn't see the gunman behind her raise his rifle. It happened quickly. Everyone dove for cover. Parents grabbed their children and held them close. Husbands and wives wrapped their arms around each other. Never had any of them witnessed such brutal violence.

In his cell phone Keller heard the blast of gunfire and people in the church screaming. "Hassid, NO! I told you, we're working on it. They're in federal custody, and a lot of people are involved in the decision to release that many prisoners."

"And I told you....we kill one hostage every fifteen minutes until I get word from my Islamic friends that they are free. Every fifteen minutes, got it? Tell that to the people in Washington and see if they can't speed things up just a little." Hassid disconnected.

"They've killed a hostage," Keller announced solemnly to the agents and officers. "This bastard Hassid is serious about his demands and cold-blooded as well. We've got to move fast." Agents and officers waited for orders. "Sergeant Miller, take your SWAT teams; move into positions. Get as close to the church as possible without being seen. Does anybody know about windows? What kind? How many? And how many entrances to the building?"

One of the police officers shouted, "I do, sir. I've been a member of Trinity for almost five years. Can't go every Sunday, but I know the building pretty well."

"I want you to brief Lieutenant Hanson and Sergeant Miller," Keller ordered. "Tell them all you can about the structure, the layout, the entrances, and the windows. Hanson, Miller, see if you can get somebody close enough to check out the explosives. If we can disarm them without being seen, we'll have one big advantage over Hassid. Start making plans for an assault. I hope that won't be necessary, but if it is, we want to be efficient. Chief and Sheriff, over here! I've got assignments for you and your men."

Several FBI men moved off on foot toward the church with the bomb squad and SWAT teams. The rest gathered around Keller, the Police Chief and Sheriff. "Chief, you and your people probably have the best knowledge of this neighborhood and the church. I want your officers to move in behind the SWAT teams and stand ready. I see two or three possibilities. One…the one I hope we can achieve…the terrorists give up and surrender. Your team will do handcuffing and arrests, read them their rights, and get them into patrol cars. Second, if there is an assault and shootout, be prepared to deal with victims, both enemy and civilian church members, when it's over. Stay in touch with fire and rescue and with the hospital paramedics. Third, if there's an explosion and the church collapses, also be ready to do search and rescue. Any questions?"

"What about our guys?" the Sheriff asked.

"Crowd and media control," Keller responded. "I know, I know, sounds lame. But believe me, this place is gonna be crazy with reporters, TV vans, and nosy neighbors. Send the media here to the school command center. We've got several square blocks and several streets to evacuate and barricade. We've got to keep people back and out of danger. Assign just a few officers to the homes closest to the church. Tell them to try not to be seen. Let people know there are explosives involved and the whole area could go up in smoke. Move nearby neighbors to the perimeter. Do you understand how important this is?"

"Yessir! I'll go instruct my units right away!"

"Shit! It's been ten minutes or more already! Shit! I've got a phone call to make." Agent Keller was thinking fast and talking as fast as he possibly could. He hoped his instructions were clear. He jotted some notes for his upcoming conversation…and dialed the terrorist's cell phone.

"It's about time, Agent. How ya doin'?" Hassid sounded cool.

"Doin' the best I can, Hassid. Can I give you my report?"

"I'm waiting…and it better be good. Fifteen minutes is up."

"First of all, I was able to get hold of the Chief of Police in Weston. He agreed to call off his units. They are on stand-by, but have been ordered not to come near the church."

"Good, very good. I haven't heard any sirens and my men haven't seen any patrol cars come by. In fact the street seems really quiet. It looks like they may have blocked all traffic on the main street past the church."

"That may be. I'm not aware of that," Keller lied coolly.

"So what's happening with the orders to release all Islamic prisoners? And don't forget immunity!"

"I've been talking to the FBI Director and I've spoken personally with the President. They are taking you seriously, Hassid. There was some initial disagreement between them, but I think they are on the same page now. At first, Director Brown refused to negotiate, but the president said he didn't want to see two hundred innocent people die. I told them you had already killed one hostage." Keller was ad-libbing to the best of his ability.

"Actually, we've killed two."

"WHAT?" Keller was shocked. He had heard the gunfire, but took Hassid at his word, that only one was killed. "You promised you'd only kill one hostage!" Keller was mad.

"One of your Christians in here wasn't too smart. He wanted to be a hero. He shot one of my men, so we had to shoot him. Too bad.... the other we shot after your first call."

Keller took a deep breath and let out a sigh. "I'm doing my best, Hassid. But you've got to be realistic. You and I would both like miracles, but these things take time to arrange."

"You're stalling, Mr. FBI. And I don't have a lot of time. Have any prisoners been released?"

Keller hated that question. "Not that I'm aware of; however," he added hastily, "I am confident the president's wishes will be followed.

The president himself said 'no more killing.' The prisoners will be released." There was a long silence. "Hassid?" Keller waited to hear a response. Hassid was thinking. Finally, he responded.

"Since we've killed two hostages, you get fifteen more minutes to make things happen. Tell your boss that the released prisoners are to call me at this number to confirm their release. Has the charter plane been reserved for Monday? One charter jet to Tehran, remember?"

"I'll get on that right away. And I will call back in fifteen minutes with progress. I guarantee it. The plane to Tehran will be ready. Hasssid… there's no need for any more killing." This time Keller pushed the button to end the call.

30

ALLAH BE PRAISED !

The gunman named Esau was assigned to stand guard outside the front of the church. Every few minutes he would descend the steps, walk to the street corner to the east, and back past the main doors of the church to the edge of the parking lot on the west. In this way, he was able to see most of the space around three sides of the church. The office area and classrooms were connected to the west side of the sanctuary. At the end of the west hall through which Elmer Johannsen had exited, there were stairs and a door which opened to the parking lot. Most members used that door when getting out of their cars. Some walked to the front of the building and used the street doors and narthex. The sanctuary was fairly light inside, but one could not see outdoors because the windows were all stained glass with a protective tempered glass covering outside. Hassid was depending on his guard outside to report any approaching police or FBI personnel.

News of the hostage situation spread quickly through the community. Teenagers were the first to be aware, as their friends text messaged from inside the sanctuary. After receiving the reassuring phone call from Elmer that he was safe, Arda Johannsen called her daughter in Elgin. She, in turn, called the Weston Police Department which had been inundated with phone calls. A newspaper reporter who was home reading the Sunday paper overheard police calls on his home scanner.

He called his editor and headed for the church neighborhood. The editor called the TV station, and within the hour, two TV vans and numerous reporters were on the scene. The sheriff's deputies directed them to Lincoln Middle School, but one van and several reporters refused to leave the perimeter. The deputies did their best to keep them on 16th Avenue behind the street barricades, but two photographers tried approaching the church on different streets looking for photo angles. From a distance they were able to see when the bomb squad and SWAT teams began moving toward the building.

Agent Keller maintained radio contact with Sergeant Miller who was directing the SWAT teams, with Lieutenant Hanson and his bomb squad, and with the Weston Chief of Police and the Sheriff.

The initial police unit which had approached the church from the north side of the property had moved on foot a little closer to the church. They found an observation sight from behind a neighbor's home on the west side, across the church parking lot. From there they were able to see a single guard patrolling the front of the church. They reported this information to the Chief of Police who relayed it to Agent Keller, Lieutenant Hanson, Sergeant Miller and the SWAT teams.

Both SWAT teams moved forward quickly and quietly. They approached from the north, based on the report that there was only one guard stationed at the front door on the south side of the church. FBI SWAT team A moved carefully into the west parking lot, using cars in the lot for cover. Officers in the parking lot could see the guard when he reached the southwest edge of the building. SWAT team B remained behind the building in the north parking lot where they could peer down the sidewalk and see when the guard reached the southeast corner of the building. They reported by radio to Sergeant Miller that they could take down the subject at either end of his patterned walk. Miller instructed them to maintain their positions out of sight and wait for orders. He knew if the guard did not report to the terrorists inside, their leader would become suspicious.

Sergeant Miller, Lieutenant Hanson, and Agent Keller were concerned about the explosives planted around the church. If Hassid's threat was real, and there was no reason to disbelieve it, the greatest loss of life might occur if those explosives were detonated. "Is there any way we can get close enough to the building to find and defuse the explosives?" Keller asked Miller.

"If we take out the guard in front of the church, we can send some men in to take a closer look around the foundation," Miller replied, "but we'll have to hurry. The guard reports to Hassid every ten or fifteen minutes."

"You're damn right we have to hurry!" Keller answered. "It's been four minutes since my last talk with Hassid."

"Hang on a second, Commander," Miller interrupted, "one of my men just spotted wires at the base of one of the sanctuary columns here on the north side of the building. Oh m'god! There's another at the corner. There are three columns on the north side. We can't see the bases of the columns along the east wall. If the terrorists planted the explosives at the base of each support column....I'd estimate four on the side of the church; that would be seven or eight possible devices to disarm...maybe more..."

"Can you or the bomb guys get to them?" Keller asked.

"Not without being seen....unless we take the guard out first."

"Hansen, are your bomb guys ready to go?" Keller hoped the bomb squad leader had been listening.

"We're behind the neighbor's house and ready to move."

"Miller, tell your guys to do it. Next clear shot; take out the guard."

"Copy that." Miller switched frequencies and notified his team leaders, "Next one to get a clear shot; take out the guard."

"He just disappeared from the east side, Sergeant, he should be headed toward the front doors," the sniper replied. Both teams had excellent marksmen. They waited for the guard to appear on the west side. The sniper in the parking lot raised his weapon and aimed at the edge of the building where the guard would emerge into view.

"Miller," Keller called, "after the guard is down, tell your men to hold their positions and prepare for an assault on the sanctuary."

"You got it," Miller replied. He switched frequencies again. "Team A, when the guard is down, take a position near the west entrance. Hold position outside the church and await orders for assault on the sanctuary. Team B prepare to assault sanctuary by entering front doors of church."

Fifteen seconds, twenty. . . the guard should be approaching the parking lot. Miller wondered if he had gone into the church to report to Hassid. Thirty seconds, thirty-five…POW! The explosive rifle shot rang through the air. The bullet found its mark. "Guard down . . . Team A approaching west entrance," their leader reported.

"Bomb squad moving," Hansen radioed as he waved his men forward. Four experts ran toward the church. Two would check the wall facing the north parking lot, and two would circle the building to disarm explosives on the east wall along 16th Avenue. There were low shrubs planted along sections of the foundation and snow shoveled against the walls of the church. The first technician headed for the one exposed area where the wires had been spotted. Each column supported a laminated roof beam inside the church ceiling. Dynamite had been half-buried in a hastily dug hole in the snow at the base of the column. A small cell phone lay on the snow next to the column with fine wires attached to a detonator. It was a crude device and easily disarmed. The wires were pulled from the detonator and the cell phone tossed aside. The technician moved to the next column. His partner finished disarming another detonator and flashed him a high sign. They radioed Lieutenant Hanson, "Three devices disarmed on north wall. We're moving south around the west side and office area looking for further explosives."

"This is Hanson, good work North Team; East Team where are you"

"East Team reporting, we've reached the front corner of the building and disarmed the fourth device here at the corner."

As North Team came around the church office they spotted explosives at the southwest corner of the church and raced to disarm the last of the devices. "Final device disarmed at southwest corner. The SWAT teams behind us are ready to move!"

Hanson replied, "Good job men. Now get the hell outa there!"

Miller began coordinating the assault, "SWAT team A, are you in position near the west entrance?"

"Problem here, Serge, the exterior door is glass. Two gunmen are visible at the end of the hall, at the sanctuary doors. If we try to go in they'll see us."

"Hold your position just outside the door, but be ready to go when the assault order is given," Sergeant Miller replied.

Ten minutes had transpired. Lieutenant Hanson called Agent Keller to tell him all the explosives had been disarmed. "Good news, Commander, my team has disarmed eight explosive devices and we haven't found any others." Hanson was not aware of the dynamite at column #9, directly beneath the men's room where the office addition met the church.

"I wish we had more time. I've got to call Hassid before he kills another hostage. All right everyone, hang tight, there's no telling what might happen." Keller was nervous. "Miller, are your men ready for an assault?"

"Ready and waiting, Commander."

Keller didn't want to lose any more lives. Two hostages had died already. One terrorist had been shot while patrolling outside. Hassid would know soon if the guard didn't report at the front doors. With fear and trembling he dialed the number.

"This is Hassid. I heard a shot fired a few minutes ago. What's going on?"

"Hassid, this is Agent Keller. I assure you, our officers are blocks away. You probably heard a car backfire. But I've got some good news for you! The president has ordered all Islamic prisoners released!" It was a lie, of course. He was flying by the seat of his pants. "Your terrorist friends should all be walking out of federal prison about now."

"I haven't heard from them. You did tell them to give the released prisoners a phone so they could call me?"

"Yes, Hassid. As per your instructions. They should be calling momentarily."

"What about immunity papers and the plane?"

"The president guaranteed me they would have a plane ready. A charter commercial plane, not a military plane, right?"

"Yes. And the papers?"

"Yes, I told them to supply the prisoners with immunity papers before releasing them. That may be the hold up. Can I call the FBI Director to check on that? I'm not stalling. I promise you, they're being released. I'll call you back in ten… no, five minutes or less."

"Five minutes, Agent Keller. Five minutes or another hostage dies." Hassid put the cell phone back into his pocket. He raised his rifle into the air and addressed his men. "Allah be praised! The FBI is releasing our comrades."

"ALLAH BE PRAISED!" they shouted in unison.

Hassid pulled a different cell phone from his other pocket. He held it above his head and addressed the congregation, "Foolish Jesus lovers! When our friends leave prison, we will leave the church. Do you see this phone? I have entered the number which will detonate explosives all around this building. If any law officers make an attempt to stop us, I will push 'redial' and BOOM! You and your church will be dust. You believe Jesus was raised from the dead? Ha! Soon you will see for yourselves! Soon you will know just how foolish is your belief in Jesus."

Hassid was pleased to hear that the warriors for Islam were being released, but he was nervous about the sound of gunfire outside. The more he thought about it the more certain he was that it had not been a car's backfire. He was about to send one of his men outside to check when the door swung open and Esau stepped into the narthex.

31

TIME'S UP

Esau stopped in the narthex and bent down to tie his boot lace which dangled loosely on the floor.

"Ahmid, get the report from Esau," Hassid commanded, "and ask about the gunfire."

Ahmid went through the open sanctuary doors into the narthex. Esau was tying his boot with his head down. Ahmid couldn't see his face. Suddenly, Esau lifted his rifle and fired, killing Ahmid. The second terrorist stationed at the door raised his weapon and stepped into the doorway. Esau's second shot spun him around. The third shot hit his head knocking him to the floor. Esau dropped to the floor and rolled behind the doors as Hassid began firing his gun toward the narthex. He knew they had been tricked! It wasn't Esau. They had killed Esau, taken his clothing and checkered head cloth, and come in by surprise.

SWAT team A heard the gunshots and slipped unnoticed through the west entrance glass doors. All eyes were on the action at the back of the church. They moved quickly up the stairs, knelt, aimed, and fired at the guards inside the sanctuary doors. Hassid turned when he heard the gunfire and saw both his men fall to the floor. Team A sprinted along the walls of the hall toward the sanctuary. Hassid opened fire.

The SWAT team officer who had posed as Esau threw a flash-bang into the sanctuary which rolled up the center aisle and exploded. Hassid and his friends were stunned temporarily. They began firing randomly toward both doors. Hassid realized they were under attack. Team A came streaming into the sanctuary. Team B was charging through the narthex. Hassid looked down at the cell phone in his hand, prayed to Allah, and pushed REDIAL.

Church members were already flat on the pews or flat on the floor underneath the pews. Paul pushed Cheri to the floor and she pulled David down with her. People were screaming at the sound of gunfire.

An explosion shook the church! Again Hassid screamed, "ALLAH BE PRAISED!" One of his men echoed, "ALLAH BE PRAISED!" Hassid was hit by bullets from two sides as plaster began falling from the ceiling near the back of the church. The column near the rear of the sanctuary began to crumble. A loud cracking sound was emitted from one of the large laminated ceiling beams as it broke loose and fell, bringing with it sections of drywall and a large chandelier. One end of the beam dropped along the inner wall and hit the floor with a loud thump which shook the church for the second time. Plaster and drywall fell over the pews. Dust and smoke were rolling through the sanctuary. People were crying beneath the pews and covering their faces.

Hassid lay in the center aisle looking upward, waiting for the rest of the ceiling to fall. He raised himself on one elbow. His eyes scanned the walls which were all still standing, and the stained glass windows, in tact except for one near the back of the church. What happened? Why wasn't everyone buried beneath the rubble? Pastor Paul could see him lying there. He saw Hassid trying to speak or pray. He wasn't sure, by reading his lips, if Hassid said, "I'll be damned, or Allah be damned." Then Hassid's eyes closed, his body rolled, and his head thudded to the floor.

Two terrorists had died at each door. One had been killed by Coach Warmowski. Hassid had been killed in crossfire. One terrorist was shot outside. Of the seven terrorists inside the sanctuary, six were dead; only one remained alive. He had fired a few rounds toward the SWAT team, but as he watched his comrades fall, threw his rifle away, and hit the floor behind the pews. He lay there waiting for the church to collapse. When it didn't, he waited, hoping to be shot in the head. He knew he was a coward. He should have died as a martyr.

When the laminated beam fell, it smashed one of the pews. Several church members were badly injured and trapped beneath the pew. One was injured by the chandelier which had fallen. Many received cuts and bruises when hit by plaster dry wall which had been blown inward by the explosion, or had fallen from the ceiling. Being beneath the level of the pew backs saved many from serious injury. One SWAT team member suffered an arm wound. They were thankful for their bullet-proof vests. As the smoke cleared they began guiding people out the doors into the hallway and narthex. Eventually, as they moved through the sanctuary, they found the one terrorist who was still alive, lying frightened on the floor. They searched and cuffed him, and dragged him outside. He wasn't injured, so they walked him to a squad car.

Paul, Cheri, and David were gently guided from the pew by SWAT team members. Paul could hear members crying, but his eyes burned too much to see anyone. Once outside on the street he began to see groups of church members hugging one another and praying. He wrapped his arms around Cheri and she returned his hug. Ambulances had moved up 16th Avenue and around the corner onto Oak. Paramedics entered the church and began bringing out the wounded.

Paul and Cheri wandered through the crowd of people. Paul spotted Pastor Barbara hugging Sheila, the choir director. Thank God, they were all right. After a few minutes ambulances began leaving for the hospital; others pulled up to receive more victims. A SWAT team member with a tourniquet on his arm climbed into an ambulance under his own power. Paul hugged Cheri again and the two stood silently watching as stretchers came down the front steps with body bags holding those who had died, two church members and seven terrorists.

Agent Hanson drove his FBI car from the Lincoln gymnasium and parked across the street from the church entrance. He had been listening to reports from Sergeant Miller and Lieutenant Hanson, from the Police Chief and Sheriff. Several newscasters were milling about, trying to get closer to the crowd of worshippers, filming ambulances as they left the scene. They were shouting at Keller asking for a report on what had happened. He put in a quick call to FBI Headquarters in Washington, D.C. where Director Bob Brown was glad to hear the crisis was over. Brown said he would call the directors of the CIA and Homeland Security. Keller turned to face the reporters and cameras.

32

MEET THE PRESS

Agent Ron Keller wasn't the only one who had to meet the press. Pastor Paul Walker was looking into more television cameras and facing more reporters than he had ever seen, including the media coverage following Brian Holloway's murder twenty years earlier. While Cheri was at home calling Randy and Chip and her mother to assure them they were okay, Paul was responding to reporters in interview after interview. The evening news on every network and television station had coverage of the terror at Trinity. Pastor Walker gave thanks for the courage and bravery of his church members, and for the courage and skillful actions of the FBI and law enforcement personnel. He asked the nation to remember those who died in the attack, and to pray for their families. He asked for prayers for the people of Islam, saying they are not all terrorists. He gave credit to the agents and officers whose quick and decisive response had prevented the loss of many more lives. All questions about the terrorists, their identity and their demands, he referred to the FBI.

Trinity Lutheran Church was once again, a crime scene. The sanctuary was sealed off with yellow tape and police guarded the front doors and west doors allowing entry only to authorized personnel. The authorities were also concerned about structural damage and the possibility of further collapse of walls or roof. A large hole had been blown in the foundation and lower part of the sanctuary wall. A section of the roof had fallen inward with the laminated beam. Most of the force of the explosion had been outward, blowing snow and debris across the parking lot and across the street.

Paul spent the remainder of Sunday afternoon in the church office, answering, what seemed like hundreds of phone calls; calling Maybelle Stewart's daughter in Ohio; and searching the records and calling people in an effort to find any relative of Coach Warmowski's. Between phone calls he found himself on the verge of tears and praying constantly. Finally, before heading home, he went to the hospital to check on church members who had been injured by the explosion. Many had been treated for minor cuts and bruises and released. Sadly, however, several members in the vicinity of the beam which fell suffered more severe injuries, concussions, broken bones, and internal injuries. Amazingly, no one had been killed by the explosion.

Howard Bardwell, who had just been elected president of the congregation, was admitted to a room on the medical-surgical unit and was being kept overnight for tests and observation. The stress of the situation had triggered an arrhythmia, and he was in deep shock when admitted. Paul prayed with him and his wife Bonnie, and then drove home.

Cheri was glad to see him; her embrace had never meant more. They smiled at each other with tears in their eyes. The adrenalin was gone from Paul's system and he felt ready to collapse.

The two of them warmed up some soup and gobbled a salad Cheri had prepared. Paul realized then that he had not eaten since breakfast. When they crawled into bed exhausted, they tossed and turned, talked to each other about their fear, their sorrow, their anger, and their blessings.

"Oh, my gosh," said Cheri, "what about Omar? Will they think he was part of this?"

"How could they?" Paul replied. "He's been in prison, or whatever they call it. There's no way he could have been involved!"

"I wonder if he'll hear about what happened today?"

"I'll call Miguel Juarez, first thing tomorrow, and ask him how he thinks this incident will effect Omar's situation," Paul answered. "How are we ever going to fall asleep?"

Cheri climbed out of bed, took a pill to help her fall asleep, and brought one to Paul. "Take this! It'll knock you out."

"I won't argue with you tonight." Paul swallowed the pill with the water Cheri handed him. "Do you think I can get through the Lord's Prayer before I doze off?" Paul joked.

As Paul prayed, they both thought again of how that prayer had sounded this morning with guns pointing at them. And finally their eyes closed and in a few minutes, so it seemed, it was morning.

* * * * * * *

In the office on Monday, Jeannette handed him six phone messages as soon as he walked through the door. Paul returned the bishop's call and one from Father Muldoon, the Catholic priest. Father Muldoon told Paul that St. Mary's Catholic Church would be available to the Lutherans if they needed a place to worship while Trinity's building was being structurally evaluated and repaired. Paul thanked him and asked if a Prayer Service could be held there on Wednesday evening. Father Muldoon said he'd be honored to host the service. "Just let me know what you need." Paul's bishop said he would drive up from Indianapolis to take part in the service.

Paul began calling his council members, and had Jeannette call chairpersons and key lay leaders. All who could make it were invited to a planning meeting on Tuesday evening. The purpose was to plan a prayer service for Wednesday evening at St. Mary's. He called the hospital mid-morning and asked to speak to Howard Bardwell. The nurse informed him that Howard had gone home an hour ago. A call to his home confirmed the fact that Howard was feeling much better, though he wasn't sure he'd make the meeting Tuesday night. Paul also called his clergy friends in other churches and told them about the service. Then he called the local radio and TV stations asking them to announce a 7 p.m. Wednesday evening Service of Prayer, Mourning, and Thanksgiving.

The Walker's son, Chip, called just to say how glad he was that "mom and dad" were okay, and to assure his dad he would keep them in his prayers. Miguel Juarez called back to inform the pastor that the FBI had a few more details to review, but that last week, before the attack on Sunday, they seemed prepared to drop charges and release Omar. He promised to keep Paul informed.

Pastor Barbara Lambert was also busy making phone calls. She was reviewing attendance records and making a list of everyone she could remember who was at church at the second service. She wanted to touch base with everyone she could reach. She began with Elmer Johannsen. Elmer told her that he had several calls already congratulating him on his "heroic escape!"

"Heck, there was nothing heroic about it," Elmer said dryly. "I really did have to go!"

"But I understand you called 9-1-1 from the church office!"

"Yeah," Elmer replied bashfully, "but I was safe and sound over at Lincoln Middle School when the church exploded! Lordy, was I glad to hear so many people came out of the church unhurt!"

"How's Arda doing?" Barbara asked him.

"She didn't have any idea what was happening until I called her from the police car. Then she turned on the television and watched the whole thing. She said she was so thankful to know I wasn't inside the church."

"If you're able to come to church on Wednesday evening, there will be a special prayer service at 7 p.m. It'll be held at St. Mary's Catholic Church. I hope you can make it," Barbara concluded. "And God bless you both."

"Thank you for calling, Pastor," Elmer said, smiling at Arda. "I think we'd both like to attend. Arda's getting around pretty well now with her walker."

* * * * * * *

When Paul and Cheri arrived at St. Mary's shortly after six on Wednesday evening, they were greeted in the parking lot by Father Muldoon and several Catholic families. Paul was a little surprised to see three mobile TV vans in the parking lot, and a gaggle of reporters already gathered near the church entrance. "We'll be doing a spot on the ten o'clock news!" one shouted. "Our station is pre-empting a sitcom to broadcast the entire service," shouted another. "Pastor, how long do you anticipate this prayer service of yours will last?" another asked. "Our network wants an uplink; no telling how many stations will use it. You're talkin' national coverage!"

"Gentlemen! Gentlemen! And ladies!" Father Muldoon addressed the media reps. "You are welcome to come inside and set up cameras. I do want to remind you that this is a church, and a service of memorial to those who died last Sunday. All I ask is that you be as discreet as possible. Please show some care about where you set up, and sit near the back if possible, so members of the church and community can fill in the front."

"Pastor Walker, do you have a statement for us?" one of the reporters asked.

"I just want to say thank you to Father Muldoon and our Catholic friends for hosting tonight's service and making their church available to us at Trinity. I'll take about five minutes for questions inside, and then I must leave you to prepare for worship." As Paul and Cheri moved toward the church they noticed several police cars parked in conspicuous locations. Several officers were talking together near the church entrance.

The air was crisp and cold; snow was forecast for the coming weekend. The parking lot filled quickly, and as worshippers filed into the sanctuary, Paul realized that Trinity would not have had enough room for everyone. St. Mary's could seat about 500 and even it might be full. He asked the ushers to give only one bulletin per family or they might run short. Father Muldoon prayed with the acolytes who went out early to light the altar candles. Several pastors from the text study group also gathered in the priest's study for prayer before the service began. The bishop was there with vestments and his bishop's cross about his neck.

Worship began with a hymn which reminded Paul of Brian Holloway, "A Mighty Fortress." Father Muldoon welcomed everyone including his Lutheran colleague, Pastor Paul Walker. Paul also welcomed everyone and expressed deepest gratitude to Father Scott Muldoon and the members of St. Mary's Catholic parish. He introduced special guests including the bishop and thanked the other pastors from the study group. The church was filled to capacity. A row of folding chairs had been set up in the aisles and a crowd of people stood behind the back pews. Pastor Paul shared a brief description of what had happened on Sunday morning. Pastor Barbara led a brief memorial service to honor Coach Bob Warmowski and Maybelle Stewart. Paul noticed that David Turner was sitting next to Cheri, as he had been on Sunday, that his head was down and he was crying. Paul made a mental note to call him after school the next day.

One of Trinity's council members introduced a power point meditation she had put together, using photos from national parks in different seasons, words from scripture, and soft flute and new-age music. It had a very soothing effect on the entire congregation and ended with quotes from the psalms and slides of creeks, streams and lakes. Paul was grateful for this beautiful devotional interlude.

Guest clergy read a variety of scripture readings, and Paul shared a meditation in which he again urged everyone to resist being overcome by fear and hatred. He talked about the challenging words of Jesus who told us to love our enemies and pray for those who hate us. He spoke about faith, as he had so often, being more than believing in God, faith as a deep relationship of trust. "Only faith and love can overcome fear," he reminded the congregation. "Some of you may be disappointed that I'm not talking more about America and patriotism, about our enemies and our need to fight. May I assure you that I love this country as much as anyone. However, I confess, I am a Christian first, an American second. And when I am most tempted to draw my weapons, I hear Jesus whispering, 'Peter, put away your sword.' But Lord, I whisper back, my name is Paul, not Peter! And Jesus simply says, 'You know who I'm talking to.' I struggle with a desire for revenge. Our church was held hostage by a gang of frightened and angry young men. I believe they misused their religion to justify their anger. And their anger motivated a desperate attempt to free their companions who remain in federal prisons. It is unfortunate, but perhaps necessary, that they had to die.

"Tonight, we are sad, and fearful, and angry, and those feelings are all legitimate. It will take a while to get through them. But I would like to focus on one more feeling which will help us overcome the others…. gratitude. I want to express my, indeed our entire congregation's, gratitude to the FBI and law enforcement officials who responded quickly and professionally. There were men who risked their lives to save ours. There were men who believed it necessary to kill our captors to prevent many of us from being killed. We owe them our deepest gratitude.

"I also want to thank the members of this church and all in our community who support each other in prayer. Without the prayers prayed silently and aloud last Sunday, who knows what the outcome might have been? Those who were held hostage showed great courage and great compassion for one another. And finally, thank all of you for coming tonight to pray with us and for us, for the families who lost loved ones, and even for our enemies, for peace in our world and peace in our hearts. Most merciful God, have mercy upon us, and grant us your peace. Amen."

The congregation sang, "Lord of All Hopefulness." The service concluded with prayers led by local clergy, and a closing hymn. At the conclusion, Father Muldoon invited everyone who could, to come into the fellowship hall for coffee, tea, cake and cookies. Pastor Walker shared his final remarks. "It is so important," he said "to talk and talk and talk about the terror and trauma so many of us experienced. And we will appreciate it when those of you who weren't present, are willing to listen and encourage us to talk. Thank you again for coming to pray with us tonight. Father Muldoon will share with us the benediction."

Several reporters cornered Paul at coffee after the service. He answered their questions politely and briefly and hoped nothing he said would appear as a stupid or out-of-context quotation.

On Thursday afternoon Pastor Walker stopped at the office at Weston High School, introduced himself, and asked if he might visit with David Turner. A message was sent to David's classroom and he was excused to visit with his pastor. While Paul waited, one of the school counselors chatted with him about David's terrible experience at the church. Paul and the counselor agreed to stay in touch and to keep a close eye on the young man who had loved his coach.

"Hello, David," Paul rose to greet him as he entered the counselor's office. "I'm sorry to pull you away from class."

"No problem, Pastor, I don't like Statistics that much anyway." The counselor shook David's hand, told David to have a seat, and excused himself from the room.

"I just wanted to touch base with you and ask how you've been feeling since last Sunday," Pastor Paul continued.

David sighed, put his head between his hands, "I don't know, Pastor. I just feel tired, exhausted…you know what I mean?"

"Yes, I do. That's not an unusual reaction to the trauma and stress and grief you are feeling." Paul waited to give David a chance to get in touch with his feelings and to feel free to say whatever came to mind.

"I think the worst part is that I feel like it's my fault."

"What's your fault, David?" Paul asked.

"That Coach got shot. I was so stupid. What did I think I could accomplish by taking out one gunman?

"Blaming yourself is also a common reaction when someone you love dies." Paul reflected again on his grief over the death of Brian Holloway, remembering how he had felt personally responsible.

"If I hadn't crawled under the pew and tried to tackle that terrorist,

Coach might still be alive!" David's grief and regret were beginning to show in his voice and body language.

"Listen to me, David. Did you have a gun in church with you last Sunday?

"No."

"Then you didn't kill Coach Warmowski. Did you grab the rifle from the gunman?"

"No. Coach did."

"Then you didn't kill Coach Warmowski. Did you kill the gunman you tackled?"

"No. Coach did."

"Then think of this. Coach Warmowski decided to grab the rifle and kill the terrorist, and one of his reasons might have been to save you."

"Yeah, I thought of that," David said timidly.

"Isn't that amazing? Kind of reminds me of Jesus. Jesus was willing to die to save you, and Coach Warmowski was willing to die to save you. They must both love you very much."

David began to cry. Paul reached over and put a hand on David's knee. "You have a lot to live up to now. Both Jesus and Coach would want you to do well in school. Become a Marine if that's your dream. They wouldn't want you to go on blaming yourself and hating yourself. That would destroy what they died for. It would make Coach Warmowski's death pointless."

David sobbed for several minutes. Paul pulled a handkerchief from his pocket and handed it to David. Finally David responded, "I guess you're right. Coach would want me to keep fighting for what I believe in. I just wish I hadn't been so stupid."

"David, I want you to repeat after me," Paul insisted. "Say these words, 'I am not stupid."

David looked up at the pastor and hesitantly repeated, "I am not stupid."

"I may have been foolishly brave…" say that.

David repeated, "I may have been foolishly brave…"

"I may have been foolishly brave, but I am not stupid."

"I may have been foolishly brave, but I am not stupid," David said with a grin.

"Whenever you start feeling guilty about what you did, I want you to repeat that sentence, do you understand?" Paul asked.

"I may have been foolishly brave, but I am not stupid."

"Exactly. You are human. You're not perfect. Coach was brave, but he wasn't perfect either. I'm not either. Foolish sometimes, but not stupid."

"I think I get it, Pastor Paul."

"I think you do too. Don't be concerned about having all these terrible and crazy feelings. They are natural and normal. The most important thing is not to bottle them up inside. I hope you'll feel free to call me, talk to me, or to my wife, or to the counselor here. We all want you to come through this, and live up to the hopes and dreams Coach had for you." Paul looked him in the eye, smiling. "You are a fine young man."

"Thanks, Pastor. I really appreciate your coming to talk with me today. I know you're busy."

"That's true, but Cheri and I both care about you a lot." Paul stood to leave. "Stop by the church any time. We're praying for you."

"I will, Pastor. Thanks."

* * * * * * *

Friday morning Paul returned to the high school to speak and pray at the memorial service for Coach Warmowski. The gymnasium was packed. A couple of cousins from Toledo, Ohio, were introduced; otherwise there was no family. Actually there was a family of nearly six hundred students, teachers, and friends. In addition to the pastor and principal, many came to the podium to pay tribute to a great teacher, coach, and human being.

David Turner could only sit in the bleachers, thinking of the courageous man who had been exactly the kind of tough mentor he needed and loved. His throat was tight as he remembered all the hours they had spent together in this very gym on the dark blue wrestling mats. He would miss Coach yelling at him.

Paul also met with Maybelle's family on Thursday to plan her memorial service for 11 am Saturday. Not since Brian Holloway's tragic death had Paul experienced such a week. He worked each day from 8 am to 8 pm or later. He knew he couldn't keep up that pace, but there were so many people and things needing his attention. He reminded himself that self-care was crucial, that he needed to talk to someone and debrief his stress and emotions. He certainly didn't want a repeat of his stupid, or better…foolish, indiscretion with Marge Holloway. As Paul reflected on the terror of the attack on his congregation, he remembered some of the same feelings of terror which had plagued him nearly twenty years ago. The difference was that he himself had been the cause of his earlier terror. This time it had come from the outside.

On Friday morning two engineers from the county met with Paul in his office to present their report on the structural damage and their recommendations for repairs. Once again he was thankful the damage had been minimized by the expertise of the bomb squad and assault teams. He would turn over the report to his building and maintenance committee to use in obtaining bids from local contractors. He called Father Muldoon and scheduled a meeting to talk about use and scheduling of St. Mary's on Sunday afternoons until repairs were completed.

The high point of Paul's week came on Friday afternoon as Paul was writing his sermon. Attorney Miguel Juarez called to say Omar Shufti was being released. Phone records and a thorough look at the computer hard drive which the FBI had confiscated convinced them that Hassid, not Omar, had been communicating with other terrorist cell groups. Paul thanked Miguel for his support of Omar, and then called Cheri at the library to share the good news about Omar with her.

"Finally!" Cheri responded. "I'm concerned about how he'll handle the news of his friend Hassid being killed."

"I'm sure he's doubly sad; first to learn that Hassid was in a terrorist cell, and second, to hear he was killed trying to blow up the church."

"I'm praying he'll find the strength to get through all this," Cheri added.

"And I'm praying Omar will still love this 'land of the free and the home of the brave,'" Paul confided to Cheri. "I've called Agent Robinson at the FBI office and told him I would give Omar a ride back to Weston when he is released."

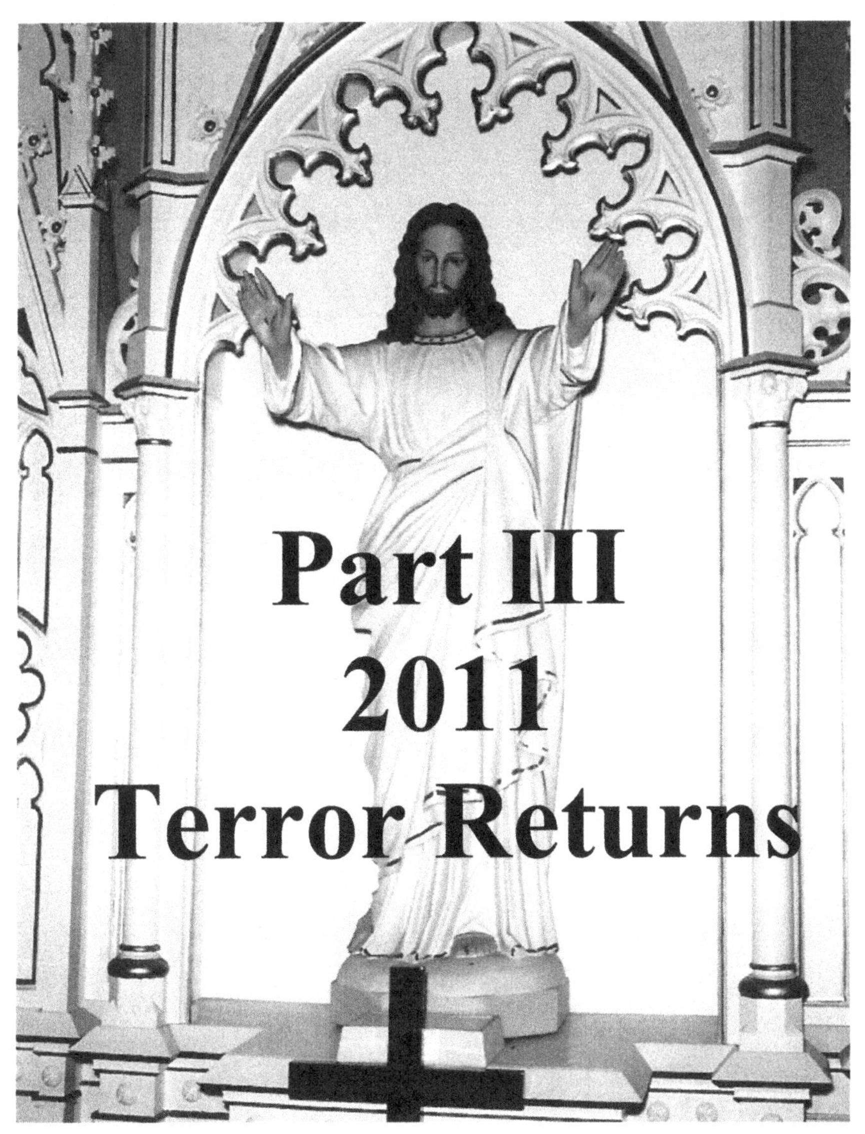
Part III
2011
Terror Returns

33

FATHER'S DAY

June 19, 2011

Paul Walker pulled into the church parking lot on Sunday morning. Over a year had passed since the terrorist attack at Trinity. Contractors had worked throughout the previous summer to complete the reconstruction project. Repairs to the foundation, brick wall, and roof were noticeable only if one were looking closely for evidence of the damage.

On February 20th, the first anniversary of the incident, another prayer service was scheduled. This time it was held in Trinity's sanctuary. Father Muldoon was one of the honored guests. Omar Shufti asked the pastor if he could speak at the service and was granted permission. He apologized for the actions of his roommate and former friend. He expressed gratitude to the members of Trinity for their support in welcoming him to America and through the terrible time of his imprisonment. He gave special thanks to Pastor Walker and to his attorney, and now his friend, Miguel Juarez. He also asked the members to continue to pray for the people of his homeland in Iran. "I pray for them every day because my family is still there, and many of my family and friends are still Muslim. They are not all bad people like the ones who came here." Both pastors led the prayers of remembrance and thanksgiving.

Today was Fathers' Day. The air was already warm and humid. Paul hoped his sons would call this afternoon, but first, he had two worship services to lead. At fifty-six years of age he felt blessed to be here. It was good to be a pastor, good to be a father, good to be alive. As Paul walked toward the entrance to the church he breathed a prayer of thankfulness for Cheri, for Chip and Linda, married three years and still no kids, for Randy and Gail and those precious grandkids, Trevor and Joy. Cheri would arrive later, in time for the second service. She was still working in the public library and still enjoyed singing in the choir.

Paul entered the church and heard Sheila playing a hymn on the sanctuary piano. He walked to his study and glanced at his sermon notes, then took them to the sanctuary and placed them on the corner of the altar. The music stopped and Sheila smiled at him, "Good morning, Pastor!"

"Good morning, Sheila. How are you today?"

"Mighty fine! Did you see my new engagement ring?"

"No! I didn't know you were engaged!" Paul walked to the piano, somewhat surprised Sheila was even dating. "Let's see that ring! … Wow! That's a beauty! Who's the lucky guy?"

"John Williamson, from Williamson Realty; do you know him?" Sheila asked, proudly holding up her left hand to show off her new diamond.

"I've spoken with him at Kiwanis meetings, but I don't know him very well. Congratulations!"

"He actually got down on one knee at the restaurant. Everyone in the place turned to stare. He placed it on my hand and everyone began clapping. Then he couldn't get up again! He grabbed hold of the table to pull himself up and knocked a glass of water on the floor. He was so…o…o embarrassed! I thought I would die laughing!"

"Poor John, I'll bet he didn't think it was funny!"

"No, his face was beet red! I got up, walked behind his chair, and put my arms around him. I whispered in his ear, 'I'd love to marry you.' He really is such a sweet guy!"

"Well, congratulations to both of you! We'll have to talk more about this at coffee hour or staff meeting."

Paul was glad to see Sheila so happy. John Williamson was a well-known business man whose wife had died some years ago. He wasn't a member of Trinity, but Paul hoped they might ask him to perform their wedding. Paul also hoped this might bring an end to Sheila's flirtatious behavior with the men here in church.

Paul's assistant, Barbara, walked into the sanctuary. "Good morning, everybody!"

"Good morning!" Sheila and Paul both spoke at once. "Did you hear the good news?" Paul asked. "Sheila is engaged to be married."

"Yes, I know," Barbara answered. "I was here in the office yesterday when Sheila came by to practice. John Williamson gave her the ring on Friday night."

"That's what I get for not being around the church on Saturday," Paul replied.

"Not only that," Barbara said, tipping her head back and staring down her nose at Paul, "but she asked if I would do their wedding!" She reached down to give Sheila a hug. Both women smiled conspiratorially at Paul.

"Do you think you might have room for me to assist?" Paul asked, feigning hurt feelings.

"We'll think about it," Barbara said, smiling at Sheila.

"It might be nice for Barbara to have an assistant for a change," Sheila mused.

"You two are too much!" Paul grinned. "Let's get our robes on, Pastor Lambert," Paul said as he headed for the sacristy.

The first service went smoothly, and after worship Pastor Barbara greeted folks in the narthex. Paul removed his alb and went downstairs to the fellowship hall for a cup of coffee. Everyone seemed to be in a good mood. Paul wished everyone a happy Fathers' Day and received many smiles, hugs, and handshakes in return.

* * * * * * *

Paul walked to the center of the chancel to welcome worshippers to the later service. Glancing around the congregation he noticed a new young family near the back of the church. He didn't recognize the couple as members. The young father was holding a baby wrapped in a blanket. The mother had long black hair and a loosely-knit shawl around her shoulders. Next, his eyes fell on another visitor, a young woman sitting alone on the side aisle. She was slender and quite attractive, handsomely dressed in a tan colored two-piece suit. She had spiked auburn hair and appeared to be in her late teens or early twenties.

"Welcome to Trinity!" Paul greeted the congregation. "We hope all of you will feel loved by God and warmly welcomed by the members of the church! We invite everyone to stay for coffee in the fellowship hall after worship."

The scripture lessons were read. The choir came to the front of the church to sing the anthem. In his sermon Pastor Paul spoke of God the Father's love incarnate in his Son Jesus. "Any time we experience genuine kindness, caring, or forgiveness, we experience God's love. Just as God's love became touchable and human in Jesus, it becomes incarnate, tangible in us." The prayers also included a petition for fathers. Holy Communion went smoothly. Pastor Lambert pronounced the benediction.

During the closing hymn, Paul walked to the back of the church and past the new couple with the baby. He smiled at them and then stood in the doorway to greet the congregation. His final words concluded worship, "Go in peace; serve the Lord."

"Thanks be to God!" the congregation replied.

Paul took a deep breath and let out a sigh. He was always relieved when the second service ended and everything had gone well. *Yes indeed, thanks be to God; everything has been perfect this morning!*

Everyone seemed in good spirits. His wife Cheri came out chatting with Annette, a mother of one of the acolytes. An elderly gentleman asked the pastor to add his wife to the prayer list. The new couple with the baby introduced themselves, Peter and Janet Scarpelli. They said they were just visiting. "This is our son, Ethan. He's six months old!

"Has Ethan been baptized?" Paul asked.

"Not yet," the mother answered, "but we plan to do it soon. That's why we're visiting different churches."

"If you don't have a church home, I'd be happy to talk with you about Trinity and about your son's baptism… perhaps during the coffee hour. Please join us downstairs in the hall and meet some of our members."

As the last of the worshippers left the sanctuary, the pastor saw one final person walking slowly and deliberately up the aisle. She was looking around the church, absorbing every detail. When she finally reached the rear doorway, she smiled and extended a hand to the pastor. It was the auburn-haired young woman who was even more striking up close.

"How do you do? My name is Brianna," she said with a smile.

"I'm Pastor Paul Walker. Welcome to Trinity!" He was somewhat perplexed by her casual, yet self-confident approach. They shook hands.

"Hello, father! After all these years, we finally meet," she replied.

"Pardon me?" Paul questioned, puzzled by her comment.

"It's nice to meet my father."

Thinking she had meant to say, "It's nice to meet *you,* Father," Paul replied, "Thank you, but in the Lutheran church we're called Pastor, not Father, like the Catholic priest."

"Oh, no, I said 'my father.' YOU . . . are MY. . . FATHER."

Paul smiled, still puzzled. "I don't think so. I have two sons, but never had the privilege of having a daughter." *Is this a joke?* Paul wondered.

"At least none you ever knew about," she added.

"What do you mean?" Paul asked, frowning.

"My mother never told you about me... did she." It wasn't a question. It was stated simply, as a matter of fact. Brianna was smiling, enjoying the perplexed reaction of the pastor. Her casual self-confidence was due to the obvious advantage she had over this older stranger.

Paul was at a loss for words. This was a ridiculous conversation. She was saying that he had fathered a daughter he never knew about? Finally, Paul stammered, "Who...who is your mother?"

"Marge Holloway," Brianna paused, letting the name sink in. "You do remember her don't you?"

"Well, yes....but...." Paul wasn't sure what to say next. "Marge and Bob Holloway were members here years ago."

"And you and Mom...?" Brianna left the thought unfinished.

"Well, um... Marge and I were good friends, but I...I...I never knew she was expecting a baby." Paul was really nervous. He realized suddenly that what this young woman was saying just might be true. He and Marge had been together, once, but he didn't want to admit it to himself, let alone to this stranger.

"It seemed so ironic today, as I sat in church," Brianna continued, "that while everyone was thinking of their father, I was staring at my dad for the first time in my life!"

Paul was suddenly aware of the perspiration beneath his arms. He glanced nervously around the church to see if anyone might be listening to this bizarre conversation. He reached inside his robe to make certain that his microphone was turned OFF. His heart was pounding. He fought to remain calm. "Maybe we should talk about this somewhere else," he suggested. "Would you be willing to make an appointment for some other time?" Paul wanted to get away from this situation as quickly as possible.

"I live in Chicago, but I could grab a bite of lunch and come back this afternoon," Brianna suggested.

"Sure, sure, that would be fine. We could meet in the church office at… say…two o'clock, if that's all right with you?"

"Excellent! Two o'clock," she said cheerily. And with a smile she was gone.

Paul stood in a daze, not able to believe what had just occurred. He stood there alone, his mind racing, trying to comprehend the incomprehensible. He focused again on his racing heart and tried to calm down. *This is so awful!* Paul thought to himself. *I thought this was over years ago. I know pastors are sinners too; but we are held to higher standards because of our position, which is as it should be.*

Paul walked in shock to the sacristy, lost in thought and prayer. *Good Lord, you know I've tried to live with faithfulness, honesty, and decency, all my life. I know I'm guilty of many sins: self-centeredness, impatience, lack of gratitude, and a host of lesser faults. But God, I thought you had forgiven me for that one terrible incident after Brian's death. Now, on this sunny day in June, the consequence of my indiscretion has appeared in church on Sunday morning. Why, Lord? Why now? Why ever? Why didn't I tell Cheri? Maybe I should have told her then. What am I going to tell her now? O God, help me!*

Mercifully, one never knows when a dark cloud from the past may suddenly turn a sunny day into a stormy nightmare. The terror had returned. A familiar knot of guilt and shame formed in Paul's stomach, strangely familiar, considering it had been gone for nineteen or twenty years.

34

BRIANNA

Thirty-two faithful years in the ministry, and now this! Paul was not sure how all of this would play out; time would tell. Slowly he turned his thoughts back to his congregation and his wife waiting for him in the social hall. In the sacristy he hung up his robe, and the stole he wore around his neck, symbol of his ordination, "the yoke of Christ." As he made his way to the fellowship hall, he could hear the noisy chatter of members having cookies and coffee. Cheri was seated at a long table with six other members, engaged in someone's good story. As Paul poured his coffee, he heard them all burst into laughter.

Paul looked around for the young couple he had promised to talk to about baptizing their infant son. He spotted them near the furnace room door, cornered by Elmer and Arda Johannsen. No couple at Trinity was friendlier, and no one was more enthusiastic about Trinity Lutheran. Arda had recovered from her hip surgery last year, and Paul was thankful she was feeling well enough to attend church. She appeared enamored with the young couple's baby. He approached the visitors and introduced himself again.

"I was just tellin' Peter that the Lutheran church ain't that much different from the Catholic church. Ain't that right, Pastor?" Elmer said.

"Well Elmer, you're right in one respect. Both churches share the historic creeds and liturgies, but there are some major differences with regard to church structure and authority," Pastor Paul replied.

"Peter was raised Catholic and went to Catholic school. He was askin' me questions about Martin Luther, but I think he knows as much about Luther as I do!"

"We're seriously considering the Lutheran church," Peter responded. "Janet went to a Baptist Sunday School when she was little, and she is a believer. She just doesn't get all this 'church' stuff. She doesn't understand why I feel it's important to have Ethan baptized as a baby."

"I have an adult class on Sunday evenings which will begin next week. There are only a handful of new people who will be there, and I'd love to have you join us. I could give you more background on the Lutheran faith and answer any questions you have."

"Thank you, Pastor," Janet smiled, "that's exactly what I was hoping to find. Is there any obligation involved if we attend the class?"

"Certainly not," Paul replied. "No commitments required and no arms twisted, I promise. I just hope you enjoy the class and find the Lutheran church as great a faith community as I believe it is."

"We'd better get Ethan home for his nap;" Peter interjected, "he's starting to get fussy."

"What time will that class be?" Janet asked.

"Seven p.m. next Sunday," Paul replied.

"We'll be there," she reassured him. "It was very nice meeting you, Pastor Walker." She and Peter shook his hand, and then turned to the Johannsens, "And it was a pleasure meeting both of you!"

"Oh, the pleasure was all ours!" Arda gushed, stealing one last squeeze of little Ethan's hand.

Peter and Janet made their way to the parking lot. Paul thanked Arda and Elmer for being such hospitable people. He refilled his coffee cup and began visiting with other members. Try as he might, he couldn't seem to focus on what they were saying. His mind kept going back over the conversation he had had in the narthex a few minutes ago. The one thing he was too nervous to remember was the young woman's name.

A few minutes later Cheri came over to where he was standing, touched his arm and told him she was going home to prepare lunch. She was wearing his favorite pink sweater and burgundy wool slacks. For a woman of fifty-five Cheri's figure was still that of a woman twenty years younger. Her short blond hair was brushed loosely and her smile was radiant. How Paul loved those dimples in her cheeks! He smiled, kissed her on the cheek, and told her he'd be home soon. He usually arrived at least a half hour later. It took ten or fifteen minutes to straighten up the sacristy and office, and talk with people who just had to see the pastor before he left. Sally and Bill were washing out the coffee pot when Paul locked up the office and main doors of the church. Glancing around the parking lot, he noticed that everything looked hot and dry under the noontime sun. He got into his white Dodge Magnum, and as he drove home, he kept saying the name over and over again .... Marge Holloway, Marge Holloway. Yes, he remembered her well. Marge and her husband Bob, and their son Brian, members of Trinity, so many years ago. How could he ever forget those years? Or that family?

* * * * * * *

At home, Cheri had prepared ham sandwiches for both of them. They were wrapped and waiting on the table. Paul ate and then slumped into the easy chair to read the comics. He chuckled at Dagwood and shook his head at the political satire in Doonesbury. After a brief rest, he told Cheri he had to see Mr. Wicklund at the hospital, and he had an appointment at the church afterwards.

The hospital was just a ten minute drive when traffic was light. Paul found his patient's room, and listened as Mr. Wicklund described the procedure he had undergone on Friday morning. He was so excited about going home only three days after his surgery, he wanted to tell the pastor every detail of his hospital stay. Although Paul was reluctant to meet with the young woman at the church, he finally excused himself and said a prayer for Mr. Wicklund's continued recovery.

As Paul drove from the hospital to the church, his mind raced. *This may be the beginning of the end of everything I've lived and worked for. She must be mistaken. I was only with her mother that one time. Bob must be her father. If not, it means I'm in big trouble. My marriage, my job, my dignity, my reputation, everything could be lost. I'll be asked to resign and my name will be removed from the clergy roster. Cheri will leave me in bitter disappointment. I guess I wouldn't blame her. Chip and Randy will be so ashamed of me. I've let everyone down. I wonder what the young woman wants? I wonder how much she knows about me? Darn, I'm so upset; I can't even remember her name!*

He pulled into the parking lot at five after two. A sporty red Honda was parked near the office entrance. There were no other cars in the lot. Paul felt waves of panic flow through his body. He parked a couple of spaces from the Honda and got out of the car. As he walked toward the door, the young woman opened her car door and got out. He smiled as she walked toward him. He unlocked the door and held it open for her as she entered the church. He knew he had made a terrible mistake by not remembering her name and decided it best to begin by honestly admitting this shortcoming. "I'm very sorry, but I've forgotten your name."

"Brianna," she replied pleasantly. "Brianna Holloway." Again she smiled and offered a handshake which Paul returned with apprehension.

"My office is just up the stairs. Would you follow me?" Paul unlocked his office door and welcomed her, "Please have a seat."

"Thank you," she said as she took a chair.

Paul moved behind his desk and sat down. There was an awkward silence as she looked around the room, again studying each detail as she had in the sanctuary a few hours earlier. At the same time, Paul studied her, his anxiety rising.

"I'm sure you're anxious about what I'm going to say," Brianna began.

"Very," Paul agreed.

"Well, first of all, I'm not here to make any trouble for you. As I said this morning, I just found out a few months ago that Bob wasn't my real dad. In fact, I never knew him; I've never even met him."

"You never...what? What do you mean? What happened to Bob?"

"Didn't my mom tell you that, either?"

"No. They quit coming to church a couple of months after Brian died. Later, I heard that they had moved out of town. I never spoke with your mom again."

"Did you know they split up?"

"No. But I guess that doesn't surprise me. Statistically, that happens a lot when a child in the family dies. By the way, I assume you know about Brian, your older brother?"

"Oh, of course! My sister told me about Brian many years ago. It was a scary secret between the two of us when I was little. Why do you think my name is Brianna? Mom thought her new baby was a gift from God to help her overcome her grief in losing Brian."

"Your sister? That's right, now I remember, Brian had a younger sister. Well, she'd be your . . . older sister. What was her name again?"

"Sarah. Sarah is thirty-three now and she has three little girls. My nieces are the cutest girls you'll ever meet. I just love'em!"

"Wow! That's great!" Paul hoped his feigned enthusiasm would relieve the anxiety he was feeling. "Good for Sarah. She's thirty-three? It hardly seems possible that many years have passed. She was only thirteen or fourteen; at least that's how I remember her."

"Sarah was fourteen when I was born, and I'm nineteen now. She was more like a mom to me than a sister… not that Marge wasn't a good mom. She's the greatest! I admire her for raising me and my sister after she and Dad split up."

"I do remember that Marge was a great mom. My wife, Cheri, always admired her." Paul reflected briefly on the friendship Cheri and Marge had shared. "We have two grown sons, and I give Cheri all the credit for how they turned out." Paul was still feeling uneasy, but so far the conversation seemed to be going well.

"I still say Dad sometimes, instead of Bob, because Sarah always called him Dad."

"So you've never had a father in your life? Your mom never remarried?"

"No, Mom had her hands full, working full-time, and two daughters fourteen years apart. She told us that Dad sent money from time to time. Oops, I did it again. For a while, Bob sent money; I suppose it was for Sarah. According to Mom, she never even told Bob about my being born. They sent Christmas cards for a while. Bob eventually remarried and stopped sending money. I guess they never even saw each other again, and Bob never found out about me."

"All those years, you assumed Bob was your father."

"That's right. I never saw him, but for nineteen years, I thought he was my father. Sarah always called him Dad, and Mom never bothered to explain that he wasn't really my dad. Until recently, that is."

"And she's sure that Bob wasn't your real father?"

"Absolutely. The way she explained it, after Brian's death, the two of them never slept together again. She told me they were both so hurt and they just didn't know how to handle it."

"Why did she finally decide to tell you all of this?" Paul asked.

Brianna looked out the window. "It's kind of a long story; have you got time?"

"Yes, I've got time. And I really would like to know. As you can imagine, I'm very embarrassed to learn that I have a daughter, if you really are my daughter. I hope your mother, Marge, explained that we were only together once."

Brianna burst out laughing.

"Why is that so funny?" Paul asked.

"I laughed because that's exactly what Mom said! 'We were only together once!' she insisted. Mom wanted me to be sure I had sorted out my feelings before coming to see you. And she insisted that she bears no ill feelings toward you."

"Brianna. I'm trying really hard to absorb all this. I am interested in knowing what happened to Marge, and to you, and why she finally decided to tell you about me."

"Okay. I'll start with my sister's wedding. Ten years ago, Sarah and Mike got married. Sarah wanted her dad to walk her down the aisle, but Mom wasn't too keen on the idea. She let Sarah write to Dad and ask him to be a part of the wedding. He had only been married a year or two, and apparently his new wife was really jealous of his family. She put her foot down and said he shouldn't try to be a father to a girl he hardly knew any more. At least that's the way Mom tells it. So Dad didn't come to Sarah's wedding. Sarah's feelings were hurt, of course. I remember listening as Mom tried to comfort Sarah and defend Bob. Sarah just ran out of the house. I remember that! I guess she needed time to work it out. Anyway, last Christmas, a wonderful man named Guy, Guy Spencer, gave me an engagement ring; and in April we began planning our wedding. I asked Mom if she thought Dad would come for my wedding, even if he didn't for Sarah's. She said, 'Brianna, you're nineteen now, and it's time for us to have a serious talk.'

"I laughed and told her I already knew about sex. She said, 'No, not about sex.... about your father. Brianna,' she said, 'Bob is not your real dad; your real father is a Lutheran pastor. His name is Paul Walker. He was our pastor in Weston, Indiana, when Brian was killed. I hope you're not ashamed of me. I just don't want to keep it a secret from you any longer.' So that's how it finally came out. I think I was in shock for about a month! I just turned twenty on June 5th and decided it was time to meet my real father."

"Wow! That's quite a story. So, Bob never even knew you were born?"

"That's right. According to what Mom told me, after Brian died, she struggled with the most difficult decisions she ever had to make. First, she had to decide whether or not to divorce Bob. And second, whether or not to let him know she was pregnant. She said if she told him, he would be suspicious, since they hadn't had sex for months. He'd demand to know who she'd been with. She didn't ever want to tell him, so she kept her pregnancy a secret. And I guess she didn't want to make any trouble for you."

"O Lord, Brianna!" Paul sighed, shaking his head. "I admit I've been feeling really nervous since this morning. I'm really ashamed about what happened. May I ask if you or your mom have told anyone else about this?"

"No, I haven't talked to anybody, and I don't think Mom has either. But I have been thinking…some time before the wedding, I want to tell Guy."

"Are you angry at me? Or your Mom? How are you feeling about what she told you?"

"Pretty excited, actually. I thought, why be angry? Or ashamed? I've been thinking about this visit for weeks. I really didn't know what to expect, but I just felt I had to meet my real father. And so far, I think Mom was right."

"How's that? Right about what?"

"You seem like a really nice man!" Brianna smiled.

"Thanks, and you're a lovely young woman!" Again, there was a long pause and Paul could feel his discomfort rise again. "I just can't believe I have a daughter!"

"I know how you feel. I can't believe I'm sitting in front of a stranger whom I should be calling 'Dad.'"

"That's sounds nice, coming from a young woman like you, but it will be a long time before I feel comfortable with it. Would you mind just calling me Pastor Walker, or Pastor Paul?"

"Not at all, if that's what makes you comfortable."

"I'd appreciate that. So, what do you plan to do, now that we've met?" Paul wasn't sure he wanted to hear the answer. He secretly wished this was the end of it.

"Mostly I was curious to get to know you... at least a little." Brianna chuckled. "But I'd also like to know what you can tell me about Brian, and about you and Mom."

Paul thought for a few moments. "Well, there's not much I can add to what you already know." Paul prayed that this would end the whole thing, but Brianna would not be deterred.

"No, I really want to hear what happened from your perspective. That way, I'd get to know you as a person, as my dad. .... Please, Pastor Paul, I really do want to learn more. I think it will help me understand myself better. And don't forget about Guy. I think I owe it to him. I wanted to meet you before the wedding."

"Brianna, I guess I'm still in shock. I respect what you've said about your reasons for wanting to know more. It's just that... that...." Paul glanced nervously at his watch. "It's kind of a long story, and right now, I really should be getting home."

"Oh, right." Brianna glanced at her watch. "I guess since it's been twenty years, I can wait a little longer," Brianna sighed. "Is it all right with you if I come back again?"

"Well... I guess.... I mean, sure."

"Is it okay if I come back to church in a couple of weeks? Maybe we can talk again after lunch like we did today."

"Sure, yeah, that would be fine." Paul grimaced, wondering again whether he would have to confess all this to Cheri.

"Sounds great!" Brianna said enthusiastically. "I'm going straight home and tell Mom what a good visit we've had." Brianna stood to leave. "See you in a couple weeks!"

Paul jotted the name Brianna on his calendar, two o'clock, two weeks from today. He stood up and reached across the desk to shake her hand. She shook it vigorously. He closed up the office and the two of them walked to the parking lot. Paul locked the church door and turned as Brianna was getting into her car. "Drive carefully on your way home!" Paul shouted, not realizing he sounded like a father talking to his daughter.

"Thanks, Dad, I will!" Brianna shouted back and giggled.

Paul glanced around to see if anyone might have overheard her, opened his car door, and slumped inside. *I thought the Holloways were history. I thought after all these years Cheri would never find out about what happened. Cheri might have believed me, if I had told her then, that Marge and I were only together once. What in the world will she do now, if she finds out I have a daughter? O God, help!* Paul glanced at Brianna's car, smiled and waved as she backed out of her parking space. Brianna grinned and waved excitedly!

35

BRIANNA'S SECOND VISIT

Sunday, July 3

As she had promised, Brianna showed up for worship at Trinity two weeks later. Paul was nervous, but kept reminding himself what she had insisted on her first visit, "I'm not here to make any trouble for you." She sat in nearly the same pew as before, perhaps a row closer to the front. Paul acknowledged her presence with a nod and a smile. After church, she came out in the midst of other parishioners to shake the pastor's hand. "Hello, Brianna," Pastor Paul greeted her, relieved that this time he remembered her name. He had written it on his office calendar for 2 p.m. Sunday.

"Good morning, Pastor Paul," Brianna replied.

"Will I see you this afternoon?" Paul asked.

"Yes, at two again?"

"That should be fine," Paul responded as Brianna moved past him.

After lunch, Paul told Cheri that he had a counseling appointment at the office. As always, she was good about respecting confidentiality and did not ask whom Paul was meeting if he did not offer. Paul drove to the church a few minutes early, and again her red Honda was already there. "Good afternoon, Brianna!" Paul said pleasantly as she got out of her car.

"Good afternoon, Pastor Paul," Brianna replied as they walked toward the church. "Do you like being a pastor?" she asked, making conversation.

"Well…most of the time. I enjoy my ministry at Trinity very much." Paul pushed the security code, unlocked the church door, and they went in. "This is a growing congregation and it keeps changing; and it keeps me very busy. But I like that. I never was good at just sitting and reading."

"How long did you know my family when they were here in Weston?" Brianna asked, changing the subject.

"Hmmm, let's see, your folks left after Brian died which was in my fifth year. So I guess I knew them for about five years." Paul opened the office door and they sat down.

"Go on….. tell me what you remember about Brian. I know he was killed in the church. I'll bet that was an awful thing to deal with."

Paul drew a deep breath, let it out slowly, and began, "Brian was the best custodian Trinity ever had." Paul thought back. "He was going to be a veterinarian. He was a very good student and was well liked in high school and in the church. He was so faithful in the job; I never heard one complaint. Oh, there was the time he burned the palm leaves, but that's a story in itself! He kept the church spotless. One night, it was during the summer, he apparently startled an intruder in the church and they fought on the stairs to the basement fellowship hall. The other guy had a knife, and Brian was stabbed and died right there. It was horrible. Your mom and dad were devastated."

"Bob's not my dad, remember?" Brianna interrupted.

"Sorry, I keep forgetting. Bob and Marge were devastated. I guess it affected me too, a lot more than I realized at the time. We got together to plan Brian's funeral. Your sister Sarah amazed us all by saying she wanted to get up in front of everyone and talk about her brother. Remember she was only thirteen at the time. She had on the prettiest dress and a ribbon tied up her pony tail. She looked like a child and yet conducted herself like a mature young adult. At the reception, everyone told her what a nice job she had done talking about her brother. She accepted the compliments like a little lady with uncommon grace. We were all so proud of her."

Brianna sat with a tear running down her cheek as she listened to the story of her brother's terrible death, the funeral, and her sister's eulogy. Paul took another deep breath and let out a long sigh. He was amazed at how clearly it all came back. "Is there anything else you want to know about?" Paul asked Brianna.

"That must have been so hard for all of you," Brianna replied. "I still have a lot of questions, like: Was the murderer ever caught? Did you love my mom? Do you know why mom divorced Bob?" Brianna shifted in her seat and stared at Paul, "Are you mad at her for telling me about you?"

"Whew! Those are some tough questions. I don't know that I'm mad at your mom; but I wish she had told me about you, Brianna, before you just appeared on my doorstep. But, I guess she had her reasons." Paul paused to reflect on the other questions. "I'm not sure I know everything that happened, or why we all acted as we did, but I'll share what I know."

There was a long silence as Brianna sat waiting expectantly. Paul finally stammered. "Are you sure you want to hear it all? It could take a while."

"Look at it this way, Pastor Paul, if you don't tell me the whole story, I'll be wondering about it for the rest of my life. I really do want to know, so I guess I've got all the time in the world."

"I'm not sure where to begin," Paul said, closing his eyes as memories swirled again in his mind.

"Did you love Mom? ....Or was it just a 'one night stand' as they say?"

Paul shifted nervously in his chair. Looking out the window he replied hesitantly, "Maybe a little of both...what I mean is, I did care about your mom very much. She was, and I'm sure still is, a wonderful woman. We were good friends, very good friends. She was very active in church and adult education. She organized our Vacation Bible School every summer. I admired her desire to learn and grow in faith. Cheri and I both admired how she was raising Brian and Sarah. Then, one horrible night, everything was thrown out of whack. When Brian died... I let my feelings for Marge turn into something that wasn't right. I wanted so much to take her pain away. I felt so helpless; and it felt so good to hold her. She and Bob were having a difficult time with their grief."

Paul stopped to reflect, "Remember, you asked if I knew why she divorced Bob? First of all, I never knew they separated. I thought they moved away together. But Marge did share some intimate details about Bob's anger and then his silence, and the wall that grew between them. So it doesn't surprise me that she finally decided to go on without him. Especially, as you said, to keep him from knowing that she was pregnant." Paul stopped to think and to watch Brianna's reaction to what he was saying.

"You said 'a little of both,' Brianna interjected. "So, how was it like a one night stand?"

"Yea, that," Paul sighed. "We were both pretty vulnerable, mostly because of your mom's grief, and Bob's inability to share his feelings. But I admit I took advantage of the situation. Marge seemed to want to be intimate with me, and even though I should have been stronger, I gave in to the temptation. In that way, it was like a one night stand."

"That's pretty crappy."

"Yea, you're right. I'm really ashamed of my behavior. I cared a lot about your mom. That's why I struggle to this day about how I could have let it happen."

"I think my mom cared a lot about you too, Pastor Paul. I think that's why she's tried to protect you all these years by keeping a secret about my real father."

Paul nodded in agreement and sighed again. What more could he say? Brianna sat staring out the window of Paul's office. She struggled to bring herself back to the present. Her mind was lost in the past, seeing her mom as a younger woman, grieving the loss of her son. She felt numb. "What about the murderer? Was he ever caught?"

"O, Lord, that's another long story. If it's okay with you," Paul suggested, "we'll tackle that one some other time."

"Sure," Brianna replied, "I've taken enough of your time. I would like to come back again; maybe later this summer?"

"Cheri and I will be gone on vacation the last two weeks in August, but any time before or after that would be fine," Paul added.

"By the way, how long does it take you to get home from here?" Paul asked.

"About an hour and a half from our apartment, depending on the traffic. Mom and I live on the north side, not too far from Wrigley Field. Oh, I almost forgot; Mom said to say hi."

"Please greet her for me also." As they rose from their chairs, Paul asked Brianna, "Do you mind if I pray?"

"Not at all," she answered.

"Heavenly Father, thank you for our meeting today. Keep Brianna safe as she returns home. You are the Redeemer of our past, our present, and our future. Forgive us our trespasses as we forgive those who have trespassed against us. Help us to come to terms with the events of the past and to live with confidence as your children. Be with us as we seek to serve you in all that we do, in Christ's name we pray. Amen."

"Okay, you'll definitely see me again!" Brianna said as she moved toward the door. As they said good-bye in the parking lot, Paul realized that he was being drawn into a relationship that might not be easy to end. At first he had hoped Brianna would be satisfied just meeting him and then would go away. He had to admit that he admired the young woman and was fascinated by her curiosity. On the other hand, the longer this went on, the more difficult it would be to keep from Cheri. Tell, or not tell. This dilemma just would not go away.

36

PLEASE DON'T TELL MY MOM

Friday, July 29

There is a rhythm in the life of a pastor. Some people might call it a rut, and like most routines it can easily become a rut if one forgets the divine purpose of that rhythm. Hospital visits, Bible study, sermon preparation, council meetings, annual stewardship emphasis. Some of the rhythms are weekly, some monthly, some annually. Yet every day in the pastor's work brings the unexpected. Paul had not told Cheri about his visits from Brianna, and kept hoping he wouldn't have to.

He was feeling rather pleased with himself for having finished his sermon preparation on Friday morning. The bulletin was printed, the prayers were written, the baptismal certificate was filled out and placed on the altar. Saturday evening, he would review his notes, remind himself about the baptism Sunday morning, and pray that Sunday worship would be uplifting for all. Paul was always a little more anxious as Labor Day approached, because church programs and activities always picked up in September. He was relieved that there would be no visit from Brianna this Sunday. She had said she'd return later in the summer, but that she would call first.

Paul straightened the papers on his desk and left the church about two-thirty. At five he began preparing dinner. Cheri enjoyed his salad and pizza on Friday evenings. After a leisurely supper they chatted a while before turning on the television to watch the ten o'clock news. The phone rang and Cheri picked it up in the kitchen. Paul heard her listening for a few moments; then she said, "Just a minute, I'll let you talk to Pastor Paul." He took the phone and glanced at the kitchen clock which read 10:12 pm. *Who would be calling at this hour?* he thought to himself.

"Pastor, this is Cindee. I'm at the video arcade a couple of blocks from the church. I need to talk to you real bad." Cindee was in high school, a delightful girl whom Paul really liked. Although her dad seldom came to church, her mom, Charlotte, was very active. Cindee was popular in school and a leader in the youth group. On the phone she sounded extremely upset.

"Shall I meet you at the video arcade?" he asked.

"No, I'm walking over to the church, please meet me there."

"Okay, I'll be there in about five minutes," Paul replied. He told Cheri where he was headed and that he wasn't sure how long this would take, but he'd be home as soon as possible. Ever since his experience with Brian Holloway's death, Paul felt uneasy going to the church late in the evening.

When he pulled into the church parking lot, he saw Cindee and her friend, Missy. Both of them were sitting on the cement, leaning against the back door of the church. He got out of the car and walked over to them. They looked so small and vulnerable in shredded jeans and t-shirts. This was not the Cindee Paul usually saw on Sunday mornings! She put out her hand and he helped her get up.

"I don't feel very good," Cindee said. "Can we go inside the church?" Pastor Paul unlocked the door and turned on the lights. Cindee and Missy stumbled up the stairs. "I need to go to the bathroom," she mumbled; and she and her friend disappeared into the women's restroom.

In a moment he heard the sound of retching and vomiting, and it dawned on him why she wasn't feeling very well, and why she had sounded troubled. Yes indeed, she was in big trouble!

Paul waited through ten or fifteen minutes of silence, punctuated with the all-too-familiar sounds of over-indulgence. Finally, Missy came out. "Pastor, Cindee wants to talk to you." Paul cautiously opened the restroom door. The smell was enough to make him nauseous. She was sitting on the floor, with her back against the stall door. He drew a little closer and sat down on the floor next to the sink facing her. Slowly, she lifted her head. "I think I had too much to drink."

"Yes, I think so too," he replied.

"My mom'll kill me if she finds out!"

"Oh, I doubt that," he said, "but it looks like you've done a pretty good number on yourself!"

Her head dropped again. "I'm sorry I made such a mess here around the toilet, and I guess I kinda lost it by the sink too."

He looked up to see a spatter of red flecks on the tile above and beside the sink. "What were you drinking?" he asked.

"Annie Green Springs....strawberry wine," Cindee answered.

"Doesn't smell like strawberries any more," the pastor added with a disgusted look on his face.

"I'm so sorry, Pastor," she moaned.

"Well, let's get this mess cleaned up; then we'll talk some more," he suggested. This was apparently enough to give her some hope because the next thing she did was call her friend Missy back in to help. The three of them did the best they could with soap, cleanser, and paper towels....the exhaust fan humming the entire time.

Cindee finally broke the silence, "Pastor, I just can't go home. I'd be in so much trouble. Could Missy and I possibly stay in the church tonight?"

"Hmmm…." he pondered. *Now I know why you wanted me to come to the church,* he thought to himself. "What will your mom think if you don't come home tonight?"

"She'll be worried, I'm sure." Paul could see the wheels turning now as she worked on an excuse. "We could call her and say I decided to stay at Missy's tonight!"

"And if she calls Missy's mom and neither of you are there, then what?" he replied.

"I don't think she will," she pleaded.

"And you'll have to call Missy's mom and tell her a lie as well?" he asked.

"Oh, Pastor, I don't know what to do! I just know I did the wrong thing; and I'm still feeling pretty sick. Please don't tell my mom!"

"Tell me about your mom," he said. "What kind of mom is she?" Paul knew Charlotte was a very good mom, but he wanted to hear Cindee's opinion.

"She's pretty nice… most of the time," she replied. "But she won't be happy about all this. I know I'm gonna be grounded."

"Why did you call me?" the pastor asked.

"Because you've always been really nice to me and my family. I didn't know who else to turn to and I knew I was in trouble. I guess I hoped you would understand and know how to help me."

"Cindee, I like you a lot. And you've got a terrific family. I know your mom won't be happy when she finds out about this, but I think she'd respect you for owning up to your mistakes. I think the best thing you could do right now is call your mom and tell her that you're at the church with Missy and the pastor, and that I'll be bringing you home in a little while. What do you think?"

Cindee pondered Pastor Paul's suggestion and tried to imagine her mom's reaction. Finally Missy spoke up, "I think, like… maybe

Pastor Paul is right. Maybe you should call your mom and tell her the truth."

Cindee looked sheepishly at the pastor, "Will you go with me and kind of explain what happened? I don't think she'll be as mad if you're with me when she finds out."

"Sure, I'll go with you; I'll take you home," Paul spoke gently. "But, you have to do all the talking," he added firmly. "Let's make the phone call first."

"Okay," she agreed. They prayed together in Paul's office. Cindee dialed her home. She talked to her mom and told her the truth. The phone conversation was subdued but went better than she had expected. Pastor Paul drove Missy home first, and then went to Cindee's. He walked Cindee to the front door. As the front door opened, Charlotte stared at her daughter. She shook her head and gave her daughter a hug; then pulling back suddenly, let out a loud, "Peeeuugh!"

Paul couldn't help but laugh…Annie Green Springs Strawberry Wine. He was glad he didn't have to write a sermon the next day. He got home a little before midnight, told Cheri what had transpired, and they both had a good laugh! Forgiving Cindee seemed like a very natural thing for him to do, and it looked like her mom would too. As Paul was falling asleep he prayed for Charlotte and Cindee. He thought to himself, *maybe it is best to own up to our mistakes and face the consequences with courage and faith.*

37

BRIANNA'S THIRD VISIT

August is usually a scorcher in Indiana, and this year was no exception. Paul and Cheri were looking forward to some cooler weather in Ontario, when they went up north to a lake cabin which they had reserved for the week of August 15th. Paul was in the office at Trinity on Friday morning, August 5th, trying to finish writing his sermon when Jeannette told him he had a call on line #2. "Hello, this is Pastor Walker."

"Hi! This is Brianna Holloway!"

Paul's heart skipped a beat when he heard the name. "How are you, Brianna?" As July slipped by he had almost forgotten her promise to call again.

"Oh, I'm fine. I told you I'd call this summer when I could come see you again."

"Yes, yes, are you planning a drive to Weston?"

"Actually, I was telling Guy, my fiancé, about my visits with you, and I was wondering if it would be okay if I brought him along to meet you?"

Paul took a deep breath as he thought about further complicating his relationship with Brianna. "Well, I suppose, if you really want to. I guess." Paul paused, "I guess…I'm still nervous about our meetings. The truth is I haven't told Cheri about you."

"Oh, that's okay, Pastor Paul," Brianna said with sweet naiveté. "Guy and I are planning a December wedding, so maybe there won't be time to meet again. I'd just wanted him to meet you, and you to meet him, before we're married."

"Sure….sure…I'd love to meet your fiancé," Paul replied with forced enthusiasm. Secretly he hoped this would indeed put an end to the visits from Brianna. The wedding, Christmas, and focus on her new husband might end her need to dig up the past with Paul. He hoped. "When were you planning to visit?" Paul asked.

"Guy said he would come to church with me this Sunday, but if we don't make it to church, we'll meet you at two o'clock again at your office. Is that okay?"

"Sure, that's fine. See you at church, or at the office at two." Paul scribbled the two o'clock appointment on his calendar.

* * * * * * *

Sunday morning was clear and sunny. It was already very hot; in fact, the heat and humidity had been unbearable for the past five days. Paul chose his lightest suit, and Cheri put on a loose fitting summer dress. The church was air conditioned, but Paul knew the electric bill would be at its highest just as offerings bottomed out for the summer. He was nervous, not only about church offerings, but also about seeing Brianna again.

Cheri noticed that he seemed more up tight than usual. As they drove to church she asked, "What's the matter, Paul? Usually you're more relaxed in the summer months."

"Oh, I don't know. I guess I don't feel really good about my sermon this morning," Paul lied. That was the first thing that came to mind ....other than Brianna.

"You'll do fine;" Cheri reassured him, "you always do."

"Thanks."

After putting on his alb, Paul entered the sanctuary and glanced around, smiled at Cheri and looked for Brianna in her usual place. She wasn't there. He remembered she had said she might not make it to church but would be there for the appointment this afternoon. He put her out of his mind and focused on the welcome, announcements, and opening hymn.

The congregation stood for the reading of the gospel Mark 3:20-35. Paul read, "And when his friends heard it, they went out to seize Jesus, for they said, 'He is beside himself.' And the scribes who came down from Jerusalem said, 'He is possessed by Beelzebul, and by the prince of demons he casts out the demons.' At that point, everyone was startled by a loud thump, and turned to see people leaning over Mrs. Johannsen who had collapsed on the pew. "Is there a doctor or nurse here?" someone called out. "Yes, I'm coming," replied Sonja Ramirez, a registered nurse. One of the ushers headed for the office to call 9-1-1 for an ambulance.

"Would everyone please be seated?" Pastor Walker announced. "Give Sonja a chance to check on Mrs. Johannsen."

"I think she just fainted," replied Elmer. "She's done this at home several times."

"Will the rest of you please join me in prayer," requested the pastor. "Heavenly Father, source of all mercy and healing, look upon your servant Arda and bring her back to consciousness. Wrap your gentle arms around her and her husband Elmer and give them your peace. We pray for your good and gracious will to be done. Grant Arda healing. Guide our nurse, Sonja Ramirez, as she ministers to her. Bring assistance quickly so that she may receive the best medical care possible. All these things we ask in Jesus' name. Amen."

The congregation responded with an Amen and sat quietly, praying silently, and waiting. In about two minutes, which seemed like an eternity, Arda opened her eyes. She looked at the group huddled around her. "What are you all staring at?" she asked in a loud, clear voice. Slowly, everyone began to chuckle.

"We were looking at you," Elmer replied. "We were worried; you passed out."

"Oh for heaven's sake, that's nothin' to worry about," she responded flippantly, "I do that all the time!" This time the laughter shook the church. The sound of a siren indicated that the ambulance was arriving. Sonja and Elmer escorted Arda out to the narthex so she could be checked by the paramedics. She was walking and talking as if nothing had happened.

"Where were we?" asked Pastor Paul. "Oh yes, the gospel."

The sermon was anti-climactic. "A kingdom divided against itself cannot stand," Jesus said. "How can Satan cast out Satan?" Paul emphasized the goodness of Jesus, and reminded everyone of the passage in Romans which says, "Do not be overcome with evil, but overcome evil with good." The hymn was sung, the offering received, and to everyone's delight, Arda and Elmer returned to the sanctuary for communion and the closing hymn.

* * * * * * *

At two that afternoon the sun was beating on the asphalt parking lot when Paul arrived at the office. There were no other cars in the lot, and Paul wondered for a moment if he was mistaken about Brianna's visit. *I'm sure she said this Sunday, but maybe something came up. It won't be the first time I've waited for an appointment that didn't show.* He unlocked the church doors and walked to his office to check his desk calendar. Her name was there on Sunday, 2 p.m. He could see the parking lot from his office, so he sat down at his desk. About five minutes later Brianna's red Honda pulled into the lot. She and Guy came into the church and found their way to the office.

"Hello, Brianna, I was hoping you wouldn't run into too much traffic this afternoon."

"Not too bad!" Brianna replied brightly. "Pastor Paul, I'd like you to meet my fiancé, Guy Spencer. Guy, this is my dad; but I call him Pastor Paul." Brianna grinned. Paul stood and the two men reached over the desk and shook hands.

"Very nice to meet you," Guy's voice was deep but gentle-sounding. "Brianna's told me how much she's enjoyed her meetings with you."

"It's very nice to meet you too," Paul replied.

"Guy and I were out kind of late last night. We are so jazzed! We spent last night talking about a honeymoon in Hawaii! Oh, I'm so excited, I can hardly wait! Just four months now! Can you believe it?" She was almost jumping up and down.

"Wow! That's great. I can tell you're excited."

"Not just excited; I'm bonkers!!" As Brianna lowered herself into the chair, she grinned at Guy who took his seat next to her. Paul sat down behind his desk. Brianna tilted her head down and looked upward at Paul. With a mischievous smile she said, "You are going to do our wedding, aren't you?"

Paul was stunned. He wasn't sure what to say. *"No, I don't want to do the wedding?" Or, "Sure, I'd love to; I'm honored you asked."* "You're kidding, I hope," is what he actually said.

"Yea, I'm kidding. Guy and I have already talked to our pastor in Chicago. We'll be meeting with him again next month. I just wanted to see what your reaction would be!" Brianna laughed gaily. "You looked a little shocked."

"You did catch me off guard," Paul admitted.

"I keep forgetting that you're really nervous about having a daughter."

"Of course. As I think I mentioned, I haven't told Cheri about you."

"Are you going to?" Brianna asked.

Paul shook his head, "The same old dilemma again. I don't know.... I really haven't decided yet."

"Well, believe me, Pastor Paul, I'm not going to tell anybody!" Brianna said emphatically.

Paul sighed, "Thank you...thank you again. I certainly hope not." There was an uncomfortable silence for a few moments. Brianna looked at Guy who simply shrugged his shoulders. "So Guy, what do you do for a living?" Paul asked.

"Commodity broker," Guy responded. "I work at the Board of Trade in Chicago for one of the brokerage firms."

"Sounds exciting," Paul said, "but that's one business I know very little about."

"Oh, it can be exciting, sometimes; but usually it's just a lot of numbers and reports and meetings and phone calls."

"Tell me, Guy, how did you and Brianna meet?"

Guy glanced at his fiancé, cleared his throat, and told the story. "Like I mentioned before, I work for a brokerage in the loop. Our receptionist left to have a baby, so I was on the interview committee to hire a new receptionist. We looked at almost a dozen resumes and decided to interview the top three. Well, Brianna was the first candidate we talked to, and I was impressed."

Brianna interrupted, "I was so nervous; I didn't even remember Guy from that first interview."

"Our committee was split between two of the candidates, so we brought them back for a second interview. Brianna seemed much more confident and at ease that time. The other candidate was late and acted like it was no big deal." Guy shrugged. "We hired Brianna."

"It took nearly a month before he asked me out," Brianna added and jabbed Guy in the arm.

Paul laughed! "Well, you two seem to be pretty fond of each other."

"We most certainly are," Guy replied, smiling at Brianna.

Brianna stared at Pastor Walker for a long moment. "There are still some things I'd like to know about."

"Like what?"

"Like....what happened after Mom left Weston? Did they ever find Brian's murderer?"

Paul stared into her young eyes. There was an intensity Paul had seen before. A few moments ago she had seemed light and carefree, but now she was serious. Slowly, Paul began sharing what he remembered about the investigation. In his mind he could still picture Detective Sean Asplund and his partner Chad. "From what I can recall, the two detectives assigned to the case did a lot of footwork before they finally found a suspect. It turned out to be a local hoodlum by the name of Terry Mankovic. He had been robbing businesses in Weston, Gary, and other cities in northern Indiana."

"What made them suspect him?" Guy asked.

"Apparently they received a tip from a neighbor about a noise she heard the night of Brian's death. She said she heard a thump on her bedroom wall and the guy next door screaming, 'I didn't mean to kill him!'"

"That must have been kinda scary," Brianna interjected.

"I suppose it was. Detective Asplund said she was pretty interested in the reward money. Maybe that helped her overcome any fear she might have had," Paul continued.

"Where did the reward money come from?" Guy asked.

"Well, that's another part of the story. First, my wife's law firm offered to donate a thousand dollars. Later, one of their wealthy clients generously offered $10,000 more!"

"Wow! Did the neighbor get all that money?" Guy was really enjoying the story.

"Not quite. A few months later, the police found a second witness of sorts who lived less than a block from the church. The new witness said he saw someone running across the parking lot the night Brian was killed. It turned out he was able to identify a photo of Terry Mankovic who lived next door to the woman who heard him screaming."

"Wow! Did they ever arrest him? Was he brought to trial?" Brianna asked excitedly.

"Well, yes, they arrested Terry and they were pretty sure they had the guilty person; but, they had to prove it at trial."

"It sounds like they had all the evidence they needed," commented Guy.

"Well, we all hoped so; but you know how trials are. If the defense can raise enough reasonable doubt, sometimes guilty people walk away free," Paul responded.

"What happened at the trial?" Brianna was anxious to hear the rest of the story.

"Brianna, I'm really sorry to put you off to another time, but I've got some phone calls to make. One of our ladies fainted in church this morning and I want to check on her before I go home this afternoon."

"Oh, I hope she's okay. We should probably get going ourselves." Brianna looked at Guy for agreement.

Guy nodded. "Yeah, we've been here quite a while. Thanks, Pastor Paul. It was really nice meeting you."

"It was nice meeting you too, Guy. I think you and Brianna make a lovely couple. I certainly wish you all the best in planning your wedding and in the years that lie ahead."

"Thanks, Pastor Paul," Brianna said, as she and Guy got up to leave.

"I may call you again in a couple of weeks. I still want to hear what happened at the trial."

As Guy and Brianna made their way down the stairs to the parking lot, Paul closed his eyes and prayed again.

38

A MAJOR INTERRUPTION

Pastors do need "get-aways." Cheri needed time away from the library. Cheri and Paul spent a week at the lake in Ontario, drifting around in a small fishing boat, not caring much if they caught fish or didn't. They caught just enough perch and walleye for a fresh fish dinner each evening. The cabin had a small window air-conditioner which was running the day they arrived. The following day it turned cool and pleasant, and the nights were chilly enough for a wool blanket. Paul felt fairly confident that Cheri would not find out about Brianna, so he decided not to say anything and ruin a beautiful week together. They came back to Weston rested and refreshed.

The week after Labor Day, Brianna called and told Paul she would be in church again next Sunday. She asked if she could meet at two o'clock and Paul agreed. She wasn't sure if Guy would be coming too. Paul hung up the phone and silently prayed this would be their last meeting. There was enough stress in his life as a pastor anyway; having meetings with a secret daughter wasn't helping!

His primary concern at this time of year was the beginning of fall programs at church. He met with Janet and her worship planning team on Thursday night and there were questions asked about Sheila Williamson's relationship with one of the men in the choir. "You'd think now that she's married, she'd stop her teasing," Janet said. Paul admitted he didn't know anything, and he warned against gossip and the spreading of rumors which may or may not be true. More stress.

On Friday his sermon preparation was interrupted by a phone call from Elmer Johannsen who sounded very upset. "I'm at the hospital, Pastor. I had to call 9-1-1 last night. It was Arda. She had another one of her spells about eight o'clock; and she didn't come out of it for several minutes. I hope I didn't wait too long before calling for help. I was really afraid she wouldn't wake up!"

"Did you get her to the hospital? How is she?" Paul asked.

"Yes, the ambulance team was so nice; they got there right away. They ran a bunch of tests at the hospital last night. She seems better this morning. I just got here and we're waiting for the doctor."

"You could have called me, Elmer, I'd have come over last night," Paul suggested.

"Naw, I didn't want to bother you until we found out more from the doctors. I'm sure Arda would appreciate a visit today, however." Elmer wasn't begging, but his voice sounded shaky and frightened.

"Sure, Elmer. I'll get over there right away," Paul responded. Pushing his sermon notes aside, Paul rose and went to tell Jeannette he was on his way to the hospital to see Arda.

* * * * * * *

Friday, September 9

On Friday evening, Cheri told Paul about her day at the library, and Paul shared his day with Cheri. "Arda Johannsen is back in the hospital with ischemia of the brain, or 'mini-strokes' as they're sometimes called. They said at her age there's very little they can do for her. Elmer is really worried. I'm sure he wonders each time this happens if it will be the last. You can see it in his face."

"Paul, you're so compassionate. Sometimes I think you hurt almost as much as your parishioners," Cheri said admiringly.

"Thanks, honey. I do have trouble separating my work from my personal life sometimes. Their pain does become mine."

"Why don't you go golfing tomorrow? Call your buddy Carl," Cheri suggested.

Paul was glad he had finished his sermon and left it on the desk Friday afternoon. A round of golf sounded like a great idea. Why not? A few minutes later, he was calling Carl, the pastor who had followed his friend Ryan Jacoby at the United Methodist Church.

* * * * * * *

Saturday, September 10

Paul had agreed to meet Brianna this Sunday at the usual time, two o'clock at the church. This morning, however, he was determined to enjoy a round of golf, and determined not to think about church business. Weston has several beautiful golf courses in the area. Paul still played his old favorite, Weston Hills, but was playing more frequently at his new favorite, Rolling Meadows. After their boys finished college, Cheri and Paul had a little extra money in their budget, so Cheri encouraged Paul to join the club there. Eighteen holes of pure relaxation…or pure concentration… which helped him clear his mind of everything else. Paul had agreed to meet his friend Carl, at eight, Saturday morning. It was cool, but by late morning the temperature would climb into the eighties. Paul had signed in and his rented golf cart was parked next to the first tee. Paul was on the practice putting green when Carl came across the parking lot.

"Hey Paul, how ya swingin'?"

"Pretty loose, Carl, how 'bout you?"

"Chilly this morning, huh?"

"Yea, but once the sun gets above the trees it's gonna warm up. It could hit 90 again today," Paul ventured.

Carl signed in and together they walked to the first tee. Paul stepped into the tee box anxious to get going. He took a couple of practice swings. Carl was swinging his driver a few feet away. They had become golfing partners about a year ago. Paul loved Carl's spontaneity; his language was very crude when he was not around his Methodist church members. In spite of Carl's vocabulary, or maybe because of it, Paul found that he was extremely comfortable around Carl, who had a heart of gold. Paul was delighted to learn that Carl loved golf as much as he did. From that point on, they were golfing buddies. Carl weighed about 250 pounds, and he could hit the ball a country mile.

Cheri met Carl's wife, Donna, at a fund-raising dinner which Paul and Carl had organized. When Cheri heard that Donna was looking for a job, she encouraged Donna to apply for an opening at the library; and somewhat to Donna's surprise, she got the job. They saw each other almost daily at the library. Paul and Cheri enjoyed going out socially with members of their congregation, but social relationships with other clergy allowed them to be even more at ease.

"How's Donna?" Paul asked.

"Great. She really likes her job; been there at the library for almost a year already. She's sleeping in today. Hell, I don't think she heard me leave this morning."

Paul swung his driver for his first shot, a clean hit up the middle. He winced as a sharp pain filled his chest. "Guess I should have taken a few more practice swings," Paul said. "Hope I didn't pull a muscle."

Carl stepped up and teed up his ball. His first swing topped the ball which bounced and rolled into the arborvitae on the left side of the tee. "Mind if I hit a mulligan?"

"No, go ahead," Paul replied.

Carl's second shot had good distance, rolling beyond Paul's drive and to the left side of the fairway. He picked up his first ball; they climbed into the cart and rode down the first fairway together. "How are the fall programs shaping up at your church? Carl asked.

"Pretty good, I think. The choir rehearsed for the first time this week and Sheila, our choir director was excited to have three new singers. How are things going at St. Andrew?"

"Same ol', same ol'....my secretary gripes from morning 'til night. Too many things get dumped on her at the last minute. She calls and can't find people at home. She can't get the information she needs for the calendar. The women's group asked her to start the coffee pot for their meeting and she resents that. Shit, I swear she gets grumpier every year!"

"And how many years have you been working with her?" Paul asked.

"Ten or eleven...but it sure as hell seems like fifty!" Carl joked, stopping the cart.

Paul pulled his three wood from the bag and approached his ball. He lined up his second shot, about 180 yards to the green. As he came through on his swing, the pain hit him like a golf ball in the center of his chest. The pain shot through his shoulder and down into his arm. He doubled over and dropped to his knees. He heard himself making a strange groaning noise.

"You all right?" Carl asked. "What happened?"

"I don't know," Paul answered, "but it hurts like crazy. I can hardly breathe."

"We'd better get you to a doctor quick. You may be having a heart attack. Damn! I left my cell phone at home." Carl reached down to help Paul up. "Can you stand up?"

"I think so, just a minute. Wait just a minute; I think the pain is easing up."

In a few moments Carl helped him to his feet and into the golf cart. Carl drove quickly back to the club house. A foursome waiting to tee off asked what was wrong. Carl told them he suspected his friend was having a heart attack. At the clubhouse, Carl jumped out of the cart to call an ambulance.

"No, no, don't do that," Paul objected. "It'll take them ten or fifteen minutes to get here, and by that time you could drive me to the hospital."

Paul and Carl climbed into Carl's Chevy Suburban. "You sure you don't want the paramedics to come?" Carl asked.

"I'll be okay… just step on it," Paul whispered in pain.

Twenty minutes later Paul was lying in the ER with a heart monitor and an IV in place. The doctors administered oxygen, a nitroglycerin drip, and morphine, and prepared him for an angiogram. Carl found a phone and called Cheri. She was a nervous wreck by the time she got to the hospital. Paul smiled and tried to reassure her that he would be okay. She kissed him on his forehead and sat by the bedside holding his hand.

Carl prayed with them both, and then went back to Rolling Meadows to check on their clubs and cart. An hour later he stopped by the ER again, but Paul was already in the cath lab having his angiogram. Carl chatted a while with Cheri and promised to check back in the afternoon. "Donna and I will be praying for both of you."

Cheri went to the cafeteria to grab a cup of coffee and then hurried back to the waiting area, hoping to hear a report soon. About forty-five minutes later, the doctor came out and told her they would prepare Paul for emergency by-pass surgery. Three of his coronary arteries were blocked 80% or more. He showed her a diagram of the heart and which arteries were occluded. "Your husband should be fine, once the by-passes are in place. Of course, there are risks associated with this type of surgery, but without it he risks another heart attack which he might not survive. We've scheduled him for four o'clock this afternoon. Do you have any questions?"

"Whew! This is all so sudden," Cheri exclaimed. "He left the house feeling fine, went to play golf, and now he's scheduled for major surgery.

This is like a nightmare! I can't believe this is really happening! Have you talked with him about the surgery?" Cheri asked the doctor.

"Yes, we talked in the cath lab. He was awake for the entire procedure. He saw some of the pictures of his arteries. We want the two of you to discuss this, and then after lunch, the surgeon will come to Paul's room to explain it again, and have him sign for the surgery. Dr.Johnstone is THE finest heart surgeon in Weston. You might have a list of questions ready for him when he comes in this afternoon." The doctor paused a minute looking into Cheri's anxious face. "Is there anything else I can answer for you right now?"

"No...I don't think so. But thank you. Thank you for doing the test and for coming to talk to me. Thank you, Doctor.... I'm sorry I didn't get your name."

"I'm Doctor Azhid. I'll be in the operating room assisting Dr. Johnstone, and I'll be checking on your husband after his surgery."

"Thank you again, Dr. Azhid," Cheri said as she shook his hand.

"You are most welcome."

Cheri was anxious to see Paul and talk with him and see how he was feeling now. She was told he would be in Cardiac Care, room 219, so she found an elevator and made her way to the room. It was empty. She went to the nurses' station and asked where she could find Paul Walker. She was told he would be brought to room 219, but that it may be a few minutes before he arrived. She could sit in the room to wait. No sooner had she returned to the room, than she saw his gurney being wheeled up the hall. She rushed to meet him and leaning between IV lines and monitors, gave him a kiss. "Please wait in the hall a few minutes while we get him transferred to his bed," the male nurse said politely. The few minutes became fifteen, and finally the nurse said, "You may go in now." At last, they would have a few hours to talk and pray and prepare for what was to come.

The first thing on Paul's mind was Sunday morning. "Cheri, I just remembered, Barbara is at a conference in Minneapolis; she won't be back until next week. You'll have to call Janet on the Worship

Committee. Ask her to call the retired pastors on her list to see if one of them will lead worship and preach tomorrow. Then see if you can reach Jeannette; she should know about this."

"I will," Cheri promised, "but please try to relax. You don't need to be thinking about your job at a time like this!"

"I can't help it. I know I'm not indispensible, but it sure seems like it sometimes."

"Paul, tell me what happened at the golf course, and what you think about the surgery that's being recommended." Once again, Cheri pulled a chair close to the bedside and held Paul's hand as he told her how the chest pain hit him on the first fairway, and how Carl had driven him to the ER.

"Are you still having a lot of pain?" she asked.

"No, I've been okay since they gave me those medications in emergency. Man, I never want to feel a pain like that ever again! It was unbelievable!"

"Doctor Azhid told me you need triple by-pass surgery. Do you want to do that?"

"I don't think I have much of a choice, sweetheart. Like I said, I don't think I could survive another heart attack, and I know I don't ever want to hurt like that again."

"Then I guess you'll be having surgery this afternoon. Doctor Azhid said your surgeon, Dr. Johnstone, will come in after lunch to talk with us."

Paul closed his eyes. Cheri waited to see if there was anything else to be said. "Bring him on," Paul whispered.

****

Cheri went home, and called Janet as Paul had suggested. Then she called both their sons Chip and Randy, and had to leave a message on

Chip's home phone. Randy wanted to drive over from Des Moines. He wasn't sure he'd get there before the surgery, but promised to be there by late afternoon or early evening. Who else? Who else should she notify? She made a list and began calling: Jeannette, the church secretary, was not in the office on Saturday, but fortunately was at home. Next, Cheri called Howard, the church council president. Then she called her sister in New York because she really needed to share her fear with someone. They talked for fifteen or twenty minutes. She felt relieved when that call was done and sat there a few minutes just thinking and praying in silence.

The phone rang, startling her, nearly knocking Cheri off the chair. It was Paul's golfing buddy, Carl, calling to ask what's up? She gave him a report, told him about the surgery, and thanked him for checking in. She tried calling Chip again but there was still no answer. She was mad that she couldn't find his work number; then she realized it was Saturday and he and his wife were probably out shopping or away for the weekend. Suddenly, Cheri realized she was hungry. She fixed herself a deli sandwich, sliced turkey, lettuce and tomato, and poured herself a glass of milk. It was all gone in five minutes, and she couldn't think of anything else she needed to do at home. She drove quickly but carefully back to the hospital wondering if Paul needed her as much as she needed to be near him.

The afternoon dragged by slowly. It was so hard waiting for something you'd rather not face at all. Paul dozed in and out of consciousness. The medications were keeping him relaxed. Cheri's eyes closed and her head nodded more than once. Finally, at a few minutes before three, the surgeon came into the room. "Hello, I'm Dr. Johnstone, and I'll be doing Paul's surgery. I just finished reviewing the angiogram and it looks like three of the coronary arteries are seriously blocked. With surgery we can graft sections of vein around the blockages and allow normal blood flow to the heart muscle through the bypass grafts. Have the two of you had a chance to discuss this and do you have any questions?"

"Yeah, Doc," said Paul, "what would my chances be if I don't have this surgery?"

"Well, I can't give you an exact percentage, but the chances of another heart attack would be very high. You were fortunate to have very little muscle damage this morning, but the next one could be fatal."

"Sounds like I'd better go through with it," sighed Paul, glancing at Cheri for her support.

"In that case I must inform you that there are certain risks associated with this type of surgery. The most common is post-operative bleeding. You'll be monitored and this situation can usually be corrected. There is also a chance of infection, but we try to minimize that with antibiotics which we started this morning. And finally, there is a very, very small chance that death can occur during surgery. In your case, you are not that old and in good health, except for your heart, so that risk is almost negligible."

"I hope so," responded Paul.

"If you don't have any other questions, I'll be talking again with Dr. Azhid who will assist me during surgery. A nurse will come in soon with a consent form and some other papers for you to sign. Mrs. Walker, let me assure you, your husband will be in very capable hands." Dr. Johnstone reached over to shake Paul's hand, Cheri's hand, and left the room.

A few minutes later the hospital chaplain came in and said a prayer. Another of Paul's pastor friends came in and said a prayer. The word was traveling fast. Paul's nurse came in with a clipboard and explained the consent form. Martha Kowalski, their eighty-two year old, next door neighbor arrived at four and insisted on sitting with Cheri until Paul was out of surgery. "That might take a while," Cheri told her.

"That's okay, dear. I remember how relieved I was when my daughter came to be with me when John had his cancer surgery. It was just nice to have someone to talk to and help pass the time. By the way, is either of your boys coming home?

"Randy said he was on his way, so he could be here any time now,"

Cheri answered. "I never was able to reach Chip. I hope Gail, Randy's wife, will keep trying."

"What time did you say Paul was going to surgery?" Martha asked.

"Originally, the doctor said four o'clock," Cheri answered.

Paul stirred in bed and opened his eyes. "What time is it?" he asked.

Cheri checked the clock on the wall, "Almost four thirty. I guess it's not unusual for them to be running late when the surgery is so late in the day."

"Four thirty? Cheri, call Janet right away!" Paul said as he tried to raise himself.

"Lie down, Paul, I already called her."

"No, I just thought of something else. Tell her that my sermon is typed out and lying on my desk. If one of the retired pastors wants to use it, he wouldn't have to write one tonight!"

"Oh, Paul, don't you ever stop thinking about work?" Cheri moaned.

"Please Cheri. I'll rest better if you'll do that."

"I will. I promise. Oh, oh, looks like they're coming to get you," Cheri said, as a team of nurses entered the room. "I'd better kiss you good-by right now, and don't forget… no monkey business in the O.R." Cheri joked, as she leaned over for a kiss.

"I'll be fine. I'm really confident this is going to turn out okay. I've been praying all afternoon."

"You have not! You've been sleeping!" Cheri chided.

As the nurses wheeled the bed from the room Paul called out, "Was not; I was praying!" Martha put an arm around Cheri, who held back her tears until Paul disappeared down the hall.

39

TRIPLE BY-PASS

Saturday, September 10

Paul and Cheri's son, Randy, quickly packed a suitcase. His wife Gail explained to Trevor and Joy that their dad had to go and see Grandpa because Grandpa's heart needed to be fixed. As he went out the door Gail reminded him to be sure to call her after the surgery. Randy left Des Moines about 12:30 and headed for Weston. The surgery was into the second hour when Randy appeared in the waiting room. Cheri jumped up to greet him with a hug and introduced him to Martha Kowalski. "Randy, you remember Martha, our next door neighbor."

"Sure do. Hi, Martha. How's he doing, Mom? How serious was it?" Randy asked.

"He's been in surgery for a little over an hour and we haven't heard any reports yet. The doctors confirmed that it was a heart attack and that there were three coronary arteries that were blocked. So they're doing a triple bypass with a vein from his leg."

"What kind of mood was Dad in?"

"Pretty good, considering. He slept, or rather dozed, most of the afternoon. And when he was awake, he kept thinking of things at the church." Cheri replied.

"Sounds like Dad," Randy joked.

"Your mom's been a real trooper," Martha added.

"She's the greatest," Randy enthused. "Have you heard from Chip?"

"No, not yet. I guess I could try again. I've got his number here in my billfold."

"Give me the number, Mom, and I'll try to reach him."

"Here it is; thanks Randy. I'm so proud of both you and Chip. And thank you for coming all the way from Des Moines. You made good time."

A few minutes later Randy returned saying he left a message on Chip's home phone. "And I left one earlier," Cheri replied.

The three of them settled down to wait. There are few times in life when time drags more slowly than it does when waiting for someone to come out of surgery. Martha helped pass the time by asking Randy about his wife and kids. Randy asked Cheri how her work was going, then about things at church. "Do you think Dad's been under a lot of stress at work? Could that have brought on the heart attack?"

"I don't think he has," Cheri answered, "at least, no more than usual. Come to think of it, I was asking him last Sunday on the way to church if something was bothering him. He seemed quieter than usual. I thought it was just his being anxious about fall activities at the church. Once things get going, he's usually busy but settles into the routines."

"Do heart problems run in our family?" Randy asked.

"Paul's dad had a congestive heart condition when he was in his seventies, but he never had a heart attack to my knowledge," Cheri answered.

A few minutes later Randy asked, "Have either of you had dinner? I'm hungry."

"No we haven't," responded Martha, "but I'm not hungry."

"Neither am I, honey," said Cheri, "but why don't you go to the cafeteria and get something to eat. I guess I assumed you ate on the way here."

"No, Mom, I was in too much of a hurry. I didn't even think about it until I heard my stomach growl just now."

"Go on, the cafeteria is on the first floor. They said the surgery would be about four hours. I don't expect we'll hear anything until 8:30 or so."

A couple of more hours passed and Cheri began to get nervous. She looked at Martha whose eyes were closed but couldn't tell if she was asleep. "It's 8:30 and we haven't heard a word," she whispered to Randy. "I'm going to check with the surgery desk." She came back a few minutes later. "They said he's off the pump, and they're closing, which means the heart pump has been removed and his heart is working on its own. The nurse in surgery said everything went well and they are closing the chest wall now. The doctor should be out in half an hour or so. What a relief!"

"That's great news, Mom. When will we get to see Dad?" Randy asked.

"I know he'll be in recovery for a while, and then they'll take him to ICU. The surgeon explained that he'd be on a ventilator to help him breathe, and they would keep him pretty heavily sedated."

At a little after nine o'clock, a nurse came into the waiting room and asked for Mrs. Walker. "Yes, I'm Mrs. Walker," Cheri replied. "There's a phone call for you; he said it's your son." Martha Kowalski opened her eyes and sat up straighter in her chair.

"Oh, thank God. That must be Chip calling from California," Cheri said to the nurse. Then she turned to Martha, "I wish I could tell him it's over, but at least I can give him a report on what's happened so far." Cheri walked quickly to the phone. Martha looked puzzled. She hadn't heard the report from surgery. When Cheri disappeared, Martha asked Randy if he had heard anything about his dad. Randy explained that the surgery was almost finished.

When Cheri returned Martha excused herself. "Cheri, dear, it sounds like everything is going to be all right. I'm awfully tired; in fact it's past my bedtime already. I'll be on my way home now, but I'll call tomorrow to see how Paul is doing."

"Thank you so much, Martha. You've been a great comfort. I'm so glad you came. You go home and get some rest now."

"Randy, it was good to see you again," Martha said, "but I wish the circumstances were different."

"Me too," Randy replied. "Thanks for keeping Mom company until I got here."

"Good night, you two. I'll be saying a prayer for Paul and your whole family."

As Martha left to make her way to the parking lot, Randy asked about his brother, "Will Chip be coming home?"

"Not right away. California is a long ways away and he's pretty busy with work. But he wants us to keep in touch, and if anything changes, he said he'd hop on a plane for O'Hare. He sends his love, to Dad, and to all of us. I just wish he wasn't so far away."

About twenty minutes later, Doctor Johnstone came into the waiting room. He looked extremely tired. "Mrs. Walker, your husband is fine." Cheri introduced him to her son Randy and the two men shook hands. "I was extremely pleased with the grafts. The veins we used were in excellent condition. There appears to be no leaking at the site of the three bypasses. Paul's heart appears to be in good condition generally, in spite of the severe attack suffered this morning. There was some muscle atrophy in the left ventricle, but the area affected is small. Of course, the first twenty four hours post-op are critical, but so far it looks good. We'll be more certain tomorrow."

"Will he wake up this evening?" Randy asked.

"Oh yes, he's awake already in the recovery room. But he'll be very, very sleepy, and of course he's intubated, and that will prevent him from talking."

"When can we see him?" Cheri asked.

The surgeon looked at his watch. "Well, why don't you go over to ICU about ten o'clock and ask if he's been brought there yet. They'll be in communication with recovery and can tell you when he'll be brought to ICU."

"Thank you, doctor. Thank you so very much. We thank you; Paul thanks you," Cheri said.

"After you folks see Paul, go home and get some rest. We'll take good care of him tonight, and he'll want to see you tomorrow morning."

"Thanks, Doc," said Randy. "I'll take care of Mom. You take care of Dad; and we'll all get through this. We appreciate what you've done."

"It's a privilege," Doctor Johnstone said, as he rose to leave. "Good night. The nurses will call you at home if there's any change in Mr. Walker's condition."

Cheri hurried back to the phone to call Chip to tell him the surgery was over and his dad was fine. Shortly after ten, Paul was wheeled into ICU. Randy and Cheri were relieved to see him. They coaxed a weak smile from him, kissed him good night, and made their weary way home.

Randy made a phone call to his wife Gail in Des Moines to let her know that Dad had pulled through. She told him the kids were already in bed. "I'll plan to drive home Sunday night if Dad seems to be doing okay tomorrow." He blew her a kiss through the phone and she whispered, "Good night; I love you."

40

TRINITY HEARS THE NEWS

Sunday, September 11

Sunday morning, the church was buzzing. Everyone was sharing the news about the pastor's heart attack and bypass surgery. Almost as pervasive were discussions about terrorism, the tenth anniversary of 9/11, and the attack last year on Trinity. Pastor Lambert was still in Minneapolis and would not be back until Tuesday. Pastor Hobart was gracious enough to fill in on an emergency basis. He was eighty years old, or close to it, and spoke so softly and slowly that older members had trouble hearing him. Those who could hear him wished he would pick up the pace and get the words out. Everyone was grateful, however, and showed him patience and appreciation for leading worship.

He introduced himself, welcomed everyone, and then told the congregation why he was leading worship this morning. "As some of you already know, Pastor Walker had a severe heart attack yesterday while playing golf. He was taken to the hospital and had a triple bypass surgery."

In the eighth pew back, sitting next to the aisle, Brianna Holloway buried her face in her hands in shock, and began to pray silently, *No,*

God, no! You can't let him die now. Please help him to be okay. I just found my dad. You wouldn't take him from me now! She realized Pastor Paul would not show up for the afternoon appointment. This was to be their last meeting before the wedding, and perhaps for the foreseeable future. She had so much to tell him. There was still so much about him and his family that she wanted to know. This just wasn't fair!

"I'll ask Howard Bardwell, the council president, to give you some more information." Pastor Hobart sat down.

Howard walked to the front of the church and spoke from the lectern. "Good morning everyone, I spoke just a few minutes ago with the pastor's wife at the hospital. Cheri reports this morning that the pastor is resting and doing okay after his surgery. She asked that flowers not be sent because of hospital regulations for the Intensive Care Unit, but I'm sure a card would be appreciated to let them know we are all praying for them. Jeannette, our office administrator, will stay in touch with the Walkers, and she'll try to keep us all informed. Please keep Pastor Paul and Cheri in your prayers this week."

The service moved through the hymns, scriptures, creed and prayers. As the retired pastor prayed for Pastor Walker and Cheri, Brianna decided she would be brave and go and see him at the hospital immediately after church. She didn't hear much of the service, the pastor talked so slowly, and her mind was not able to focus on what was happening in church. She thought of the conversations they had had so far, the stories he had told about Brian and her mom and Bob. It really helped her understand why she and her mom and sister were so very close. And though she couldn't fully comprehend what had happened between her mom and the pastor, it had happened. And she whispered to herself, *I'm glad it happened. I wouldn't be here otherwise.* Then she prayed again for Paul, for her dad. *Please God, let him pull through. Let him recover so he can enjoy the fact that I'm getting married and want to have a family of my own.*

When the final hymn was over, Brianna left quickly and avoided shaking hands with Pastor Hobart. She headed for the parking lot and got into her Honda. In less than half an hour she was at the hospital, in front of the information desk, asking how to find Pastor Paul Walker.

The nurse indicated he was in ICU and that visiting time there was limited. She was told to check with the nurse on duty, and given directions to the unit.

At the intercom outside the ICU doors, she spoke nervously, "I'm here to see Pastor Paul Walker?" "Just a moment please," came the response. A few seconds later, the door opened automatically and she walked through. It was scary. There were half a dozen rooms with sliding glass doors, and a large nursing area with computers and phones on the desk. She approached the unit secretary. "May I see Paul Walker?" she asked hesitantly.

"Are you a family member?" the secretary asked.

Brianna hesitated a moment, then answered, "Yes, I'm his daughter."

"Mr. Walker is in room D, right over there. His nurse will answer your questions."

Brianna walked slowly toward room D. Her knees felt weak. She stood at the doorway and stared at the equipment. A funny clicking, whooshing noise was all she could hear. The nurse was typing notes on a computer. Noticing the slight movement near the door, she turned and asked, "May I help you?"

"I came to see … my dad," Brianna answered from the door.

"Come in. Your mom was here just a few minutes ago, did you see her?" the nurse asked.

"No, I just got here. How is he?" Brianna didn't really pay attention to what the nurse had said; her mind was focused on Pastor Paul.

"Actually, your dad is doing very well. He was awake for quite a while this morning. He's not able to talk because of the 'trache' which is helping him breathe. These wires are monitoring his heart. There's a continuous reading of his blood pressure, and the IV line is to keep him hydrated. He's also on IV antibiotic to prevent infection. Have you ever been in an Intensive Care Unit before?"

"No...I haven't. He almost looks ... d...dead!" Brianna stammered, on the verge of tears.

"I assure you, he is doing quite well. This equipment just helps support all his systems while he's resting and recovering."

"Can I talk to him? Will he hear me?"

"Yes, come up next to him and speak clearly. He may even open his eyes. Would you like a few minutes of privacy?"

"That would be nice. Thank you," Brianna said, managing a weak smile.

"Just be careful of the lines and tubes," the nurse instructed as she left the room.

"I will," Brianna said as she moved toward Paul's bed. Tears came to her eyes. "Oh, Daddy. This is so strange. I've been enjoying our talks so much. I was looking forward to this afternoon." Paul's eyes remained shut.

As his nurse moved behind the main desk, Cheri returned, coming through the ICU doors as they hissed open. "Oh, Mrs. Walker!" the nurse said, "Your daughter just arrived."

"Did you say my daughter?" Cheri asked with a puzzled frown.

"Well, she said she was your daughter," the nurse responded.

"I don't have a daughter!" Cheri replied. "I wonder who she is? Maybe my daughter-in-law came from Des Moines." Cheri was perplexed as she walked to the doorway of room D. She stood at the doorway a moment and stared at the back of a young woman leaning over Paul's bed. *I suppose she's a church member, but I don't recognize her.* She listened as the young woman spoke to Paul.

"You're not going to die, are you? The nurse said you're getting better. Dad... can you open your eyes? I know we're still just friends, but I hope God will let us have more time together. I really want to get to know you. And I want you to get to know me. I am so excited about the wedding! And I'm so glad you got to meet Guy. I knew you'd love him. He's a wonderful man.... Just like you." Brianna was trying hard to control her emotions.

Cheri stood in stunned silence.

"I know I'm not supposed to visit very long," Brianna continued speaking to Paul. "I'm not sure what to say, or if you're able to hear me. I guess I'll just say a prayer and go. Dear God, I believe there is a reason you have brought us together. Please help my dad recover. There's so much I want to share with him. Please God, make him better. Amen."

Paul opened his eyes. Brianna gasped, "Did you hear me?" Paul nodded to indicate he had heard. Brianna's eyes filled with tears. "You're going to be okay. I just know you're going to be fine. I love you, Dad." She leaned over the bed and gave him a kiss on his cheek.

Cheri backed out of the doorway toward the nurses' desk. She was dumbfounded. *What in the world did I just witness?* Brianna came out of room D and walked toward Cheri. "Who are you?" Cheri asked, her voice quivering.

Brianna looked at her with a puzzled expression on her face. Then she realized whom she was facing. *Oh my God, this must be Pastor Paul's wife!* "Hi, Mrs. Walker? My name is Brianna."

Cheri stared at her for a few moments. "I heard you speaking to my husband a few moments ago. You were calling him 'Dad.' What's going on?"

Brianna started shaking. "Maybe we should find a place to sit down."

"There's a waiting room just down the hall," Cheri said, somewhat annoyed. "My son Randy is there. You've got some explaining to do!"

As they left ICU and walked down the hall, Brianna said, "Pastor Paul told me he had two sons."

"That's right," Cheri replied curtly, "Chip and Randy. Chip is married and lives in California. Randy is married and lives in Des

Moines." They entered the waiting room and Randy stood up to meet them. "Randy, this is ....what did you say your name was?"

"Brianna Holloway." She put her hand out; Randy shook it.

"Holloway?" Cheri questioned. "We used to have members of our church named Holloway."

"Marge Holloway is my mom," Brianna responded.

Cheri looked startled and puzzled as she remembered the name. Her mind began racing to put the pieces of the puzzle together. "Marge was a very good friend of mine. How is she?" Cheri, Randy, and Brianna sat down in separate chairs, Randy next to Cheri, and Brianna across from them. Sunlight was streaming brightly through the waiting room window.

"Mom's fine, really great. Right now she's excited about my wedding! I'm getting married December 10th."

"Congratulations!" interjected Randy. "Who are you visiting here in the hospital?"

"Your dad," Brianna replied.

"You know my dad?" Randy asked.

"I guess she does;" Cheri cut in, "she was calling him 'Dad'."

"What??!" asked Randy, really confused.

"I overheard her in ICU. She was leaning over Paul's bed talking to him. She called him 'Dad.' And if my eyes weren't deceiving me, she gave him a kiss on the cheek! I'd like to know, young lady, what's going on?" Cheri's voice was icy cold.

"It's a long story," Brianna began. "My mom and dad, I mean Marge and Bob, separated after Brian was killed. Then my mom had me. Then...let's see...then I was planning to get married this year and mom finally told me that Bob wasn't my father; Pastor Paul was."

"I don't think so," Cheri replied angrily. "Paul and I have been very happily married for almost thirty years, and to my knowledge he has NEVER been unfaithful!" Randy stared at his mom, then at Brianna. The two of them were staring at each other.

"I know that Paul never told you. He didn't even know I existed! He and I have been meeting in his office on Sunday afternoons for several months now. He was as shocked as you are when he found out! I'm terribly sorry to have to tell you. He was struggling with whether or not to tell you about me. I promised him that I wouldn't say anything to anyone. I'm so sorry."

Cheri continued staring at Brianna. She couldn't believe what she was hearing. *A daughter? Marge Holloway? How? When? Why?* She struggled to find words, to sort out the barrage of feelings that flooded her soul. "You're telling me that Paul and your mom had an affair?" she finally asked.

"No....not exactly," Brianna stammered. "They both told me the same thing...that they were only together once! It was right after Brian was killed. Mom was so upset! She said Pastor Paul was just trying to comfort her; and... well... one thing led to another. Mom said that Paul never knew she was pregnant. She moved to Chicago and that's where I was born. Mom never told Bob either."

"This is too much! Marge and Paul? I can't believe it! ARE YOU SURE?" Cheri asked. She wanted to verify this story with Paul, but he was in no condition to deal with a situation like this!

"I know Mom wouldn't lie to me about something as important as this! She let me assume that Bob was my father for many years. I guess when I told her I was getting married, she decided I was old enough to finally know the truth."

"Whoa!" Randy finally spoke. "If that's true, then I guess that means you're my sister...or half-sister ...or something like that. Whoa! This is crazy!"

"I know," said Brianna. "I thought it was crazy too; that after all these years I have another family that I didn't even know about. Originally, I just wanted to meet my real dad and get to know him a little bit. I liked Pastor Paul the first time I heard him at church. Then, after we talked in his office, I really appreciated his helping me understand what happened to my mom." Brianna paused as Cheri continued staring at her. Slowly, and reluctantly, Cheri was beginning to believe that what Brianna was telling them was the truth. "I'm sorry. I never meant for you to find out," Brianna confessed, looking at Cheri.

"I can't believe Paul never told me about meeting with you! And I'm sick that he never told me about what happened with Marge!" Sick was only one of the feelings Cheri was struggling with. Betrayed was another. Embarrassed for Randy was another. Confused, another. Cheri stared blankly at the patterns made by the sunlight on the waiting room floor. *Paul never told me. Paul didn't trust me? Paul and Marge?*

Brianna's head was down; she too was staring at the sunshine on the carpet. Neither was really seeing it.

Cheri's mind was racing back twenty years to that terrible time when their church custodian, Brian Holloway, was brutally murdered in the church. *It was a crazy time; everyone in the church was upset. I remember admiring Paul for holding up so well under the strain. Ha! Chip and Randy were so young. I had all I could do to cope with being a wife, a mother, and a business manager in an office full of crazy attorneys.* Suddenly her mind jumped back to the present and she felt anger beginning to rise again. *I wonder if Paul's heart attack was brought on by the stress of finding out he had a daughter?*

"How long has Paul known about you?" Cheri asked.

"We've met three or four times. The first time was in June, about three months ago. We were supposed to meet this afternoon, but then I heard the announcement in church this morning about his heart attack."

"Was he upset when he found out? I mean about having a daughter?" Cheri questioned Brianna again, not remembering what Brianna had said about Paul's first reaction.

"Well, at first, he was shocked, and he admitted he was worried about what I'd do."

"Then?"

"Then? Well, ...I told him I didn't want to cause any trouble. Then he kind of calmed down and we just started talking. You know, like, getting to know each other. I wanted to hear what happened to Brian, and how it was between him and Mom."

Realizing she was angry, Cheri struggled to be polite. "Forgive me if I've been rude. I guess this is pretty shocking to me too." Cheri fought to keep her feelings under control. She wanted to scream or cry or run; she didn't know which. She wanted to scream, cry, AND run!

"It's not the end of the world, Mom," Randy interjected.

"I certainly hope not," Cheri said icily, as she shot a rather disgusted look toward her son.

"I'm the one who should apologize," Brianna responded. "I didn't mean to cause trouble. I was just curious, mostly. ...I'm really sorry."

"Just give us some time to think this through," Cheri said as she continued struggling to gain her composure. The sun streaming through the windows caught her attention again as it reflected brightly off an end table and lamp.

Brianna knew there was nothing more to say. It was slowly sinking in that she had betrayed a trust, broken a promise, and quite possibly ruined a marriage. "I guess I'll be going. Please tell Pastor Paul I'm sorry."

Cheri sat shaking her head. She couldn't bring herself to get out of the chair as Brianna rose and moved quietly down the hall.

"I'm really sorry, Mom," Randy said as he reached over and put a hand on his mom's arm. "Do you believe her?"

"I guess. I'm not sure. I think I'm just in shock."

"You still love Dad as much as ever, don't you?"

"I guess, honey.... I guess."

They sat staring, Randy at the floor and Cheri at the window. "I'm going into ICU to see Dad," Randy finally said.

"Don't say anything about this. Your dad can hear, you know."

"I know, Mom, I know."

41

PAUL'S RECOVERY

Sunday evening Paul showed signs of stability; he was still on the ventilator and couldn't talk. No bleeding problems had developed in the area of his surgery. Around 7 p.m. Randy came into the unit for his final visit. Paul grabbed his hand and held it firmly. "Dad, I want to tell you how glad we are that you're doing so well. I told Gail that if you were doing well, I'd drive home this evening, so I think I'll head back to Des Moines."

Paul put his palms together, pointed his hands toward Randy, and closed his eyes.

"You want me to pray?" Randy asked.

Paul nodded yes.

"Heavenly Father, we are thankful for Dad's progress today, and for the care of the doctors and nurses in this hospital. I know he is in Your hands and that Your will is always for healing, and so I pray Thy will be done. Bless Dad and Mom, and our entire family, and the people of Trinity. Help Dad not to worry. Grant me a safe trip home to Gail, Trevor, and Joy. Amen."

Paul reached out again and squeezed his son's hand. Then he put his own hand to the oxygen mask and blew Randy a kiss.

"Thanks, Dad, I love you." Randy could feel the moisture in his eyes and a lump in his throat as he left the room, the eerie sound of the respirator echoing in his ears.

****

Cheri's job as financial manager for the public library was funded by the county. It was much less stressful than at the law firm and the benefits were good. She called the library on Monday morning to let everyone know that Paul's recovery seemed to be going well according to the nurses and doctor. She told them she would spend the morning at the hospital, then come by and work a few hours in the afternoon. "Paul might be more awake today," she said.

In ICU Paul looked like a new man. Doctor Johnstone had removed the stomach tube and the ventilator. "He's breathing on his own," he said to Cheri as she walked by the desk. "He'll be on IV's for another day or two, and then he can start eating, slowly. He should be home by the end of the week."

"That's wonderful news," Cheri sighed as she walked to Paul's door. It was time to "put on a happy face," as her mother used to say. Paul's face lit up as she came through the door.

"Look, honey, it's me!" Paul nearly shouted, hoarsely but proudly. "I'm alive and I'm almost human again! No more tubes!"

"Yeah, you look a lot better than yesterday," Cheri smiled and leaned over to kiss him. "Look at all the cards that came in the mail! Some were brought from the church by Howard Bardwell," she said as she set the pile of greetings on the bedside table.

"You know, the nurses got me sitting up on the edge of the bed this morning. I thought they were trying to kill me! My chest hurt from the incision and so does my leg."

"They sure don't waste any time, do they?" Cheri sympathized.

"My nurse says they'll move me to Cardiac Care tonight or tomorrow."

"That's great, sweetheart. I'm so proud of you!" Cheri's heart skipped a beat as she heard what she had just said. *Proud of you? What a lie! Right now I am nothing but ashamed and mad. How could I have said that? Well, I am glad he's recovering, but right now, PROUD wasn't the word to use.*

She spent the morning sitting next to him, and the nurse didn't say anything about limiting her visitation times. As long as Paul was fairly quiet, it didn't seem to matter. Cheri had brought a book, and made an occasional comment to Paul. He was dozing most of the time and responding with a sleepy, "Uh-huh." About one in the afternoon, Cheri slipped away for lunch and a trip to the library office. She worked a few hours, drove home and fell asleep on the sofa. She woke an hour later and realized how emotionally exhausted she must be. She looked in the refrigerator for something to eat but didn't feel hungry. Finally, she scooped some ice cream into a dish, wolfed it down, and drove to the hospital. Paul was watching a game show on TV which meant he was a little more awake. Cheri took her seat next to the bed and stared blankly at the TV screen. Around nine o'clock she could see him dozing more and more deeply. She kissed him good night and went home.

* * * * * * *

The next day, Paul was transferred to the Cardiac Care Unit where they continued to monitor his heart. "Time to get you walking," his nurse said as she arranged the monitor leads and IV. Paul felt extremely dizzy as he stood next to the bed. "Just wait 'til the dizziness passes," the nurse said patiently. "I'll steady you when you're ready to take a step or two. We're only going to the door and back."

Cheri stopped at the library, reviewed some book purchase orders, and then headed to the hospital. She was delighted to see that Paul had been moved to CCU and was up and walking. The sun was shining brightly through his window. He seemed alert and talkative, and she knew she couldn't hold her new information any longer. "Paul, I have something to tell you. I hope it doesn't kill you; but let me tell you, it nearly killed me!"

Paul could tell Cheri was serious and thought at first that the doctor must have given her some bad news about his heart. A look of concern filled his eyes. He tried to prepare himself for the worst. "Go ahead, tell me."

"I met your daughter." Cheri waited. She stared at Paul, but saw no reaction. "I met Brianna, Brianna Holloway…Marge's and your daughter!" Cheri could feel her anger welling inside her. She waited for a response from her husband. Paul closed his eyes. The truth he had dared not share was out. What could he say?

"This is probably not the best time to tell you this, Paul, but I am shocked and disappointed and hurt and…. I don't know what else," Cheri stammered, "and angry!" Paul's eyes remained shut. "Paul!" Cheri shouted, "Are you listening to me?"

"Yes…yes, I've heard everything you said. I just don't know what to say except, I'm sorry. I am so sorry."

"How could you? How could you have done that? And not told me," Cheri was on the verge of tears.

Paul began to cry. His emotions were already on edge from the surgery. "I am so sorry. I never meant to hurt you." His sobbing increased. "I am so sorry. Please believe me, I'm so sorry," Paul sobbed. The pain he had been trying to avoid was suddenly here, the pain in his stomach and the pain in his heart. The secret he had hoped to keep…. was no longer a secret.

A nurse came through the door. "We're getting some unusual readings on the monitor at the desk; thought I'd better check." Paul and Cheri were silent. The nurse examined the leads, put her fingers on Paul's wrist to check his pulse and compared it to the monitor. "Your pulse is way up there. How do you feel?" she asked.

"I'm a little emotional right now, but I'll be okay," Paul answered.

"That happens a lot after surgery," the nurse replied. "We'll keep an eye on you, and please let us know if there's anything you need." With a smile and nod to Cheri, she left the room.

At this point Paul was more concerned about his wife than about his heart. His good wife, worried about his health, now had to cope with yet another blow. "God help me," he prayed aloud, "and God help and bless Cheri."

Cheri leaned back in the hospital chair and closed her eyes. Neither said a word for the next hour. Their emotions were raw, and neither knew what to say next. Finally, Paul spoke, "How did you find out?"

"Brianna Holloway was apparently at church Sunday morning when your heart attack was announced. She came to the hospital after church to see you, and that's when I met her. That's when she told me about you and Marge."

"What about Chip and Randy? Do they know?" Paul asked regretfully.

"Randy already knows; he was here Sunday when Brianna introduced herself to us." Cheri looked at him, "So I guess I'll call Chip and fill him in as well."

"Cheri, I'm so sorry I never told you. I tried to, I really did, but I didn't want to hurt you. I should have trusted you. I should have known you'd find out eventually." Again Paul began sobbing.

"Take it easy, Paul. You need to concentrate on your recovery. We can always talk through this Brianna situation another time. She told me she's getting married soon."

"Yeah, how 'bout that." Paul smiled weakly. Tears flowed down the cheeks of both of them, and Cheri noticed that the sun was shining brightly through the window and reflecting off Paul's tears and wet cheeks.

* * * * * * *

When Paul was released on Friday Cheri made her decision to take the following week off work. Part of her wanted nothing to do with Paul, the betrayer; but her conscience told her she should care for Paul, her husband. Before leaving the library Friday morning, she told the director she wouldn't be in on Monday, but to call her at home if she needed anything. It had rained overnight and the wind had brought down a lot of leaves and small branches. The streets were glistening from the rain and the sky was still overcast.

Paul was glad to see her and glad to be going home. The hours in the Cardiac Care Unit had passed so slowly, and yet Paul could hardly believe he was going home less than a week after his heart attack and surgery.

At home he was amazed to see several bouquets of flowers scattered around the living room and one in the bedroom as well. "The ones in the living room are from church members, mostly; that one's from the library staff;" Cheri told him, "and the bouquet in the bedroom is from Chip, Randy, and me."

"You didn't need to do that," Paul sighed with embarrassment. "You've done plenty with all your hospital visits, and everything else to keep my spirits up."

"It was Chip's idea really. He asked me to buy the flowers and then Randy said he wanted to chip in, and I decided to make it a three-way deal."

Paul tugged Cheri's arm and kissed her on the cheek. "Thanks, sweetheart, the flowers are beautiful."

"By the way," Cheri responded, "did I tell you, Chip and Linda have decided they are definitely coming for Christmas?"

"No, but it'll be great to see them. Still no baby on the way?" Paul asked.

"Not that I've heard," Cheri replied.

That afternoon, Paul took a long nap in the bedroom while Cheri baked a batch of chocolate chip cookies. When he came out to the living room he could smell the first batch of cookies which Cheri had just taken out of the oven. Paul was dressed in blue jeans and a loose fitting sweat shirt. "Well look at you!" Cheri said with a smile. "You decided to put on some clothes?"

"I was so sick of the hospital gown and pajamas! I decided since I was home that it was time to get dressed." Cheri sat down with Paul in the living room and they talked about how blessed they were, though Cheri was still feeling uncomfortable. Paul was concerned about church, and Cheri reassured him that everything was being taken care of. "Howard has called every day to ask about you and to report on committee meetings at the church. Jeannette has called a couple of times and said Pastor Barbara is back in town and is ready to lead worship this Sunday. The bishop called and said he put your name on the synod prayer list. Your golfing buddy, Carl, called again last night just to see how you were doing. Please, Paul, no church business for at least another week," Cheri pleaded.

"I suppose that would be best. I know I'm weak, but I could make phone calls."

"No phone calls! No nothin'!" Cheri shouted.

"Okay, okay. I'm sorry," Paul said sheepishly. "It's so hard to let go."

"Oh, stop apologizing all the time! I get sick of listening to you saying you're sorry, you're sorry!" Cheri realized immediately that she was angry, not just about Paul's apologies, but was still upset about the Holloway situation. Paul also sensed that something else was bothering Cheri, and he was pretty sure he knew what.

After a while he spoke, "Speaking of apologies, I need to get this whole thing about Brianna out on the table."

"You need to? You need to?" Cheri said sarcastically. "What about my needs?"

"Well," said Paul hesitatingly, "that's precisely why I never told you about me and Marge."

"I don't get it," Cheri said, her teeth still clenched.

"Let me tell you, first of all, why I never told you about it. Then, if you want me to, I'll tell you exactly what happened between Marge and me."

"I'm listening," Cheri said, staring into Paul's eyes.

Paul thought for a few minutes to get his thoughts in order. He wanted to be honest. He wanted to be open and forthright, but not say any more than necessary. "My friend Isaac, you remember the rabbi, asked me whether I needed to tell you because of MY guilt, or whether I should tell you because YOU needed to know. My need or your need? I decided I needed to forgive myself, and perhaps, you didn't need to know."

"Yeah, right. So, what exactly was going on between you and Marge?"

"A month or so after Brian died, I can't remember exactly how long, I went to see Marge at home. She wanted to be held, and I wanted to console her."

"But, Paul, you don't console someone by going to bed with them!"

"I know, I know. I was selfish and curious, and weak and stupid. Please believe me; it was only one time."

"Yeah, right. It's always…only one time," Cheri said sarcastically.

Paul knew it was pointless to argue. "Maybe I should have told you at the time, but I hoped it would never come to this."

"Just like you hoped Marge wouldn't become pregnant. I still don't understand why you didn't tell me. Don't you trust your wife?"

"I do trust you…. and I did then. I didn't know Marge was pregnant. But I knew my failure would hurt you. And… the bottom line is… I didn't want to risk losing you…" Paul choked back his tears, "…then… or now."

Cheri thought for a few minutes. "I guess I see the logic. You were afraid that if you told me, you might lose me. But don't you see that not telling me means you didn't trust that my love was strong enough?"

"Well, yes, I see that now. I kept hoping you would never find out. As the months went by, the guilt and shame gradually faded. I knew God forgave me, but I struggled to forgive myself. The Holloways moved away, and I thought the issue would never come up again," Paul continued. "It seemed like the rabbi was right."

"Until Brianna," Cheri interjected.

"Until Brianna," Paul agreed.

They sat together in silence, listening to the rain which had started again and was drumming on the roof. "Is there anything else I can do or say?" Paul asked remorsefully. "Is there anything else you want to know?" Paul waited for Cheri's answer.

"Not right now," Cheri replied. After a few minutes she got up and went to the kitchen, came back and set a plate of chocolate chip cookies on the end table next to Paul. Without a word, she returned to the kitchen and began washing the bowl, baking utensils and pans.

* * * * * * *

On Sunday afternoon Paul and Cheri had several visitors from church. First, Howard, the council president, stopped by. He brought a card signed by all the council members. Paul's emotions were extremely fragile. He cried easily, overwhelmed by the caring and support of those for whom he cared so much. Next, Sheila, the choir director, and her husband John, came to visit. She shared how worship had gone and told Pastor Paul how much they missed him. Cheri was extremely watchful for signs of flirtation, but Sheila was sincere, and well-behaved in her husband's presence.

Pastor Barbara dropped by later in the afternoon, prayed for Paul and Cheri, and gave them communion. She could not know that Paul and Cheri were thinking not only of his surgery, but also of his shame.

As she spoke the words, "The body of Christ given for you," Paul could not hold back the tears; and seeing Paul cry made Cheri's eyes fill with tears also.

* * * * * * *

Over the next few weeks Paul regained his strength and energy. He was thankful for Pastor Barbara and the fine work she was doing during his recovery. Cheri drove him to Dr. Johnstone's office for a follow-up appointment and the doctor gave him permission to drive and to return to work, no more than twenty hours a week, beginning one month after the date of his surgery. Paul was elated. He was tired of reading library books, and his twice a week conversations with Jeannette didn't satisfy his need to get back to the office.

There was no further word from Brianna, soon to be Mrs. Brianna Spencer.

42

A TIME APART

As Paul regained his strength, Cheri urged him to follow the doctor's advice on his diet and exercise. The habit of an ice cream sundae two or three evenings a week was the first to go. The Friday evening pizza routine was changed slightly as Paul began making larger salads and smaller pizzas. Paul vowed to walk every evening after supper and invited Cheri to join him. She agreed from time to time, but on some nights she chose not to walk, preferring to stay home to wash dishes.

In November Paul tried working full time, but found that he was extremely tired by three or four in the afternoon. It was especially difficult to go back to the church after supper for an evening meeting. The autumn days became shorter as did the conversations between Paul and his wife. He sensed that Cheri was still upset about Brianna, but she wouldn't talk about it. She seemed to be withdrawing, and Paul was reminded of how painful it had been for Marge when Bob withdrew from her. Much to his chagrin, Paul found himself thinking about Marge more than seemed appropriate. Perhaps it was seeing Brianna, and hearing about her mother, after not thinking about her for nineteen years, that made Paul curious to see Marge again. He dismissed the thought as both foolish and dangerous. He certainly didn't want to make Cheri any more upset than she already was.

It was getting dark at four-thirty when Cheri came home from work. Paul set the table, warmed up some leftovers, and opened a can of fruit. He and Cheri sat down to eat a little after five. He asked how her day had gone and learned that the library board of directors had contracted with an architect for an enlargement of the children's library. Cheri talked about how that would impact the present facility and staff, and finally asked Paul how things were going at church.

"The letters have gone out to the congregation for the fall stewardship emphasis. We hope to have commitments returned before Thanksgiving. In fact, I've got a meeting tonight with the steering committee planning Commitment Sunday."

"Will you have time for your walk?" Cheri asked.

"Sure, we're eating early tonight," Paul replied.

"I think I'll do the dishes while you're walking," Cheri responded.

The two of them cleared the table, and Paul went into the bedroom to put on his walking shoes and a light, down-filled jacket. As he came back through the kitchen, he passed by the sink and gave Cheri a kiss on the cheek. He was disappointed that it wasn't returned.

* * * * * * *

The wind was blowing and the air was chilly; the first snow could be expected any day. Paul walked briskly, thankful that his strength was returning after surgery. He could still feel a tightness across his chest, more from the incision than from his heart. He was in no hurry, since the meeting wasn't until seven o'clock, so he added another block to his usual route.

Upon arriving back at the house he overheard Cheri on the phone in the guest bedroom. "That sounds great!" she was saying. "You know I'm not fussy about meals. ....That's right; I really need to get away." Paul kept listening as he went into the master bedroom to remove his jacket and change his shoes. "No, you don't have to worry about that. C'mon, you know me better than that!" He tried to imagine with whom she was talking. "Yes, I think the timing is perfect! I appreciate it so much! ....Love you too."

"Is that you, Paul?" Cheri hollered after hanging up the phone. "How was your walk?"

"Great, but kind of chilly," Paul answered. "Who was that on the phone?"

Cheri came into the bedroom where Paul was putting on shoes and a sport coat for the meeting at the church. "I just got through talking to Randy. He and Gail have invited us to come to Des Moines for a week including Thanksgiving."

"That's nice, but I've got services on Sunday, and on Wednesday evening, Thanksgiving Eve. And I really hate to take a week off when it's the busiest time of the church year!"

"I know," Cheri looked at Paul with a devilish grin. "So I told Randy that I'd come by myself. Besides, I really need some time away."

"Away from me?" Paul asked, feeling rather hurt.

"Away, away. Just away from everything here, not just you. I need some time to think. And pray."

Paul was getting more and more nervous. "You're not thinking of leaving me permanently, are you?" Paul asked hesitantly.

"I'd be lying if I told you the thought hadn't crossed my mind," Cheri said.

"Ouch!" Paul replied.

"Yeah, ouch!" Cheri repeated.

"I've hurt you, I know. And it doesn't seem that anything I say can make up for what happened," Paul admitted defensively.

"No, there isn't. Not at this point. I think the ball's in my court," Cheri answered.

Paul was really uncomfortable. "I guess I'll get going. I'll probably have to unlock the church before the committee arrives."

"Have a good meeting." Cheri turned and walked from the bedroom to the living room, picked up the remote and turned on the evening news.

* * * * * * *

Cheri cleared her schedule at the library and left for Des Moines on Friday, a week before Thanksgiving. Paul told a few key people that Cheri was going to visit their son and family, and knew the word would travel by word of mouth through the church community. Everyone figured it was timed with Paul's recovery and his ability to care for himself. Only Randy and Gail, and of course Paul, knew Cheri's very personal reason for getting away.

The next ten days were some of the longest and loneliest in Paul's life. It gave him reason to think deeply about his relationship with Cheri, and about the error in judgment he had made twenty years ago. Evenings at home seemed especially dark and long. Some nights he dismissed his fears as silly worry. *Cheri wouldn't leave me; we've been married too long. We have too much invested in our life together.* But some nights he was certain that his marriage was about to end. *The trust has been betrayed and broken. I can understand why Cheri might feel she can never trust me again. I'm simply going to have to face the possibility that my life will be different from now on. I'll have to adjust to being divorced and single again. I can do it! Yuck!* Without Cheri beside him in bed at night, Paul slept restlessly and prayed for her return, and the return of her trust and good spirits.

Cheri was also finding it hard to sleep. She was having her own ambivalent thoughts and feelings. She wanted everything to be the way it used to be, but she knew it couldn't be, and never would be, quite the same. *Paul has a daughter. Not my daughter; Marge's daughter. How will I ever accept that? How will I ever get through this? I love Paul, but will I ever trust him again?*

* * * * * * *

Thanksgiving Day dawned bright with a thin layer of fresh snow on the ground in Des Moines. Cheri didn't sleep too well, thinking about Paul and the Thanksgiving Eve Worship at Trinity. She was up early, dressed, and had the coffee made before any of the kids awoke. Randy and Gail dressed the children for an early church service at nine a.m. They asked Grandma Cheri to play with Joy and Trevor while they got dressed and ready to go. Randy drove the five of them to the church, and the children threw a few snowballs at Grandma in the church parking lot! Cheri loved having Joy on her lap during part of the service, and helping Trevor with his crayons and coloring book. She fought hard not to cry throughout the service as her heart overflowed with thanksgiving for her sons and their wives, and these two precious grandchildren.

After church, Gail and Cheri got busy in the kitchen preparing the Thanksgiving turkey while Randy played some games and then ended up wrestling with Trevor and Joy on the living room floor. While the kids were resting in their beds for an hour or so before dinner, the phone rang. Cheri thought for sure it would be Paul and listened as Gail answered.

"Oh, hi Chip! Happy Thanksgiving to you too!"

Cheri was excited to talk to her other son, but Gail yelled, "Randy, get on the other phone!" Cheri could only stand by and listen.

"No!.. Really?....Wow! Oh my gosh! Congratulations! Oh, that's wonderful news! Hold on a minute, I'll put Cheri on the phone!" Gail handed the receiver to her mother-in-law.

"Happy Thanksgiving, Chip and Linda!" Cheri shouted, "Now what's the good news I'm overhearing? ...You're expecting a baby? When? ...Oh that's great! I'm so happy for you! Have you picked out any names yet?" Cheri could hardly contain herself. "Linda, how have you been feeling?"

There was one more question Cheri was anxious to ask, "Are you still planning on coming home for Christmas? ...You are? ...Oh, I'm so excited! What? No, Dad's not here; he's at home. He had a worship service last night. ...No, I've been here a week. I've had a wonderful visit with Gail and Randy and the kids!"

Chip and Linda had a request, "Can you keep this a secret until we come home? We'd love to tell Dad and see his reaction! … Sure, you can tell him we're definitely coming for Christmas."

Cheri promised, "I won't tell Paul about the baby. It'll be hard keeping my excitement under control for almost a month, but I'll do my best!"

****

After dinner, Cheri played with Joy and Trevor while Randy helped Gail clean up the kitchen. When Randy came in the living room to watch a football game, Cheri excused herself and said she'd like to spend some time alone in her room reading and praying. Gail cuddled up next to Randy until half-time and then had to break up a squabble between Trevor and Joy.

After tucking the grandchildren into bed, Cheri returned to her room and put on a nightgown. She lay on the bed, thinking and praying again about Paul, and Marge, and Brianna, and how very bad it all was. It was during this time of meditation late on Thanksgiving Day that a strange peace began to come over Cheri. She thought at first that it might be emotional exhaustion. *I'm so tired of trying to decide what to do!* Then she realized it was something much deeper. *Life is messy; so what? Marge dealt with her messy situation as best she could. Paul got himself in trouble, but he dealt with his mess as best he could. I'm in a mess right now, emotionally, deal with it. Stop feeling sorry for yourself. Brianna is getting married; she deserves a good life and as much support as possible. Her life will be messy too someday. Paul and I have so much to be thankful for, and excited about. I don't want to ruin any of that. I don't want to leave Paul, not for Randy and Gail's sake, not for Trevor and Joy's sake, not for Chip and Linda's sake…and last but not least, what the heck good would it do for me? Why leave? To punish Paul? Because I never want to be hurt again? No, I'm staying, and I'm going to be happy again. I'm not going to let this thing from the past ruin my future! I won't!* Cheri began to cry.

The peace she felt settled in. It felt right. It felt good. She felt like crying, so she let herself cry. She grabbed the pillow from the bed and buried her face in it and let the tears and sobs flow freely. This time, her tears were full of joy and gratitude. Cheri cried herself to sleep. For the first time in a long time, she felt right and it felt very good.

* * * * * * *

The roads were clear when Cheri drove back on Sunday. She left Randy's house after worshiping with them once more. She was looking forward to seeing Paul. It would be like a new beginning for them. As she approached Weston, she prayed that her peace would bring him some peace as well. *What did the Jews call it? Shalom.* She was excited about preparing for Christmas.

43

CHRISTMAS AT THE WALKERS'

The Advent and Christmas seasons at Trinity were always beautiful. A large fir tree with white lights and white chrismons stood in one corner of the chancel. The choir was at its strongest and best, with all the rehearsals for a Christmas cantata. Sheila seemed more focused on rehearsals and less on men. The children were busy preparing for a Christmas pageant. The Walkers had many reasons to celebrate. Paul was feeling like his old self again and back to a full time schedule at church. Cheri seemed happy decorating and baking for the holidays, and there was no evidence of any bitterness toward Paul.

Chip and Linda arrived from California on the 22nd and couldn't wait to share their exciting news. Cheri pretended to be hearing it for the first time. "Linda and I are expecting a baby! We had an ultrasound done just before we came, but it was too soon to tell if it's a boy or girl! The baby is due in June. You'll be grandparents again!"

"What wonderful news!" Cheri exclaimed.

For reasons even Paul could not fully understand, he began crying.

"C'mon Dad, we thought this would make you happy!" Chip exclaimed.

"I am happy," Paul laughed through his tears. He was thinking to himself how he might not have lived to hear this exciting announcement. Wine was poured and Paul made a toast to the new, first-time parents! Linda politely declined the alcohol, but lifted her glass of water.

Randy and Gail, Trevor and Joy, arrived from Des Moines on the 24th. They confessed to Paul that they already knew about Chip and Linda's baby. As everyone visited, Randy and Chip began acting like teenage brothers, poking each other, teasing and taunting. Linda and Gail spent most of the day with Cheri in the kitchen. Paul made a visit at the hospital and went to church by himself for the early Christmas Eve service at 5 p.m. The children's choir sang a couple of Christmas carols to everyone's delight. Afterward, Paul came home for a delicious dinner with his family.

The late service was at 11 p.m. Gail woke Trevor and Joy who had fallen asleep with their clothes on. Randy helped the kids get into the car and drove his family to Trinity. Chip and Linda rode with Paul and Cheri. It was a beautiful service! Cheri sang with the choir which was accompanied by a string ensemble. Sheila had a few too many drinks before the service. After the service she hugged everyone she could get her hands on, or her arms around. Her husband was used to it by now.

After the late Christmas Eve service, the Walker family gathered around the tree at home and since everyone was now wide awake, agreed they would open their gifts. "Before we do that, may I offer a prayer?" Paul asked the group. "Sure, Dad, why not," Chip replied.

"Heavenly Father, I am so grateful for my family and for my recovery. As you smiled when Mary gave birth to your Son, smile on our family this Christmas as we prepare for the birth of our new grandchild. Watch over Linda and Chip and help her to have a healthy pregnancy and a flawless delivery. Bless Randy and Gail, Trevor and Joy. We are grateful that we all can be together. Thank you, God of healing, for my recovery from surgery and keep me strong and healthy so I may continue to serve the people of Trinity for many years to come. Thank you for my loving wife Cheri, for her strength, her patience, and her wisdom."

He paused for a long moment, and everyone waited for the Amen. "Finally, Lord God, I want to ask your blessing for a young woman whom we met for the first time this year, Brianna Holloway. I can't remember her married name right now, but I ask your blessing for her and her husband, Guy, as they begin their first year of marriage. These things I ask in Jesus' name. Amen."

With an "amen" from all, packages were passed around and the gift opening began. It was almost 2 a.m. when they all headed for separate bedrooms and a good night's sleep.

Two days later Randy, Gail, and the kids, drove back to Des Moines and arrived just ahead of a blizzard bringing heavy snow across the plains states. Chip and Linda flew back to California on January 2. It was a wonderful Christmas at the Walkers'!

44

BRIANNA AND GUY'S WEDDING

The second week in January, Paul got home one afternoon ahead of Cheri, opened the mail and found a letter from Brianna. Paul sat at the kitchen table and read the hand-written epistle.

Dear Pastor Paul and Cheri,

I debated about sending you a Christmas card, but decided that was too impersonal. I've been praying that you recovered well from your heart attack and surgery. I even called the church office anonymously to ask how you were doing! The secretary assured me that you were recovering well.

Next, I want to apologize sincerely for any trouble I might have caused by coming to see you. I feel so badly about that day at the hospital when Cheri found me in your room. Guy has helped me to see how selfish I've been by intruding into your life. I am so sorry.

Along with my apology, I want to thank you, Pastor Paul, for sharing the stories which have helped me understand my family's past. I think this has been helpful in my relationship with Guy as I've shared these stories with him.

Now, about our wedding. It was wonderful! We enjoyed the ceremony at the church; our pastor did a beautiful job! And...we went to Hawaii like we had planned. I even got to go snorkeling, which I've never done before! We've purchased a small house in Arlington Heights and I'm fixing it up.

Finally, I hope there are no hard feelings, because I really would like to see you both again. Guy and I wish you both a very Happy New Year.

Love, Brianna Spencer
(847) 437-3290

Paul finished reading the letter and stuffed it back into the envelope, and left it with the other mail for Cheri to read when she got home. No more secrets. That evening, Cheri went through the day's mail and found the letter from Brianna. She gave a deep sigh and sat down in the living room with Paul to read it.

When she finished, she turned to Paul and asked, "What do you think? How do you feel about her?"

"Each time she came to see me at the office," Paul answered, "my stomach got knotted up. I was so ashamed to learn I had a daughter. I was so afraid you would find out. She was always pleasant enough, and I guess she was just curious. I don't know."

"How do you feel about her now?" Cheri repeated.

"I feel badly about how all this has affected you. But as I've acknowledged, that's really my fault, not hers."

"Would you like to see her again?" Cheri asked. "After all, she is your daughter."

"I think that should be up to you, Cheri. I wouldn't mind, but if it makes you uncomfortable, then we should just ignore her letter, or send her a polite but brief acknowledgement. The important thing is… how do YOU feel about her?"

"I told you last month. I was angrier at you and at Marge, than at Brianna. I've told you, 'I forgive you,' and I mean it. But it'll probably be a long time before I'm really comfortable again. Maybe seeing

Brianna again would help me get over my fears....maybe not." They agreed to put the letter aside and discuss it at a later time.

The following week, after another hour of discussion, Cheri agreed that Brianna could come, and told Paul that he should make the phone call. They discussed the best time and place for the meeting. They agreed that Brianna and her husband should both be invited to come to their house. Cheri suggested after church for lunch, or on Sunday afternoon for a dinner she was willing to prepare.

Paul made the call; Guy answered, and handed the phone to Brianna. She was delighted to receive the invitation. They discussed several dates and chose February 12th. They would come to the pastor's home for dinner on Sunday at 3 p.m.

* * * * * * *

Sunday, February 12, 2012

It was snowing lightly but the sun was shining as Guy and Brianna drove from Arlington Heights to Weston, taking the Tri-State Tollway around Chicago. Guy was nervous, but Brianna was brimming with excitement. "I'm so glad Pastor Paul and Cheri invited us to their house. When I left the hospital back in September, I didn't think we'd ever see them again."

"It just seems strange, the way this all happened," Guy replied. "I can't believe they are still willing to see us."

"Thanks for coming with me, sweetheart. Maybe I won't mess things up so bad with you along!" Brianna giggled. "I'd still like to hear what happened at the trial; Pastor Paul didn't have time to finish that part."

"Didn't your mom ever tell you?" Guy asked.

"No, she said she doesn't know and doesn't want to know! She told me that once her mind was made up to move to Chicago, and to leave

Bob, she never wanted to hear another thing about Weston. She said her memories of Brian were precious; and she didn't want them soiled with worry about his killer."

When they arrived at the Walkers', Cheri opened the door and invited them in. "So good to see you again, Brianna!" she said with genuine warmth. At that moment, Paul came through the living room.

"Cheri, Pastor Paul, I'd like you to meet my husband, Guy Spencer!" Brianna announced proudly.

"Good to see you again," Paul said, as he shook Guy's hand and hung up their coats. Cheri invited them into the living room to be seated.

"Thank you for allowing us to come today," Brianna began. "I would have understood if you had turned us down."

"Our pleasure," Cheri responded. "Paul and I agreed it wouldn't be decent to cut you out of our life, now that you're a part of it. Remember, your mom and I were good friends, and we all felt so badly about what happened to your brother. You have a right to know all you can about him. Now that you're married, we agreed we wanted to meet your husband and wish you both a happy life together."

"Thanks, Cheri." Brianna felt there was something very genuine in Cheri's voice. She was relieved to feel so accepted. "Pastor Paul met Guy one time last year, but I don't think they had time to get well acquainted."

"Would the two of you care for coffee or cider?" Paul asked. "We got hooked on the cider over the holidays."

"I'd like some cider," Guy said. "And I'd like a cup of coffee, black," Brianna added.

As Paul went to the kitchen to pour drinks for everyone, Cheri asked how they had enjoyed the holidays.

"Oh, it was the greatest!" Brianna bubbled. "We started looking for a house a month or so before the wedding, and found the cutest bungalow in Arlington Heights."

"We were able to close and move in right before Christmas," Guy continued, "so Brianna was in her glory decorating for the holidays!"

Paul returned with beverages. "Brianna, you haven't told us about your wedding! We got your letter, but you didn't go into much detail."

"Oh, Pastor Paul, I wish you could have been there; it was so..o..o beautiful! My dress was off the shoulder and I carried a fall bouquet with orange and yellow roses and dark red maple leaves. Guy looked so handsome in his tux with a copper colored cummerbund and tie. My attendants wore cream chiffon dresses accented with burgundy and copper."

Guy jumped in, "You should have seen her at the reception! I don't think I've ever seen her so off the wall! We rented a hall and had the greatest DJ on the north side of Chicago! We danced with each other, with our parents, and all our friends! I might have had too much to drink, I don't know, but my buddies just ragged on me all night long."

"You did drink too much, and you know it!" Brianna interrupted. It was a good thing our flight to Hawaii didn't leave 'til the next afternoon."

"How many guests were there?" Cheri asked.

"Over a hundred, maybe a hundred and fifty, at least that's what my mom says," Brianna answered. "And best of all, my grandma was able to come in her wheelchair. We wheeled her right up to the front of the church and mom says she cried the whole time. After the wedding, mom was going to take her home, but she insisted on coming to the reception! Guy had her out on the dance floor, spinning her 'round and 'round in her wheelchair. She was laughing so hard; I don't think I've ever seen Grandma have so much fun!"

"Brianna and I didn't leave the reception 'til 1 a.m.," Guy added.

"Then what did you do?" Cheri asked with a grin. All four of them burst into laughter!

"Tell us more about your honeymoon in Hawaii," Paul continued.

"I don't even remember what happened after I got on the plane," Guy joked. "I think I slept for six straight hours."

"I had to wake him up when we landed in L.A. We walked to another concourse, and waited for our connecting flight and he fell asleep again in the waiting area!" They all laughed again. "I think he slept all the way to Hawaii, but I'm not sure 'cause that's when I slept!" And they all burst into laughter again.

"We spent the first night in Honolulu, and the next day we flew to Hawaii. We had a fabulous hotel room on the big island," Guy went on. "We rented a car and drove around the island sightseeing."

"We drove up to Kilauea, a real volcano! And we saw the Kalapana Beach that had black sand!" Brianna added enthusiastically.

"We also spent a lot of time in the pool and lying in the sun."

"But my very favorite thing," interrupted Brianna, "was the afternoon we spent snorkeling. A small boat took us out to a reef where there were lots of fish. Pastor Paul, you wouldn't believe how clear the water was! And Cheri, the tropical fish were unbelievably beautiful! A big fish started following me around. At first I was scared, so I swam over to where Guy was. He told me it was a grouper. They're not dangerous; but I didn't know that. Guy told me it wouldn't hurt me. Anyway, it followed me around for the longest time. I called him my 'groupie!'"

Guy interrupted, "I finally got jealous; so when I started swimming next to her, the grouper took off."

"Our last night, back in Honolulu was the most romantic of all. We were on Waikiki Beach watching the sunset. We enjoyed a traditional Hawaiian luau, feasted on seafood and watched Hawaiian natives dance the hula. It was such a beautiful night; I wished it would never end!"

"It sounds like a wonderful honeymoon," responded Cheri.

"It was; and it made me so excited to spend the rest of my life with this man," Brianna put her hand on Guy's knee. "That's the best part of all!" She leaned over and gave him a kiss on the cheek.

"I'm happy for both of you," said Paul.

"And I'm so thankful that you got through that heart attack and your surgery," responded Brianna. "Oh my gosh, I forgot to ask how you've been feeling!"

"Really great, in fact, better than ever! I feel like I'm thirty-five again," Paul answered. "Thanks for your concern."

"Dinner's ready;" Cheri interjected, "would you all gather around the table in the dining room?" During dinner there was more discussion of the Christmas holiday. Brianna described the wonderful Christmas day they had at her sister Sarah's home with their mom and three rambunctious granddaughters. When dinner was finished, they moved again to the living room.

"Pastor Paul, you promised to tell me what happened with the investigation to find Brian's killer, remember? You said they arrested a suspect, but you didn't tell me about the trial."

"Let's see," said Paul, "that was before my heart attack. Where did I leave off? Did I tell you about the $10,000 reward that was offered by Brian, the CEO from Jerusalem Steel?"

"No, but did you say Brian?" Brianna asked.

"Yes, the CEO from Jerusalem Steel Corporation was also named Brian. Honey, what was Brian's last name? I'm so bad at names," Paul confessed, turning to Cheri.

"You know, I don't remember either....but he sure was handsome; I remember that!" Cheri and Paul both laughed together. Guy and Brianna chuckled. "Oh, yes, now I remember," Cheri added, "it was Randall, Brian Randall."

"He didn't want any publicity, but he hoped the reward would help the investigation, and it did," Paul continued. "Both informants hoped they'd get a share of the reward. Anyway, the detectives got a search warrant for Terry's apartment. Once they found the knife, they felt they had enough to go to court. So they arrested Terry Mankovic, and the trial was held in August, just a year after Brian was murdered."

"Keep going," Brianna urged, glancing at Guy and squeezing his hand.

45

THE TRIAL

Brianna and Guy were still listening attentively to Paul's story.

"Just before Christmas that year, Detective Asplund called the church to inform me that they had a suspect, Terry Mankovic, in custody. He reminded me to be very careful to refer to Terry as 'the accused' or 'a suspect,' because Terry had not yet been tried and convicted."

"What kind of person could stab another in cold blood?" Guy asked.

"Why would anyone do such a thing?" Brianna added.

Paul nodded and continued his story. "I was wondering the same thing; and I had several other questions I wanted to ask Terry Mankovic, like: Why was he breaking into the church? Was he guilty and did he feel any remorse? I told Cheri I was planning to visit the jail, and she wasn't too happy about that!"

Cheri interjected, "I remember asking Paul if he really wanted to get involved with a murderer! 'Why don't you just let the police handle it?' I said."

"I've given this a lot of thought," I assured her. "I've prayed about it and remembered what Jesus said about visiting those in prison. I'm not sure what I'll feel like afterward, but I really believe I should go."

My first visit with Terry was in June. I was relieved that Sunday School was over, confirmation classes were done, and that summer would give me just a little free time. The weather couldn't have been better, so there were no excuses for not going to see Terry. What I found surprised me. Terry sat down in a booth and picked up the phone for communicating through the thick glass that separated us. I felt more apprehensive than Terry appeared to be. My first impression was negative. Terry looked tough and ugly and dumb. I felt anger rising inside. *"Judge not!"* came a warning voice in my head.

"Good morning, Terry, I'm Pastor Paul Walker from Trinity Lutheran Church."

The conversation began with small talk, and finally Terry asked, "I suppose you're wondering why I stabbed the stupid kid?"

I could hardly believe it. He was admitting he had done it. *Brian wasn't a stupid kid,* I thought to myself, *but I think I'll let that slide.* "Yea…a lot of people are wondering why."

"'Cause he came after me, that's why! Fuck, I was scared. I thought he was going to bash my head into the stairs. He was bigger than me, you know? I was just tryin' to get out of there. If I hadn't tripped on the stairs I woulda been out of there clean. I had to defend myself, man! I never meant to kill him."

My heart was pounding. I reflected for a minute on what Terry just said. "Have you told anyone else what you just told me?" I said.

Terry buried his face in his hands and shook his head back and forth. "Only my attorney, Mrs. Santana, and she said not to admit anything in court."

"It sounds to me like you regret what happened."

Terry looked up. "Hell, yes, I regret what happened!"

It wasn't exactly the kind of humble confession I've heard from parishioners, but it had a ring of sincerity that I couldn't deny. Maybe Terry just regretted getting caught. I spoke to Terry about the grace of God and the forgiveness that Christ offers to us from the cross. Terry slipped back into his defensive shell. "Yeah, yeah, I know about all that."

I visited Terry again in July and promised I would pray for him and be at the trial which was coming up. The trial was set for August 5th, a little less that one year from the date of his fateful break-in at Trinity.

* * * * * * *

August 5, 1991

The day of the trial was hot and humid. Everyone was complaining about the heat, and glad to get into the air-conditioned court room, everyone except Terry. His attorney had brought him a white shirt and tie, telling him not to grumble; at least he didn't have to wear a suit or sport coat. Terry looked nervously at the members of the jury and felt the sweat under his arms, even though the room was cool. Pastor Paul Walker was near the back of the room. He scanned the court room, but saw no sign of Marge or Bob. He did see several other church members seated a couple of rows behind the district attorney.

Detective Asplund was pleased when he heard that Judge Julia Mendez would be hearing the trial of Terry Mankovic. Knowing what he did about her toughness on the bench, he believed she would also be very sympathetic toward the victim and his family. Susan Santana, a public defender, was appointed for the accused, and the state was represented by Jeremiah Goode, Assistant District Attorney.

After calling court to order, Judge Mendez heard the case for the prosecution. Mr. Goode, the prosecuting attorney, made an opening statement describing what happened evening of August 10th last year. Then he began calling witnesses. First, the county coroner testified that the cause of death was hemorrhaging caused by a stab wound to the chest. Photos from the autopsy were entered as Exhibit A, and the coroner described the size and shape of the wounds made by a rather large knife or other sharp instrument. “There were two puncture wounds, one of which pierced the stomach; the other severed a large branch of the aorta. One laceration was found on the victim’s left hand, and there were multiple bruises to the arms and face, indicating a struggle. Some of the bruising may have occurred when the victim tumbled down several stairs.” The defense attorney declined any cross examination.

The next witness to take the stand was Anthony Montano who identified Terry in court as the man he saw running from the church on the night in question. “When I saw the photo the detective showed me, I said right away, ‘That’s him; that’s the guy I saw.’” Jeremiah Goode had a large and very professional diagram of the intersection, the church parking lot, the location of the white jeep, the street lamp, and the apartment building where Anthony lived. He pointed at the relative location of each feature to assure the jury that the witness could see clearly. The diagram was entered as Exhibit B.

Susan Santana began her cross examination. “You testified that you could see the defendant clearly as he ran across the church parking lot. Were you able to see his face at that distance?”

“No, he was too far away; I just saw him running and that caught my eye.”

“You said a few moments later you saw him walking around the corner of the building across the street. In other words, he was out of your sight for a minute or so?”

“Only a few seconds.”

“Didn’t you say you walked from your jeep to your front door?”

“Yes.”

“And how long would that take?” Susan pointed again to the diagram showing where the jeep was parked.

"I don't know, maybe ten or fifteen seconds."

"Is it possible that the man you saw running across the parking lot turned the other direction after crossing the street? And that someone else strolled around the corner toward your apartment?"

Anthony hesitated. He hadn't thought of that possibility. "Is that possible?" Susan asked again.

"I …I suppose, but...but there wasn't anybody else around," Anthony stammered.

"Yes or no, Mr. Montano, is it POSSIBLE that someone else came around that corner?"

"No."

"You just answered, 'I suppose,' why did you change your answer to 'no'?"

"Because he was the same height, the same build, and wearing the same sweatshirt as the man who ran across the parking lot," Anthony said confidently. "I'm sure it was the same man!"

That was not the answer Susan wanted to hear. She stopped a minute to compose herself. She picked up her notes and started a new line of questioning. "How did the police first contact you? Or did you call them?"

"I guess they were going door-to-door in the neighborhood. An officer rang my buzzer and said he was a detective canvassing the neighborhood about the homicide at the church across the street," Anthony paused to take a deep breath.

"Did you go to the door and talk to him face to face?" Susan asked.

"Yes. I told him about seeing that man (Anthony pointed to the defendant) running away from the church on the night of the murder."

"How did you identify the defendant to the officer?"

"The detective had a picture of him."

"A photograph of Terry Mankovic?" Susan feigned a look of surprise.

"Yea, he showed me the photo and I said, 'That's the guy!'"

Susan paused for a few moments, walked toward the jury and then back toward the witness stand. "And you later identified him in a police lineup, is that correct?"

"Yes, I picked him out of about six guys."

"The same person you saw in the photo held by the detective?"

"Yes, I told you that."

"Your Honor," Susan said to Judge Mendez, "it seems to me that this witness was prejudiced by the photo shown to him by the detective. Once he saw the photo, he became convinced it was the person he saw in the darkness. He was able to identify the defendant in the line up, because it was the same person as in the photo, not necessarily the person who ran from the church. I'd like to move that this witness' testimony be declared inadmissible."

Judge Mendez spoke calmly, "This witness made a very positive ID from the photo, saying, 'That's him, or that's the guy!' He testified that the light from the streetlamp made his face clearly visible. I find Mr. Montano's testimony believable and compelling, and therefore, deny the motion." Judge Mendez looked at Susan. "Do you have any further questions for the witness, Ms. Santana?"

"Not at this time, Your Honor." Susan was disappointed that her motion failed, but she hoped she had planted seeds of doubt in the mind of the jurors.

* * * * * * *

Judge Mendez declared a recess for lunch. Pastor Walker made his way to the aisle to meet some parishioners who greeted him warmly. They worked their way to the exit and out onto the street. News reporters were gathered around the court house filing reports on the first couple of hours of the trial. He and his friends walked a couple of blocks to a nearby Burger King and ordered lunch. "How do you think it's going so far, Pastor Paul?" Sam asked.

"It's too soon to tell," I replied. "I'm just glad this day is finally here."

"We heard you've been visiting Terry Mankovic in jail," Lydia commented.

"Yes, I've seen Terry twice, and I've been praying for him."

"What about the Holloways? Have you seen either of them?" she asked. "I haven't seen them here at the trial."

"No, not for a long time. I think it was last Christmas Eve, but I've been praying for them too."

As they set their trays and burgers on a table, Sam spoke up, "I'm really relieved that things are working out at the church. I was really worried about you for a while, Pastor."

"Thanks, Sam. I think God has had a hand in all of this."

"I thought the way the bishop handled everything really brought clarity to the situation, and hopefully some healing to our congregation," Lydia said, smiling at the pastor.

"Yes, I think we've all learned a lot from the tragedy. I feel badly that a few members decided to leave, but perhaps now there will be less opposition to our neighborhood outreach. And by the way, I think it's great that you've started bringing Maria Olivera to church on Sundays."

"It's nothing, Pastor. She lives just a few blocks from the church, and she seems so excited about coming. She's making new friends, and she's quite a character!" Sam said enthusiastically. "We gave her a ride to the court house this morning too. She said the district attorney would provide her lunch." When lunch was finished, we strolled back to the court house for the afternoon session.

****

The third witness called by the prosecution was Maria Olivera, Terry Mankovic's next door neighbor. Once again Terry's defense attorney made a valiant effort to discredit her testimony. "Ms. Olivera, you said you woke up in the middle of the night and heard screaming. We've all had nightmares; I've certainly had my share of them. Have you ever had such a terrible dream that it woke you up?"

"Sí, Señora," Maria replied.

"Have you ever awakened and found that you were the one crying out in your dream?"

"Sí, I have."

"Maybe you had a nightmare last year; maybe even a nightmare caused by the report of a homicide in your neighborhood; and you woke yourself up screaming from fear."

"Your Honor, my colleague is leading the witness," Jeremiah interrupted.

"Objection noted," commented Judge Mendez. "Be careful, Ms. Santana."

Susan turned again to the witness, "Is it possible that you dreamt the whole thing about hearing someone screaming?"

"No! No, like I say, I woke up when he kick the wall between our bedrooms, and then a few seconds later I hear him scream again."

"And he was screaming, what? 'I shouldn't have killed him!" Susan continued.

"No, Señora, I t'ink he say, 'I deedn' mean to kill him!" Maria insisted.

"Or did he say, 'I never meant to kill him!'?" Susan asked again.

"Maybe… somet'ing like that," Maria said, somewhat flustered.

"Or maybe, 'He's trying to kill me!' Or maybe…Terry was just having a bad dream himself. No further questions, Your Honor."

Mr. Goode rose for permission to redirect, and the judge allowed Jeremiah to further question the witness. "Ms. Olivera, I'd like you to relax a minute and close your eyes. Go back to the night in question and picture yourself lying there in your bed. Are you back there, almost a year ago? Good. Now I want you to yell or scream exactly the way it sounded coming from next door."

Maria's eyes popped open, "It was awful cry! It woke me up! I lay there and listen. Then I hear it again." In a quavering voice Maria screamed, "I deedn' mean to kill him!" She lowered her voice, "Then about five or ten seconds later I hear it again." Her voice was shrill again as she shouted, "I deedn' mean to kill him!"

"No further questions, Your Honor." Jeremiah returned to his seat and the witness was dismissed.

Finally, the coroner was brought back for questioning about the murder weapon found on Terry Mankovic. He testified that the knife, labeled Exhibit C, found on the defendant at his apartment, was the correct size and shape to have made the wounds in the victim's abdomen.

"Was there any blood found on the knife?" Susan asked in cross exam.

"No, we found no traces of blood."

"And there were no fingerprints on the knife?"

"Yes, there were fingerprints on the knife and they belonged to Terry," the coroner answered.

"Of course, of course, he owned the knife. But did you find any matching prints at the scene of the crime?"

"No, none that we could match to the accused."

"So you have no conclusive proof that this knife is the murder weapon; is that correct?" Susan asked.

"Without a blood match, I guess I'd have to say yes, that's correct," the coroner answered.

There was a long silence in the courtroom. "I thought the case might be lost right there," Paul said to Brianna and Guy. "Then, suddenly, the prosecutor asked for a side bar, permission to speak to the judge off the record. The attorneys all huddled near the judge's bench. The prosecutor apparently asked the judge permission to cut open the sheath for Terry's knife. Jeremiah picked up the knife and sheath and began cutting the leather sheath apart, slitting the leather ties which laced it together. He held up the pieces for the judge to see and asked for a recess in the trial. "Granted," said Judge Mendez. "Court will resume next Monday at 10 a.m."

It dawned on me as I sat there, stunned, what the prosecutor had done. He had realized the police had not looked inside the sheath for blood. When he cut it open, he showed the judge the dark brown stains of dried blood. With DNA tests, it would be enough to link this knife to Brian.

****

In closing arguments the following week, the prosecuting attorney strung the evidence together, and now had the proof that Terry Mankovic's knife was the weapon that killed Brian Holloway. It looked to me like there was no room for any "reasonable" doubt. In her closing, the defense attorney repeated the questions and doubts she had raised during testimony, and then called Terry Mankovic to the witness stand.

"Your Honor, I have repeatedly advised the defendant not to take the stand, but he insists on it."

"Go ahead, Ms. Santana," said Judge Mendez.

"Mr. Mankovic, is there a statement you would like to make to the jury?"

"Yes, there is. I know my attorney has tried to convince you that I wasn't even there that night, but that's bullshit. The truth is… I was. The truth is… I didn't mean to kill him, just like my neighbor Maria said, when I was screaming that night. The truth is he chased me through the big room and caught me on the stairs. He was yelling and screaming at me, and I was scared he might kill me! I thought he might have a gun or a knife or that he was gonna hit me with a pan from the kitchen. So I pulled out my knife just to protect myself. When he caught up with me on the stairs, I nicked his hand with my knife. I just wanted him to let go, that's all. It was self-defense. That's the truth, it was self-defense."

"Is there anything else, Terry?" Susan asked.

"Yea," Terry's head dropped as well as his voice. "I'm sorry it happened."

"Your honor," Susan stated, "my client can not be found guilty of murder, or even manslaughter, and enters a plea of not guilty by reason of self-defense."

There was another long silence in the court room. Finally Judge Mendez dismissed the witness and instructed the jury how the State of Indiana defines the legal difference between first degree murder, second degree murder, and voluntary manslaughter, each with different sentencing guidelines. The judge sent the jury to deliberate and declared a recess. After dinner it took the jury only two and a half hours to return with the verdict.

Judge Mendez asked the chairperson, "Has the jury reached a verdict?"

"We have, Your Honor; we the jury, find the defendant guilty of voluntary manslaughter."

46

REWARD CEREMONY

"I was surprised that neither Marge nor Bob was at the trial," Paul continued. "I was furious that Terry's attorney could plead not guilty for reason of self-defense. Self-defense? Can you believe that? Brian was unarmed and was chasing the intruder out of the church. Terry was armed with a knife and had a prior arrest for burglary. Then, she tried to confuse the witnesses and the jury by questioning everything."

"But he was convicted of murder," Brianna said, asking for confirmation.

"Not exactly. He was charged with second degree murder. Under Indiana law that's defined as, 'kills another human being while committing or attempting to commit arson, burglary, and so on.' Actually, he was found guilty of voluntary manslaughter, which means that anger or 'sudden heat' was a mitigating factor that reduces what otherwise would be murder. Terry hadn't planned to kill him. It just happened in a scuffle on the stairs, and the jury was convinced that Terry just reacted in fear and anger."

"So is Terry still in jail?" Brianna asked.

"Let's see, he was given 15 to 20 years, and it happened, what, twenty years ago? I imagine he's out by now."

"Wow, that doesn't seem fair!" Brianna shook her head.

"In a way, no," Paul replied, "but would you like to spend 15 years in prison?"

"No way," Brianna answered.

"He's paid his debt, and hopefully learned a painful lesson. He served the time the law requires, so let's hope his life takes a new and better path."

"Amen to that!" replied Guy.

"Anyone want another cup of coffee or cider?" Cheri asked.

"Oh, no thanks," Brianna answered. "We really should be going."

"Here, have a little more cider, Guy. Paul, do you want more?" Cheri asked as she finished refilling Guy's cup.

"Sure, thanks," Paul replied.

"Paul, why don't you finish by telling Guy and Brianna about the reward ceremony. That might be a little happier ending," Cheri said, as she refilled Paul's cider.

"That's right. Didn't you say there was a $10,000 reward offered?" Brianna asked.

"Actually, it was $11,000 counting the money offered by Cheri's law firm. About a week after the trial, I called the bishop. I knew he wanted to come to Weston to help with the reward presentation."

* * * * * * *

"Indiana Kentucky Synod office, this is Julie."

"Good afternoon, Julie, Pastor Walker here; is the bishop in?"

"Just a moment, please."

"Good afternoon, Paul, this is John, how are you?"

"Well, Bishop, I'll make my confession. I took the morning off and played golf, so I'm feeling pretty good this afternoon."

"Good for you! What's new?"

"I'm calling to ask a favor, John. I'm sure you've heard the news that Terry Mankovic was convicted of manslaughter for killing Brian."

"Yes, I read the newspaper articles on the trial up there."

"We're cleared now to make the reward presentations to the citizens who gave leads to the police. One of them, Maria Olivera, has even joined our church!"

"Hey, that's great news! Have you got a date for the reward ceremony? You know I'd love to be there," the bishop said enthusiastically.

"Not yet, I wanted to check with you first. Cheri is checking with the businessman who put up the reward money. He said he didn't want any publicity, but we wanted to invite him to participate in whatever way he chooses. We, meaning the council and I, talked about doing it at Sunday morning worship. Then we discussed media involvement and decided that would be disruptive to worship. So we're going with a potluck followed by the ceremony at one o'clock again. That worked well last time you were here."

"Which Sundays are you looking at?" the bishop asked.

"October 13th, 20th , or 27th," I replied.

"I've got commitments in Kentucky on the 13th and 27th, but I could make it on the 20th and I'm sure I can get to Weston by one o'clock."

"Great! We'll look forward to seeing you on the 20th."

Cheri called Brian Randall. Brian was also available on the 20th and he promised Cheri he would come for worship at Trinity that day. "I've told Paul what a great guy you are," Cheri told him. "I'm glad he'll get to meet you, finally."

"Is it okay if I bring a lady friend?" Brian asked.

"Why, of course!" Cheri enthused. She was so glad to hear that Brian had found a woman friend. She prayed it was a good match and that it would provide the companionship Brian needed. He was a very good catch!

****

Sunday, October 20th

The day of the ceremony there were TV and newspaper reporters swarming around the church, inside and out. The parking lot was filled with vans and visitors. Today's publicity was going to be a lot better than the sad story of Brian's murder. Maria Olivera was dressed in a pretty new outfit, a wool skirt and beautiful rust colored sweater, accented by a large white beaded necklace. Church members crowded around her congratulating her on her reward and telling her how delighted they were that she had joined Trinity! The only sad thing was that she had no immediate family to share her joy.

Anthony Montano, on the other hand, had every Catholic relative from the entire Chicago metropolitan area with him at church that morning. His sister, Ann, was sitting next to him, and reminded him that they had been to the movie together on the night he saw the guy running from the church! The women of Trinity worried that there might not be enough food to feed all those relatives of Anthony's!

At the ceremony held in the sanctuary, TV reporters were asked to set up their cameras in the balcony. Newspaper reporters sat behind the presenters and recipients. Police Chief Jed Wilson and detectives Sean Asplund and Chad Skiles were in the front pew. The second pew held Scott Etheridge and his wife from the law firm, and his friend Brian Randall from Jerusalem Steel. The blonde woman sitting next to Brian appeared to be ten years younger, but poised, not flighty. Cheri, Paul, and the boys sat with Maria Olivera on the other side of the center aisle.

Pastor Walker asked Bill Trogdon, the council president, to welcome everyone and begin the introductions. Bill introduced Scott Etheridge whose law firm had posted the first $1000 reward. Scott stood and turned and bowed while everyone applauded. "An additional $10,000 was posted by a generous donor who wishes to remain anonymous. So, whoever you are, and wherever you are, thank you!" The congregation applauded again, and the blonde sitting next to Brian Randall squeezed his hand.

Bill introduced Pastor Walker who scanned the congregation as he stepped to the microphone. Near the back of the church he spotted the bishop, who had arrived late, but was there as he had promised!

"This will be a brief ceremony with a mixture of feelings. First, there is sadness still, as we remember our good friend and fine custodian, Brian Holloway. We thank God for his presence among us, even if for too short a time. Second, there is gratitude and joy as we give thanks to those who helped bring his killer to justice. I will introduce those people in a moment, but first let us offer a word of prayer. Please stand.

"Called, gathered, and empowered to serve, let us pray for the church, the world, and all those in need. We pray for bishops, and our good bishop John Ferguson, for pastors, associates in ministry, diaconal ministers, secretaries and custodians, and all the baptized. Focus our hearts on your will so that we might be ready to serve you like Martha and listen at your feet like Mary.

"We pray for all of creation, that the walls and barriers that divide our lands may be removed, and your people and animals be freed to share your earth with peace and respect for one another. We pray for those who have not yet heard the gospel. Empower us with this mission as we live our baptismal vocation in word and deed. We pray for those who feel forgotten in their suffering or who need your special care, that they might receive your healing touch and know your everlasting peace.

"Lord, we commend to you the young man who is now in prison for the death of Brian Holloway. Have mercy on him and help him to amend his life.

"Finally, dear God, we pray for this congregation, that you may keep us focused on Jesus Christ, the head of the church, so that we might maintain unity amidst our diversity. We pray for all who mourn the loss of a loved one, especially the family of Brian Holloway. Show us clearly the mystery of life and resurrection which you revealed to Mary Magdalene and all the saints through the power of your Son, Jesus Christ our Lord and Savior. Amen. You may be seated."

Pastor Walker then introduced Chief Wilson from the Weston Police Department, and Detectives Asplund and Skiles, and invited them to the microphone. They came forward accompanied by applause. Chief Wilson acknowledged the fine work of Sean Asplund and his partner Chad Skiles, and then spoke about the cooperation needed between the police and community if problems were to be prevented and crimes solved. Next, the chief turned the microphone over to Detective Asplund.

"Ladies and gentlemen, we shared your grief and outrage when Brian was killed. It was a senseless act. The person who did it is now behind bars thanks to the assistance of two people from this neighborhood. On behalf of every police officer who struggles to bring criminals to justice, Maria and Anthony, thank you!" Once again the congregation broke into spontaneous applause.

Pastor Walker stepped back to the microphone and added his thanks to the police department on behalf of the church. Then he introduced the honored guest Bishop John Ferguson and invited him to come into the chancel with the other presenters. Everyone applauded politely for the bishop. Finally, the pastor introduced and called the recipients forward, first, Maria Olivera, who was presented with a check for $5500. The congregation rose to their feet to applaud. Then, Anthony Montano, rose from the midst of his family and came forward. As he was handed the $5500 check from Scott Etheridge, his family group began hooting and whistling and shouting! "To-ny! To-ny! To-ny!" Anthony smiled in embarrassment.

Maria tugged on Paul's sleeve, "Pastor, may I say somet'ing?" she whispered in his ear.

"Of course," Paul said, and bent down to listen.

"Een the microphone," she insisted.

"Oh, pardon me, of course," the pastor said apologetically.

Paul turned quickly to Anthony, asked if he wanted to speak, and gestured toward the microphone.

Anthony turned toward the mike, grinned, and said into the microphone, "I just want to say Thanks!" He held his check high in the air, and his family hooted and hollered again!

Then Paul spoke into the mike, "Maria Olivera would also like to say a few words."

Maria stepped up and pulled the microphone down to speak, "I also want to say thanks. And I want to say thank you for my beeg reward!" Everyone clapped, and even a few of Anthony's relatives hooted. "And I wan' to say thank you to thees church for making me feel so welcome! I am very happy now to be a new member here. Maybe I not supposed to tell thees, but the pastor's wife Cheri tol' me that if the reward money had not been geeven to us, it would go to Trinity's scholarship fund for young people. So I teenk I like to geeve $2000 of my reward to the scholarship fund!" Once again the entire congregation stood and applauded. Maria beamed, so proud of herself, and so happy with all her new friends.

Paul concluded his story. "So, the crowds departed from the church to make their way home. The TV cameras were removed to their respective vans. I said a silent prayer thanking God for so many things: for my wife and sons, for this fine congregation, for my bishop, for the police, for Maria and Anthony. I prayed again for the Holloways, even though they weren't there. And I hoped as I had always hoped that maybe… just maybe... Trinity's neighborhood mission was touching and changing lives."

* * * * * * *

"Wow! Thanks, Pastor Paul, that's quite a story," Brianna responded. "I'm glad it turned out so well for the church." Brianna put her coffee cup on the table and looked out the window. "It's snowing again. We really should be going." She looked at Guy for agreement. "I really appreciate the fact that you let us come and hear the rest of the story about Brian. I think I feel better now."

"Not only that," interjected Guy, "but if we don't overstay our welcome, perhaps you two will come to Arlington Heights and have dinner at our new home some night."

"That's awfully kind of you; we'd love to," said Cheri.

"It looks like the snow is starting to accumulate on the streets," Brianna commented, as she and Guy got up to leave.

"It's been great getting to know you Pastor Paul, and you too Cheri," Guy said.

"We'll look forward to seeing you again," said Paul.

"So will we," Brianna smiled again as she gave Cheri and Paul a hug. Guy shook Paul's hand and gave Cheri a hug. They put on their coats and stepped out the front door.

Paul could not have imagined a visit like this, six months ago. He and Cheri stood on the front porch watching Brianna go down the steps with Guy's arm around her. Paul had been so embarrassed, so afraid to tell Cheri, so uncertain of what might happen. He looked up at the snow falling slowly from the dark gray sky, wrapped his arms around Cheri, and knew God was behind it all.

Brianna and Guy brushed snow from the windshield and climbed into the car. It was getting dark, so Guy turned on the headlights and backed out of the driveway. They waved good-by to Paul and Cheri standing there in the twilight, and headed back to Arlington Heights as the light snow blew against the windshield.

"I hope our marriage will be as good as Pastor Paul and Cheri's," Brianna said to Guy as he pulled onto the tollway.

"I'm sure our marriage will be fantastic!"

"Be careful on this fresh snow;" Brianna warned, "I don't want you driving like a holy terror!"

"You're the holy terror in this family!" Guy teased.

Brianna laughed, "That's what my mom used to call me!"

STUDY GUIDE

Questions and Issues for Discussion

1. **Chapter 1** A violent death is always shocking, perhaps even more when it happens inside a church. Could such a thing possibly happen in your church or community center? We live much of our community life based on trust, the trust that others will not harm us. Discuss examples such as schools, traffic laws, paying taxes, etc.

2. **Chapter 1** Brian was considered "the best janitor we ever had" in spite of burning the palm branches. Do conscientious people made mistakes? How did the church members deal with Brian's mistake?

3. **Chapter 1** Did Brian make a mistake by chasing the intruder? What would you have done in that situation?

4. **Chapter 1** Discuss Pastor Paul's ministry on the night of Brian's death. What might you have done differently?

5. **Chapter 2** Now that we know a little more about Terry, discuss how you feel about him. Tragedy among poorer families is always compounded by lack of financial resources. Is it right for the church to be concerned about social justice as well as about forgiveness? Was Jesus concerned about social justice? Give examples from his action or teachings.

6. **Chapter 3** A Mighty Fortress. Discuss the role that music and hymns play in worship.

7. **Chapter 4** How does a pastoral call differ from being hired for secular employment? Discuss the issues in Paul's interview at Trinity. What boundaries do you feel should be kept between a pastor's work and her or his family?

8. **Chapter 4** The parishioners could not see Paul's prayer life... Faith is lived out through prayer and practice. What role does each play in the living of our faith?

9. **Chapter 5** Discuss the Community Fair. Was it a good idea? Was it effective? Is effectiveness the only way to measure ministry?

10. **Chapter 7** Is the Holloway's grief typical or strange? Marge's grief can be blamed for her loss of self-control. Did Paul have an excuse? It's easy to say what Paul should NOT have done. What should Paul have done?

11. **Chapter 12** In what ways were Cheri's feelings toward Brian the same as or different from Paul's feelings for Marge?

12. **Chapter 13** Paul experienced a knot in his stomach. Was it due to his feelings of guilt and shame or to his fear of being found out?

13. **Chapter 13** Paul thought Cheri was about to accuse him. How often do we get "caught up in ourselves," thinking that others are aware of some weakness we are struggling with, when actually they are struggling with their own problem? Discuss.

14. **Chapter 13** What is the difference between shame and guilt? How would you define shame? What is the effect of shame? Did Paul feel shame in this story? How did Paul refer to himself after Cheri told him about her feelings for Brian?

15. **Chapter 15** Paul confesses his immoral behavior. Do church seminaries adequately prepare pastors for dealing with temptation? If you were a bishop, what would you do if a church member reported to you that their pastor had acted immorally? How is justice consistent with the gospel of forgiveness?

16. **Chapter 15** Confession and Confidentiality. What role does confidentiality play in dealing with people's sins and mistakes? Do you agree or disagree with Rabbi Chevitz advice to Paul?

17. **Chapter 16** Why did Bob lash out so angrily after forgetting Marge's birthday? What is the difference between controlling

our anger, suppressing our anger, and managing our anger? What techniques work best for you in managing anger?

18. **Chapter 18** Did the police have sufficient evidence to arrest Terry? Do you anticipate problems during the trial?

19. **Chapter 19** How would you describe Pastor Paul's antagonists? Do you believe they are motivated by good intentions? Or were they being self-centered? Who is responsible for listening to, working with, and reconciling with antagonists? The pastor, the council, or all the members?

20. **Chapter 20** When people are frustrated, they tend to take matters into their own hands. Discuss why this happens. Why is this generally not a good idea? Are there circumstances in which this is justified? Hitler in Nazi Germany?

21. **Chapter 21** Do you agree with the bishop's insight that these members are grieving "the death of the church as it used to be?" How often does this happen? How can pastors help people cope with change? The church's continual "dying?"

22. **Chapter 21** Do you consider the bishop's sermon and recommendations "heavy handed?" Do you see other possibilities that might not have resulted in members leaving?

23. **Chapter 24** Is Omar as innocent as he appears to be? Why do you think that?

24. **Chapter 25** Can you put yourself in Hassid's place? To what extent do you agree or disagree with his plan?

25. **Chapter 26** Is Elmer Johannsen typical of anyone you know? Share your story.

26. **Chapter 28** Is David Turner typical of anyone you know? Share your story.

27. **Chapter 30** Agent Keller tells Hassid lies about the release of prisoners. Is this justified? Hassid taunts the congregation about their faith. How does this make you feel?

28. **Chapter 32** A hectic week in Pastor Paul's life. How did it make you feel? How did Paul handle the many responsibilities he faced?

29. **Chapter 33** Paul didn't want to believe Brianna was his daughter. The first reaction to any trauma is often shock or denial. Have you ever experienced, or observed irrational denial? Describe and discuss. Is this the same denial as seen in addiction?

30. **Chapter 36** In what way is this little incident a reflection of Paul's dilemma?

31. **Chapter 38** Cheri chides Paul about his compassion. To what extent is empathy Christ-like? At what point does it become debilitating, weakening the care-giver? Was Jesus weakened by empathy?

32. **Chapter 38** In Paul's case, was his heart attack sent by God as punishment for his indiscretion? Or was it due to diet, lack of exercise, genetic predisposition, or stress? What percentage would you assign to each of these four contributing factors? Discuss.

33. **Chapter 40** Brianna is understandably upset to hear about Paul's heart attack. When confronted by Cheri at the hospital, Brianna started shaking. How do you think she felt on her drive home to Chicago?

34. **Chapter 40** Cheri demonstrates amazing composure in the shock of meeting Brianna. Point out several specific examples of her wisdom, honesty, faith, and love.

35. **Chapter 42** Cheri struggles to forgive. Compare her thoughts on Thanksgiving night with Jesus' prayer in the Garden of Gethsemane. How are they similar? How do they differ?

36. **Chapter 41** Paul is finally confronted by Cheri. Did Paul try to defend himself? Why or why not?

37. **Chapter 42** Have you ever struggled with a really difficult decision? If you are willing, tell the story of your struggle.

38. **Chapters 44** Cheri Walker is a strong, independent woman. Discuss her strengths and the ways in which she is a good partner in Paul's ministry. Could it be said that Cheri is the real hero in this story?

39. **Chapter 45** Public trials strive for justice while protecting the rights of a defendant. Did the procedures described in this trial seem fair? Give examples.

40. **Chapter 45** Terry took the witness stand to tell "the truth." Was he believable? Was he truthful? Why or why not? Does the jury's verdict seem fair to you?

41. **Chapter 46** Does the web of human relationships described in this novel accurately reflect reality? Discuss. If forgiveness seems to be at the core of our relationships, what does this say about sin? If Jesus died so that sins would be forgiven, why is it so important for us to forgive others? Doesn't Jesus forgive them?

42. **Chapter 46** If God forgives us, and the person we wrong forgives us, why do we find it so difficult to forgive ourselves? Do we still want to be punished? How does "not forgiving ourselves" deny the gospel?

ACKNOWLEDGMENTS

This book is lovingly dedicated to my wife, Carmen, who has been a faithful and supportive partner in all aspects of the journey we have travelled together. Her enthusiasm has always been an inspiration, and I have admired her initiative to make and maintain friendships.

A word of thanks to my sons, Keith and Joel, for their struggle to grow up as pastor's kids, **and to my parents, Jim and Bernice,** for the spiritual and moral foundation they laid for my life.

Appreciation is expressed to the members of congregations the author has been privileged to serve as pastor. Many have become life-long friends. Their support and love and encouragement have enriched our family's life in ways that words cannot express.

The story is fiction, and any similarity between characters in this novel and real persons is purely coincidental. The author has received permission from several former church members to tell the story of minor incidents which occurred when the author was their pastor.

Appreciation is also due to many friends and family who reviewed and made suggestions for improvement on this story: Bishop Ron and Ellie Hasley, Chris and Bobbi Brown, Erling Lindstrom, John Ohst, Charlie Slightam, Gary and Debbie Bornzin, Carmen Bornzin, Joel Bornzin.

Churches should be sanctuaries. All people, especially women and children, should be safe in the church building, and in the midst of God's people, and in the presence of priests and pastors. We all know, however, that sin is never banished in this world, no matter how good people try to be. Pastors and priests should be, and are being, held to higher standards and accountable for their actions. Hiding shameful secrets has too often led to more tragedy and greater harm. The failure of the clergy to maintain high moral standards is a weakness the church must confess and deal with, in a just, yet merciful manner. Bishops in every denomination are well deserving of our prayers.

ABOUT THE AUTHOR

Jim Bornzin is an ordained Lutheran pastor, married and living in Silverton, Oregon. During forty years of ministry, he has served six congregations in Oregon, Washington, and Illinois. Jim has also served as a hospital chaplain in Spokane, Washington, and Silverton, Oregon, and as a volunteer police chaplain in Coos Bay, Oregon. All of these experiences have influenced his current novel, Terror at Trinity.

He has worked with numerous community agencies, both as a volunteer and board member. These include: Habitat for Humanity, Helpline Information and Referral, Temporary Help in Emergency House, and Rockford Area Lutheran Ministries. As a parish pastor, Jim appreciated forming deep and lasting relationships with church members, often walking with them through crisis situations.

Jim received his bachelor's degree in Science Engineering from Northwestern University. Working several summers in various engineering departments convinced him that he should seek a career in something more people-oriented. Further education included two Masters degrees (MDiv and STM) from the Lutheran School of Theology at Chicago, and three quarters of Clinical Pastoral Education. He was ordained in 1967.

His wife, Carmen, is a registered nurse with experience in a variety of hospital and clinic settings. Together, they raised two sons in the Pacific Northwest, and as a family enjoyed traveling, camping, and hiking. Jim also enjoys playing golf. His love of detail has found expression in scissor-cutting (scherenschnitte), oil painting, cabinet work, photography, and creative writing, including a collection of poetic sermons.